It's Getting Hot in Here

Jane Costello has written ten books, with another five written under the name Catherine Isaac. Jane's books have been translated into 26 languages, have been Sunday Times bestsellers, have been selected for the Richard & Judy Book Club and Jane has won a Romantic Novelists' Award twice. Jane was born in Liverpool and still live there with her husband Mark and three ridiculously tall sons.

Sign up to Jane Costello's newsletter by
scanning the QR code below

JANE COSTELLO

It's Getting Hot in Here

**HODDER &
STOUGHTON**

First published in Great Britain in 2024 by Hodder & Stoughton Limited
An Hachette UK company

This paperback edition published in 2024

2

A CIP catalogue record for this title is available from the British Library

Paperback ISBN 978 1 399 73934 4
ebook ISBN 978 1 399 73935 1

Typeset in Plantin by Manipal Technologies Limited

Printed and bound in Great Britain by Clays Ltd, Elcograf S.p.A.

Hodder & Stoughton policy is to use papers that are natural, renewable
and recyclable products and made from wood grown in sustainable forests.
The logging and manufacturing processes are expected to conform to the
environmental regulations of the country of origin.

Hodder & Stoughton Limited
Carmelite House
50 Victoria Embankment
London EC4Y 0DZ

The authorised representative in the EEA is Hachette Ireland, 8 Castlecourt
Centre, Castleknock Road, Castleknock, Dublin 15, D15 YF6A, Ireland

www.hodder.co.uk

This book is dedicated to Helen Wallace, aka The Prof.

Chapter 1

To-do list

- Find maths tutor for Jacob
- Book appointment for HRT
- Find solution to Leo's 2am gaming sessions – Wi-Fi timer? Cattle prod?
- Cancel direct debit for Total Pilates studio
- Order 37 pieces of cheese for PTA wine tasting
- Start DIY panelling in living room
- Return jumpsuit, leather trousers and weird bandeau thing to ASOS
- Disable online purchases after 9pm on a Friday
- Buy age 10–11 school trousers, GSCE Chemistry textbook
- Find a baseball club for Jacob
- Reinstall Drinkaware app
- Switch energy provider
- Buy socks (both kids)
- REMEMBER TO TAKE STUPID EXPENSIVE COLLAGEN
- Descale kettle

'Is that kettle *really* still on there?'

Rose shakes her head, amused, as she glances at my phone. 'Go on, just delete it. You *know* it's never going to happen.'

'Yes, it is,' I say defiantly. 'One day. I've already bought the descaler tablets. Not sure where I've put them, but still . . .'

The first time I came to hospital with Rose, I felt like a spare part. I couldn't really work out what my role was supposed to be as we sat in the waiting room and I could only waffle on about nothing of consequence. I felt as if I should be providing words of wisdom, advice, or at least a discussion more profound than *First Dates Hotel*.

It took a couple of appointments before something became clear. I wasn't there for wisdom. The waffle was the whole point. I suppose cancer is a shit topic of conversation for anyone, especially if you're the one who's got it. Since then, on the occasions when I've accompanied her for appointments with her consultant breast surgeon, or now, for radiotherapy, it's been the same story. We've talked a lot about what she's going through since her diagnosis, but quite often she prefers to stick to subjects she actively *enjoys* slagging off, such as my ex-husband.

'He bought the boys *what?*' she asks when I tell her about Brendan's latest gift.

'A hamster,' I reply.

'Idiot,' she mutters, then catches my eye. 'Sorry, but he is.'

I've tried to resist becoming a stereotypical man-basher since the divorce, no matter how tempting it is sometimes. Staying amicable with my children's father is the least I can do for them. When the marriage fell apart, my overwhelming regret was not for me, but them. I felt like I'd failed them in some way. Rose thinks I let Brendan get away with murder as a result. She says I deserve better – and always did. But then, she is married to someone who considers himself the luckiest man alive to have found her – which sets the bar impossibly high. She thinks I deserve the same love and happiness that have been lavished on her; in fact, she thinks everyone does. This would make her a romantic if she wasn't so cynical about almost everything else.

'Doesn't he think you've got enough to look after, between a full-time job, two kids and a kettle to descale?' she adds.

'It'll all get a bit easier once I've got the PTA Wine Quiz out of the way,' I tell her, knowing that, since we've been in here, I've probably accumulated 16 new WhatsApp messages on this very topic.

'Well, you know my view on that. You've only got yourself to blame for signing up. *Why* would you volunteer to organise something like that?'

'I've got an affliction,' I tell her. 'If someone asks for a helper, I can't bear the sound of silence. My hand shoots up before I can stop it happening.'

'You need to knock *that* on the head immediately. So, this hamster. What made Brendan think it was a good idea?'

'Oh, Jacob's been banging on forever about wanting a pet. Brendan took him for a Happy Meal on Saturday and I think he had a rush of blood to the head. He'd said he was taking him for a new toy. I was expecting some Lego.'

'Well, that's typical. He gets to look like Santa Claus, while you're left to pick up shit after a rodent.'

'If you're attempting to wind me up about this, you're succeeding,' I tell her.

'Good. Did you point out to him that he should've consulted you in the first place?'

'Of course. His response was: "At least it's not a puppy".'

'Personally, I'd tell him to take it back,' she says.

'I don't think it's like returning a pair of chinos to TK Maxx. Anyway, Jacob loves the thing, so I'm just getting on with it. To be fair, I've never seen him so happy. He's christened it Alan.'

'Rose Riley?'

The nurse who calls her name is cheerful, with grey hair and large hips that would make her look like someone's nana if it weren't for a small tattoo on the inside of her wrist.

'How are we today, darling? Let's get you started, shall we?'

Rose is here for radiotherapy, which she's been having every day for the last week and a half. The treatment doesn't take long – she was gone less than thirty minutes last time – and as I wait in the hospital café for her, I find myself trying to work out how many years we've known each other. The answer turns out to be 25. Which is ridiculous . . . especially because, in my head, I'm still only 25 years old.

Time does a weird thing as you get older. When I was a teenager, there were a handful of middle-aged women that I admired: an inspiring history teacher, Alexis Carrington from *Dynasty* and a rebellious aunt who'd travelled around the Greek islands on a motorbike with a handsome hippie who looked like Jesus. But I never quite pictured being in my forties myself. I knew on a theoretical level that one day it would happen but it felt so far removed from reality that I couldn't get my head around it.

I'm 47 now, which should have been enough time to get used to it. Yet, my outlook remains suspended around the time Oasis were in the charts and Tony Blair was running the country – even if the same can't be said for my pelvic floor. It was back in the heady 1990s that Rose and I shared a house with two other BBC trainees and a landlord who – judging by how high he kept the heating on – must, with hindsight, have been running a cannabis farm in his loft.

Even then we looked like physical opposites. I'm five foot five, average build, with blue-grey eyes, full lips and thick, brown hair that has been every style and shade under the sun over the years, but now sits just below my shoulders. Rose inherited her pale skin, fine features and long, red hair from her mother, but gets her height from her dad's side. She's a full five inches taller than me, with slender hips and a narrow waist, which means she never faces the constant battle I have to find jeans that fit.

I don't know if I'm too old to have a 'best friend' now. The phrase feels better suited to little girls in playgrounds. But there's no question that I love her. She's the sister I never had; the wife I would have married had I not had the misfortune of being heterosexual. She's my wing woman both in life *and* in work. For near enough the last decade we've both been employed by the rapidly growing UK outpost of MotionMax+, a streaming service with more than 76 million subscribers worldwide.

Throughout the whirlwind of the last couple of months – Rose's diagnosis, then lumpectomy – she has remained resolutely positive. But as we head downstairs after her treatment session, it's clear just how much the radiotherapy has wiped her out. She has 10 more days of this – and she already looks broken.

'Silly question, but how are you?' I ask. 'Under the circumstances, I mean.'

'Under those, I'm positively tickety-boo. Eurgh . . . sorry. I'm just exhausted. And my skin feels hideous. I was warned it might burn where I'd been treated but it's gone all the way up to my neck,' she winces, reaching up to the angry-looking patch.

'Oh Rose . . . do you want to go for a coffee before I take you home?' I ask.

'I haven't got the energy to even lift a cup right now. Is that all right?'

'Course it is,' I say, gently.

It's just as we're heading across the huge hospital concourse that she says something I'd been expecting long before now.

'I think I'm going to have to take up that offer of more time off work, aren't I?' she sighs.

'Personally, I think that would be the wisest option.'

'I'd just really wanted to try to keep some normality in the midst of this shit show,' she says. 'Does that make sense?'

'It does but some things are more important, Rose. Getting better, for one thing.'

'The timing's awful . . .'

'Oh seriously, who cares?' I protest.

'*I* care.'

'I know, but this is temporary. You need to make yourself the priority now.'

Her feet come to a stop and I realise there are tears in her eyes.

'Oh, come here, you,' I say, beckoning her in for the most careful of hugs, which she accepts. She squeezes me briefly, then, conscious that we're blocking the corridor, pulls away and sniffs. We start walking again.

'Have you spoken to HR about how long they'll let you stay off?'

'I'm allowed up to six months on full pay but by the time I added my holiday entitlement, it's more. They'll have to bring someone in to cover, which I don't like the sound of.'

'Why not?'

'What if my replacement is terrible? Or – worse – *really good?*'

'They won't be as good as you. You are too hard an act to follow.'

We step outside into the first decent phone reception since we arrived and a blaze of notifications appear on my screen. One of which is a voicemail from my mother, who was picking Jacob up from school in my absence. I bypass her message – it usually takes several minutes and an update about something she's just read in the *Daily Mail* before she gets to the point – and call her mobile instead.

But it's Jacob who answers.

'Mum!' he gasps breathlessly. 'You won't *believe* what's happened!'

Like all 10-year-olds, it doesn't take much to excite him. He once called me in the middle of a Content Bundling workshop I was leading to tell me that they'd started selling a new flavour of Prime in the newsagent at the end of our road.

'What is it, sweetie?'

'Alan has given birth!'

Blood drains from my face like sand from an egg timer.

'Is this a joke?'

'No, it's real!' he giggles excitedly. 'Grandma let us in to the house and I ran over to Alan's cage and found the hamster babies. All nine of them.'

Chapter 2

Morning all! Just a quick one to say there are only a handful of tickets left for the PTA Wine Quiz. Drop me a line to snap one up before they all go – it should be a fabulous night! Also, a quick follow-up to my earlier messages to see if there is anyone else who might be interested in a hamster? They are free to a loving home, easy to look after and very cute! Eight have been rehomed so there's now only one left. Let me know!

I press send on my WhatsApp message and wonder if the exclamation marks are a dead giveaway for how desperate I am. It already feels like a miracle that I've managed to get rid of eight of them within three weeks of their birth. Apparently, if you leave hamsters together any longer than that, they start killing each other or, worse, reproducing.

Obviously, the pet shop where Alan was purchased was uninterested in our plight and, although Brendan said he was horrified and would immediately ask around to see if anyone wanted one, I haven't heard a peep from him since. So I was forced into the hard sell to anyone with a child, touting my wares at the school gates, Scouts, work, on social media and, in one case, to my neighbour's acupuncturist. In another life, I could have been a used-car salesman.

Only now the end is in sight – with only a single baby currently homeless – I am completely out of ideas. I even texted my hairdresser, who responded with, No thanks Lisa and don't try and tip me with one after I've done your lowlights! x

Unless I can get rid of it, I'm going to have to buy a second cage tonight after work. Which I really, really don't want to do. Yet I'm horribly aware that, even now, they could be multiplying; every time I open the front door, I live in fear of being confronted by a scene straight out of *Gremlins*.

'Why couldn't we have just kept them?' asks Jacob, as I straighten his school tie in the hallway.

'Because I think 10 pets is too many, even for an animal lover like you.'

'I'd have looked after them,' he protests.

I kiss him on the head and push a bit of his fringe that refuses to stay down. He's got light brown hair, the same shade as his father, but that's where the resemblance to Brendan ends. Despite being 10, Jacob still has the same lovely squidgy cheeks that he had as a baby, and huge blue, puppyish eyes that occasionally mean he can wrap me round his little finger. But not about pets. On this, I am not changing my view.

'When you leave 10 hamsters together for longer than a couple of weeks . . . how can I put this? *Bad things happen*.'

'What sort of things?'

I wonder what I should break to him first – the cannibalism or the incest.

'They fight, that's all. They're better off on their own.'

'But that's so sad. *Everybody* needs *somebody*, Mum,' he says, earnestly.

'Not everybody. And definitely not Alan. Alan is an independent woman.' The name has stuck despite it now being clear that our hamster is very definitely female. 'And she's really happy that way.'

I glance at my watch and realise we're nearly 10 minutes late thanks to my teenage son, who has yet to grace us with his presence.

'That's *it*, Leo,' I yell up the stairs, for what must be the ninth time. 'Unless you're down here in 20 seconds, you'll be walking.'

His school is two miles away. It's raining heavily. The register will be called in 15 minutes. The likelihood of him making it in any other way than by car is zero. But this is now beyond a joke; enough is enough and he *cannot* be allowed to go on like this. Which is precisely what I say every morning.

'Are we really going without him?' Jacob asks, looking up at me anxiously.

I pull up the hood of his raincoat.

'I hope not,' I whisper. 'Because then I'll drop you off, feel guilty and have to turn around to go and pick him up. Leo! NOW!'

He finally appears at the top of the stairs, half asleep and looking like a drunk who's just crawled out of a nightclub. At 15 years old, my son is six foot one, athletic and handsome, which I *think* is true even taking maternal bias into account. He also currently has no shoes or socks on, his shirt is undone and the top button of his trousers is hanging open. The only element of his appearance that he's attended to is his dark blond hair, which is styled to perfection. Of course it is.

'Have you seen the time?' I say.

He closes his eyes and inhales deeply as he heads down the stairs.

'Would you *please* stop shouting.' He has the air of someone whose patience is being tried by an incompetent customer service operator. I feel my simmering blood rise to a slow boil.

'I. Was. Not. Shouting. I'm merely trying to get you out of the house without making everyone else late. I've got an important meeting first thing.'

'There's plenty of time,' he shrugs, sitting on the bottom step and tugging on a sock in a manner so leisurely you'd think he was lying on a beach in Acapulco.

'*There isn't!*' I say, with rising exasperation.

'You say that every morning and I'm literally never late.'

'That's only because I have to drive like a maniac to make up for lost time!'

He stops and looks at me. '*WHY* are you shouting?'

'I'M *NOT.*'

'Oh, really?'

'Well . . . NOW I am! Good *God*,' I huff. 'Just get in the car. *Please.*'

I love my eldest son more than I can express. I am often dazzled by how clever, thoughtful and fun he has the ability to be. But he's none of these things in the mornings. If you catch him before 9am on weekdays – and early afternoon at weekends – he seems determined to forge a reputation for himself as a giant pain in the arse.

He hasn't always been like this. He was the sweetest little boy you could hope to meet, the first to want a cuddle or a bedtime story. I thought I'd got away lightly with his teenage years at first, but then he hit 15. The transformation happened like the flick of a switch . . . or, more accurately, Godzilla rising from the deep, ready to wreak havoc on everything in his wake.

I turn Jacob around and march him out of the house to the car, clicking the lock and piling in the bags.

'Have you put anything nice in my packed lunch?' he asks.

'What do you mean? You have school meals.'

'But there's the museum trip today,' he reminds me. I feel a gust of breath leave me. 'You haven't forgotten, have you?'

'Of course not. You jump in the back and I'll go and get it.'

In the kitchen, I throw the first edible things I can find into a Tupperware box, before running back outside.

'What have I got?' Jacob asks eagerly. 'We are allowed chocolate as a treat because it's a special day.'

'I had to work with what I had available,' I say, only imagining his disappointment later when he discovers some carrot batons, last night's prawn crackers and three cold cocktail sausages.

I turn out of our street and head into the centre of the leafy, tree-lined suburb where we live. Roebury Village is full of big Victorian houses and has a tram stop twenty minutes from the centre of Manchester. Thanks to the botanical gardens and pretty shops, it's always been considered a nice place; when I was growing up, it was where the kids at my school lived if their parents were lecturers, lawyers or, as in the case of one of my classmates, their dad had had a one-hit wonder in the mid-seventies which had led to a brief flirtation with fame and a lifetime of royalties. It's a few miles from where I grew up, which was in a significantly less posh but nonetheless pleasant neighbourhood with a betting shop on the corner of our street, as opposed to the artisan bakery I've managed to acquire these days.

I switch on the Radio 4 headlines as they're discussing an item about a national shortage of HRT following the 'Davina effect'. Which is great news when I've only just started taking it to combat my own headaches, palpitations, raging PMS and the odd bout of insomnia. I am never sure whether this is caused by my time of life or simply the fact that there really needs to be two of me to run a career alongside our family. But I decided that if there was a tube of gel I could rub onto my arms to lessen *any* of these problems, I was all in.

'Jacob, I forgot to say. I've got some good news about the club you wanted to join. I heard from the coach last night.'

Jacob has made a hobby out of collecting hobbies. You name it, he's tried it over the years – football, drumming, Scouts, climbing. I told him after he'd signed up for fencing classes last year that that was it – no more.

But he has been banging on about wanting to join a baseball team for so long now that I promised to at least look into it. Unfortunately, there aren't that many baseball teams in the UK and it's been nigh on impossible to get him even onto a waiting list. But it's been worth the effort for seeing how much his little face lights up now.

'Did you get me a place?' he says, so delighted that I can't help feeling a bit pleased with myself.

'I did. You're now a proud junior member of the Manchester Baseball Club.'

His expression falls.

'What's the matter?'

'I don't want to join that.'

'I'm sorry . . . what?' I say, failing to keep the exasperation out of my voice. 'You *cannot* just keep chopping and changing like this. How many clubs have you joined over the years? Have you got any idea how hard it was for me to get you into this thing? There're hardly any baseball teams in the UK.'

He blinks, looking a bit shellshocked. 'I know but—'

'But *what?* It's not on, Jacob. Enough is enough.'

He slinks down into his seat dejected and mutters something under his breath.

'What was that?' I snap.

'It was basketball I wanted,' he whispers. 'Not baseball.'

Leo lets out a long, derisory snort. 'Nice one, Mum,' he says.

Chapter 3

I finally dispatch the kids to their respective schools then catch the tram to Salford Quays. I'm waiting at the station as a notification appears on my phone informing me that I haven't logged my breakfast yet – the one I haven't had time to eat – followed by another one pointing out that I have 14 incomplete tasks on my personal list and a full day of meetings ahead of me. A final ping arrives from Asana Rebel, inviting me to take a relaxing meditation. There isn't an option that says, 'Are you taking the piss?', so I swipe it away and get on.

I have a phone full of apps like this. They each represent a crucial ball in the great juggling act that is my life, even if there are times when they feel more bossy than helpful. I'm not complaining about how things are, by the way – the fact that I seem to spend my life organising not merely myself but everyone around me.

This is my modus operandi; it's how I've always been. Former school milk monitor. Brownies Sixer. Head girl at secondary school. I did well academically not because I'm some genius, but because I had a *system*. Every piece of revision was neatly filed and colour-coded, so that by the time I came to my exams, it would have been harder to fail than not. But even I have limits. And these days I have so much 'on' that I occasionally feel less like a well-oiled machine than a wonky shopping trolley whose wheels are threatening to come off.

I step off the tram into one of those bright, cool mornings, the kind where shards of thin sunlight bounce off the water-front. Media City might be a couple of decades old and now home to more than a few of the BBC's and ITV's flagship programmes. But it still feels young and buzzy, an energy that's in keeping with its industrious history. The site sprawls alongside the Manchester Ship Canal and is surrounded by docks that had been operating for centuries. It was through here that the city was once supplied with tea, fruit and oil, raw cotton, grain and timber. But there are no ships now.

Instead, the old stone walls are surrounded a complex of office and residential blocks, purpose-built TV studios and state-of-the-art production centres. In the midst of all this is the UK headquarters of MotionMax+, where I work as Factual Entertainment Commissioner.

It's my role to find new, unscripted programmes about everything from DIY to dating, alongside fly-on-the-wall documentaries and 'social experiments' like *The One*, which was our twist on the 'hot people on a desert island' show (every channel must have one – it's the law). Five years ago, this division had a portfolio of nine shows a year. Now, it's twenty-four. All of this means my job is constantly expanding, which on the one hand means I'm vastly overworked, but on the other is great because, at its heart, I love what I do.

I glance at my watch and peep through the window of Liberica coffee shop, where three baristas are behind the counter, with not much of a queue. Deciding I need a caffeine kick before my first meeting, I step inside and get a notification on my Drinkaware app asking me if I'll commit to a wine-free day. I click on the tick and stand in line as a text arrives from my boss Andrea.

Did you manage to arrange a meeting with Rose's replacement?

I bristle at the description. 'Replacement' sounds permanent and this is only going to be for a few months.

Yes, I'm seeing her *temporary stand-in* this morning.

Oh good. Fill me in on how it goes, will you?

She knows as well as I do how important our working relationship is with Scheduling, the department Rose worked in before her diagnosis and subsequent leave last week.

It is her job to create the final transmission calendar that goes out to viewers and as such her role and mine are entirely interdependent, with constructive co-operation the name of the game. But not only is her judgement impeccable, she loves the same kind of show as me: joyful, escapist, emotional watches which make viewers want to binge until it's coming out of their ears.

I have no idea what to expect from her understudy – who I learnt only yesterday is on a transfer from the US office. I'm about to reply to Andrea when I realise that I'm no further down the line, thanks to the fact that two baristas are busy comparing manicures, while the other is making such a meal out of his cappuccino foam you'd think it was a Turner Prize entry. There was a time in my life when I wouldn't have said anything. When I'd have reacted to an unconvincing 'Sorry about your wait,' with the standard British response – i.e. waving away their apology and reassuring them all that I can see they're absolutely rushed off their feet.

But I've reached an age when, British or not, I just don't have time for this sort of thing.

'Excuse me. Sorry to interrupt but is anyone available to serve?' I ask. I am pulling my most pathetically apologetic expression, but the glance they exchange still suggests they think I'm a snotty cow. At least I'm finally served though.

Coffee in hand, I dash across the piazza, making several turns until I reach the entrance of our building and push through the revolving doors. Teddy, the security guard, is on jovial form as ever. He's an ex-marine, even though he looks like Santa Claus and is such a big softy that it's hard to imagine him ever killing anything other than a sausage roll.

'Morning, Lisa, and no I don't want a hamster,' he says, chuckling at his own joke.

'Ha! Are you *sure*, Teddy?' I smile. 'I bet you'd provide a very loving home.'

'Yeah, and my wife would never speak to me again.'

If only Brendan had been so considerate.

I take the lift up to the fourth floor. MotionMax+ has a swanky workplace by anyone's definition, bright and mostly open-plan, with glass doors on the meeting rooms and thoughtful modern art chosen by someone who knows about this stuff. If I was being cynical I'd say it's also designed for a company that's conspicuous about looking after its 'people', hence the bowls of fresh fruit, well-stocked fridge and soothing meditation room (designed for yoga but mainly used as an extra storeroom).

My workspace sits amidst a quadrangle of desks, all of which are occupied by 8am, to my perpetual dismay. I hate being last in. It might be totally within the company's family-friendly policy and it means I can do the school drop-off first. But I can't shake the idea that it makes me *look* like a part-timer when I'm anything but. I can't remember the last evening I didn't spend at home catching up on work.

'Morning all,' I say, taking off my coat.

Daisy looks up from her computer. She's 25 and peach-skinned, with a dress sense that is eclectic to put it mildly. Some days she turns up looking like Molly Ringwald in *Pretty in Pink* – all floral fabrics and oversized glasses – on others, the look is closer to Gru from *Despicable Me*, in dark, tent-like ensembles. Today is a Molly day, hence the lace dress, fuzzy cardigan and DMs.

'Before you say anything, I can't have a hamster.'

I tut and take a seat. 'This is getting silly. You're the second person to say that and I didn't even ask.'

'I know but I'm *so* easily persuaded,' she says. 'My land-lady had an Ann Summers party the other week. Have you heard of them?'

'Er . . . yes.'

'She insisted my flatmate and I went. I won't even tell you what they ended up selling me . . .'

'I can't help thinking I'd have better luck selling nine vibrators than nine hamsters. Just let me know if you've any friends who might be interested, okay? I've only got one left.'

'Oh, I will,' she says eagerly, going back to the computer she's no doubt been burning up since arriving at 6.30am. Daisy is *very* keen. In that sense, she reminds me of myself at the start of my career, always willing to go the extra mile, refusing to shy away from hard work and determined to hit on the next big idea. But that's where the comparison starts and finishes. Because, despite poor Daisy's best efforts, she hasn't yet come close.

'Did you try out the air fryer recipe for fish tacos, Daisy?' Her face brightens at the sight of Calvin, our intern, who appears from the staff kitchen dunking the bag in his mint tea up and down. He's slightly younger than she is, very tall and slim, with light brown skin and an immaculate haircut with short dreads on top and a fade around the sides.

'Yes and they were amazing!' she replies. 'The flat was a bit smelly mind, but they were almost as good as the halloumi popcorn . . .'

If ever I needed proof of how much things have changed since I was in my twenties, it's the amount of time these two spend discussing their air fryers.

I realise they're both broke – in Daisy's case she's saving up for the deposit on a flat, which is likely to take her until 2065.

But I'd love one – ideally both – of them to come in one morning and tell me they went out, got drunk, shagged someone they regretted and stumbled home at six in the morning with a hangover the size of Pluto.

That doesn't seem to be how twenty-somethings roll these days. If Daisy really wants to push the boat out, she'll go home on a Friday night to a glass of Blossom Hill, her cat and some knitting. When I was 25, this would've made me tragic, but it's somehow become entirely normal.

But then, we used to regularly go to the pub over the road when I was at the BBC and have a half a lager with various journalists, who'd then roll back to work, presumably half-cut and primed to resume an afternoon of newsgathering. Nobody batted an eyelid.

I don't say any of this, of course. All it would do is make me look very old.

'Oh, is that the time?' I mutter, realising my meeting should have started a minute ago. I grab the coffee, my bag and laptop before heading to the stairs and taking a couple of flights up. I'm almost at the meeting room when my phone rings and I recognise the name flashing up as Jacob's fencing coach. I silence the call when a text arrives a moment later.

Hi Lisa, my sister is about to buy a hamster from Pets R Us for her little girl's birthday. Did you say you had some? She's in the shop now so if you've got any left, can you let me know? Like now.

Chapter 4

Rose's temporary replacement is called Zach Russo. He looks
different in the flesh. When I did my homework (because
obviously I did my homework), the profile picture on the US
office's 'Leadership' page showed a man who was dark-haired
and handsome, with generous lips and high cheekbones. He
gave the impression he'd been asked to cross his arms and
smile by the photographer, in a bid to make him look relaxed.
It had the opposite effect.

The picture I saw was obviously taken several years ago,
because now his thick, wavy hair is infused with salty grey.
Also, what was not previously evident is just how tall he is
– six foot three at a guess – and, how can I put this? He's
buff. Leo cringes when I use this word because he thinks I'm
trying to sound 'down with the kids', but there isn't a better
description of his sturdy-but-lean torso, muscular shoulders
and well-honed biceps.

Given he's come direct from LA, I shouldn't be surprised.
I tend to go there once a year and you'll never catch *anyone*
in the US office scoffing Bacon Sizzler McCoys when they
get the 3pm munchies. I suspect that, without the pre-flight
spray tan and crash diet I feel compelled to go on before
every visit, I'd be turned away at Customs.

In Zach Russo's case, though his broad frame can almost
certainly be attributed to genetics, it also suggests a dedica-
tion to working out that – in principle – I find unappealing.
I tend to like men intellectual enough to have a squidge in

their belly. The juxtaposition between Zach's six-pack and the dad bod Brendan had during most of our marriage couldn't be more pronounced. Nevertheless, physically, it's impossible to look at him and not appreciate the view.

'Lisa Darling,' I say, as we shake hands. 'Sorry to be late. I had an emergency to deal with.'

I don't go into further detail, even though I have a spring in my step after finding a new mummy for the last of Alan's babies – an eight-year-old girl whose goldfish died last week (of natural causes, not neglect. I did check).

'Zach Russo,' he replies, distracted by something on his phone.

'Thanks for agreeing to meet before we get into anything more formal. I thought it would be beneficial given how much we'll be seeing of each other. I had a very good relationship with Rose Riley, who you're standing in for. It would be great if we could foster a similar level of co-operation.'

He's still looking at the phone, but eventually tears his eyes away.

'I agree.'

'Great! So have you been to the UK before?'

'Many times.'

'Worked for MotionMax+ long?'

'Two years.'

'And before then?'

'ABC.'

'Ah,' I reply, as if I didn't already know this. I have, in fact, approached my research to Zach Russo's background like a rookie detective trying to solve the clues to a murder. His credentials are impressive – confusingly so. He's over-qualified for this job, which is at least one and possibly two steps down from the position he held in the US. Also, when I quietly asked my opposite number over there about him, she was far from reassuring.

'He has his fans but it's not a universally held opinion,' she'd said.

'What made you decide to move this side of the Pond?' I ask, noticing that his leg is tapping up and down impatiently. 'We don't get as much sun here as in LA. I hope someone's warned you that—'

'Sorry, I need to wrap this up by 9.30,' he says.

This meeting was supposed to be for an hour. He's looking at his watch now. It's expensive, the sort of thing advertised in the pages of Sunday supplements, aimed at overpaid executives who once dreamt of being James Bond, but had to make do with a career in accountancy. 'I read your email so shall we just cut to the chase?'

He's clearly bored already and I haven't even started.

'That's fine,' I say curtly. '*I'm* busy too.'

I can't help feeling that this is very unlike any greeting I usually encountered at the American office, where they're all open arms, brilliant white smiles and, 'Heeey Lisa, how's it hanging?'

'As I said in my email, I thought it would be useful ahead of the meeting next week to bring you up to speed on those projects that are furthest along. One in particular – *Our Girl In Milan* – is ready to be green-lit. Rose was involved in the development all the way along and she was fully on board.'

His eyes pinch at the sides. 'Yes. I read about that one.'

The monthly content planning meeting is when my department updates internal stakeholders on our current projects, so they can have their input. The dream scenario is that everyone around the table is happy, give or take a few suggestions, meaning we can see it all the way through from development to screen.

It rarely happens like that. Questions are asked, objections raised, further work requested, all of which is part of the process. Yet there have been extreme but by no means unheard of cases when someone has put a spanner in the works when it's literally *days* from the start of production. It's a risk with every project. But if Rose were still here, *Our Girl in Milan* would be getting the green light next week, so the last thing I want is her stand-in getting any ideas.

'As you read in my email, the concept will follow a young British model all the way from her discovery as an unknown teenager – where viewers will see her plucked from obscurity on the street – to her first runway show in Italy.'

'Hmm. I read that.'

'We're billing it as perfect for fans of *Emily in Paris* and—'

'That was dramedy.'

'Exactly the point,' I say. 'There's a gap in Factual Entertainment. The tone will be fun and colourful. It is a great financial proposition and has excellent long-term prospects. We're the perfect home for it. *Everyone* thinks so. Two other streaming services were chomping at the bit for this.'

'Huh,' he says, ponderously. Then he puts his elbows on the desk and presses his forefingers together, drawing attention to his muscular forearms, which flex when he releases them, and sits back in his chair.

'Let me rewind just a moment,' he says. 'Is the purpose of this meeting for you to illicit some kind of *guarantee* that I'll nod this through next week, no questions asked?'

Frankly, that would be ideal. Not that I can say it out loud.

'I wouldn't expect you to do that, obviously,' I laugh lightly, as warmth spreads to the tips of my ears.

'Okay, good,' he says, nodding. 'Because if I do have concerns, I obviously need to voice them.'

I feel my spine tighten. 'Well, *obviously*. I was simply asking you to bear in mind that this particular project is ... well, it's really far along,' I say, hoping to emphasise what a massive pain in the arse, not to mention waste of money and time, we'd face in the event of major problems now. 'It would make life very difficult for all concerned at this stage if—'

'But it hasn't yet been green-lit?'

'Well, no.'

'Then it's still all to play for. And I might as well tell you: I do have concerns.'

My expression darkens. I strongly suspect his only genuine 'concern' is that I've had the audacity to approach him privately about this. But what was I supposed to do? Allow him to sweep in at the last minute and smash up my sandcastle?

'I see,' I say, gritting my teeth. 'Well, I hope you realise, I was not suggesting anything other than . . . pragmatism.'

'Right,' he drawls, but it's not the kind of 'right' that suggests he's buying this. 'I can understand why you wouldn't want any nasty surprises at the content planning meeting. Equally, I'm not pushing this through just because it'd be inconvenient for you. Assuming that's what you're asking me to do?'

Heat blooms on my chest. Fucking perimenopause.

'I don't believe I said that,' I say, coolly. At some point, we seem to have become engaged in a staring contest, one I'm determined to win. 'I simply wanted to give you the opportunity to see what I'm working on – the projects Rose was involved in – so that you have a chance to . . . take it all in before we're in front of a wider audience.'

He looks me directly in the eye, apparently equally determined. 'Consider it taken in.'

'Look. Mr Russo—'

'My name's Zach,' he says. 'I think we can use first names if we're going to be working together, don't you? Unless you'd prefer *Ms Darling*?'

'Lisa's fine,' I say with a wave of dread. Do I *really* have to work with this guy? Even for six months? I don't like him. *At all.* I want Rose back.

He crosses his arms and looks down at his phone again as I register how he smells. The aftershave isn't overpowering. In fact, I don't even know if it is aftershave. I can't put my finger on any of the top notes beyond saying that it's masculine and soft all at once. I look away briefly and when I glance back, he's standing up and putting his jacket on.

'I gotta cut this short, I'm afraid,' he says. This isn't just short, this is ridiculous.

'But I haven't told you about—'

'I know. I apologise. I did read your email . . . with interest,' he says, heading towards the door. As he's about to leave, he turns around. 'I'm sorry if you were hoping for a yes man, Lisa. But I'm not one of them.'

'Clearly not,' I reply, with a saccharine smile, deciding I'll move my drink-free night to tomorrow instead.

Chapter 5

He's an arsehole. I am counting the days until you're back. Honestly, he's going to be very unpopular around here x

I press send on my text as I march across the building towards the lift.

Rose responds immediately.

Does nobody like him then? Not that I'm feeling insecure (much!)

Nobody. You have NOTHING to worry about around here

The lift doors open and I step inside. As I turn and press the button, I spot Zach Russo on the opposite side of the office holding court with several members of senior management, among whom is my boss Andrea. She's in her early sixties, with a neat figure and dress sense like that of a Tory politician. Today, she's in a tailored pencil suit, silk scarf knotted at the side of her throat, while her feathered blond bob has the kind of fibreglass lustre that can only be achieved with a *lot* of hairspray. I have no idea what they are discussing, but at one point they all throw back their heads in an explosion of raucous laughter.

The doors are closing when Zach, apparently possessed of a sixth sense, glances up and catches me looking at him. From all the way across the room, we lock eyes. A bolt of adrenalin causes heat to prickle under my arms, yet I'm frozen, a rabbit in headlights. I'm about to look away when I see the corner of his mouth turn up. It's an almost imperceptible gesture, but if I didn't know better I'd say it was a smile.

The lift closes.

As it descends, I exhale, feeling so overheated that I have to sniff my blouse to ensure I'm not too fragrant, before pulling myself together to focus on my next meeting. I barely have a gap between them. I don't know when I'm supposed to go to the loo exactly, let alone eat lunch.

When I was a trainee in the BBC Drama department, there was a certain mystique around the senior executives and what exactly happened when they disappeared into a conference room. I imagined a hotbed of creativity, of fiery debate, of women with heels and swishy hair flinging around ideas and quips as sharp as their suits. Basically, I imagined a scene from *Ally McBeal*.

What I discovered when I was senior enough to be invited into those same meetings was that I hadn't been missing much. No offence to my colleagues, but the world seems to have gone meetings mad, or MotionMax+ has at the very least. Nobody can order new paperclips around here without having a Zoom about it.

The rest of the afternoon is taken up with a finance update that drags on for so long that I'm forced to break it up with a few pelvic floor exercises, followed by two further appointments with companies pitching new ideas for what they hope will be the next big TV hit. The first one wasn't bad, certainly worthy of a second look, though the second – for a celebrity pigeon-racing show featuring Boris Johnson, Geri Halliwell and somebody who used to be in a boy band (none of whom had confirmed) – didn't set anyone's heart alight.

It's 3.45pm before I get to eat the now soggy Pret sandwich I'd bought for lunch, hunched over my desk as I simultaneously correspond with the fencing coach about a convenient time to come and collect the hamster.

'How was McDreamy?' Daisy grins, plonking down at her desk opposite, with a glint behind her glasses.

'Who?' I ask.

'*McDreamy*,' she repeats, as if this should mean something to me. 'Don't you think the new guy in Scheduling looks like Patrick Dempsey in *Grey's Anatomy*?'

'I've never seen *Grey's Anatomy*,' I tell her, though you'd think from the way she gasps afterwards that I've just told her I've never eaten solid food.

'You don't know what you're missing! I've watched all 19 seasons. You need to get *right* onto it, Lisa.'

'Daisy,' I say, patiently. 'I don't have time to watch 19 *minutes* of anything, let alone seasons.'

'Right,' she says, not really listening. 'He's *very handsome*, don't you think?'

'He's old enough to be your dad.'

'He is not!' she protests before her eyebrows knit together as she rethinks the statement. 'Hmm. Maybe you're right. What about you then? You're not past it, Lisa, despite what you've said. Surely you could make an exception?'

I choke on a piece of crust. 'I don't think I ever used the term "past it".'

'Well, *good*,' she says, emphatically. 'Because you're still pretty. I hope I look like you when I'm 50.'

'I'm 47.'

'Oh, you know what I mean,' she says, dismissively, as if they amount to the same thing.

Chapter 6

I grew up in the 1980s, the era of strong female icons such as Madonna, Martina Navratilova and Margot Kidder's Lois Lane. So I've never particularly suffered from imposter syndrome and never thought I didn't deserve a successful career because I wasn't as clever or capable as any of the men I worked with. There is one intellectual challenge, however, that is guaranteed to fill me with existential self-doubt . . .

'What on earth is a Carroll Diagram?' I huff, clicking on the latest maths homework that's been set for my 10-year-old on the dreaded See Saw app.

It doesn't help that I've only just been able to sit down after spending half an hour cajoling Jacob to get off the game he was playing, trying to throw together his swimming kit for the following day and flogging several more PTA Wine Quiz tickets via WhatsApp. 'That didn't even exist when I was at school. Who was it who changed maths and *why?* What was wrong with how it was?'

'Does that mean you can't help?' Jacob sighs and picks up his iPad.

I take it off him. 'Absolutely not. We don't give up that easily.'

'Even when we don't know what we're doing?' he asks.

'*Especially* then.'

Leo pops his head around the living room door. 'Have we got any Pot Noodles?'

'No. We're having a crackdown on ultra-processed foods.'

He huffs. 'There is literally *nothing* in this house to eat.'

'I'm sure there is, Leo,' I say, aware of the divergence in our respective expectations. He eats like a horse and seems to think it's my job to keep the cupboard full enough to whip up a Tudor feast at the drop of a hat.

'Not that I can see. And where's the Coke? Or Doritos? You said you'd get some.'

'Have some fruit,' I say, distractedly, googling something that might shed some light on the next maths question.

'Nah. I wanted something good.'

To think this is the child I bothered pureeing organic broccoli for when he was five months old because I naively believed that it would lead to a lifetime of healthy eating. But then, that's not the only way in which Leo has changed recently.

Until the beginning of this school year, he wasn't just one of the brightest students in his class, he was diligent too. There wasn't a spelling test that Leo didn't prepare for.

Unfortunately, the start of his two-year GCSE studies seems to have coincided with a major re-evaluation of his priorities in life. Now, he has a total disinterest in exams, has to be threatened, bribed and cajoled into doing his homework and seems to place as much value on studying as he does on picking up wet towels from a bathroom floor.

Far more important to him these days is developing his skills on the PlayStation and playing any sport available – including but not limited to Brazilian Ju-Jitsu, tennis and, above all, rugby.

Obviously, I'm glad he's looking after his physical health, if you can say that about a sport that has resulted in several black eyes and a broken wrist (and that's just the tennis). I think it's fantastic that he has passions. Equally, he's a clever kid who is going to blow these exams completely if he doesn't get his act together.

'Do you know what a Carroll Diagram is, Leo?' I ask, more to satisfy my own curiosity than anything else.

'Course,' he shrugs.

Something occurs to me. 'Great! Come and sit down. You can have a Pot Noodle if you help Jacob with his homework.'

'I thought you said we didn't have any?'

I don't tell him it's my emergency stash. 'Chicken Curry?' I offer instead, standing up to head to the kitchen.

'Ooh yeah,' he replies eagerly, as if I've just offered him a Michelin-starred meal. 'Thanks Mum.'

I sometimes think I should be stricter, that the backchat I've been dealing with since he turned 15 is my own fault. Perhaps I made this bed in the aftermath of the divorce. When Brendan left, I felt an almost primal need to lavish them with affection and tenderness. With hindsight, I probably spoiled them, but I wanted the message to be loud and clear: your dad might no longer live in this house, but I've got more than enough love to fill it with.

I don't get time to watch TV after Jacob has gone to bed – I've got too many emails I need to catch up on in the spare room. This doubled as my office at the height of the pandemic and still does on the odd day when I work from home.

The boys and I live in a four-bedroom Edwardian semi that my dad and I redecorated from top to bottom when we first moved in. I wouldn't describe it as my dream house; that would be one of those rambling country cottages in the Cotswolds where Jilly Cooper's books were set. But there is a lot to love about it that goes beyond the desirable postcode. Original features. A good garden. A fitted kitchen, complete with double oven, pendant lights and a flexi-spray sink tap that I got very excited about when it was installed 18 months ago.

It's gone 11pm before I finally close my laptop, at which point I'm too shattered to do anything except head to the bathroom to take off my make-up. Back in my twenties, I'd happily scrub it off with a disposable wipe, slap on a bit of supermarket moisturiser and that was that. I can't claim that my skincare routine has changed enormously, though there are dozens of jars in my cabinet and they cost more, though I suspect all these AHAs and retinols are probably no better than a good night's sleep.

Full disclosure: I have had Botox. Not because I want the skin of a twenty-year-old but because I have frown lines above my nose that, without an injection a couple of times a year, make me look permanently angry and irritated. And I'm only that some of the time. I'm not brave enough for fillers, though, mainly because there's a woman on reception at our doctor's surgery with lips you could stand a potted cactus on.

Beyond that, my quest to be the best forty-something version of myself is half-hearted at best; I am no Gwyneth Paltrow.

I think every woman reaches a stage in her life when she vows to *Be More Gwyneth*. I'd love to be irritated by her. To dismiss her vagina-scented candles and bone-broth diet as evidence that she's ga-ga. But at the end of the day, she's running a multi-million-pound empire and she still has time to meditate, scrape her tongue and dry-brush her thighs every night.

As if on cue, another Asana Rebel notification pops up on my phone, reminding me that if only I'd devoted 10 minutes to their exercises today, I'd soon be on the way to an iron-clad core and inner peace. I don't really have the temperament for Pilates or yoga, preferring the endorphin high and convenience of a thirty-minute run, which I can slot in a few evenings of the week when Jacob is at one of his clubs. The only trouble is, running does not love me these days, judging by the sound my joints make the day after a 5k. Like someone in the vicinity is opening a bag of crisps.

Yet, I know I should be doing the holistic stuff at my age, aimed at strengthening and suppleness. A bit like the collagen, oils and powders I should be knocking back, to balance hormones, suppress carb cravings and basically do everything a busy woman needs short of highlighting her hair. But I'm now too shattered to manage anything close to a warrior pose, so I swipe away the notification and vow that tomorrow will be the day I commit to the Pilates – and the start of the new, more supple and grounded me.

Daisy's words suddenly pop into my head.

You're not past it, Lisa.

It was clear she wasn't talking about the flexibility of my joints, but about how hot I am – or otherwise. I don't really think about that these days, at least not as much as I once did. I suspect I can still turn the odd head with a push-up bra and the right lighting, but that's as far as I'll go.

Someone like Daisy – who's in her mid-twenties – might find it impossible to believe, but I am really not on the look-out for romance like I was at her age. On the contrary, I am not merely comfortable about the idea of being single for the rest of my life – I'm actually *relieved* by it. The pressure's off.

I did a little bit of dating before I met Brendan. It was fun, I can't deny it – but it was also stressful. I can't be alone in thinking this, surely? That I've devoted too much time over the years to over-thinking men's behaviour, analysing their texts and worrying about whether I'm being ghosted. I've been there, done that. And while I refuse to beat myself up about anything in my past, including the two failed marriages, one thing is certain: there will never, ever, *ever* be another.

Chapter 7

To-do list

- Offer 1.5 x going rate to maths tutor to end Carroll Diagram misery
- Take the sodding collagen – it's not hard
- Catch up with eight days of Asana Rebel
- Buy battery-powered candles, catering roll and print out guest list for PTA Wine Quiz
- Return five bras to Pour Moi
- Measure cup size to avoid wild guesswork in future
- Buy more socks (both kids)
- Reply to school email about geography field trip
- Reply to school email about end of term photos
- Reply to school email about consent for flu jabs
- Reply to school email about careers open evening
- Consider giving up full-time work in order to reply to school emails
- Start DIY panelling – for real this time
- Find one of at least six scientific calculators we have in this house
- Ditto protractors
- Uninstall Drinkaware
- Descale kettle

There are some meetings during which you accept calls and interruptions from nobody – and I'm about to step into one of them. I'll be presenting to other key heads of department and have been dreading it ever since my tête-à-tête with Zach last week. But no matter how important, when the contact that flashes on your phone up reads, 'JACOB SCHOOL', you answer.

'Nothing at all to worry about,' says the school secretary breezily. She begins all calls with these words. She'd say it even if your 10-year-old had absconded, hot-wired the Principal's Mondeo and was currently en route to the airport with a ticket to Fiji. 'However, you'll need to come and collect Jacob as soon as possible please. There's been an incident.'

Fuck. 'What's happened?'

'I'm afraid he's put a Polo mint up his nose.'

'Oh, thank God. I thought it was something serious,' I exhale.

'Well, it's not *ideal*,' she points out, as I feel a ripple of panic.

'*Is he all right?*'

'He's fine. Just says his nostril is very cold, so it obviously can't stay there. Has he done it before?'

'Not since he was two, but that was a Tic Tac. It came out with a good blow.'

'I believe that's already been tried,' she says.

'What about tweezers?'

'Mrs Darling.' I decide now isn't the time to say – again – that I'm a *Ms*. 'Nobody here is going to put a pair of tweezers up your son's nose,' she adds, not unreasonably.

'No, of course not,' I mumble, chastised.

'You'll need to collect him straight away.'

'Of course,' I mutter, glancing into the meeting room, where most people are already seated.

Andrea's face appears in front of the door and she taps her finger on her watch furiously. I nod and return to the call.

'I'll see if I can get Jacob's granddad to come over straight away. Leave it with me.'

I push open the glass door as Andrea turns around. 'One minute! Sorry!'

Her glowering face is the last thing I see as I step outside again to phone my parents. Mum answers and I fill her in, before asking if Dad is available. In case it isn't obvious, this is far from the first time Grandma and Granddad have had to step in.

'Well, if their own father hadn't moved to the Peak District, he might be able to pull his finger out,' she huffs, never missing an opportunity to slag Brendan off.

'I know. He's a dick.' She doesn't usually approve of language, but *always* makes an exception for my ex. She can turn the air blue with some of the insults she's thrown his way over the years. 'So can Dad go?'

'He can't, love. He's got the chiropodist here. She's having a hell of a time with his heels.'

I hear a noise in the background that resembles the kind of power tool you'd need to fell an oak tree.

'Is there any way you can go? I'm sorry to ask,' I grovel. 'It'll probably just pop out the moment you see him, but if not, he'll have to go to the NHS walk-in centre. I'm really sorry.'

'Oh, stop saying sorry. I would but it's Aquarobics on a Tuesday.'

A cry escapes from the back of my throat before I can stop it.

She tuts. 'Oh, all right then. I'll go Thursday instead, though the instructor isn't as good as Pauline.'

'Sorry.'

'Stop it. I'll go and get him now.'

'Mum, you are a star,' I say emphatically.

'I know,' she sighs.

As I step into the presentation room my eyes are drawn automatically to Zach.

He is talking to Bram Gullit, our Dutch-born head of Digital, but briefly looks up at me, prompting a treacherous flash of heat in my belly. I slip into the only free seat directly opposite him at the conference table where there are twelve of us, from departments ranging from Marketing to Drama, Legal to Reality.

Andrea clears her throat.

'Now we're all present and correct, we should get started. Before we proceed, Zach, would you introduce yourself to anyone you haven't yet met?'

He's had his hair cut. It's very short at the sides, but he's got some kind of product on top so it sweeps forward in a thick wave. His jaw is clean-shaven and smooth, enhancing the tiny dimple in his chin. He's wearing a pale blue shirt that is very simple but nonetheless looks expensive. Everything about him does.

'Sure. Well, I'm Zach. As you may be able to tell, I'm not local.'

Compared with the clipped British vowels of the rest of us, his accent is like honey. Deep and smooth, with no hard edges.

'I was born in New York but studied in the UK, before returning to the US to work for ABC in LA. I worked there for most of my career, before joining MotionMax+. I've been here a week so far and have been grateful for the warm welcome. I must say, I'm impressed with your operation.'

'Flattery will get you *everywhere*,' says Andrea, with a seductive giggle.

'Ha,' he says, though it's closer to a cough than a laugh. 'Well, this is already sounding like some cheesy speed-dating introduction, so I'll leave it there. Oh, except . . . I'm aware I'm stepping into a big pair of shoes here. I hear wonderful things about Rose Riley and she's left me a comprehensive handover. Still, my aim in the few months I'm here is that I can make a contribution that's . . . meaningful.'

'I'm sure you will,' gushes Andrea as I try not to roll my eyes. 'Well, let's move on, shall we. Could somebody take notes?'

She glares at the side of the table where I am sitting, between our Chief Talent Officer Karen Mariko and Head of Comedy Angikka Bayu, before looking to the end, towards Emily Reig, the new hotshot in Digital. The only women in the meeting, aside from her.

I can imagine what Rose would have to say about this. It would be something about the patriarchy and how Andrea is not merely an unwitting collaborator, but a raging sexist in her own right. Despite having smashed more than a few glass ceilings herself, Andrea thinks the #MeToo movement is a 'lot of fuss over nothing'. If there's a cup of tea to be made, she considers it the job of one of the women in the room, no matter how senior. I've even seen her leap up to make a Darjeeling more than once amongst a group of men, all more junior than her, simply because she's the only female available.

The note-taking is a case in point and I can almost hear Rose in my ear: it's *fine* to be asked, as long as the men are too. We're senior managers, not 1950s secretaries. But Andrea, in all the years I've worked with her, never has. Worse than that is that I, just like when I was a six-year-old milk monitor, cannot *bear* the sound of silence.

'Shall I do it?' I offer. I'd kick myself if I didn't already have one member of the family en route to a doctor.

'Thank you, Lisa,' she says, as I reach into my bag for a pen. Unfortunately, it's only as I click the top that I realise the only one at my disposal is a battery-powered Spider-Man biro that flashes when you write. I briefly attempt to hide it behind my hand, but it just looks as if I'm stopping someone from copying my answers in a spelling test.

'Let's start with daytime, shall we?' says Andrea.

At this point, my pen starts flashing, first red, then blue. I glance up quickly and realise that Zach is looking at it, then me. He raises an eyebrow. I purse my lips. Then, I click on the end decisively and vow to ride this out with as much dignity as if I was holding a Mont Blanc fountainpen.

Chapter 8

The first part of the meeting involves a discussion of the Autumn schedule, a new adaptation of *Anne of Green Gables* and a recently green-lit reality project based in a cosmetic surgery clinic, pitched as '*ER* meets *Real Housewives of Beverley Hills*'. There's a review of our competitors' performance and a lot of discussion regarding a feature in *Deadline* about what's in the pipeline over at Netflix.

When it's my turn to present, I push aside any unease and try to ignore Zach's ominous words. '*I might as well tell you . . . I do have concerns.*'

How is he going to play this? Am I about to be stitched up? Or might he have dwelled on what I said and decided it's not worth making an enemy of me, especially given that he's only here for a short time?

'I'll begin with *Our Girl In Milan*,' I say. 'As you all know I've been working on this for six months and it's a project that we're lucky to have a chance to be involved in, given the intense interest from our competitors. The minor rights issues I mentioned last time we met have now been ironed out and if we can keep everything on time and on budget, we can assign a slot alongside a key date in the fashion industry calendar, creating significant PR opportunities.'

I can hear my own heartbeat thundering in my ears. Zach says nothing.

'All this effectively means we're ready to give this the go-ahead, assuming everyone around this table is happy.'

'Really great work on this one, Lisa,' interjects Andrea. 'This is very exciting. We'll all look forward to seeing it come to fruition.'

'Thank you.' I am reaching for the mouse when a voice makes my spine prickle.

'Before you move on, could I make some observations?'

It sounds like a question, but it isn't. Zach's *observations* are going to be made whether I like them or not.

I look up and glare at him. For a short moment, the atmosphere feels charged, almost gladiatorial.

'Could you please skip back one or two slides, Lisa?' His softly melodious voice is in sharp contrast to my rigid smile.

'Certainly.'

I click as Zach leans in, his eyes on me. Some knot forms in the hollow of my chest. In the moments that follow, I pray for kindness, for him to say, '*What a great idea, Lisa, you nailed it!*'

'I realise I'm late to this party, but it would be wrong of me not to share the fact that I have some reservations about this concept.'

Bastard.

Andrea blinks. 'Really, Zach? Then you must share away,' she urges him.

'Well, at its most basic level, this is an area that's been done before too many times. It's unoriginal,' he says, bluntly.

'That's ridiculous,' I interject. 'This concept is brand new.'

'Apart from *The Face*, *American Beauty Star*, *Model Behaviour* . . . and any number of copycat shows since *America's Next Top Model*? Does the world *really* need another one of those?'

'I see what you mean,' murmurs Angikka.

'Another *America's Next Top Model*?' I say, unable to believe my ears. 'Would that be the incredibly successful franchise that spawned 22 seasons, dozens of spin-offs and still regularly has viewing figures that exceed 1.2million? Frankly, if you think you could do better than that, I'm sure we'd all love to hear it.'

'Well—'

'Either way,' I say, cutting him off, 'I fundamentally disagree with the idea that this is some kind of copycat project. It's completely different. The only overlap is that it features models. But no single show has exclusive rights over the subject matter.'

Zach is unfazed.

'The fact that this *is* a wannabe is only one problem with it,' he continues. He's not talking to the rest of the room now, only me. There's something about those inky eyes of his that have a deeply unsettling effect. You feel as if you're captured by them, as if he's got an invisible lasso around your waist and he isn't going to let you go anywhere.

'Given that one of MotionMax+'s stated strategies for the next 12 months has been to try to reach a young adult audience, I can see the thinking behind this,' he concedes. 'Nevertheless, it's *precisely* in that context that I feel like this concept is a little . . . off.'

'*Off?*' I repeat, as if we're discussing an out-of-date chicken madras.

'Yes,' he says, unapologetically. 'You're talking about plucking some girl from the street and telling her you'll make her dreams come true, if only she can squeeze into that size-zero dress and never eat a brownie again. I don't feel comfortable with glamorising an industry that is well known for manipulating vulnerable young women.'

I let out a huff of disbelief, then realise that several people around the table appear to be murmuring their agreement.

'Look. I would be the first person to agree with you if there was anything *manipulative* about this show,' I leap in. 'I feel qualified to say that, not merely as someone who has been involved in it from the start, but also as someone who once was herself . . .'

'A model?' asks Giles from Legal, clearly impressed.

'*A young woman,*' I say.

I cross my arms, awaiting Zach's comeback. Surely the only trump card available to him at this point is that *he too was once a young woman.* Anything's possible these days, of course, but it still seems unlikely.

As he says nothing, I continue. 'Also, since when was it our job to moralise? We're here to *entertain*. And I am confident that this has huge appeal. Any teenager would love it.'

'That's what concerns me.'

'Oh yes, how awful to create something popular.' A slam dunk.

But annoyingly, while *my* adrenalin is fizzing, he seems completely unruffled.

'I've seen the trailer for it. The girl in question . . . she's, what, 17? Must have a BMI of 15, 16 tops.'

'She's 19 actually,' I say, even though I have literally no idea if this is true or not. All I know is that I have to stop this shit show, or at least work out how and why he's doing this.

At that point – finally – the penny drops. I can't believe I didn't see it before now. It's obvious what's going on here. This guy doesn't want to just keep Rose's job ticking over. He wants the position for good. And he's not going to get that without making a name for himself. What other possible reason could there be for what's going on here?

He's still banging on about this when I drift into my own head, roll up my sleeves, consider everything Rose is going through – and glower at him.

Not on my watch, *mate*. No. Fucking. Way.

'This is all very noble of you,' I say, coolly, in the first gap in conversation. Now I understand what's going on here, the gloves are well and truly off. 'However, I'm not sure it's appropriate that anyone in this group to pull the plug on a show based on their assessment of a woman's body shape.'

Giles, who is nearing retirement and permanently terrified that he'll say or do something that isn't politically correct, says: 'Hear hear'.

Andrea's brows knit together. 'Well, none of this is ideal at this stage, of course. But I can see where you're coming from, Zach.'

I turn and glare at her, trying to work out if I'm hallucinating this. Five minutes ago, she thought this programme was 'very exciting'. On Tuesday, we had a conversation about the potential for foreign rights. She has backed this whole concept from its inception. Now, the moment she's sitting in front of some smooth-talker from LA, New York or wherever, she starts batting her eyelids and can 'see where he's coming from'.

'I'm sorry, Lisa,' she says gently, as if she's withholding a lollipop from a small child. 'I know how much work you've put into this, but there are some good points being made here. Are you getting them all down?'

She nods at my notepad, where my Spider-Man pen has stopped flashing. I haven't written a single thing in the last ten minutes. Right now, I feel like drawing a cock and balls on the paper then holding it up to say: 'Yes. Here is a summary of my notes so far.'

Instead, I start attempting to write. Only now, the bloody thing has run out of ink and despite the dozen or so angry circles I draw on the side of my pad, nothing appears to be happening.

'I'll take notes.'

Zach reaches into the pocket of the jacket on the back of his chair and pulls out a pen.

'Oh, you don't have to do that,' Andrea leaps in.

'It's fine,' he says, clicking the end of it.

He looks up at me, apparently waiting for me to comment. 'You were saying?'

'It's all in the execution. We can make it clear to the production company that if there is anybody who shows signs of struggling with an eating disorder, then they will have to act. Also . . .' I start flailing around for anything now, 'if it makes you feel better we could put a helpline number at the end.'

'Won't work,' Zach says, flatly. I glare at him. 'Sorry, but it won't.'

'Well, I agree with Lisa,' says Giles. I flash him a grateful smile. 'It's just silly to say that we can't make *any* programming about a whole industry. That it simply can't be done. Sensitive handling is the key.'

'Giles, with respect . . .' Andrea begins, which is how she always begins a sentence when she's about to tell him he's a complete arsehole.

I can only describe the scene that ensues as a pile-on. Andrea and Angikka side with Zach, along with Simon from Drama and Julian from Reality. Karen and Giles side with me, alongside Suzy from Acquisitions and Chris from Comedy. Emily throws in a random anecdote about her brother's niece working as a hairdresser at a fashion show in Barcelona, while Elias Caliskan from Finance simply keeps shuffling around a spreadsheet and saying, 'Can I interest anyone in a budget breakdown?'

The whole thing is a shambles.

'Look, look,' says Andrea, calling the room to order. 'There's only one way to resolve this. You're going to have to take it to Krishna Chowdhury, Lisa. It's up to him to adjudicate in instances such as this.'

Krishna is Chief Content Officer. Mr Big. The final decision is his.

The thought of all the extra work a presentation to him will involve, not to mention the fact that until this morning I was convinced I'd have this over the finish line, makes me almost fall to my knees and start to weep. Instead, I close my notepad and push out my chair.

'Fine. I'd be delighted to,' I say.

I throw Zach a withering glare, then get to my feet, pick up my Spider-Man pen and take my leave.

Chapter 9

A disturbing thing happens on Saturday morning. I have a dirty dream. Which would be fine in itself. Delightful, even. Except that it's about Zach Russo. It's during that mysterious point of sleep when you're not quite awake, but conscious enough to apparently stumble into your own personal porno.

It's been a few years since I had one so vivid. I'd assumed they'd dried up at about the time adverts for caffeine shampoo began to pop up on Facebook. Aside from a short revival courtesy of the hot priest in *Fleabag* Season 2, there really haven't been many to write home about for a while.

Now, though, my inner goddess appears to be back with a vengeance.

In the dream, I'm in a luxurious hotel room. Imagine a slick, cream-carpeted suite in a nineties movie starring Sharon Stone or Kim Basinger. It's the sort of place where, in the days when I read *Cosmopolitan* as a teenager, I once firmly believed I'd be hanging out *all the time* later in life. The lighting is subdued, the furnishings plush, the mood seductive. There's an unfeasibly large bed and a floor-to-ceiling window, beyond which the lights of Manhattan glitter against an obsidian sky.

Zach leads me into the room by the hand, anticipation rising in my chest. The apples of my cheeks are flushed, the taste of multiple whisky sours lingers on my lips. I'm in a midnight-blue slip dress, which pinches at my waist and reveals the soft, heavy outline of my breasts.

He's in a tux, or at least he *has* been; the jacket's now gone and his tie hangs loose around the collar of his shirt, top button undone. The smooth skin of his Adam's apple is begging to be kissed and I am indescribably hot for him. He closes the door behind us and draws those dark eyes slowly down my body. The way he looks at me makes something liquify in my core. Like he wants to devour me.

'God, you're beautiful.'

The statement comes from deep at the back of his throat, before he slides his hands around my waist and pulls me into him. I lift my chin as his lips sink into mine, full and tender. An undulating heat rises from my belly as I run my hands across his back, feeling the swell of his muscles. Something twitches against me and I push my pelvis into him, registering not merely how hard he is, but how big.

He places his hand on my jaw and tips back my head, sliding his mouth to the sweet spot behind my ear, searing me with silky kisses. Then he runs his fingertips all the way to the slope of my neck and down my shoulder, before they skim the side of my breast. Forgotten parts of my anatomy spark into life. My need for him is so intense I can hardly breathe. I stand on my tiptoes and cup his face in my hands as I kiss him, sliding my tongue gently inside his mouth until he groans.

We are ferocious after that, tugging at his shirt and flinging it to the floor, until his beautiful, honed torso is bare and one strap of my dress has fallen off my shoulder. I run my hands over the ripples on his triceps, feeling the strength of him beneath my fingers. Then we make our way to the bed and I lie back, lifting my arms above my head in surrender as the silk of my dress gathers up around my thighs.

He climbs on top, straddling me, his knees at the side of my hips as my hem rides higher. He kisses me again, our foreheads pressed together as he slides a hand between my legs, where a warm pulse is already throbbing. He gently pushes aside my knickers and slips a finger inside, drawing it gently downwards in a slow vertical line. It begins as soft as a whisper, before building slowly into something more insistent, drawing me deeper and deeper under some kind of spell. I hear myself groan and think, *Fuck me*, though I'm too inside my own head to know if it's an exclamation or a request. And then—

'MUM!'

Someone is shaking my shoulder. I wake up to find Jacob standing at the side of my bed in his pyjamas, a tuft of hair sticking up from the top of his head. 'Did you hear me?'

'Huh? Oh. Yes!' I say, wiping sleep from my eyes.

I push myself up, blinking as I fully register that I'm not in a hotel room with Zach Russo about to make me come so hard that I forget my middle name.

Jacob's face brightens. 'So does that mean . . . *we can?*'

'Can what?'

'Can get one of them,' he says, as if I'm being a bit dense.

'Get one of . . . what?' I ask, feeling as if this conversation has taken an ominous turn.

'*A parrot.*'

'What?!' I exclaim. 'No, Jacob. No, no, no. Absolutely not.'

His brow furrows. 'But you *will* think about it?'

'No,' I say, firmly. 'It's out of the question. Why would you want a parrot when you've already got a hamster?'

'You *can* have more than one pet. Bella's got three cocker spaniels.'

'The answer's *no*, Jacob.' I peer at the clock. It's 5.38am. 'Why are you up so early?'

'I had a funny dream,' he tells me.

'Me too.'

'Was yours about a giant frog as well?'

'Something like that. Anyway, off you go and jump back into bed.'

'Can I get in with you?'

'Oh, go on then,' I say, lifting up the duvet. He curls into my arms and I kiss his head. The best feeling in the world.

'How's your nose, by the way?' I ask.

'All right now,' he says. 'It's stopped tingling.'

'Why on earth did you do that, anyway?'

'It was a dare.'

'Of course it was,' I sigh. '*Promise* me you won't do it again.'

'I promise.' He snuggles into my arm and looks up at me with those big eyes and their long lashes. 'I love you, Mum.'

'I love you too,' I whisper.

'Are you sure about the parrot?'

'Absolutely. And don't even think about asking your dad.'

Chapter 10

I give up on the idea of returning to sleep at six, largely because Jacob's favoured position is horizontal and with a toe up my nose. I flick around on my phone for a while, googling, 'Is it possible for perimenopause to actually increase sex drive?' The answer is that – despite its libido-dampening reputation – it's very possible, if an Australian women's health website is to be believed. The lengthy explanation can be summed up in one word. Hormones.

I might have known. To read the internet you'd think hormones are responsible for everything from mood swings and blackheads to soil erosion in sub-Saharan Africa. In this case, it's something to do with the relative rate of testosterone decline versus oestrogen. If the former is going down slower, it ends up being dominant. Hence you feel friskier than you have for years. At least that explains one thing. The fact that Zach Russo – of all people – is the object of my temporary lust remains a complete mystery. No wonder I've made so many terrible decisions in my life.

Jacob stirs and pushes me further to one edge of the bed, so I decide to make the best of the situation and start on some of my weekend jobs. Sunday will be devoted to starting my new presentation for Krishna, but I don't want to work both days if I can help it and I vowed I'd start panelling this living room today if it killed me.

I'd planned to begin weeks ago and have all the gear from B&Q ready and waiting. Only, the dozens of mundane day-to-day tasks I end up doing most weekends – not to mention driving the kids to various sporting venues – suck up time. Housework and laundry are of course necessary evils, but I do hate getting to Sunday evening without anything to *show* for my efforts. At least with DIY you have something concrete.

Plus, I'm relatively handy around the house these days, on the rare occasions when I get the time. When I bought my first flat in my twenties – back in the day when you could get on the housing ladder at that age – I basically renovated it myself. The work required was more aesthetic than structural, admittedly – mainly stripping the maximalist maroon walls so it felt less like I was living inside a womb. But with a lot of help from Dad (who, despite being an ex-mortgage adviser in his seventies can rewire a semi and plumb in bathrooms), we got the whole thing looking great in no time. Same thing happened when I moved into the house we're in now.

During my marriage to Brendan, though, we somehow ended up with a very unoriginal division of labour. Despite being a *Guardian*-reading liberal who liked Suzanne Vega and had a man-crush on Stanley Tucci, he still colonised the garage and considered certain jobs to be his domain. Anything with a drill, basically. He never attempted anything too ambitious, but still liked nothing more than to flex his macho neurological pathways by putting together an IKEA flatpack, after which he'd expect the sort of praise that I'd give the children during an egg-and-spoon race. I sigh. He wasn't perfect, but nobody is – and he definitely wasn't as bad as Rose and my mum would have you believe. But then I suppose they don't know the sorry story behind our break-up – not the whole of it anyway.

I pick up my measuring tape when I hear a WhatsApp ping, followed by another. I try to ignore it, but their arrival is like the two black crows in *The Omen* which denote the imminent arrival of the anti-Christ. I glance at the clock and realise it's 7am and the 'Do Not Disturb' setting has been lifted, just as another ping arrives.

I tell myself that just because I forgot to mute them doesn't mean I have any responsibility to answer them. I don't even have to *read* them. Not at the weekend. Not at 7am.

Ping.

I write down a measurement.

Ping.

I stretch out the tape.

Ping.

Oh, who am I kidding? I last four minutes before abandoning my task to pick up the phone. The PTA events committee group is lit up like a Christmas tree.

Can I confirm somebody is on top of the catering roll @lisadarling? asks Denise Dandy, Chair of the PTA. **Also, we have apparently sold 94 tickets but only have payments through for 89. Can you explain @lisadarling?**

I got involved in the PTA last term, largely because of my guilt at having hitherto avoided it. There was a good and very practical reason for this – namely, I have absolutely no spare time. But every time I said those words out loud I hated the sound of them. It felt like a flimsy, pathetic excuse, so I caved in and joined the ranks, as 'Communications Secretary', the perfect role for someone who works in TV.

In some ways, I am an ideal candidate to join the association. People who are creative, hard-working and prepared to roll up their sleeves and get stuck in are exactly what they need. Unfortunately, at the hands of the PTA, this is a lethal combination, as I discovered at the first meeting when I came up with about seven fundraising ideas that everyone enthusiastically agreed were brilliant . . . and then expected me to implement.

The latest of these is the Wine Quiz, of which I have somehow been left at the helm because Denise – aka Our Leader – will be in Paris for her 15th wedding anniversary. It's not a complicated event. I've managed far bigger budgets than this, which is likely to raise less than £1,000. Yet Denise, instead of packing her La Perla negligee and booking tickets for the Moulin Rouge, thinks she needs to micromanage me from afar.

There's another ping as one of the other mums writes: Someone bought tickets yesterday asked what time the food is served. Does this suggest that the poster might not have been clear that it is NIBBLES ONLY and not a three-course meal??

Denise doesn't miss a beat.

Could we send out a clarification to all ticket holders ASAP @lisadarling?

I feel as if I have joined a cult. I am desperate to get out, but am chained to them for dark psychological reasons that I can't fully explain. In fact, if you told me that Denise Dandy was not in fact the co-owner of a microblading clinic and mother of a girl in Year 5, but actually the leader of a group that made animal sacrifices and chanted in the woods, I wouldn't doubt it for a second.

Chapter 11

'How are you feeling?' I ask Rose later that afternoon as I place down a tray with two flat whites.

'Truthfully? Still pretty grim,' she says. 'Oh, don't get me wrong, I'm glad to see the back of the radiotherapy, but I'm exhausted. Just wiped out. I've never felt anything like it.'

'Did they tell you to expect that?'

She nods and picks up her coffee to take a sip. 'I have to have this injection in my stomach called Goserelin, which has put me straight into the menopause. Overnight. So no periods for me, ever again. When I first heard that, I thought, well, that's not a bad thing. I can get it all over with in one go. Now I'm starting to miss the cramps and Tampax.'

'Why, what's happening?'

'Oh, I just feel like I've been hit by a ton of bricks. Anxious. Lethargic. All that fun stuff.'

'You didn't have to meet up today, you know. If ever it's too much, just cancel on me. You know I won't hold it against you.'

'Oh, I wasn't missing this. You've got to keep hold of some of the little rituals.'

As young TV execs in London in our twenties, Rose and I gravitated to one particular café on Clapham High Street every Saturday afternoon. If we were lucky enough to get a seat by the window we would never feel inclined to move and could stretch out a single coffee and cake for hours. These days it's not just the location that's changed – to a new favourite next to a second-hand bookshop in the centre of Roebury that's equidistant between our two houses. It's everything.

When someone your age, your best friend in fact, has a diagnosis like hers, it hardly feels real. Even now, more than four months later, I can't get my head around it.

She went to see her GP initially having found a puckering of the skin under her armpit. It was subtle, she'd said, only visible in a certain light, which was one of the reasons she was convinced it would turn out to be nothing.

The other was that she'd had cysts before. None of them had amounted to anything troublesome. So when she was referred to the breast unit, she assumed she'd get the same message as a couple of years previously – that it was benign and nothing to worry about. She'd even only mentioned the appointment in passing, as if it was nothing more important than getting her roots touched up.

But an examination, then a mammogram gave a consultant cause for concern. She requested a biopsy and Rose received the news that same day: she had cancer. I got a text from her as I was about to go into a meeting on the fourth floor that she herself was due to attend.

I'm not going to make it at 3.30. Can you give my apologies to Andrea? Will explain later x

There was something about the message I immediately didn't like.

Weren't you at the hospital today? How did it go? I asked.

Three dots undulated on the screen for too long. When she finally responded, it was with four short words.

Not according to plan x

Worse was that Rose's husband Angel was over in Spain visiting his mum. Yes, he's really called Angel. The standing jokes you might expect – about whether he took her to heaven and back – were all duly forthcoming when she first started seeing him 15 years ago.

The funny thing is, he lives up to his name in all the ways that count. He's one of the kindest people you could meet, a sweet, energetic primary school teacher, avid Real Madrid fan and owner of the biggest smile in south Manchester. He's impossible to dislike and would do anything for Rose. Except on this occasion, stuck in another country, he couldn't do much.

His only option was to frantically book a flight back to the UK the following day. I couldn't let her be alone that first night, so my mum came over to watch the kids while I stayed at her house. Rose wasn't ready to break her news to anyone other than me at that stage, including her dad, the only one of her parents still alive. She planned to phone him later in the week, when she'd be less liable to burst into tears and 'give him a heart attack, which would be the icing on the fucking cake, let me tell you'.

I felt helpless. All I could do was bring wine. Order pizza. Arrange the supermarket flowers I'd grabbed on the way there in a vase on her kitchen table. We were quite drunk by the end of the evening, but neither of us very sleepy, so we flicked around on TV until we landed on *Dirty Dancing*. An absolute favourite for both of us.

'On any other day, this would be a great sleepover. We must do it again,' she said, through reddened eyes.

'I agree. We can watch *When Harry Met Sally* next time and I'll bring some yogurt face packs.'

'Done,' she said and managed to smile.

At that point, they weren't able to give a prognosis, but reading between the lines, it seemed relatively positive. She was told that the lump – because underneath that puckering there *was* a lump – was only 1cm in diameter. Small and contained.

A few weeks later, the story changed.

The operation to remove the tumour revealed that it was twice the size they'd originally thought. Worse, it gone into one of her lymph nodes. Even accounting for the fact that the surgeon thought they had managed to get it all out, her anxiety was through the roof. Quite understandably, it still is.

'I went to see a counsellor this week for group therapy,' she says.

'How was that?'

'Bit odd. All that sitting in a circle with a bunch of strangers. But . . . it was good on balance. I think it was the first time I've really stopped and thought about everything that's happened since December. What a crazy time it's been.'

'I think the way you're handling this is incredible, just for the record,' I tell her.

'Oh, I don't know about that,' she sighs. 'I'm just handling it. What other option is there? I just keep reminding myself throughout that all this could've been worse. I mean . . . I don't need chemotherapy, so that's something. Did I tell you what the first thing I thought of was when they told me I had cancer?'

'Your hair,' I say.

She smiles. 'So I did tell you. How silly is that?'

'It's your crowning glory,' I say, nodding to the silky pre-Raphaelite tendrils spilling over her shoulders. 'I don't know anyone who'd want to lose that.'

'Well, Angel thinks that's very weird.'

'I think what he means is he'd love you just as much, with or without your lustrous locks.'

She presses her mouth into a smile and lowers her eyes. 'I feel lucky to have him at the moment. Honestly, I don't know what I'd have done if I'd had to go through this by myself.'

The next thought seems to occur to both of us before she'd even finished her sentence: if this had happened to me, not her, that's exactly what I'd have been. By myself. Obviously, I'd have my parents, kids and friends, all of which counts for a lot, I know. But there would be no life partner to hold my hand in the middle of the night or kiss away my tears whenever things got too much.

'I mean, I'd have coped,' she adds, hastily. 'And family makes all the difference, doesn't it? Anyway, tell me about what's going on at work. I want every last bit of gossip.'

I briefly fill her in about a few major work-related developments before getting down to the stuff I know she really wants.

'Andrea's had to start wearing flat shoes and compression tights because she did something to her Achilles playing golf.'

'She won't like that.'

'No. She's quite short without her heels. Oh, Nice Nigel from Marketing – the one with the quiff – is now very serious with a woman who works at Sky Sports and is friends with Clare Balding. He's been to Clare's house for drinks – *twice*.'

'Blimey.'

'Daisy has joined a club for vintage postcard collectors who meet at a café in Chiswick. She's got very into vinyl. I offered to lend her a *Wet Wet Wet* LP I had knocking about somewhere but she didn't seem all that excited.'

She chortles into her coffee.

'So what about my stand-in, the handsome Mr Russo? Is he still unpopular?'

I bring my cup to my lips and take a sip, buying some time. 'What makes you think he's handsome?'

'*Obviously*, I've had a good snoop at his profile picture.'

I feel my neck redden. 'I think that's got a filter on it.'

I'm partly stalling for what to tell her about him. I don't want to let her know that he's clearly got aspirations to keep her job permanently. She's got enough on her plate as it is without that.

'Well . . . Andrea fancies him,' I offer.

'She fancies everyone with a Y chromosome.'

'Exactly.' She waits for more information. 'Oh . . . he's being a pain in the bloody neck, if I'm honest – and causing me a lot of trouble over *Our Girl In Milan*.'

She frowns. 'Oh no, really?'

Why can't I learn to keep my mouth shut? Because now she wants to know about his objections and we end up talking about what he said about glamorising an industry that 'manipulates vulnerable young women'.

'Seems a little extreme. Maybe he's not entirely wrong, though.'

I pull a face. '*Yes*, he is. The whole thing is ludicrous.'

'I wonder what his problem is?' she says. 'Maybe he just likes the sound of his own voice.'

If only it was nothing more than that. Either way, if he does think he's getting Rose's job, he's got another thing coming.

Chapter 12

The whole of the following week is spent trying to magically squeeze my preparation for the meeting with Krishna – who is in LA until Monday – into an already crammed diary. It's unclear how I'm supposed to fit this in between half a dozen pitches from independent production companies, writing script notes for a new reality show, watching cuts of another and generally undertaking the small daily miracle of making sure everything is delivered on time and on budget.

Matters aren't helped by the fact that I'm premenstrual which, despite my new HRT routine, left me feeling woolly-headed and flu-like for four days, even if – promisingly – I haven't had a full-blown migraine in as long as I can remember. Thankfully, the clouds are parting, my brain feels sharp again and I finally get the opportunity to concentrate on my presentation after asking Mum to watch the kids so I can stay late on Wednesday. I've only just opened it when a shadow appears at my desk. I look up and the first thing in my eyeline is Zach Russo's crotch. I feel my chest redden.

'Got a few minutes?' he says, pulling up a chair to sit at the side of my desk before I can say no.

This should feel like an invasion of my personal space, yet something weirdly pleasant stirs in my belly. It's the way he smells, I think. It's part citrus, part cedar, part undiluted pheromones oozing from his every pore. I don't know how much of this is to do with my filthy dream the other day, but I can't deny it: he is almost offensively hot.

'Did you get my email?' he smiles.

'I'm afraid I haven't had time to read it,' I say curtly, eyes fixed on my screen. 'Not now that I'm having to do another presentation.'

The bit about not reading it isn't true. *Obviously* I read it. It said something about how he's sorry we got off on the wrong foot and he wondered if we could discuss a way forward. He has some 'thoughts', apparently. Frankly, I've had enough of those.

'Well, it was about *Our Girl In Milan*,' he continues breezily, not taking the hint. 'I felt like I ought to explain a few things. Also, I'd like to clear the air. We got off to a bad start.'

'*Did we?*' I say, with a vinegary smile. 'Are you referring to the fact that in our first meeting you clearly had far better things to do than talk to the likes of me? Or that you're intent on trashing a project I've worked on for months?'

I sound like a bitter bitch but from the raised eyebrow he seems to think this is banter. 'I think you gave as good as you got in that meeting.'

'Not good enough, apparently. Though this isn't over yet,' I warn.

He crosses his arms, with a challenging glint in his eye. 'Well, I apologise for wanting to move that first meeting along. Nothing personal. My ex got a flat tyre and we were trying to arrange someone else to pick up my daughter from kindergarten but couldn't make it happen. I was a little distracted.'

I push aside my first instinct, to feel sympathetic. 'If you expect me to applaud you for darting out of work for a family matter, you're talking to the wrong person. If *I* did that, my commitment to the business would be questioned.'

'No applause necessary,' he says, entirely missing my point. 'And regarding my comments about your modelling show—'

'Can I stop you there? I really do have to get on with this.'

He leans forward, elbows on the edge of my desk. It takes all my will not to look at those forearms. 'I know you do. But I also need to talk to you about it before you meet Krishna.' He's serious now. The banter, it would seem, is over. At least I thought so.

He leans back in the seat again. 'How about I buy you a drink after work tonight?'

I think my jaw might actually drop.

'Come *on!*' he grins, as if he's trying to persuade me to jump into a swimming pool. 'Let's get to know each other. We gotta work together, after all.'

He looks at me expectantly, almost daring me to say yes. In the split second that follows, I have a vivid flashback of my dream. His hands on my breasts. That full mouth on mine. The insistent throb between my legs. My eyes drop automatically to his lips and he clearly registers something odd in my expression.

'Sorry,' he sits back, holding up his hands. 'I didn't mean to unsettle you. I wasn't suggesting a . . . *date*, just to be clear. It was strictly work.'

'I didn't for a moment think you were.'

'All I'm saying is, we got off to a bad start. And that's not going to work long-term.'

'There isn't going to *be* a long term,' I remind him. 'Rose will be back in a matter of months.'

'Six. That's a long time to be enemies.'

'We're not enemies. I don't give you enough . . . thought for you to be my enemy.'

He laughs. Anyone would think he was enjoying this. 'You *really* are good at the put-downs.' He leans in. 'What's this all about? I know you're pissed off about *Our Girl In Milan*, but is there something else too?'

I look at my screen, ignoring him momentarily as I bite the inside of my lip. Then I turn to him and decide to come straight out with it. There's no other way. 'Are you hoping to keep hold of Rose's job permanently?'

He sits back, as if surprised by the question. 'No,' he says flatly.

'Because you know she has breast cancer, right? But she's going to get better, then she's coming back. So, if you have any ideas about keeping this position for good, then you need to just put them straight out of your mind. Like, now.'

He crosses his arms, as if something all makes sense. 'Okay, listen to me. I do not want this job permanently. End of story.'

I feel my back slump. 'You're sure? Because—'

'I'm sure.' His gaze is so intent that it silences me. 'There are *many* reasons why I will not be even attempting to keep hold of it. I won't bore you with them, but you have my word. When Rose's six months are up . . . that's assuming she—'

'She's definitely coming back,' I tell him firmly.

'Of course.'

'Because she'll be better and you'll be gone.'

'Precisely.'

I don't know why exactly, but I believe him. He really doesn't seem to want to stay around here for good.

'Now we've got that out of the way, can we please put aside any lingering hostility, for the sake of both of us?'

I'll give him this: he's persistent. I hate to say it, but he's also right. I haven't got the energy to continue like this for five months.

Chapter 13

I'm lying in bed that same night, flicking around my phone, when a name appears on Facebook as a 'Friend suggestion'. Danny Brookbank. I swipe it away – and not for the first time. The app seems to be convinced I want to buddy up again with my first ex-husband and keeps making him pop up every time I open it I have nothing against the guy. Equally, some things are better left in the past.

Mistake marriage number one happened when I was 22. Far too young to get married. But at that age, I wouldn't be told. I was completely convinced that love conquers all and hadn't experienced enough slaps in the face to know any better.

I was the last person anyone expected to do something wild because I had been a shy child and an embarrassingly un-rebellious teenager. My mother might tell a different story; I did slam a few doors and would argue at the dinner table about anything from Section 28 to whose turn it was to wash up. But there was no shoplifting of lipsticks from Boots, bunking off school or going behind the bike sheds to do whatever people did back there. While friends had experimented with smoking and in some cases soft drugs, the only illicit substance I ever recall buying was a sachet of Harmony Highlights temporary hair dye.

Shortly after my twenty-first birthday and in my final year at the London School of Economics, I met Danny. He was studying Fine Art at Goldsmiths, trying to hide an upper-class accent and had a look of Michael Hutchence, with soft curly hair and to-die-for brown eyes. He was gentle, sexy, romantic. The term 'falling in love' had never been more apt. I was like a supernova, or Alice plummeting down the rabbit hole: euphoric, a little scared and not entirely sure if any of it was real.

We were obsessed not just with one another but the sheer wonder of being in love. He'd travel across London between lectures just so he could be with me for twenty minutes. We'd spend every spare moment in each other's company and when he wasn't there all I could think about was him.

Trouble is, falling so hard for someone that young makes you a bit selfish. So I did the first truly shocking thing I'd ever done in my life: I agreed to marry in secret. Danny and I took off to a registry office with just the two of us and a witness we picked up on the street – an Argentine exchange student who looked completely bewildered throughout.

I was too loved-up to stop and think how upset my parents would be. I'm still not proud that I was so obsessed with Danny that I failed to think of anyone else. Though I distinctly remember a thought running through my head as I walked down the aisle, in clunky Top Shop heels and a bias-cut dress: *This isn't going to last.*

We moved in together and quickly proved the inevitable: that chemistry does not guarantee compatibility. For all his sweetness, Danny was also chaotic, lazy, entitled and frankly unhygienic. I did all the cleaning, cooking, laundry and household admin. I was the one who made us tuna bake every night (my signature dish). The one who changed the bedsheets, picked his dirty underpants off the bathroom floor and fished his pubes out of the shower plughole. Not because he asked me to, admittedly, but because they'd have been there forever otherwise, a bad impression of a Tracy Emin's bed exhibition at the Tate.

I told myself that none of this mattered because we were in love. Then I'd catch myself and think: Jesus, Lisa! You're supposed to be a feminist. We're heading towards a new millennium. This is *not* 1959.

So I'd try to broach the issue and he'd accuse me of nagging, fireworks would ensue, we'd make up and the process was repeated, at first monthly, then weekly, then daily. After six months of marriage, I had literally no idea how *anyone* made this institution work. If Danny and I couldn't when we'd been so mad about each other, how did anyone else?

Despite knowing it wasn't working at all, I was heartbroken when he finally left. He left only a note, telling me that he'd always love me but this wasn't meant to be. I couldn't argue with that really. I felt the same.

For a time, I felt like I'd been lanced in the gut. But I learned something all women discover, sooner or later. It doesn't matter how bad something or someone makes you feel, you can't stay at rock bottom forever. Whatever depths you're in, at some point you'll rise to the surface again, like it or not. The only question is whether you fight it or do as my Mum liked to say: pull yourself up by your bootstraps and give it a helping hand.

And, once the dust had settled post-Danny, I had the time of my life as a single woman. I had a fabulous job. A brilliant group of friends. I enjoyed my twenties to the full. Singledom suited me. It always has, which is why I'm perfectly content with my current romantic situation (or lack of).

I didn't see or hear from Danny for years afterwards. Only his mother had ever been in touch to reassure me that he was alive and well, working in a beach bar in Koh Samui and very sorry. As he never requested a divorce and I was not planning to marry again any time soon, it was ages before I thought I might as well send off the paperwork.

His family had been wealthy, so I was probably entitled to half of Bedfordshire, but I never even went to see a lawyer. I didn't want his money. That marriage had not been real, I told myself. It should never have happened. When I finally did settle down with someone and start a family, it would be forever.

Ha.

Chapter 14

The day of the school PTA cheese and wine has finally arrived and the only thing keeping me from a job lot of cheap plonk and brie is a determination to make sure my presentation with Krishna is perfect before I leave for the week. It's just after I've put the finishing touches on it that I spot Zach on the other side of the office, chatting to Andrea. My initial instinct is to shut down my computer and run out of the building, before he gets the chance to try and offer his 'thoughts' again.

But as they finish their discussion and she walks away, he looks over at me and we lock eyes. Something inside me twists and turns, as I remember his comment a couple of days ago.

Five more months is a long time to be enemies . . .

I am clearly going to have to a grown up here, no matter how painful this is. I straighten my back and give him a stiff little wave, hoping this at least shows I'm prepared to be civil. He takes this as his cue to walk over. My heart spikes as he approaches my desk.

'How's it going?' he asks, with a big smile.

'Good, thanks. I just wanted to . . . well, I'm sorry I didn't have a chance to hear you out the other day, but honestly no more discussion is necessary. You don't need to worry about me misrepresenting your views towards Krishna.'

'I wasn't worried about that.'

'Oh. Well . . . good.'

'We could talk now, if you're free?' he suggests.

'I can't,' I say quickly, saving my document. 'Genuinely. I've got to leave right this minute. I'm organising an event tonight.'

As if her ears are burning, another message from Commandant Denise Dandy pings on WhatsApp.

'SUCH a shame you didn't manage to sell out ☹. Only one ticket left too! So near and yet so far @lisadarling !!! Was there *really* nobody else you could work your charms on? If it helps, I could authorise 50p off the price of the last ticket and make it £19.50. Could be an incentive?'

I blow out my cheeks, slam the phone on my desk and stand up, grabbing my coat.

'Anything exciting?' he asks.

'The Roebury School PTA cheese and wine. Unless you're prepared to buy a ticket for that, I'm afraid that's where I'll be otherwise indisposed . . .'

'Sure. Why not.'

I look up at him and blink, trying to work out if I've heard him right. '*What?*'

He shrugs. 'I drink wine. And who doesn't like cheese? Come on, *Darling*.'

'It's *Lisa*.'

'I know but Darling really is a great name. Surely people call you only by that all the time?'

'Not if they want to keep their solar plexus intact,' I say, saving my document. 'It was a throwaway comment, Russo. I was not being serious. The event is in a sports hall. In my children's school. It's to raise money for a new sensory garden, though God knows why anyone needs one of those . . . '

'Sounds like a hell of a night. How much is a ticket?'

I'm about to send him on his way, when I hesitate. I cross my arms. 'Eighty-five pounds.'

His eyebrows rise. '*Per person?*'

'Yep.'

'And what would I get for that?'

'Three pieces of cheese from Aldi, eight half measures of wine and the company of a load of strangers you have nothing in common with and are never likely to meet again.'

He flashes me a smile. 'I'm sold.'

Then he takes out his wallet and begins counting out nine ten-pound notes and stands up as he plants them on my desk. 'Keep the change. Sounds like a good cause. Text me the details and I'll meet you there.'

We only get access to the school sports hall from 6pm because a Year 10 basketball competition is taking place immediately beforehand. This means that a crack team of parents has just one hour to transform the entire sweaty cesspit into 'an intimate and atmospheric space.' Those are the words of Denise Dandy, as part of the lengthy instructions she left on the WhatsApp group, like a turd on my doorstep, before disappearing to Paris.

I shouldn't rise to this. But, given that she'll be scrutinising any photos posted at the first opportunity, I am determined to make the place look like The Ivy. A bit of dim lighting should help; she doesn't need to know about the lingering whiff of old trainers and armpits. Still, an hour, it turns out, is not a lot of time for such a transformation.

'Sorry I'm late,' says Jeff, taking off his coat and placing it on the back of a chair as he looks me up and down. 'Love the outfit.'

'First thing I threw on,' I say, which is true, albeit this is a staple: wide-leg trousers from Sézane, white pumps and a satin shirt.

'Oh, *as if.*'

'Okay, you got me,' I say. 'I went for a full body massage this afternoon, had my hair and nails done, then I spent a looong time browsing my walk-in wardrobe to curate my outfit . . .'

'Well, you *look* like it and that's all that counts. Anyway, that's enough compliments. We've got cheese to organise. What can I do?'

Jeff and I first met through our respective 10-year-olds, when they were much younger. His daughter has been one of Jacob's best friends ever since his first week at juniors, when he came home and told me, 'Bella has two dads and three cocker spaniels.' I'm not sure which he'd considered the most impressive. I get on well with most of the parents around here, but Jeff is one of the few I'd consider a true friend, someone I'd go out of my way to spend time with even if we hadn't been thrown together at the school gates.

He is an accountant, but that's about the only boring thing about him, no disrespect to accountants. He is one of those rare men who turn more heads in their late forties than in their twenties, though even Jeff admits – proudly – that looking as good as him requires a lot of effort. He works out religiously, owns more cashmere jumpers than anyone I know and has an edgy haircut and immaculate goatee that he models on David Beckham.

'The beer needs to be brought in,' I suggest. 'Unless you'd prefer to do the table centrepieces?'

'Think I'll give the flowers a go,' he decides.

'Great. There's your material.' I gesture to a bucket of foliage standing next to one of the chairs but he looks underwhelmed. 'What am I supposed to do with a bucket of twigs?'

'Hannah's mum supplied them. They're from some ornamental tree in her garden. She reckons she often arranges branches around a few tealights for dinner parties and they look lovely.' He looks sceptical. I can understand why. 'Admittedly, you might need to work a bit of magic.'

'Who do you think I am, Harry Potter?'

'Just do your best, Jeff.' I pat his shoulder reassuringly and head off in search of some platters.

With half an hour to go before the guests arrive, the room takes on the frantic air of a *Great British Bake-Off* finale. As I'm trying to find someone to wash and dry the side plates, the double doors open. There, in the unforgiving sports hall glare, stands Zach Russo.

Good God. He actually came.

He's wearing a monochrome sweater, cotton trousers and desert boots, that posh watch loose at his wrist. I wonder if this was the first thing out of his wardrobe too, because somehow it's both nothing special and the perfect off-duty ensemble all at once.

I raise my hand and wave awkwardly. His face breaks into one of those heart-stopping smiles as he walks towards me. There are a few odd seconds in which I don't quite know where to put my eyes, so I keep frowning down at my clipboard, as if there's something terribly important on there. Yet my gaze is repeatedly drawn back up to him until he's standing right in front of me.

'Nice place,' he says, looking about.

'The hottest nightspot around right now.'

He laughs and a series of little lines fan out from his eyes.

'What *are* you doing here? Seriously?'

'I bought a ticket,' he says, innocently.

'I left the cash you gave me on your desk. Under your keyboard. I thought I'd made it clear that I had been joking about tonight. It was an off-the-cuff comment. I know you Americans aren't supposed to understand sarcasm, but still.'

I'm teasing, though I wonder if he'll realise.

'I do know when someone's being sarcastic. *And* patronising. But I had nothing better to do tonight. I'm the new kid in town and I know virtually nobody around here. And it was clearly the only way I was going to get to speak to you before you see Krishna. So, I thought, what the hell?'

'You're mad. I'm *not* going to be able to talk about work any time soon. I'm way too busy.'

'I can see. It's why I came early; thought you might need some help. I know how these things work.'

'I doubt that, somehow,' I say.

He stops and narrows his eyes, scrutinising my face.

'Do you *really* not want me here?' he says. I detect genuine hesitancy now. 'Because if this is some kind of privacy infringement then . . . I don't want to be that guy. And I'll just go.'

I open my mouth to respond, without knowing exactly what I'm going to say, as one of the attractive Year 4 mums – Jessica or Sarah or somebody – passes by and touches Zach on the arm.

'Could you come and help me with the wine crates? I can't carry them all by myself. It'd be such a help. Follow me,' she urges him.

Then she marches off in her skin-tight jeans, a thick ponytail of dark, glossy hair swishing behind her.

He looks back at me, waiting for a cue.

'Don't be silly, Russo,' I say, nodding after her. 'Roll up your sleeves and get stuck in.'

Chapter 15

The lights are turned down and the room is soon packed with mingling guests. I've put two sixth-formers in charge of shoving a glass of Prosecco in the hands of everyone who steps through the door, before most of the parents in attendance are seated with their respective teams.

'All set at our end, Lisa,' says this evening's host, a guy in his early sixties who owns a local wine shop. 'If you jump on stage to say a few introductory words, I'll take it from there.'

'I didn't realise you wanted a speech.'

'Not a *speech*, as such. You just need to explain what you're raising money for and tell people that if a fire alarm goes off, they should run for their lives.'

'Leave it with me. I'll find someone.'

Although I've done plenty of public speaking over the years, I can't say it's my favourite thing in the world, especially to an audience of this size. Thankfully, I know just the man to step into my shoes.

'Can I ask a favour?' I say to Jeff, as he's about to sit down.

'As long as it has nothing to do with babysitting a hamster.'

'Could you jump on stage and do an introduction?'

'Me? I wouldn't want to take your glory, Lisa. *You're* the one who masterminded this extravaganza. If Denise were here, she'd be straight up there with the mike. . .'

'Honestly, I don't mind. The limelight is all yours.'

'You won't need to ask him twice when you put it that way,' drawls Andy, Jeff's husband.

'Oh, go on then,' Jeff says, pushing back his shoulders heroically. 'What do I need to say?'

After a short briefing, I take a seat on our table – just as one of my other favourite people arrives.

Nora is head coach at Roebury Tennis Club so most clothes look good on her athletic physique. But tonight's blue shirt dress really compliments her pale skin, oval face and silky dark hair.

'Well done on the decor, Lisa,' she says approvingly, looking around the room. 'It looks almost . . .'

'Like a dimly lit sports hall?'

She chuckles. 'Well, yes, but to be fair you didn't have a lot to work with.'

For the first few months of our acquaintance, I didn't really know Nora beyond what I'd seen from the clubhouse terrace, when I'd sit and watch her lessons with both of my boys. But I could instantly see why she was loved by adults and kids alike – for her infectious enthusiasm, encouragement and a superhuman ability to find something positive to say, no matter how bad the player or atrocious the shot.

I knew that her son Charlie was in the year below Jacob at Roebury and she'd also mentioned an older daughter, Isabelle, who is now at Bristol University studying Dentistry. But it was quite by chance that I discovered she and Rose were friends.

After that, it automatically followed that she and I would be too and, along with Jeff, we became a solid foursome, members of a WhatsApp group he set up with the name: 'Roebury Besties'. All of which makes our mutual friend's absence tonight all the more evident.

'Have you seen Rose this week?' Nora asks.

'Only at the weekend, but we texted today. She nearly came tonight, but decided at the last minute to save her energies for something more salubrious.'

'Poor thing. She's really going through it, isn't she?' she says, with a small shudder. 'Still, I bet Angel is looking after her.'

Nora's husband, Iain, runs a freight business that has grown exponentially in the last few years, at least judging by the number of ski trips they started taking. He is a nice guy, although I can't claim to know him particularly well. I've always thought of him as a bit of a closed book and he's often away on business these days, so even at an event like this Nora is on her own.

'Listen, sorry I couldn't make it in time to help set up tonight,' she continues. 'Work is suddenly crazy now the summer league has started. I'd love to join the PTA but I don't know how I'd fit everything in. You and Jeff are making me feel very guilty.'

'Why, because of his floral arrangements?'

'Hasn't he told you he's offered to do their end-of-year accounts?' Nora says.

'No! See . . . this how they suck you in,' I say, under my breath. 'Take my advice and stay well clear. You've got enough on your plate.'

'So have you, haven't you?'

'I know, but I've been weak. There are forces at the PTA that I'm powerless to challenge,' I say grimly.

She hoots with laughter. 'Oh, Lisa . . .'

'May I?' We look up in unison.

Zach has his hand on the seat next to me.

I clear my throat. 'Of course.'

As he sits down, his arm brushes against mine and the nerve endings on my skin begin to tingle.

Nora is looking at him with an odd expression – part surprise, part delight.

'I'm Zach,' he replies, convivially. 'Pleased to meet you.'

'Hi there!' she grins, then flashes me a look that says: *Where on earth did you find this guy – Planet Hunk?*

'Oh, sorry,' I say, realising I was too unsettled by this entire bizarre situation to remember to introduce them. 'Zach, Nora. Nora, Zach.'

'I had no idea you were seeing someone, Lisa,' she says, astonished.

'Oh, God, I'm not,' I say hastily. 'He's nothing to do with me. I mean . . . we're not seeing each other. Are we?'

'Not that I'm aware of.'

'This is my . . . colleague,' I continue, for some reason at twice my usual speed. 'He's from Los Angeles.'

'Via New York,' he adds.

'We work together. *That's all.*'

'Right,' she says slowly, still looking a bit confused. 'New York. How exciting.'

'It has its moments, but then . . . so does Manchester, as I'm already discovering.'

I'm saved by the sound of a knife tapping a wine glass. Jeff has taken the stage.

'Good evening and a very warm welcome to this special venue,' he begins, as if he's watched *The Greatest Showman* one too many times. 'I'm sure you'll all agree that, when it comes to glamour, the Met Gala has nothing on us. So much so that Lady Gaga is hoping to make an appearance later, though sadly we've just had a message from Nicole Kidman's agent to say she's washing her hair. . .'

Nora leans in. 'You do realise that you'll *never* get the mike off him now, Lisa.'

She's not wrong. Considering Jeff's job was predominantly to detail the location of the fire exits, the rest of the speech is worthy of a stand-up slot at the Edinburgh Fringe. After a round of applause, he returns to the table.

'I quite enjoyed that,' he confesses.

'You'd never guess,' laughs Nora. 'You'll want to announce the raffle winners next.'

'I've already got Miss Bennett on the case.'

'Is that the elderly French teacher?' he asks. 'Tell her I'll arm wrestle her for it.'

I'm usually not bad at quizzes. I grew up in a family in which my teenaged cousins and I relished taking on the adults at Trivial Pursuit and these days I can usually manage a passable score in our local pub quiz. But this particular challenge – to test the subtlety of one's nose – turns out not to be my forte.

The idea is that we have to match eight small samples of wine with the host's descriptions, identifying for instance which of them is 'dry, fruity with balanced acidity and tannin levels' (and therefore a Merlot) and which is 'rich and spicy with mouth-watering notes of apricot, peach and honeysuckle' (and is therefore a Viognier). On the basis of all this, my palate, it seems, is about as subtle as a brick. And my partner's – because for these purposes that's what Zach is – is not much better.

'Pretty sure it's a red,' says Zach, frowning as he swishes the liquid around his glass. 'Possibly with top notes of gasoline and grape Jell-o.'

'*That's* what you're getting from this?' I reply.

'Definitely. I'm going to say it's a . . . Zinfandel,' Zach declares.

'There's no Zinfandel on the list.'

I take a sip, swish it around my mouth and swallow. 'I can definitely detect some alcohol.'

'You two are useless,' laughs Nora. 'We're never going to win the bottle of champagne at this rate.'

'It's Prosecco,' I tell her. 'Not that I'd be able to taste the difference between that, champagne and 7-Up, apparently.'

'Then I give up,' Nora says, abandoning the sheet. 'So tell me, Zach. How long have you lived in the UK?'

'Three weeks exactly. At least, this time around.'

'You've lived here before?' Jeff asks, leaning in and *way* too interested.

'Yeah. A long time ago.'

It turns out that Zach spent four years as a student in Edinburgh, which was where he met his wife, from whom he is now separated, pending a divorce. I concentrate on taking another sip of red and mark it down on the sheet, pretending not to listen to the conversation around me.

'She's originally from Manchester, though she moved to LA with me when we got together. Only now her dad is really sick with late-stage cancer. Sadly, it looks like he's not going to make it,' Zach explains.

'Oh dear. That's sad,' Jeff says.

'Yeah. It is. He's a great guy, a real sweet man. She understandably wants to be here with him at a time like this – and support her mom. Except, we have a daughter, Mila. And . . . because her mom's here, she has to be here too. Which I *get* . . . except,' he takes a breath, 'I just *cannot* be a whole continent away from her. That's not even an option for me.'

'I see,' Nora says. 'So that's why you've come to live and work here?'

'Exactly. Only for a short while.' He shrugs. 'It was never part of the plan, but it is what it is.'

There's something about the way he says it that sounds as if, all things being equal, he'd prefer not to have left the US.

'How old is Mila?' Nora asks.

'She's four.'

Nobody around the table could fail to notice the sparkle in Zach's eyes as he almost automatically picks up his phone, unlocks the screen and is about to thrust it in front of Nora before withdrawing self-consciously.

'Sorry,' he smiles. 'I sometimes forget that *nobody* is interested in other people's kids, no matter how besotted you are.'

'Not at all,' protests Nora, as she pulls out her own mobile. '*I'm* interested. How about I'll look at yours, then you can look at mine?'

'Hand it over,' he grins.

I catch a glimpse of a picture on his screensaver of a small girl sitting on top of Zach's shoulders. She has soft, curly hair and exactly the same dimple in her chin as her father.

He glances at me and I clear my throat.

'Very cute,' I say, feeling caught out.

Jeff, on my left, leans into whisper. 'The kid's sweet too.'

The evening is a triumph. Proof that, despite the less-than-salubrious venue, if you are surrounded by good company and a lot of plonk (even if I suspect some of these bottles fell off the back of a lorry) you can still have a wonderful time. And Zach, it is undeniable, *is* good company.

He manages to charm everyone, without dominating the conversation. Though it's fair to say that our concentration on the quiz itself wanes the more the evening progresses. Eventually, we find ourselves discuss anything but wine. The reformation of Bananarama. Exactly how popular soccer is in the US these days. How Nora reckons that my moody 15-year-old not only has a superb forehand slice, but in *her* presence is never anything other than pleasant, polite and engaging. Dr Jekyll, basically.

As the evening draws on, we're also treated to the revelation that Jeff is considering a hair transplant.

'I don't think you're thinning that much, are you?' I say, surprised.

'Are you joking? I feel like a Scotch pine on Boxing Day. There'll be nothing left soon.'

'You exaggerate.'

'Not at all,' he says. 'As soon as my dad started thinning, it happened very quickly. All his teeth went next. I'm not going through that.'

Nora is finding this hysterical. 'Well, now you've revealed your secret. If you'd gone ahead and said nothing, none of us would've noticed.'

'They cost about £15k, don't they?' asks Zach. 'For that you'd want *everyone* to notice.'

'Exactly,' laughs Jeff.

Zach seems easier to get along with outside the context of work. But then, perhaps we all are. I certainly couldn't accuse him of not getting into the spirit of things.

'Oh look, you've won!' Jeff exclaims, nudging Zach and pointing at one of the many raffle tickets he's bought.

'Wow,' he smiles. 'Glad I came.'

'Well, what are you waiting for? Go and collect your prize,' Jeff says.

'Don't get too excited,' I call after him, as he pushes out his chair and walks towards the stage. I turn to the others. 'I think the only prizes left are a Thermos flask and an Imperial Leather gift set.'

In fact, Zach soon heads back carrying a tin of tennis balls, the kind that cost about £9 from Sports Direct. He places them on the table in front of him before sitting down.

'I hope you weren't hoping for a new iPhone,' I say.

'What are you talking about?' he grins. 'I'm having the time of my life. Forty-three years old and I swear I can't remember winning anything. Apart from an Emmy, that is.'

My mouth drops. He looks at me, with a smirk. 'That's a joke. Sadly.'

'Oh!' I smile, taking a sip of wine.

Forty-three.

Four years younger than me.

An age gap.

Why the hell am I thinking this?

'So do you play?' he asks me. 'Tennis I mean.'

'I used to,' I say.

'And *she still should*,' Nora interjects. 'Lisa is a lovely player. I'm constantly trying to persuade her to get on a court, rather than just watching her kids.'

'I'm *not* a lovely player. I'm a rusty one. I haven't picked up a racket in years. These days, it's the same old story.'

'You just don't have time for it?' he says.

'How did you guess?'

We come second to last in the quiz. I can't say I'm surprised. Then, before we know it, someone points out that it's 11pm and therefore my job – as event co-ordinator – to start turfing everyone out. This is easier said than done. Because it turns out that eight glasses of wine – even 'tasting' sized – is quite enough to make everyone reluctant to tear themselves away.

I eventually flick all the lights on, prompting a scene reminiscent of a Hammer Horror, in which daylight melts the flesh of a room full of vampires. But it at least empties them out, before I – along with Zach and a handful of PTA stalwarts – blearily put away tables, wash glasses and get ready to lock up.

'I still can't actually believe you came here tonight,' I say, as I put my last tea towel in a bin bag to take home to wash.

He picks up the final crate of unopened wine as we walk towards the door, which he opens for me. I flick off the lights then step outside to lock up.

'I paid £85 for the privilege.'

'No you didn't. I gave you that back. It's hidden under your keyboard. I told you.'

'Yes, but I bought 190 raffle tickets.'

This, for some reason, is one of the funniest things I've ever heard. It might be the eight tasting glasses of wine. Either way, when I start laughing, he joins in and soon we can't stop. We walk across the floodlit car park and I click open my boot.

I'm obviously not going to drive home, but I'll leave the vehicle and its contents here overnight and either get a lift from my dad in the morning or – if I'm feeling bright-eyed and bushy-tailed enough – go for a run to collect it.

I throw in the last bag full of junk from the evening, while Zach places the final crate in. I'm about to close it when I grab a bottle of Chenin Blanc and thrust it into his arms.

'Here, take this. It will make me feel less guilty for swindling you out of so much cash.'

'Well, at least it's for a good cause. What was it again?'

'A sensory garden.'

'Cool. How far away is your Uber?'

I look at my phone. 'Twenty-five minutes. Friday night. It takes forever. What about yours?'

'Thirty.' He looks at his bottle and holds it up. 'One for the road?'

I plan to say no. I swear I do. But for some reason that's not what comes out of my mouth.

'Oh, why not?'

Chapter 16

It's a peculiarly warm night for the end of April, with a trea-cle-coloured sky. We take two paper cups and the bottle before climbing up the hill behind the sports hall overlooking the rugby field and cricket pavilion. Zach takes off his coat and lays it down for me to sit on, apparently unconcerned about grass stains on his own backside.

He unscrews the wine and pours some, first for me, then himself. I'm pretty woozy already, but the fact that I've had more units than I'd dare confess to my Drinkaware app only makes me think I've nothing to lose by having another.

There's something nostalgically thrilling about loitering on school grounds after hours. It adds an odd frisson to the situation, which is silly because it's not as if we're about to share a Silk Cut, sniff some glue or do anything else . . . illicit.

Nevertheless, the warmth that spread through my belly when Zach put his hand on the small of my back to guide me up the slope had nothing to do with the setting. Now, an amber glow from distant street lamps falls gently on his face, casting shadows across his cheekbones and the sensual curves of his throat. Whatever I think of him personally – and I'm still trying to work this guy out – physically, he is impossible not to admire.

'Cheers,' he says. We tap cups and each take a sip.

'Your kids play sport here?' he asks, nodding towards the field.

'My 15-year-old plays rugby. He's called Leo.'

'Is he any good?'

'He's not bad at all, actually. Though I'm not allowed to come and cheer him on these days. I'm too much of an embarrassment to him.'

He laughs. 'I have 14- and 16-year old nieces. My sister says they're exactly the same. She seems to spend her life worrying about them . . .'

'Oh, I get that. With Leo it's not just broken limbs and missing teeth that keep me up at night. That's before we even get to his total disinterest in exams.'

'I guess some kids aren't academic.'

'Oh, he's bright enough. He'd just prefer to be chucking a ball around.'

'Wouldn't we all?'

'So what about your daughter – Mila is it?'

His face brightens, as if he thought I'd never ask. 'She's adorable. V*ery* smart. Shy at times but a little sassy too. She has no trouble standing up for herself, that's for sure. She wants to be a scientist when she grows up – like her mom, who's a biology teacher. I mean, Mila loves dolls, but she's happiest when trying to extract DNA from a banana.'

'I like her already,' I say. 'Is she a daddy's girl?'

'A little. But she *loves* Sara too. She's a great mom.' He looks down at his hands and I detect a wistful note in his voice.

'So, did you learn much about wine tonight?' I ask, feeling the need to change the subject.

He slides his eyes towards me. 'Mainly that I'm better at drinking than analysing it,' he says.

'You and me both. Hey, thanks for helping me clear up.'

'Anytime, Darling.' I shake my head at the mischievous glint in his eyes, in the full knowledge that he's doing this to wind me up.

'That's *it* now, isn't it? You're *never* going to stop calling me Darling.'

'No way. It's too good to waste.'

'It is better than my married name, I suppose.'

'Well, now I'm intrigued. Come on, spill.'

'Smedley.'

He grimaces and a laugh gusts out of me.

'I am *very* offended by that look, Russo – just so you know. I only used it on my bank account and things. I kept my maiden name for work.'

'Good decision. *Lisa Smedley*,' he says, trying out the sound of it, before shaking his head. 'No. Doesn't suit you at all. You're *definitely* a Darling. That why you divorced him?'

'No!' I laugh. 'I didn't feel *that* strongly about it.'

'Could've been worse, you know. There was a kid in my class in middle school called Calvin Titball.'

'Oh, the poor thing.'

We're both laughing now. Everything tonight feels quite funny for some reason.

'Yeah,' he sighs. 'Still, he runs a tech company and drives a Ferrari these days so it didn't turn out all bad for him.'

Only now appreciating how exhausted I am, I slip off my shoes and wiggle my painted toes, stretching back my neck to let my spine decompress. The moment I become aware he's watching me, heat rushes up my body.

'You do realise that you've succeeded in preventing me from talking about the very thing I've been attempting to discuss with you for, like, four days?'

'So I have. Maybe that's because every time it comes up it results in more work for me.'

'Well, what I wanted to say was very simple. I'm going to drop my objections.'

I sit up straight and blink, wondering if I've heard him right. 'What?'

'If you want to pursue *Our Girl In Milan*, then I won't stop you. You can make it clear at the meeting with Krishna on Monday that you have the full support of Scheduling.'

'I don't understand. Why would you do that?'

He inhales, as if he's about to confess something. 'Because I may have allowed my personal feelings to cloud my judgement.'

He disliked me *that* much in our first meeting? As much as the sentiment was mutual, I'm a little bruised at the thought. I wonder when he decided I was less of a twat?

'For the record, though,' he continues, 'I think you've got a better concept up your sleeve. If I was going to choose one of those shows to actively champion, it'd be the second one in your presentation.'

'*My Teenage Bombsite?*'

He nods. 'I loved that idea.'

In a nod to *How Clean is Your House?* – the hit Channel 4 show that made stars out of two housekeepers, Kim and Aggie, back in the 2000s – each episode would focus on one young person's filthy bedroom. A crack team of cleaners would initially assess levels of grime, test for E coli, salmonella and other gruesome bacteria usually found on dirty dishes lurking underneath beds. They'd fill skips full of the old shit found at the back of wardrobes and in sock drawers and do it all while accompanied by a dramatic score of horror movie music. Then, they'd undertake a transformative deep clean, leaving the place so sparkling you could safely conduct open-heart surgery.

'My youngest niece Ivy is a delight. But her mom would say she has the most disgusting bedroom on earth. We all know a kid like that. We probably all *were* a kid like that. That's why people would love it. It's relatable, about real people and – unlike your modelling show – it would make viewers laugh. I'm telling you, it's a winner.'

'Hmm. I mean, I like it too. But the production company has little in the way of a track record.'

'So they're new,' he shrugs. 'You can get a more experienced firm to godfather them. We all needed someone to take a chance on us at some point in our lives, don't you think?'

I get a sudden warm waft of his aftershave and something snags behind my ribcage.

'Well, either way, you've already outlined the objections to *Our Girl In Milan* to the rest of the team. I'm not sure I'll be able to put the cat back in the bag now.'

He flattens his mouth. 'Sorry.'

'Ah, you did your job,' I'm forced to concede, deflecting the apology. 'It's up to Krishna to decide now.'

'Well, let me know if I can be of any assistance.'

'Oh, you've done *quite* enough, thanks very much,' I say, only half kidding. He smiles anyway. 'So how did you swing a transfer from the US office? Who's doing *your* job while you're here?'

'That is a sore point.'

'Oh?'

'Since Susan Fleming became group CEO a couple of years ago, she made a big deal about how MotionMax+ is a global company and teams ought to share talent and experience. So I approached her and she was all for it. Some of my fellow senior execs, however, didn't see things that way. To them, this is just a satellite office.'

'What a cheek,' I say, even though it's obviously true. Still, we are the biggest outside the US.

'Couple of people made no secret of thinking that I'd left them in the shit.'

I remember that conversation I'd had about him before he arrived. *He had his fans but it wasn't a universally held opinion . . .*

'It was like they thought I was here to have some long vacation,' he says.

I snort. 'Have they seen the average spring temperatures in this part of the world? None of us tend to do much sunbathing in Salford at this time of year.'

Now he laughs too. I'm so busy looking at the way his face illuminates that I totally fail to notice that he's topping up my paper cup until it's too late. As I shift my bodyweight forward, oblivious, I manage to spill about three-quarters of it, most of which lands on Zach's trousers.

'Shit.'

I grab the closest thing to a cloth that I can find, which happens to be my linen scarf, and I automatically start to mop it up. Then I realise what I'm doing and that I'm touching his leg. I freeze. We are suddenly very close. The warm curve of his thigh is still against mine. I can feel his eyes on me, almost before I look up, a fact confirmed when I do so and they drop unexpectedly to my mouth.

It strikes me that all I'd need to do is lean forward an inch, maybe two, and it would be an invitation for him to kiss me. I could brush those lips, taste the wine on his tongue. A flood of liquid desire spreads through my body. I can't work out if it's simply some trick or refraction of moonlight, but it feels as though we're already drawing closer towards one another. Time seems to stand still. And then—

Ping.

I clear my throat, pull back and register the vehicle drawing into the car park.

'Looks like that's your ride,' he says, his voice slightly hoarse.

'Yes. Sorry about your . . . trousers.'

The faintest smile. 'No problem.'

We both get to our feet.

'Don't forget your tennis balls.'

'I wouldn't dream of it.'

'You are *way* too pleased with those. You must have a very boring life.'

'Not as boring as I'd like,' he mutters, suggesting some hidden irony.

Facing me, he suddenly seems unfeasibly tall. The sort of guy you'd have to stand on your tiptoes to kiss.

Why are you thinking about kissing him?

'Thanks for tonight. I had fun,' he says.

'You don't have to be polite.'

'And you don't have to be so cynical.'

'I was simply pointing out that you're a single guy, it's a Friday night, and believe me when I say this city has more to offer than a school wine quiz.'

His eyes drift over my face. 'I'll bear that in mind.'

I swallow. Then I take a step back and flap my arms in a weird way, like I don't know what to do with them. 'I'll see you around, Russo.'

'Take it easy, Darling.'

He raises his hand.

I turn around and make my way down the hill to the Uber, crossing the car park and opening the door to get in, feeling Zach's distant gaze on me all the way there.

Chapter 17

To-do list

- Finalise accounts from PTA Wine Quiz
- Check on subscription to Asana Rebel
- New shoes (Jacob)
- Download new school meals app
- Sew Leo's blazer pocket
- Buy outstanding items for Leo's Duke of Edinburgh expedition (whistle, rucksack liner, blister pads, titanium cutlery, head torch, collapsible bowl, dry wash gel, sock liners)
- Buy shares in Mountain Warehouse
- Buy more socks (Jacob)
- Mum birthday present
- Mum birthday cake
- Mum candles
- Check with Dad if she is 73 or 74
- Organise outfit for 'Rock Star Day' at school
- Start DIY panelling. COME THE F*** ON
- Search *Vinted* for black jacket he wants for birthday that costs £480 when purchased new. Failing that, go on the game
- Descale kettle

Jacob has a new-found passion for the music of Kate Bush. Which I'm thrilled about because a) it's Kate Bush and b) it's not the German version of 'The Gummy Bear Song', which at one point he was playing around the clock, absolutely screwing my Spotify algorithm.

At least, that was what I'd thought, before we sat in the car on the way home from fencing club on Saturday morning and we listened to 'Wuthering Heights' approximately 18 times. Now, as I pile laundry into the washing machine, I find myself singing along to the earworm in my head. It really isn't a song you can just hum gently along to, is it? You can only give it all you've got.

I belt out the first line, a suitably rousing and high-pitched impression of my favourite Eighties songstress, which echoes through the house . . .

'UHMIGODDD. Mum. Seriously?!'

Leo is at the utility room entrance in full muddy rugby kit, his face twisted into an expression that suggests he doesn't appreciate my vocal skills.

'No offence, but you sound like a tortured cat,' he huffs.

'Glad you said, "No offence" because I might have found that insulting otherwise,' I reply, but he can't dampen my mood. It's only this morning that I realise how much more energetic I'm feeling since my HRT started to kick in.

Then I notice the kitchen floor, which is literally covered in mud from his boots.

'Oh, Leo! Look at the state of the tiles!'

He casts his gaze over them and shrugs. 'Calm down. It's only a bit of muck.'

'Yes, but I mopped it an hour ago.'

'It's not like it won't come off,' he huffs, heading to the fridge.

'You're right. The mop's in the utility room. Off you go,' I say, nodding to the door.

He tuts and emerges with a block of cheese. 'Can't you do it? I'm busy.'

'Doing what?'

'The match is about to start.'

'Well, I hate to disrupt your hectic schedule, but no, I can't.' I fetch the mop myself and thrust it into his hand as I go in search of Jacob, who is in the garden bouncing on his trampoline.

'Come on, sweetheart. You really need to get this maths homework done. I've asked you twice this morning already.'

I finally managed to get Jacob a maths tutor, who would only do video calls rather than in-person lessons, and seems to be doing very little to stoke my son's enthusiasm for the subject.

'I can't. I've got a headache,' he shouts back, before performing three progressively higher bounces that culminate in a full 360-degree somersault.

'Maybe stop trampolining then.'

'That makes it feel better,' he says.

'Jacob, get in here,' I say, tersely. 'You've got twenty seconds.'

He ignores me as a text arrives from Denise Dandy.

Hi Lisa. Just back from Paris and was going through the inventory of PTA equipment following the Wine Quiz in my absence. There seems to be one trifle bowl and a fish slice missing. Can you explain please?

What I really want to do is reply with: Thanks for asking – the event went well and we raised a record £1,300! Also, we only ate cheese and drank wine. Trifle and haddock weren't on the menu.

I decide to be the better woman.

Sorry, Denise. I don't recall seeing either. Hope you had a nice anniversary.

Outside, Jacob is still bouncing. 'Right, young man. I'm cutting off the Wi-Fi on your iPad for the rest of the day unless you come and do this.'

I hear an amused snort from Leo's direction.

'What does that mean?' I ask.

'Just that you always say that and never do it.'

My chest inflates with indignation, though that's partly because I've been caught out.

As anyone knows, the number one rule of effective parenting is never to make idle threats that you can't see through. That's fine in theory. But the only thing my kids are bothered about is the Wi-Fi and sadly, despite multiple attempts, I still haven't worked out how to block individual devices without turning the whole system off. Given that I want to watch *Strictly* tonight – and that both kids seem to have a mystifying talent for getting around any 'parent safe' gizmos I attempt to install – the only one who tends to be punished . . . is me.

'This time I will,' I declare, with an ominous glare. 'You just watch.'

I go to the patio door again. 'Jacob. *Now* please!'

He begrudgingly climbs off the trampoline and trails inside. 'I don't know why you always have to shout, Mum.'

I turn around, take a deep breath and see that Leo is gone, having apparently completed the mopping. I know this because the muddy smears he'd left on the tiles are now just as muddy, but also awash with dirty water, the mop is lying on the floor and the bucket is next to it. On top of that, every bit of paraphernalia he's used to make his cheese sandwich – butter, bread, knife – is spread out across the worktop.

'LEO!' I call up the stairs.

'I'm in the shower!'

Defeated, I start to clear up myself, silently apologising to any future wife of his – if there is one, that is – for failing to raise him as the feminist ally I always SWORE I would. Am I the only woman in the world whose kids are running rings around me? I am grappling with a sense of my own inadequacy when a text arrives. It's from Zach.

I have four new tennis balls and nobody to play with. Could you be tempted into a hit? Fully prepared for you to kick my ass.

For a brief moment, I feel a lightness beneath my breastbone. It's the oddest, stupidest schoolgirlish feeling, like getting a Valentine's card from a boy in sixth form. I bite the inside of my mouth and type back.

Don't think you need worry on that front. You should give Nora a ring. She really is an excellent coach.

I might just do that. Either way, I wasn't lying last night. I really did have fun.

I start writing: Me too, then I stop myself.

What the hell do I think I'm doing? I can't send something like that. Something . . . flirty.

I remind myself that this man has made life very difficult for me as a result of his 'reservations', whether he's now backtracking or not. More importantly, aren't my flirting days over? They certainly should be.

I decide not to respond, instead clicking on Instagram. I bypass all the reels it seems to send my way these days. Serums for thinning hair. Interiors accounts featuring women running their fingers along immaculate kitchen tops to a whimsical, acoustic track. And various ADHD accounts which the platform seems to have diagnosed me with all by itself. I search 'Zach Russo' and to my astonishment . . . there he is, with a public account. I click on his profile.

There aren't masses of photos. He's clearly one of those people that dips in and out of social media without much conviction. The majority are of him and his daughter Mila. He was right about her being adorable, even I'll concede that, despite my long-held conviction that no child on earth could possibly ever be as cute as my own were.

There aren't many captions, which usually amount to just one or two words – 'My Girl', or 'In training', below the selfie of them at a baseball match. I keep scrolling, and there's a black-and-white photo of him cradling her when she was tiny. It takes me a moment to realise what it reminds me of – that famous old Athena poster, 'Man and Baby'. Zach isn't bare-chested; he's wearing a white T-shirt and his hair is a little longer than now. But she looks so tiny, cradled in his big muscular arms, and the tender look in his eyes would melt anyone's heart.

I continue down his feed, past a couple of cityscapes of New York and LA, before coming across a clutch of posts from five years ago. They're photos of an attractive young woman with dark hair and a bright smile, with a charity logo overlaid on top of them with the initials: the Jenna Russo Memorial Fund.

I look more closely and read Zach's caption.

'I'll be running the Boston Marathon this year in memory of my twin sister Jenna, who tragically died aged 27. Please read our JustGiving page and donate if you can.'

The link is still in his biography.

I click on it to find that, over the years, $34,746 has been raised by 431 supporters through a variety of 'Russo Family Memorial Walks' and other charity challenges. I continue to read.

Story:

We have decided to raise funds in Jenna's memory for the NEDA – the National Eating Disorder Association. Their mission is to end the pain and suffering caused by eating disorders, something we know Jenna felt passionately about.

Jenna suffered with anorexia nervosa for more than 13 years. She developed it in her teens when she was still at high school and had just been scouted by a high-profile modelling agency at the age of 15. Over the course of her illness, Jenna had over 25 hospital admissions.

When she left modelling, she went on to study for a degree in psychology at Colombia, but living with this chronic illness meant she was unable to start a career, despite her intelligence and drive. Nevertheless, she was always determined to continue to fight and was still able to enjoy her life, friends and family, right until the end.

The pain of seeing someone you love suffer in the way she did is devastating. It had the potential to tear apart our family, but instead it made us stronger and love each other even more. Our story is by no means unique and if there's one legacy we know Jenna would want, it's to help others like us.

Chapter 18

It's a bank holiday weekend, but the boys have decided against staying with Brendan in the Peak District. They don't hate it over there by any means, but I can't say they love it either. There was a time when I thought their lack of enthusiasm could be attributed to Melanie, his partner. But they assure me she's 'all right', in the same way you'd describe an average, inoffensive sort of biscuit, a custard cream as opposed to a Chunky Kit Kat.

Truth is, while they're usually pleased to see their dad, at this stage in their lives, it's clear where he stands in the hierarchy of their friends, sport and gaming consoles.

So, he's driven here to spend the day with them, though that seems to have turned into an afternoon, because it's nearly 12pm by the time he arrives to collect them. He's in his cycling gear – head-to-toe Lycra, fingerless gloves and a pair of those funny shoes that make him sound like Fred Astaire when he's walking up the driveway.

'I'm a bit sweaty,' he says apologetically. 'I've come straight from a ride. I won't come in, I stink.'

'Oh, don't worry, it's fine. Don't stand out on the step,' I say, beckoning him in, though part of me regrets that when he enters the hallway and starts to overpower the Febreze plug-in. 'Do you need to use the shower?'

'No, I'll get one in the leisure centre before I get in the pool. I'm going to take the boys swimming.'

I can't deny he's looking good for all the exercise. Trim, healthy, glowing. My ex-husband has become very enthusiastic about cycling in the last couple of years, which surprises me because he'd be the first to slag off 'gym bores' when we first met. A lot has changed since then.

Brendan and I were introduced by one of my neighbours, whose husband had shared a house with him at university when he was studying Computer Science. He had dusty brown hair, fair skin that turned pink and peeled in the summer and a gentle face, shaped like a love heart. This gave him the appearance of being closer to my age – 29 – than his – 37.

It was refreshing to meet someone who didn't work in the media and, although he was a small business owner and clearly doing well even before he sold his little credit checking firm to a much bigger global concern, he had the air of someone who was slightly surprised at his own success. I found that quite endearing. After we moved in together, then got engaged, I can only say that he lived up to his glowing Google reviews: he was trustworthy, consistent, reliable. I never really felt like a grown-up until I married Brendan.

But if any of this is making him sound boring, then I'm doing him a disservice. He can be quite funny when he wants to be. And he knows a great deal about things I don't, like volcanoes, algorithms and the early albums of Tom Petty.

We had fun together in those early days and he could surprise me on occasions. On a mini-break to Amsterdam, it was he who suggested we share a joint in a coffee shop then venture into the red-light district. Just to tick it off the bucket list, of course. We stayed about seven minutes, laughed awkwardly at a few things in a souvenir shop, then agreed to go to Anne Frank's house instead.

Falling in love with Brendan felt completely different from the first time. Compared with the whirlwind of Danny, it was slower, more cautious. Having your fingers burnt makes you less starry-eyed, less vulnerable, less, frankly, stupid. I think it's a matter of self-preservation. Nevertheless, three years later, we were married with a mortgage, a baby on the way and, just to complete the royal flush of domesticity, a dog.

How I loved Tilly. She was a seven-year-old rescue with curly hair and a – usually – soft, dopey nature that I found impossible to resist. She was perfect in all ways but one: she loved *me* a little too much. In practice this meant she refused to tolerate Brendan going anywhere near me. She would become agitated and growl if he so much as held my hand. A kiss would result in frantic barking and, at the onset of any foreplay, she'd howl like there was a full moon. She once scampered into the bedroom when he was attempting penetration and her response resulted in the neighbours calling the RSPCA.

In short, she wreaked havoc with our sex life. We tried putting her outside the door but she'd scratch and bark until she was nearly hoarse and the hinges were creaking. We introduced a baby gate to keep her downstairs, but she'd go so ballistic that, even with 'Wicked Game' by Chris Isaac on full blast, it really was hard to get in the mood.

We eventually worked out that she thought Brendan was attacking me, which was sweet in some ways, though funnily enough he didn't see it like that. We never really found a solution. I mean, there isn't a palatable one, is there? Beyond the odd quickie when the boy opposite asked if he could walk her to save up for his gap year. But the reality was that having sex became hugely stressful and not really worth all the hassle. So long past that, by the time Tilly died and the coast was clear for us to resume relations, it all seemed like such a distant part of our lives that we never really got going again.

Brendan called time on the marriage shortly after Jacob's first birthday. There were all sorts of complex reasons why we'd both stopped loving each other. But I'm fairly certain that the lack of intimacy was the final nail in the coffin for him.

If I'd been willing to add 'Fellate husband' to my to-do list twice a week, it may well have persuaded him to stay.

That's partly why I don't ordinarily rise to Mum and Rose when they slag him off. They don't know this detail. It's hard to say out loud that your marriage failed because of a jealous crossbreed with curly hair and intermittent explosive disorder.

'Are you still having the kids over half term?' I ask Brendan now.

'Yes, I've booked some time off work so we can all do something. Melanie too,' he adds, then catches himself, as if he thinks I'm still liable to burst into tears every time I'm reminded of the woman who's taken my place in his life.

There was once a point when that was the case, but we're long past it. It's not as if she was the cause of our break-up. They only met a year after he'd left, when he'd already started cycling long distances at weekends, got a tattoo on his upper arm that read '*Freedom*' and bought a pair of leather trousers that Rose said made him look like Suzi Quatro.

I'll admit that when I discovered his new girlfriend was eight years younger than me, I imagined some Monroe-esque sex kitten. But Melanie is actually an averagely pretty but by no means exceptional woman who works in a gift shop and has stencilled the words 'Live, Laugh, Love' above the sofa in their living room. I only know this because she made a half-hearted attempt to become an influencer a few years ago and made several videos in which she demonstrated how to apply mascara, before moving onto interiors, then giving up altogether.

'Thing is,' he continues, 'I know I was supposed to be having them for a few days, but I'll have to drop them off on the Tuesday now.'

'Uh . . . okay, that's fine,' I say. In truth, I don't love being away from the kids for this length of time anyway.

'It's just, Melanie got us tickets for a concert that night. Drake.'

I am tempted to ask if he actually knows who Drake is, but keep my mouth shut.

'I'll work from home that week or make sure Mum's around,' I tell him.

His inhales visibly at the mention of my mother. She despises him with the sort of passion most people reserve for military dictators and Monday mornings. I'm sure he can already imagine the conversation, in which she'll accuse him of expecting *everyone else to drop everything for his convenience*. I sometimes think I'm the only one who doesn't hate him.

Or maybe it's just that my mum feels the need to remind me what terrible taste in men I've got. Which I absolutely can't dispute, especially when I compare her experience with mine. She met my dad when she 15. They became sweethearts at 17. While she claims they've had their 'ups and downs' over the decades, it's clear that she can't work out why my generation – with our startling divorce statistics – has made such hash of something that used to be so straightforward.

Chapter 19

Calvin and Daisy are having a discussion about an approach from a production company that she's picked up. They have an idea for a new show that has piqued her interest.

'It's called *Haunted Supermarkets*,' she says.

'Right,' says Calvin carefully, looking hesitant. 'Are there *many* haunted supermarkets?'

From the look on her face, she can't believe he even has to ask.

'Loads! There's one grocery store in a village in Iceland where staff are regularly assaulted by flying potatoes. Also, in a Sainsbury's in Exeter, they've had several sightings of this weird creature. It's meant to be part lizard, part dog, a sort of poodle.'

'A loodle?' Calvin grins.

I snort, unable to stop myself. Daisy crosses her arms.

I straighten my face. 'Do they have a presenter lined up?'

'Yes, actually. They wanted someone big and thought a recognisable face from the eighties would be good, ideally a bit of a heartthrob.'

'Interesting,' I say idly, focusing on my emails.

'Have you heard of a band called A-ha?' she asks.

I stop typing and look up. 'Yes.'

'Well, they had a lead singer who apparently lots of people fancied back in the day.'

'Morten Harket?' I say, astonished and impressed. *'Have they got him?* I used to have a poster of him on my bedroom wall that I'd got from the middle of *Smash Hits*.'

'Well, no. They've got *Harten Morket*. He's in a tribute band – a really successful one though. You'd hardly tell them apart. Look.'

She spins around her computer and shows an image of what I can only describe as a Lidl version of Norway's best-known musical export. He's wearing all the same clothes as in the 'Take On Me' video. Leather jacket. Tight white T-shirt. Unfortunately, this guy also has a dad bod and his luxuriant bouffant hair looks as though it could disappear in a strong breeze.

'Is he actually Norwegian?' I ask.

'No, he's from Rhyl,' she confesses, then clearly registers my expression. 'Oh, you don't like it, do you?'

I decide not to break it to her publicly that it's the worst idea since we were approached about a *Love Island*-style dating show set in the Arctic Circle, in which contestants wore expedition gear and balaclavas. They were apparently oblivious to the fact that skimpy swimwear was the whole point.

'Maybe we should have a meeting about it later?' I say diplomatically, as I pick up my folder and laptop and head towards Krishna's office.

Andrea looks up from her typing as I'm en route. 'Good luck. You can do it,' she says, as if encouraging one of the girls in a lacrosse team.

'Thanks, Andrea.'

'Oh, and Lisa?' She glances over her shoulder and leans into me, quietening her voice. 'Might be worth unbuttoning your blouse a little.'

'Andrea,' I hiss, 'this is the 21st century. I'm not showing my cleavage.'

She tuts and mutters something about woke snowflakes, before returning to her work. Even if I were willing to stoop to such a level, I can't envisage a scenario in which Krishna Chowdhury would be remotely interested in anything other than the subject up for discussion. I once read an interview which said he'd grown up in a traditional Indian household and had been expected to go into medicine. His diversion into television had been an act of rebellion and was the driving force behind both his personal ambition and that of the company. Even though his family are fully reconciled with his choices these days, there's clearly still a part of him that wants to prove himself. And he does it in spades.

Krishna is a born leader and a driven workaholic with an eye for spotting brilliant, popular shows that audiences love. That's not to say he hasn't worked on one or two turkeys over the years, of course – we all have – but his judgement is second to none.

I step inside his office, closing the door behind me. It has the same expensive, over-designed air as the rest of this place, but a patterned rug makes the room look a little less clinical. There's also a picture on the wall of Krishna at his daughter's decadent, vibrant wedding, looking as proud as punch.

'Lisa, come in and take a seat,' he says. 'Great to see the ratings for *Pawn Again* doing so well. My wife is obsessed.'

'Oh, thank you,' I say, feeling a swell of pride. 'I'm glad to hear it.'

The show is one of our most successful projects of the last twelve months. It's a fly-on-the-wall format set in a pawn shop, focusing on the heartbreaking, comical and frequently life-affirming human stories behind some of the items being bought and sold.

'Well, sometimes you are just presented with a gift and that was one of those times,' I say.

'You fought for that show and it paid off,' he corrects me. 'Now, let's discuss this controversial modelling programme of yours.'

I take a seat opposite him and open up my laptop. Then I click on my first slide and begin my rundown. I've put so much into this, I could do it backwards. But when I reach the slide with an image of a woman on a catwalk – one I'd picked out myself – I hesitate.

It's just a random model, from a show in a previous Milan Fashion Week. I have no idea of her name and when I added the photo, nothing had seemed out of sorts to me. Now, all I can think about is how unbelievably thin she is. It's such a normalised thing that it had never even occurred to me. Maybe that's the problem.

'Everything all right?' Krishna asks, wondering why I'm stalling.

I think back to the picture of Zach's sister Jenna. She *has* to be the reason why he was so against this format. His 'personal feelings' weren't about me at all.

I remove my hand from the mouse. 'Can I level with you, Krishna?'

He raises his eyebrows. 'I'd say that's exactly what you were here for, wouldn't you?'

Chapter 20

I have a rare night to myself on Friday. Jacob is at his best friend's house for a birthday sleepover, while Leo is away for the weekend on his Silver Duke of Edinburgh expedition.

I can't begin to tell you the amount of preparation this trip required. I'm convinced I'd have a shorter kit list to get someone ready for six months on the International Space Station. I also spent most of last night traipsing around the supermarket (while he was allegedly 'studying') to purchase as many lightweight, high-carbohydrate food options as possible. I returned home laden with energy bars, instant oatmeal and Super Noodles, at which point Leo informed me that I'd failed to provide him with a mosquito net and water purifying tablets and if he came home from the Lake District with malaria then it was all on me.

I tell myself I'm going to really make the most of the breathing space. Perhaps I could get round to reading that novel I keep opening and managing half a page of before falling asleep? I could give myself a pedicure, have a long soak in the bath, or finally manage that elusive two-day streak on Asana Rebel.

Instead, I end up staying late in the office. It's not exactly 'me time', but I do get a lot done – including an overdue clear-out of my desk drawer. I'm shocked at some of what I find in the back of it: out-of-date Well Woman supplements, a couple of Fox's Glacier Mints and a menstrual cup that I was once convinced I'd lost in my actual vagina. I was on the verge of seeing the GP about an ultrasound but, after a rummage in the ladies' loo, concluded – rightly as it turned out – that I must have left it elsewhere.

I slip it in my bag, when a light flickers on the other side of the office and Zach walks in, heads to Andrea's desk and places something in her in-tray. His shirt is burgundy, a colour I never ordinarily like. Yet, on him, I could look at it all day. The way it warms his tanned skin and skims over the swell of his biceps and shoulders, the sinews of his neck just visible beneath the collar.

He spots me just as he's about to leave and responds with an unselfconscious smile, all cheekbones and twinkly eyes. He makes a beeline for my desk.

'Haven't you got a home to go to?'

'Haven't *you?*'

'I was planning to head to the gym, but lost interest. What's your excuse?'

'The kids are both away tonight. I had a lot to catch up on.'

'*Surely* you had somewhere better to be than this place?' he says.

'Well, I did have a ticket for the opera in Paris but had the option to stay here looking at a proposal for a show called *Haunted Supermarkets*. There was really no contest.'

'Sounds it. So, come on. Don't keep me in suspense. How'd the meeting with Krishna go? Did I ruin your week or did you manage to get things back on track?'

I'm about to answer, but hesitate. 'How about I tell you all about it over a drink?'

When it becomes apparent that Zach has seen little of Manchester, we take a short tram to Piccadilly Gardens, before I show him the way to one of my favourite places to go for a drink. The distance from the office feels like a bonus because I don't want anyone to see us. Not that I've got anything to hide, but still – I don't want people getting the wrong idea. And while there's no chance of bumping into Calvin or Daisy on a pub crawl, I wouldn't put it past Andrea to be propping up some bar with a Richard Madeley lookalike she met at last year's Baftas.

The brasserie's decor is so apparently contradictory that you'd never think to put them together – manor-house-style wood panelling and comfy leather chairs, with brutalist metal pipes on the ceiling and huge plants spilling out of free-standing pots.

'I think we need a cocktail menu,' he decides, as we climb up on two stools. They're the only ones left and we're at the end of the bar, tucked away in a relatively secluded spot.

'You're a bad influence.'

'I like to think so.'

He picks up the card and I notice how beautiful his hands are: strong fingers with tanned skin and neat nails.

'What's yours?' he says.

'Something fruity. A cosmopolitan maybe.'

As he studies the choices, I am assaulted by a vivid memory of my dream again. The way he slid his belt slowly from his trousers, the taste of that drink on his lips.

'Whisky sour?' I suggest, before I can stop myself.

'No, I'm not a fan. I'll take a dirty martini.'

He gestures to the bartender with a single finger, who appears immediately to take our order. I don't know if it's Zach's size, or something else less easily defined, but he has a kind of *presence*. He really isn't easy to ignore.

'Come *on*. Don't keep me in suspense about Krishna any longer,' he says.

'Well, I put up a good argument, I think . . .' I begin. 'But then I kind of stalled.'

He looks surprised. 'Doesn't sound like you.'

'Rather than going all out and fighting for *Our Girl In Milan* – which part of me still thinks would have been the sensible thing to do – I said I was going to outline the pros and cons of both that . . . and another show.'

He raises his eyebrows, hopefully. '*My Teenage Bombsite*?'

I nod.

'You are full of surprises. So what did he think?'

'He likes both. As do I. But on balance, we've decided that we wouldn't want to plough on with *Our Girl in Milan* without further investigation into a couple of things. Which basically meant, when I telephoned the producers . . . we've lost the show to YouTime.'

He exhales. 'I don't know what to say. Sorry? Thanks?'

'I think you were right about it being unoriginal. I'm big enough to admit that,' I confess. I don't want to admit I've been snooping around on his Insta. 'I still think I might have lost a massive hit though.'

'We'll never know.'

'Until it appears on YouTime. So you'd better be right, Russo,' I warn, with a smile.

'I'm always right,' he says, dismissively.

'Really?'

He shakes his head and scrunches up his nose. 'No.'

I laugh.

'But on *this* occasion . . . you did the right thing. I'm sure of it.'

Our drinks arrive and I take a sip of my cosmopolitan. A fuzzy, electric warmth spreads through my chest and I find my eyes drawn to that dimple in his chin again. A ripple of laughter rises from the other side of the room, while the opening bars of a soft piano tune drift from a distant corner. I feel suddenly quite warm and go to remove my jacket. As he helps me shrug it off, his fingertips brush through the sleeve of my shirt and something flutters in my belly.

'I am not supposed to be drinking on weeknights,' I say, tapping on my phone.

'Says who?'

'Me. I still feel pickled after that night at the school.'

'Well, it *was* a Wine Quiz. What are you doing?' he says, glancing on my app.

'Logging my alcohol units,' I tell him.

He looks amused. 'That's *very* disciplined of you.'

'Not really. It's been days since I did calories . . . and don't even get me started on water intake.'

'Do you have an app for everything?'

'I draw the line at bowel movements.' He bursts out laughing.

'Sorry,' I cringe, feeling myself blush. 'I have *no idea* why I said that.'

But he's still grinning. 'You are hilarious, Lisa.'

'Yeah. Thanks,' I say, pulling a face.

'Hey, what's wrong with hilarious?'

I lean in, elbow on the bar. 'Nothing. Though I think most women have a list of adjectives they'd prefer over that.'

He narrows his eyes, mimics what I've done with my elbow and faces me as he lowers his voice. 'You're not fishing for compliments, are you?'

It strikes me that this moment – everything about it – is so far removed from anything that's happened to me for . . . oh, *years*, that it feels almost cinematic. Like when you go on holiday to New York and everywhere you look makes you feel as if you're in a movie. Except here I am in a cocktail bar, twirling my straw and stealing sideways glances at a guy who looks like the love interest in a big-screen blockbuster.

This is not my life.

My life is budget meetings and parents' evenings. It's standing at the side of muddy fields in the rain, watching kids play rugby. It's crashing into bed every night with a to-do list that only grows and grows. It isn't flirtation. It isn't attraction. Only, just being here next to him, so close that I see the direction of the tiny hairs on his neck, has awakened some fire inside me that I really need to put out. But something is stopping me and all I want to do is bathe in the warmth of its flames.

'I *do not* fish for compliments,' I whisper back.

'Good. Because you shouldn't need to.'

Chapter 21

One cocktail turns into three, or possibly more. I couldn't exactly say how many because the one thing I know for sure is that I stop logging any of them on my Drinkaware app. Instead, I sit, watching the light in Zach Russo's eyes as he laughs, and concluding decisively that he might one of the most handsome men I've ever encountered. The longer I talk to him, the more details of his face I notice. The way the hairs on one eyebrow go in crazy directions. The slight asymmetry of his cupid's bow. The tiny lines that fan from his eyes when he smiles. Individually, they amount to nothing more than quirks; together, they make a masterpiece.

Over the course of the evening the bar has become slightly busier. It's full and a little noisy and, when two guys arrived earlier, Zach had to shift his stool towards mine. Now, he's close enough that I can see the pattern of veins on the inside of his forearms. That when he reached for a napkin, his hand accidentally brushed mine, causing a ripple of pleasure to sweep up my skin. That every so often I get a warm waft of his aftershave and have to fight the urge to close my eyes and just inhale.

'So, what's your story, Russo?' I find myself asking, as I slowly stir the ice in my glass, then lift it out to suck the straw. His gaze drops to my mouth every time I do this, and the subsequent prickle at the base of my spine gives me no incentive to stop.

'My *story?* You'll have to be more specific.'

'Well, how long were you married?'

'Oh. That's what we're doing now, is it? Delving into our sordid pasts?'

'Yours is sordid then?'

'Actually, it's kind of uninteresting,' he sighs. I doubt it somehow, but either way, there's a long enough pause for me to regret my question.

'Sorry. I didn't mean to pry.'

'You didn't,' he says, taking another sip of his drink, before lowering it onto a coaster with a ponderous look on his face. 'Sara is a very nice, smart, *likeable* woman – and a wonderful mom. But we're very different people in lots of ways. The ways that count.'

'So, you're *not* very nice, smart and likeable?'

He laughs. 'I'm baring my soul to you here, Darling.'

'Sorry,' I say sheepishly, though in truth making him laugh feels just too nice to stop.

He tells me that he and Sara had been casually dating for less than a year when she fell pregnant. It was a huge shock to both of them. But he'd always wanted kids and to be a husband. 'So . . . in all honesty, I was over the moon. She's from a kind of conservative, traditional background – her mom is a devout Catholic. My folks are nothing like that, but I did grow up in a very loving family environment. I felt as if my child deserved that privilege too. Does that make sense?'

'Of course.'

'So I asked her to marry me. I thought it was the right thing to do, even though I always knew I wasn't the love of her life. And she wasn't the love of mine. We were more like good friends who happened to share a baby and a house together, which we hoped might be enough.' He looks up from underneath his eyelashes. 'It wasn't.'

'No?'

He shakes his head. 'Turns out love, passion, desire . . . they're kind of important.'

I'm not sure what he sees in my expression that makes him narrows his eyes. 'You don't think so?'

'Well, yes, I mean . . . of course they're all great,' I shrug. 'But I don't think being in the throes of lust is the be-all and end-all. Certainly, when you've been married for a long time.'

'That's very practical of you, Darling.'

I laugh. 'Sorry if that's disappointing.'

'Actually, I agree with you, in the main. But I *still* think that if you're planning a whole lifetime together, then at the start, a little passion is the minimum requirement.'

There's a short, loaded pause in which I realise that my palms are slick.

'Anyway,' he says, concentrating on his coaster. 'She had an affair, which was about as shitty a discovery as you might imagine.' He mumbles the words, like it's a throwaway line.

'Oh,' I hear myself say. 'I'm sorry, Russo. That sucks.'

He shakes his head. 'Don't be. It's in the past. We did our fighting in the aftermath, there were plenty of pyrotechnics, and I got to take the moral high ground . . . though that was way less enjoyable than you'd think,' he says with a flat smile. 'Truth is, she did us both a favour. Hey, how the hell did you get me spilling my story of woe?'

'Sorry. Didn't mean to be a Debbie Downer.'

'Your turn now.'

'Mine?' I take a sip of my cocktail, then another, blatantly stalling for time. 'Oh, I'm a disaster area.'

He tuts. 'I find that hard to believe. I know you've had a divorce, but it's hardly the end of the world.'

I look up. '*Divorces*. Plural.'

Some small, inscrutable reaction filters in behind his expression. 'Huh. So exactly how many . . . *divorces plural* are we talking about? Do I call you Joan Collins from now on?'

'I prefer "Darling". The answer is *twice*. I've been married and divorced . . . *twice*.' I repeat it just to make sure he's got the message. It doesn't matter how many times I say this, though, I still feel as exposed as if I was declaring: 'My name is Lisa Darling and I'm an alcoholic.'

I find myself watching him, working out exactly what thoughts are shuffling in behind his eyes. Believe me, I've seen them all over the years. Pity. Intrigue. That peculiarly smug kind of satisfaction when you know someone is congratulating themselves for not being feckless enough to lose not one but two husbands.

Zach, however, is impossible to read. 'Could be worse,' he says eventually.

'I know. Still, it's not ideal.'

'Nor are most things in life. You must have worked that out by now?'

I smile, feeling oddly grateful for this reaction. 'So what do you think of the UK? Do you like living here?'

'Hmm . . . it has its pros and cons,' he says.

'Go on?'

'Well. Things I love: universal healthcare, hardly any gun crime, the fact that everyone is funny. Some of them even intentionally.'

'Ha! And what don't you like?'

'Being away from my family. Not being able to buy ranch dressing. Oh, and obviously . . . the weather.'

'Oh, don't be a wuss. It's not that bad.'

'It's *terrible*.'

'We've had a chilly spell lately, that's all. Anyway, the sun was shining when we walked over here. I'm surprised you didn't get a tan.'

'I'd be more likely to get one of those from a 40-watt light-bulb,' he says.

I'm not sure what it is that makes me finally look at my phone and realise that we seem to have lost hours here.

'Urgh. I really need to get going,' I sigh, failing to muster any enthusiasm.

'Are you kidding me? You have no kids tonight. By rights you should be going dancing, or to a strip club, or an all-night poker game.'

'Maybe some other time,' I smile sleepily.

I gather my belongings and slide off my stool as he stands and helps me shrug on my jacket. It's a strangely old-fashioned gesture and I like it more than it probably deserves. We step outside into a dark, dank night and I lead the way through the amber glow of cobbled backstreets, the sound of distant revellers and music echoing through the city sky.

'There's a taxi rank this way,' I tell him. 'It'll be cheaper than an Uber on a Friday night.'

We've barely walked twenty feet when I feel spots of rain. I try to pretend it isn't happening at first, but it gets very heavy, very quickly. I'm getting rapidly soaked until he removes his coat and drapes it over me, so it's covering my hair. The lining is warm, dry and smells deliciously of him. As our steps quicken, he turns to me, blinking rain out of his eyes.

'What was it you were saying about the weather?'

I turn to him, peering out from under his coat. 'Like I said . . . *not that bad.*'

I'm silenced by a groan of thunder and within moments, the only way to describe the conditions is *torrential*. One of those nights when every attempt to avoid a puddle only results in stepping in a bigger one until, eventually, you're soaked through.

'Exactly how far away is the taxi rank?' he yells.

'About five minutes. Maybe a little more if we're—'

Before I've finished my sentence, he has me by the elbow and is guiding me in the direction of a covered doorway. It's a small space – not very deep and no more than five feet wide – but enough to provide temporary shelter and give us a moment to catch our breath. I look up, meeting his gaze at the precise moment when it seems to occur to both of us exactly how close we are.

'You're still getting wet,' he says, as he places a hand on my lower back to shuffle me around, shielding me from the rain. His touch is momentary, but I feel his imprint tingling through my clothes even after he's removed it. Drenched and illuminated by the street lights, he is so damn gorgeous that it makes my chest constrict. The soaked, translucent fabric of his shirt clings to his muscular shoulders. Trails of water snake down the skin on his neck, disappearing into his collar. I feel a sudden urge to trace them with my fingertips, to follow them all the way down.

Instead, I wipe water from my lashes, checking the edge of my hand for mascara.

'Have I got panda eyes?'

'No,' he says gently. Then, in a different, lower voice: 'Actually, you have beautiful eyes.'

It occurs to me that I should feel cold. My teeth ought to be chattering and goosepimples should be prickling up my back. But none of those are the case. Quite the opposite. I am soaked through – yet I am on fire.

'You're getting very wet. Here, step in,' I whisper, briefly taking him by the wrists and gently pulling him towards me. It's only then – when he's as close as he could be without us touching and I'm facing his chest – that I get a full sense of the size of him. The ripples on those forearms, the sheen on his biceps. When I look up, his eyes are unmistakably heavy with desire. He seems to contemplate me for a moment, before he slides both hands around my waist and draws me into him. I tilt my face towards his as some deep, hidden part of me ignites.

The first touch of his lips is whisper soft. I press myself into him, a heartbeat pulsing in my ears, as I submit to the feel of his mouth and the way it moves with mine. The warm wetness of his tongue creates an agonising kind of bliss somewhere in my core, which spreads through my limbs and all the way to my toes. The kiss deepens as my nails dig gently into the flesh on his lower back and I become intensely aware of the sensitive swell of my breasts against his damp shirt.

He moves his lips to my temple, where he kisses me tenderly, then on my forehead, my jaw, that soft dip behind my ear. When our mouths meet again, the kiss becomes urgent. I feel out of control. I slide my palm over the skin at the bottom of his spine, as he releases a soft breath from the back of his throat. Then his hand moves down until he's squeezing my backside as if it's the delicious flesh of a ripe peach.

We are fully clothed, we are in public, we are doing little more than kissing. But I feel as if I could explode with desire. And then . . .

I don't know what it is exactly that causes my rush of clarity. The sobering quality of the rain. The beep of a distant taxi. The sheer, fucking insanity of this situation – being here, drunk and snogging in a doorway on the edge of town like I'm 18 years old and have stumbled out of a club.

He senses my hesitation and gently pulls back an inch, searching my eyes.

'Y'okay?' he says softly.

I nod, but struggle to look at him as I clear my throat and step back to create more distance between us. He still has hold of my hand, as if he doesn't want to let me go and is slowly rubbing the wrinkled pad of my thumb in circles. Still undoing me.

I take a deep breath, pull away my hand and force a smile. 'I'm fine. Definitely need to go and get that taxi though.'

He smiles and gives a curt nod. The inch between us now feels like a mile. 'Sure. Let's go find one.'

Chapter 22

I am mortified. Waking up the next morning, I have the worst case of The Fear that I've ever experienced. What the *hell* did I think I was doing? I know Zach is charming, easy on the eye and all those things that made last night feel like a good idea. But I've got to work with this guy. We're not twenty-something interns. We're senior managers, with staff and budgets and *reputations*.

I have never done anything like this with a colleague, unless you count one minor indiscretion at a BBC Christmas party, when I sang 'Yes Sir, I Can Boogie' on karaoke with one of the maintenance guys who serviced the printers. And while there is a part of me that would love to say I don't give a toss about what anyone thinks because I'm a grown-up and it's nobody else's business, the reality is, I do. I really, *really* do.

I am a mother of two. I take my career very seriously. It's bad enough that people know I'm twice divorced and make all the judgements about my baggage that they do (Rose thinks I'm being paranoid about this, but she's wrong). All of this brings me to one conclusion.

This cannot get out.

The only saving grace is that it's the weekend and I don't have to see Zach until Monday. In fact, I might try and rearrange some meetings so I can work from home. In the meantime, I decide I'm going to try and put him out of my mind entirely. It's a largely futile exercise, especially when a text arrives from him minutes after I've met Rose for a walk in the park on Saturday afternoon before the kids get back from Brendan's.

I've changed my mind about the British weather. I enjoyed last night very much. Z x

I feel my breath suspended somewhere in my chest and quickly stuff my phone in my pocket, without replying.

There was a point in my life when I was never away from this park. It's only five minutes from our house and when Leo was little it was the one guaranteed way of letting him expend some energy. I've been here in bitter winters and glorious summers. Now, it's somewhere in between, a spring day that can't make up its mind, dry but with glimmers of cool sunshine pushing through grey clouds.

'I keep meaning to ask,' I say, deciding to change the subject, 'what have you decided to do about the work on your house?' Rose and Angel were due to have their kitchen knocked through and extended this month. They'd been waiting almost 14 months for a slot from the in-demand builder their architect recommended.

'Oh, I've put it on ice. I couldn't face it.'

'I'm not surprised. You can have the nicest, most reliable builder in the world but having your house full of dust and burly blokes every day is a nightmare at the best of times.'

'Exactly. They've been really nice about it and said we don't have to go to the end of their list though – it's booked in at the end of the year, when I'm hoping to feel better equipped.'

I glance across to her. 'You already look a lot brighter, you know.'

'Do I?' she says, clearly pleased. 'I've been trying a bit of mindfulness, which is helping. Didn't you do that once?'

'Yes, I had an app for it. It was so bossy it drove me mad. It would be pinging every hour of the day telling me it was time to relax. I don't have the temperament for meditation.'

She chuckles. 'No, I think you're a lost cause, Lisa. I *am* feeling perkier though, now you mention it. Maybe we could meet for a drink next time. I don't fancy more than a glass at the moment, but it'd be nice to go out.'

'Oh, then we must do that,' I say, deciding not to mention the vow I made this morning to never touch alcohol again in my life.

'Or if you can get someone to watch Jacob, Keanu Reeves has a new movie out,' she says.

'If anyone's going to perk you up, it's him.'

Rose always said Keanu was the main reason she wanted to work in broadcasting. At 14, she thought it was her best chance of meeting him. I've assured her that there are far less noble reasons for choosing a career but, regardless, she's never come within a sniff of him. As Jeff points out, though, there's still time.

We spot a free bench and take a seat.

'Listen, I know I've said this before, but I really am grateful for all your support throughout this, Lisa. Having you there with me at all those appointments, especially the early ones, really helped.'

I tut. 'Don't be silly – you don't need to thank me. I owe you, remember.'

Rose was the first person I phoned after Brendan told me he was leaving me. Just thinking about that evening makes me feel tense, even after all these years. It was on 6 January. The first day back at school for the kids and peak season for divorce lawyers. Brendan is nothing if not conventional.

Things had been strained between us for three or four months and Christmas had been difficult. I felt as if I was permanently pretending everything was okay, even though I had an ominous knot in my stomach that had nothing to do with brussels sprouts.

I couldn't work out what had changed exactly, or why we were suddenly not getting along. Brendan had never really had a temper, but he was suddenly, inexplicably vile – picking fights at the slightest thing, complaining resentfully at basically everything. I couldn't do a thing right and I literally didn't know why.

We could not have continued like that but I hadn't appreciated how unhappy he was until, in a heart-to-heart at some point between Christmas and New Year, he suggested we go to couples' therapy. That alone shocked me to the core. I couldn't believe it was happening. But I booked an appointment, absolutely certain that this would be the thing that would make Brendan snap out of it – whatever 'it' was.

Only, on the day in question, he didn't show up and I had to sit awkwardly with a nice woman called Deborah, chatting about how much I liked her jumper, which she told me she'd got in the Oliver Bonas sale.

When it became clear he wasn't coming, she suggested I go home, make myself a cup of tea and not to worry, she wouldn't charge me. Which was kind of her, because I suspect she already knew she was unlikely to get any repeat business out of us. When I arrived home, Brendan was sitting at the table, nursing a can of lager. It was 11am. We were supposed to be doing Dry January.

He looked up at me and his bottom lip was trembling. He said something trite and soap opera-ish, about how *he couldn't do this anymore*. The row that followed was short, explosive and may possibly have broken a world record in the number of expletives crammed into three minutes.

I yelled. I cried. I told him I couldn't believe he was going to do this to our kids, our family . . . and for what? A midlife crisis? Couldn't he have been a bit more original?

I absolutely lost the plot with him that day. I was fuming. I can only imagine what Brendan tells Melanie about it all:

that I was ranting, hysterical female and he couldn't wait to get out of there fast enough. Maybe that's why I'm so determined to prove how reasonable I am these days. A rational, calm woman. That's me.

At the time, my most vivid recollection is sitting on the kitchen floor, unable to catch my breath, as I pulled up the only number I ever phoned in a true emergency. Within twenty minutes of Brendan's departure, Rose's Peugeot hatchback screamed onto the pavement outside like it was taking part in a drive-by shooting.

I sobbed into her arms that day, for the first of what would be multiple occasions. Of all the friends who supported me during that horrible time – when I had to tell my parents, then the kids, then move house and essentially deconstruct my entire life – she was the one who was easiest to be around. She was my scaffolding, propping me up when all I wanted to do was crumble.

I always knew I'd do the same for her. But I suppose I never thought I'd have to.

'Fancy seeing you two reprobates here.'

We look up and spot Jeff walking towards us, with one of his cocker spaniels on a lead. He's wearing an expensive-looking rib-knit sweater, with pale blue and white stripes that make him look ridiculously stylish.

Jeff is also dressed well.

'Love the dog's jumper,' Rose says. 'Where are the other two though?'

I bend down to stroke the animal and its tail begins to wag.

'They're at home. Because for some reason, Pascal here hates me, so Andy thinks we need some time together. *To bond*,' he says ominously.

'I'm sure he doesn't *hate* you,' I argue. 'Look at him. Those eyes! The little waggy tail! He's so cute!'

'Yes and I treat him like a prince. I don't know what I've done to deserve it. Watch.' He bends down to pet Pascal, who turns his head away with a disdainful curl of his top lip. 'I had a boyfriend whose mother used to look at me like that,' Jeff sighs, standing up. 'Come on, let's walk together. You two might put him in a better mood.'

We continue our stroll and the first thing that Jeff brings up is the one subject I'd rather avoid. 'I haven't seen you since the wine night, Lisa. You're a dark horse, aren't you? Your date was an absolute *delight*.'

Rose looks at me, astonished. 'What date?'

'It wasn't a date,' I assure her.

'Looked like it to me,' Jeff says, leaning around me. 'It was someone you guys work with. Zach?'

Rose's feet come to a standstill. 'You went on a date with Zach? My stand-in?'

'It wasn't a date,' I repeat firmly, refusing to stop walking. 'It was a stupid school event. I only let him come because I needed to flog the last ticket.'

'But I thought he was an arsehole?' she says, scurrying to catch up with me.

'I've warmed to him. Slightly. But it still wasn't a date.'

I suddenly realise that I'm blushing. It does not go unnoticed. 'Are you all right? Your cheeks have gone very pink,' says Rose.

'Must be a hot flush,' I reply, looking straight ahead and focusing on a toddler terrorising a mallard with some crusts.

Jeff raises an eyebrow. 'If that's a hot flush, it's a delicate one. Our poor office manager Adele looked as if she'd stepped out of a shower the other day. I had to go out at lunchtime to buy her a mini fan.'

'That was nice of you, Jeff,' Rose says.

'Hmm. I think it would've been more likely to propel a Boeing 747 than cool her scalp down. Still, hopefully it's the thought that counts.'

'Exactly. I'm sure she feels like she's got an ally,' Rose continues. 'And it's good that we can talk about the menopause openly these days. My mother never even mentioned it when I was growing up. It was like a dirty secret. You just had to get on with things.'

'Oh, mine never stopped talking about it,' Jeff says. 'She went through a phase of constantly losing her car keys – we found them in the freezer behind some peas once – and she would say, "Oh, this is it. It's happening. It's *The Change!*" I was only about nine and very worried about what the hell she was going to change into. A lizard?'

I laugh, as Rose decides to return to a subject she is far from finished with. 'So tell me about Zach, Lisa. Is he good at his job? By which I mean . . . *my* job?'

'Not as good as you,' I tell her. 'So don't be worried, because you have no reason to be.'

'You don't think he'd try and keep it, do you?' she asks.

'Absolutely not. One hundred per cent certain. I've already told him I would have to kill him if he tried to do that.'

'Well, if that's the case then I think you should go on a date with him.'

Jeff sniggers.

'It. Was. Not. A. Date,' I say, looking up just in time to witness her winking at him.

'My car is up there, so I'm going to head off,' Jeff says, turning to Rose. 'Give me a hug, you brave woman. Now, I know you keep saying there's nothing we can do for you while you're having your treatment, but there must be *something*.'

She shakes her head. 'There isn't.'

'Oh, *come on*. I'm sure you can think of something. Let me run an errand for you,' he says.

'I don't have any errands that need to be run.'

'Well, let me make you a lasagne,' he insists. 'Or a shepherd's pie. Go on, please.'

'You're vegan,' I laugh.

'I know but turning up on the doorstep with a tofu stir fry doesn't have the same ring to it.' He looks down at Pascal. 'Does it, my little chickadee?'

Pascal raises his eyes, lifts his leg and promptly empties his bladder.

Chapter 23

I technically could have waited a couple of weeks before my HRT review, but this way I kill two birds with one stone: tick an important task off my to-do list *and* avoid Zach after Friday night.

As I step into Dr Willoughby's room at the surgery, it's nice to be able to give her some good news.

'My symptoms have definitely eased,' I tell her.

'Oh good!' she says, delighted.

Dr Willoughby is a couple of years older than me and one of the new GPs at the practice where I've been registered for over a decade. I'd only seen her once before – when Jacob had tonsillitis. But when I finally got round to booking an appointment about my perimenopause symptoms back in.

The doctor is a couple of years older than me and one of the new GPs at the practice where I've been registered for over a decade. I'd only seen her once before – when Jacob had tonsillitis. But I finally got round to booking an appointment about my perimenopause symptoms back in March. It had been a long time before I finally accepted that I needed to do something about them, though it's hard to pinpoint exactly when they'd begun. Eighteen months earlier? Two years? Maybe even longer. I just know that what had initially amounted to the odd headache and a day or so of feeling low before my period turned into something far more invasive.

Palpitations that I thought were a heart attack. Migraines that made it hard to lift my head off a pillow. PMS that lasted for a week and made me sad, angry and paranoid, convince I was a bad mother, friend and daughter, that I was bad at my job, that I was, quite simply, the worst.

I remember having a conversation with Nora in which I felt genuinely tearful because Jacob had been told off by a teacher at school for failing to wear the correct team socks during rugby. It had been me who'd packed them in his bag. She looked at my tortured expression as I apologised for being 'a bit hormonal', before putting a hand on my arm and saying: 'Have you considered having a chat with Dr Willoughby?'

'Our GP?'

She nodded. 'She's also a registered menopause specialist.'

I don't know why I'd left it so long. It's certainly not down to any mistrust of medical science. We've got the NHS to thank for fixing everything from dad's dodgy back to saving Leo's life when he got a nasty chest infection as a baby and needed three days in hospital.

'Your palpitations are better then?' she asks now.

'Completely gone. Same with the migraines. I still have PMS symptoms and feel a bit foggy just before my period but they're not as severe. I've generally got more energy.'

'Well, that's great news. Stress levels?'

'Hmm. I do live with a teenager . . .'

'Say no more. But a general improvement across the board, you'd say?'

'Yes. Apart from the hot flushes.'

She looks at her computer. 'I don't think you reported those at our first appointment.'

'No, they . . . seem to be a new thing. Nothing I can't live with, though.'

'Hmm. Okay.' She types it in. 'Anything else. Vaginal dryness?'

I nearly say *quite the opposite*. 'No.'

'What about your sex drive?'

I shift in my seat, feeling slightly awkward. 'I think the best description of that would be . . . off the scale.'

'It's gone up?'

'Through the roof.'

She looks very pleased. 'That'll be the oestrogen.'

'Should I be *concerned?*' I ask.

'Oh no. I'd say the only thing that need concern you now,' she says, spinning round to reveal a wry smile, 'is having the time of your life.'

I'm not one of these people who has a general distrust of the medical profession, but as I walk home after the appointment, I do know that on this particular issue Dr Willoughby is way off the mark. The time of my life indeed.

The truth is, I make terrible decisions after having sex with people and I always have. The sex in question doesn't even need to be that good. I read somewhere once that this is something to do with oxytocin levels in the aftermath of the event. I might have known it would be a hormone.

I've convinced myself I've fallen in love with so many people after a roll in the hay over the years that I realised a long time ago I simply cannot be trusted. It's taken time and two failed marriages for me to recognise this, though Danny and Brendan are far from my only mistakes. They're just the most drastic examples. I had a single one-night stand at university and was so gutted when he wanted nothing to do with me in the cold light of day that it took about two terms to get over it.

I put my key in the door as a response to my earlier email arrives on my phone from Andrea.

From: Andrea.boden-smith@MotionMaxplus.com
To: Lisa.darling@MotionMaxplus.com

Lisa,

Today's fine but don't make a habit of home working, will you? Zoom can be handy, but it doesn't bring out the best in any of us. Remember Giles flashing his pyjama bottoms at the Public Policy Director of Ofcom? Also, don't forget the 'Future of Streaming' day tomorrow. We definitely need you here for that.

Andrea

I feel a surge of dread at the reminder. Zach will be presenting at that. It will be impossible for me to avoid it. Which is unfortunate because so far my main approach to Friday night's events has been to try and pretend he doesn't exist.

This really isn't like me. Ordinarily, I never bury my head in the sand. I roll my sleeves up, have a difficult conversation and sort it out. I am the last person to avoid an issue. Unless that issue involves a handsome American who has caressed my behind in a dark, rainy street – something I have singularly failed to stop replaying in my head ever since.

'Eurgh,' I groan, heading to the bathroom. I'm washing my hands after using the loo when I look in the mirror and register a couple of wrinkles that I'm sure never used to be there.

I'm not especially obsessed with the way I look, which I think can partly be attributed to the fact that there was no such thing as a selfie in my formative years. Only a handful of pictures even exist of me in my twenties, largely because of the effort it took to buy a film, get it developed, then come to terms with your disappointment when the only vaguely decent photo had been hijacked by your dad's thumb.

But I like to take care of myself as much as the next woman. And while it goes without saying that I never, ever plan to kiss Zach Russo again, when I look in the mirror, the first thought I have is both inexplicable and overwhelming.

I need to up my game.

I return to my desk and make a phone call.

Chapter 24

The woman who does my Botox is an attractive fifty-some-thing ex-NHS dermatology nurse called Liz and is, in the words of Jeff – who recommended her – a miracle-worker. I'm not sure about that, but she is willing to err on the side of caution and subtlety. Judging by some of the foreheads I've seen at the school gates, this is not a universal quality in her profession.

She had a cancellation this afternoon at her clinic, which is great except that I can only go directly after picking up Jacob from school.

'Can't we go straight home? I've got so much to do,' he says, climbing into the passenger seat.

'A lot of homework?' I ask, starting the engine.

'No, I'm just about to complete a new level on Roblox. Where is it we're going anyway?'

'It's . . . a *beauty* appointment,' I say vaguely.

But he's not listening, too busy scrolling through Spotify to find 'Wuthering Heights' again.

The clinic has that sterile, all-white look similar to how set designers in the 1970s imagined all living rooms would be fitted out in the future. Jacob sits on a chair outside the treatment room, next to a well-dressed woman of indeterminate age. They smile at each other, before he picks up a copy of *Aesthetic Beauty* magazine and starts flicking through it.

I ask for 'my usual' and tell Liz I need to be quick if she doesn't mind, which she takes as her cue to start telling me all about the limestone render she's having replaced on her Georgian terrace and try to flog me an at-home skin tightening device.

'I haven't seen you for *ages*, Lisa,' she says, peering at the lines above my nose with an expression that suggests I've allowed myself to become a gnarled old crone. She pulls back with a ponderous expression and I'm slightly concerned she's going to pull out a syringe the size of a nuclear warhead. But instead, she snaps on a pair of latex gloves and asks, 'Have you got something special coming up?'

'Yes, an award ceremony in a few weeks,' I say, which is at least true.

The actual injections are relatively quick and, contrary to popular belief, fairly painless, at least for anyone who's ever been through childbirth.

'Usual advice,' she says afterwards, 'no exercise or alcohol for twenty-four hours.'

'Why *is* that?' I ask, pulling on my coat.

'Oh, any increased blood flow can cause the toxin to migrate to the surrounding areas. Worst-case scenario, you'd end up looking like Droopy. Oh, don't worry,' she laughs, sensing my alarm. 'Just don't be going into a sauna, running a 5k – basically anything that makes your face go red. It will take two weeks for you to see the full effects so we'll book you in for a review then.'

I head out into the waiting room, where Jacob is now regaling a woman dressed in head-to-toe Marc Jacobs about why Manchester City's new striker has the best left foot in the Premiership.

'Ready, sweetheart?'

'Yep,' he says, slapping his hands on his knees before standing. Then he looks up at me and frowns. 'No offence, but you don't look any different.'

We head home and I'm pulling into the driveway when a text arrives from Rose.

Feel free to ignore this but given what you've been saying about Leo lately, I thought I'd forward this. My cousin swears by it.

I click open the link to an e-book called *The Book You Wish Your Parents Had Read*, by Philippa Perry.

Interesting – I'll give it a go. Are your cousin's children perfect, as a matter of interest? x

I wouldn't go that far, but she says it's helped. On another subject, the Keanu movie is sadly meant to be a stinker x

Do you care? I thought your devotion to him transcended all that!

It does, as my *Feeling Minnesota* DVD proves! Might be better to stick to the new wine bar in the village instead though x

I smile to myself as we go inside, pleased to hear she's even considering this.

Then I enter the kitchen and my expression dissolves. The devastation in here is the kind that can only be attributed to the recent detonation of a nail bomb, a minor earthquake . . . or alternatively a teenager who has decided he wants to make a cheese toastie. Every item – from a little-used cucumber spiraliser to what, worryingly, looks like it might be the PTA trifle dish – has been removed from a cupboard and is now sprawled across the worktop alongside half the contents of the fridge.

'For God's sake,' I mutter, heading into the hallway. 'Leo! *Will you please get down here to clean up this mess?*'

No response.

'LEO!'

No response.

'ARE YOU UP THERE, LEO?'

His bedroom door opens. 'WHAT?'

Ah. The monster lives.

'Can you please come and clean up your mess.'

He exhales. 'FINE.'

I return to the kitchen and put the kettle on to set about making myself a cup of tea. By the time I've made it and put away the milk, he's still not down here and the sight of this mess is burning my retinas.

I begin to clear up, amidst a tornado of huffing and puffing. I am acutely aware that I should dig my heels in and wait for him to do it. But I am still apparently compelled by some mysterious force that simply won't allow me to even look at this.

Once I've put the first few items away, it's very clear he's wilfully 'forgotten' about the whole thing. I return to the hallway and call up the stairs.

'LEO!'

'WHAT?'

'Get down here and clean up the mess.'

'I'm busy.'

'SO AM I!'

I try to remember a couple of breathing techniques and remind myself that he's got a lot on at school this year. Maybe I need to cut him some slack. I count to 10 and tell myself I need to let this go. There are more important things. Just put the stuff away, let him get on with his schoolwork and fight this battle another day. So I do exactly that. Only, just as I've cleaned the surface of the worktop, my phone beeps.

Notification: Principal's detention

Your son has been given a Principal's detention, for non-attendance of his recent Faculty detention, for failing to submit GCSE Art coursework. Detention must be served on Monday from 15:00 to 16:00. Yours, Mr C Stowell

My eyes begin to blur as I attempt to count the number of times the word 'detention' is used and work out exactly how many my son has been given. Then, I head into the hall again and stride upstairs two at a time, before giving three sharp knocks on his bedroom door and opening it.

It's a complete state, but I've seen it all before. Like a scene from a documentary about people with hoarding disorders, only instead of old newspapers, my son is collecting empty Pot Noodle cartons, dirty underpants and a spaghetti heap of USB cables on his floor. I remind myself of a scientific study sent to me by one of the producers of *My Teenage Bombsite* which said teens' bedrooms are messy because 'as their childhood starts to succumb to the confusion of adolescence, so does their sense of order.' So they're not just bone idle then.

'CAN'T YOU KNOCK?'

I look up at him, crouching at the window, and realise that he's shouting because he's panicking. And the reason for that is that I've caught him red-handed, surrounded in a halo of melon-flavoured nicotine vapour.

'*What . . . are . . . you . . . doing?*'

It's my Darth Vader voice. Deep, menacing, designed for intimidation.

He starts coughing and spluttering like a backfiring lawnmower. 'Nothing! I'm not doing anything! What are you doing in here? JUST GET OUT.'

I step forward and hold out my hand. 'Give me that. NOW. Please.'

'What?'

'The vape that you've just been smoking.'

'What vape?' he says as something drops from the window, clangs on the conservatory roof and clatters down to the patio below. He holds out his hands. 'There. No vape.'

'You've just dropped it! Honestly, Leo, you must think I was born yesterday,' I say, my voice rising.

'I have NO IDEA what you're talking about,' he protests, marching to the door and holding it open for me. 'Now will you just get out!'

He has red cheeks and the guilty, cornered air of someone who's farted in a lift, but the only available tactic to him is to brazen this out. Unfortunately, he is no Talented Mr Ripley.

'I'm talking about you vaping. But that wasn't even why I came here.'

'This is MY ROOM.'

'And this is MY HOUSE,' I say, realising as the words come out of my mouth that all I'd need is a batwing jumper and a Lady Di haircut to turn into my mother, circa 1989.

'Look, don't yell at me,' I say, feeling my temperature rise and my temples throb. 'We will get onto the vaping later. That's quite bad enough, but I wasn't even here to talk about that.'

'I know,' he huffs. 'You were here to have a go about your AWFUL DELINQUENT CHILD leaving a bit of cheese on the counter.'

'Well, yes, there was that too. But the main thing I was here to discuss with you was . . . THIS.'

I thrust the phone at him, showing him the notification about the detention.

He peers in. 'That's me and Jacob in Disney World.'

I glance back and realise my screensaver has flipped on. 'Not that.' I try again. 'THIS.'

Only now, the bloody thing is refusing to unlock – presumably because my facial recognition can't cope with the steam coming out of my ears. I hit a few numbers in a bid to type in the code and, when that doesn't work, abandon the phone and just come out with it.

'Leo. You have a *Principal's detention* . . .'

He releases a long sigh and rolls his eyes. 'Is that all? You'd think I was wanted by the FBI.'

'. . . and the reason you have that is that you'd been given a different detention and didn't show up. And the reason for that – apparently – is that you haven't submitted your coursework for the Art GCSE.'

'I mean . . . it's only Art.'

Stay. Calm.

'It is a GCSE. If you're going to do A Levels, you need to get enough points right across the board to stay in your school's exceptionally good, highly oversubscribed sixth form.'

He's not looking at me now. Instead, he's sitting on the bed, putting on one of his trainers. Once he's got that on, he starts looking for the other. Unfortunately, it's concealed somewhere under the rubble of his life, buried probably for eternity like the lost Ark of the Covenant.

He starts throwing bits of paraphernalia around to try and find it.

'Have you got nothing to say for yourself?' I ask.

'Nope.'

Then, having failed to find the shoe, he stands up and pushes past me.

'Where are you going?'

'Out.'

'Oh no you're not, young man. We need to talk about this. You've only got one shoe on for a start.'

'*UHMIGODDD!* WOULD YOU JUST STOP MICRO-MANAGING ME.'

'Fine!' I say, hurtling after him down the stairs. 'But you can't go out, you've got homework to do or you'll end up in yet another detention.'

There is a pleading note in my voice now, but it's too late. 'Look, we can talk about the vaping. I can help you give those up – I'll get you an app. But please. Your exams . . . this is your whole future. You need these grades if you're going to get into sixth form and—'

'I'm not going to sixth form. You'd know that if you bothered asking me.' He reaches the door and turns around.

'What? What are you going to do then?'

'I'm going to apply to a rugby academy instead.'

I let out a laugh before I can stop myself, but when I realise he's serious, manage to turn it into a cough.

'But . . . what about your A levels?'

'I'd get a BTEC in Rugby Union Studies instead. I don't need anything else. I'm going to be a full-time player.'

'But . . . but . . . Leo, only a tiny proportion of people are able to become professional sports people.'

'Oh, thanks for your support. That's just *great*, that is.'

I resist pointing out the irony of this particular delusion when he's just been caught sucking that rubbish into his lungs. Instead, I say: 'Leo. Listen to me. You're a *really* clever kid. I will support you in whatever you want to do. And I'm not saying give up on your sporting dreams but—'

'Then don't. Don't say anything.'

'I'm your mother! It's my job to say something!'

'Whatever,' he replies, before striding out of the door – in his one shoe – and slamming it behind him. I look in the hall mirror. My face is the colour of a beetroot.

Chapter 25

In a bid to avoid Zach, I move about the office the following morning like a shifty double agent. The only thing missing is a brown mac, a trilby and a pair of dark glasses, possibly with a fake beard for good measure. I am on edge the entire time, refusing to walk around corners without first checking the coast is clear. I manage to make it through the morning without encountering him, but realise that this charade cannot be maintained when Calvin thrusts a Tupperware box in front of me and I nearly jump out of my seat.

'Sorry. Didn't mean to startle you. They're just vegan brownies,' he smiles. 'I baked them at the weekend.'

'They're *so* delicious,' gushes Daisy, as I take one. 'What did you put in them, Calvin?'

As I take a bite, the first ingredients that spring to mind are treacle, turnips and Castrol GTX.

'Sweet potato, prunes, avocado oil . . .'

I resist the temptation to say something about the wholesale demonisation of carbohydrates having a lot to answer for, but realise Calvin's big, puppyish eyes are looking at me expectantly.

'Abmoludey *gorggus*,' I mumble enthusiastically, suspecting it will take most of the day to unstick this small morsel from the roof of my mouth. 'Well done you.'

Fortunately, neither he nor Daisy notice as I fold the rest into a napkin as they're now too busy discussing the highlights of last night's *Antiques Roadshow*. Most of today is tied up with presentations, but I have a few minutes to send a couple of emails, including to the production company of *My Teenage Bombsite*.

I'm still not entirely sure about this project. While it showed so much promise when we held a recent brainstorm with them, they're digging their heels in about us wanting another, more experienced firm to get involved to hold their hand. They clearly resent the implication that they're not capable of running the show, although, as I pointed out to Andrea, they'll soon get over themselves if we end up with a hit on our hands.

After I've hit send on the last one, I pick up my bag and check the coast is clear before I cross the office to head for the stairs. There's one hairy moment when I spot someone I *think* could be Zach chatting near the gents' toilets, but I manage to conceal myself behind a large potted fig until they've gone. I dart towards the lifts and hit the button as Brendan phones.

'I'm about to lose reception,' I tell him, 'but have you managed to speak to Leo?'

As a sign of how desperate I was, I phoned my ex-husband immediately after Leo had disappeared last night and told him what had happened. He's his father, after all. Leo might live with me but I think my mum is right on this one: his father needs to know. In fact, ideally he needs to *Do Something*.

There was a short pause when I said those two words.

Then, after a long inhalation, he declared bullishly: 'Leave this with me.'

Now, he tells me he phoned Leo at lunchtime and 'had a good chat'. He sounds *very* positive.

'Do you think you got through to him about staying at sixth form?'

I spent last night googling the sports academy he wants to go to, determined to keep an open mind. Its academic performance is atrocious. I'm sure he'd have enormous fun there – which *obviously* I want for him, just not at the expense of his whole future.

A place like that is going to close all his options, not widen them. How do I get through to him that he needs to put the work in, get the grades, then make an informed decision about what he wants to do with his life? All this sounds so sensible I'm almost boring myself to tears.

'No doubt about it,' he says confidently. 'Although, are you absolutely sure he was vaping? He was determined you'd got that wrong and you didn't see anything of the sort. Are you absolutely *sure* you saw it?'

'Yes,' I say, through gritted teeth.

'It's just, I really think I'd know if he was lying. He seemed very genuine, Lisa.'

'I bet he did,' I mutter, though I question myself a moment later. Maybe I'm *not* sure. Maybe this is the dreaded brain fog I've heard all about. It makes people feel as if they're losing their mind, apparently. I can't deny I feel like that quite a lot lately.

'Either way, I don't think you're going to have any more problems,' Brendan says confidently.

'Really? Well, that really is . . . great. So thank you. I'll be honest, I felt like I was hitting my head against the wall last night. There was no getting through to him.'

'I think some things simply need to be dealt with man to man.'

I feel a stab of indignation. Or is it jealousy? It's not good, either way. The thought that *I'm* the one who has raised this child – single-handedly, give or take the odd weekend in the Peak District – yet all it takes to get Leo to start listening is for Brendan to sweep in and talk to him. *Man to man.*

I shake the thought from my head. This is no time to be petty. It really doesn't matter whether it's me or Brendan who makes him see sense. The only important thing is that our son gets his act together.

'So . . . what did he say exactly? That he's going to start revising?'

'He's got the message, don't you worry. Trust me Lisa, it's *all sorted.*'

'Right,' I say, exhaling. 'Well, that really is brilliant, Brendan, thank you.'

'Any time,' he says, with a Supermanish air.

I end the call just as the lift doors open. And I come face to face with Zach Russo.

He looks me in the eye as if daring me to glance away and some odd feeling swoops in my gut that I can only compare to the first big plummet on a fairground ride. He's wearing a suit. I've never seen him in one before. Our office dress code is like most places in these post-pandemic days – smart but with mostly open collars.

Zach has a tie. Midnight blue, the same colour as his eyes. It's juxtaposed with a white shirt that looks specifically designed to highlight how tanned and smooth the skin on his neck is. Meanwhile, his jacket, in a steely grey, emphasises the breadth of his shoulders, with a single button that meets precisely in the middle of that muscular torso.

He looks like a Hugo Boss model, all polish and attention to detail.

He looks – there's no other way of putting this – insanely hot.

I consider running away, but as the lift begins to close, he puts his hand against the door to stop it.

'Getting in?'

I swallow, then nod. 'Yes.'

I step inside and the doors close.

We both look straight ahead for a few silent seconds and the only thing that fills my head is the intense, now familiar smell of him, with top notes of something else.

'Like a mint?' he asks, offering me a Tic Tac.

So that's what it was.

'No thanks,' I say, followed by a stab of paranoia that my breath smells.

He turns his head to look at me.

'I texted you a few times,' he says.

I fix my eyes on the doors. 'I know.'

'Are you feeling a little . . . *weird* about what happened on Friday night?'

Weird is one word. Horny is another.

All I can now think about is the slide of his tongue against mine. The feel of his triceps beneath my fingers. The warm wetness of his mouth on my neck. An unwelcome heaviness settles between my legs.

'I am, yes.'

I keep my eyes firmly ahead until I can resist no longer.

'Are *you*?' I ask.

'Sure,' he shrugs. 'But *nice* weird. You are one hell of a kisser, Darling . . .'

His eyelashes lower to my lips. My breath hovers somewhere in my chest. *Oh my fucking hell.* I want to kiss this man so badly. I want his hands on my behind again. The muscles of his chest pressed against my breasts. I want to tilt my face and relinquish myself so his tongue can move deeper and deeper into my mouth. I realise from the look on his face that something, if not identical, then certainly similar, is running through his head.

The doors open.

'Ahoy there!' says Giles, who shuffles in between us.

The presentation is taking place in our largest meeting room – in front of more than 100 people. I've never felt entirely comfortable with an audience of this size – too many flash-backs to being cast in the school play, as one of Miss Hannigan's orphans in *Annie*. But Zach looks so relaxed you'd think he was on vacation.

I slink to the back and take a seat next to a twenty-something bearded guy I recognise vaguely as being new in IT. He's watching a trailer for the Japanese *Godzilla* on his phone, looking very much as if this is the last place he wants to be.

I sit next to him and, recognising me as someone senior, he coughs and puts his phone away. I consider reassuring him that I too have been known to multitask during meetings. But he probably doesn't want to know about my pelvic floor exercises, or that I had to stop when Rose pointed out I'd never entirely mastered the art of doing them without simultaneously pulling strange facial expressions.

Krishna is on first, for an introduction about the need to take time out of our day-to-day jobs and 'future proof' the business. This is followed by a session with some guy from a consultancy, presenting his research about 'the viewer experience', before we split off briefly for a break. Then it's Zach's turn – to deliver a talk called 'Innovations in free ad-supported streaming TV'.

I already suspected he'd be polished, confident and slightly overfamiliar, because everyone in the LA office is. At the risk of sounding like a West End theatre reviewer, he is that – but also more. He's engaging and funny. Whip-sharp and charismatic. And, above all, he has substance. Even the IT guy next to me – who during the first part of proceedings was unquestionably listening to a true crime podcast on his ear pods – is enthralled.

When he's finished talking, he takes questions. The first, he works through with the same cool confidence as his presentation. But then someone from marketing puts his hand up and asks a question.

'Don't you think it would be better to focus less on what will be going on in this industry in the future and more on now?'

'We need to focus on *both*. Every business does, just as every industry does. Assuming you want a job in five years' time?'

Zach fails to hide the fact that he considers it a stupid question and the guy blushes and sits back in his seat. Perhaps that's another reason why 'not everyone is a fan', then.

I try to hold that thought for the rest of the day. To make it bigger in my mind than it possibly deserves. To tell myself that, he might be fanciable, hot and oozing charisma, but he's arrogant too. Which is yet another reason – as if I needed one – to stay away from him. To push him right out of my mind. Immediately.

It proves to be easier said than done.

As I'm driving home that night, I am determined to keep all sexy thoughts, especially flashbacks – well and truly out of my mind. Except at one point when I click on Spotify. I press play and when 'Wuthering Heights' comes on, unable to listen to it one more time, I skip forward to the next Kate Bush song.

'The Sensual World'.

I feel my spine prickle and consider moving on, before chastising myself. Come on, Lisa. You're enough of a grown-up to listen to *a song* without letting your mind drift to places it shouldn't be. I click on the indicator and drive as a dreamlike sound fills the car. The soft, swirling woodwind and breathless vocals make the hairs on my forearms stand on end. My imagination ignites. Her voice meanders to one particularly stirring line – something about slipping between breasts – and I'm forced to slam my hand on the off button. Then I turn down our street and see Leo with a group of friends, puffing on a vape.

Chapter 26

I spend a restless night tormenting myself about the way Zach looked in the lift, convinced in the cold, lonely hours between 3am to 5am that this cannot be normal at my age, HRT or not. Aren't I supposed to be drying up, thinning out and starting to find the idea of sex repellent? Maybe if I spent more time focusing on being a Mother – capital M – then perhaps I wouldn't be having this much trouble with my 15-year-old . . .

Still, at least when Leo came in last night, he said sorry for his behaviour the previous evening and promised me there will be no more detentions. Clearly, he's saying what I want to hear, but let's not split hairs. He did the right thing and gave me an apology – a proper one too, not just one of those teenage grunts that mean nothing. I didn't then want to ruin the mood by discussing the vaping, though that's clearly the next fun item on my agenda that I need to grapple with.

Even accounting for the dark places to where insomnia can lead your thoughts, I realise that if I were counselling a friend I'd say this was a harsh assessment; that my fancying Zach has nothing to do with what goes on at home. Part of me already knows that a woman can wear many hats in her life – Mother, Daughter, TV executive, Friend, Ex-wife (x 2), PTA Communications Secretary – and suspects that adding, 'Snogger of the Office Hottie' to that list is neither here nor there.

But I'm not counselling *someone else* – only *me*. And the gloves are off.

I decide to give up on the idea of sleep at 5am, so turn on the bedside lamp and remember the link Rose sent me – to Philippa Perry's *The Book You Wish Your Parents Had Read*. I suddenly feel slightly ashamed that I've been devouring Reese Witherspoon's book recommendations, instead of this sort of thing. I've never thought of myself as a 'bad parent' per se but maybe that's because I've never truly been tested. My failings are certainly apparent now.

The book promises to 'break negative cycles and patterns', 'handle your own child's feelings' and 'learn what you can do about your own mistakes'. I can think of so many of the latter that something must shut down in my brain because after an hour or so I finally start to drift off. At which point, the alarm goes off, like the insertion of a knitting needle in my ear. And another morning unfolds in which Leo is late and ill-tempered, which consequently makes *me* late and ill-tempered. Above all, I feel as if I need to get my priorities straight.

PRIVATE AND CONFIDENTIAL

Dear Zach,

This is an excruciating email to have to write, but here goes. Could I please ask that you keep what happened on Friday night strictly between you and me? At the risk of sounding precious, I've worked for this company for a long time and take my reputation seriously. What happened was unprecedented and not something I plan to make a habit of.

I don't know you well, but I very much hope that you feel the same way as me on this subject. I'd like to reassure you that, from my point of view,

it will go no further. As far as I'm concerned, the
matter is confidential – and now closed.
  Best wishes,
  Lisa

I hit send and think about it at random times throughout
the day. As Andrea and I are waiting to meet a production
company about a TV flower-arranging competition show –
floristry's take on *The Great British Bake-Off* – I find myself
scrolling through my email sent box to reread what I've written, praying that he'll respond and put me out of my misery.

But, for hours, there's nothing.

I wonder briefly if this is what it means to be ghosted, then
realise I'm not sure that's possible when I've aimed to give the
impression I wish to never set eyes on him again. An email
only finally arrives at the end of the day, as I'm prodding
my eyebrow in front of the mirror of the ladies', pondering
whether my conflagration with Leo – and rush of blood to
the head – will result in any major facial disfigurement.

Hi Darling,
  Okay, I get it. I'm not the kind of guy who needs
to be told twice. I wouldn't dream of spilling this,
but, for the record, that's not because I think we
did anything wrong. Consenting adults and all
that. Plus, it was just a kiss. A damn good one
too, as far as I'm concerned. Nevertheless, message received, loud and clear. Confidential – and
closed – it is.
  See you at work tomorrow.
  Zach

I feel a twist of something in my stomach which I want to be
relief. Oddly, though, it feels closer to disappointment.

Chapter 27

I have plenty to occupy my mind over the next couple of days, both in and out of work. Not least the PTA Bounce-a-thon. This extravaganza is the brainchild of Denise Dandy and involves the hiring of a local trampoline park at some obscure, off-peak time in order to fill it with pupils from the prep and pre-prep school.

The cost of a ticket is vastly inflated in the name of fund-raising. But most people don't mind paying an extra £6 because it offsets all their mum guilt if they've never quite made it to the Halloween disco to volunteer on the tuck shop dressed as a Ghostbuster.

As far as I'm concerned, it's one of Denise's better ideas; simple and straightforward, with little in the way of preparation. Even if, at the last PTA meeting, when nobody else offered to co-ordinate the post-event collection of 140 small, sweaty socks, I heard myself say, 'Oh, I don't mind doing that.'

Part of me had thought that, in my Communications Secretary role, I wouldn't have a great deal else to do for this one. All that was required was a flyer that could be circulated on school WhatsApp groups and the weekly Principal's newsletter. Or so I'd thought . . .

Because while whipping up a poster on Canva took only half an hour, what I hadn't counted on was Denise appointing herself in an unofficial role of 'Artistic Director' to critique my handiwork.

Just a few thoughts off the top of my head @lisadarling, she begins, after I shared the electronic flyer, naively assuming my job was complete. I think it's a nice idea overall but what happened to the school logo? Can we fix pls. Also, regarding the three little characters bouncing on the trampoline, I wonder if we should be more inclusive? Perhaps we can include a wheelchair somewhere? Finally, the expression on the little boy on the right is odd. Creepy almost. Can we alter his facial expression?

I'm biting my knuckle so hard I almost draw blood when another one pings – from some random woman I've never heard of.

Excellent points @denisedandy. Also – is it me or is the background a bit drab? What do others think? Maybe we could produce a few different versions and vote on which looks the best.

'Are you fucking kidding me?'

'Language!' says my mother, appearing behind me in the kitchen with a gravy boat.

'Sorry,' I mutter, as another message pings on WhatsApp. This one has been posted by Nora, who finally caved in and joined the PTA last week.

@NoraCTennis I think it looks fabulous. To make best use of everyone's time, wouldn't it be better to leave jobs like this to those in the group who have experience of them? Seems counterproductive to be picky when we could focus our energies on raising more money.

I click to text Nora.

Have I ever told you I love you? Thank you xxx

Pleasure. I've only been in this group for five minutes and suspect my name is already mud! Creepy? FFS! Xx

I smile and look at the poster. Now she mentions it, maybe Denise has a point . . .

I decide to have a look again later tonight because right now, my priority is the family dinner I've cooked to celebrate my mother's 72nd or possibly 73rd birthday – I'm not sure she remembers herself and, clearly, it's too late to ask now. I dart to the oven to check on the roast potatoes.

'They're fine. Just need another couple of minutes,' says Mum.

'Mum, sit down and put your feet up. Please. Let me top you up with some Prosecco.'

'Well, I'd never say no to that,' she says, holding out her glass, as I take the bottle out of the fridge.

'Where's Dad disappeared to?' I say, grabbing a pair of oven gloves to remove the chicken.

'Oh, he's fixing your gutter.'

'What?'

I lower the roasting dish onto a trivet and crane my neck so I can see out of the bifold doors. My father is currently at the top of a ladder, which he presumably helped himself to from the garage in order to undertake a little light roofing before his meal.

He's had this compulsion ever since Brendan left. Every time he walks through my door, I can see him scanning the fittings – on the lookout for wonky skirting boards and dripping taps – to see what DIY tasks might be required now there is no longer a Man of the House.

I have tried to tell him that Brendan was useless on that front anyway, that his leaving hasn't made the slightest bit of difference and that, while I'm very grateful, he *is* allowed to just come over to see us all sometimes without firing up a Black and Decker. It falls entirely on deaf ears.

'What's wrong with my gutter?'

'Oh, I don't know. He said something about the "fall" not being sufficient.'

I look out again as he starts doing something with a spirit level.

'Well, will you tell him to get in here and have a beer instead?'

She walks to the door and opens it up. 'Lisa says stop interfering.'

'I didn't say *that*,' I call out. 'But I'm about to serve up.'

I wipe sweat from my forehead as Mum puts her glass down.

'What else can I do?' she asks.

'Nothing,' I reply, which she takes as her cue to start doing *everything*. Both of my parents are doers by nature. He's the sort of man who taught himself to rewire a house and plumb in an entire bathroom back in 1978 using nothing more than a Collins manual. She makes her own jam, compost, biodegradable wet wipes and can offer you seven different tips for getting stains out of a linen tablecloth.

There is no doubt I have inherited these sensibilities but I have somehow ended up living a life in which there isn't a minute in which to put them all into practice – hence the jam recipe she wrote down for me two years ago is still pinned on our corkboard, entirely redundant.

By the time both parents and my children are at the table in front of what – if I do say so myself – is a damn good home-cooked meal, I feel a small twinge of smugness. I feel sure Philippa Perry would approve. So much so that I get a rush of blood to the head and, deciding to emulate the kind of nice, functional families you see on TV, I say—

'Shall we say grace?'

Leo's face scrunches up like a bull mastiff. 'Why? You're an atheist.'

'You're not, are you?' Mum gasps, nearly dropping her Prosecco.

'What's an atheist?' asks Jacob.

'Someone who doesn't believe in God. And no, I'm not. I'm agnostic.'

'What's agnostic?'

I sigh. 'Shall we just dish up?'

The dinner represents one of those rare, blissful occasions when everyone is both on excellent form *and* well behaved. Plates are scraped clean, conversations are civilised, nobody fights or complains. My mother seems to be having the best 72nd, or possibly 73rd, birthday anyone could ask for. She loves her cake, even though it's only my old faithful red velvet recipe and falls some way short of the three-tier, knitting-themed spectacle Jacob found on YouTube and suggested I whip up after work one night.

'There's not long till your own birthday, Jacob,' says Dad. 'Have you had any present ideas yet?'

'Well, I was thinking of maybe a 3D printer,' he says, 'or a freeze-drying machine.'

'What on earth do you want those for?' I ask.

'You can use them on bananas,' he explains, apparently impressed.

'You can print out a banana?' Mum asks.

'No, but you can freeze-dry one,' he clarifies.

'They cost about two grand, Jakey. Bit of an expensive snack,' says Leo, catching my mother's eye so they can share a conspiratorial chuckle.

'Then maybe a Padel racket. I was thinking of joining the club Rowan is in.'

I lower my cutlery. 'Jacob, you *cannot* join any more clubs.'

'You're in *everything*, mate,' Leo laughs, ruffling his little brother's hair.

My eldest son, it seems, is having a good day. Just like he always does when he's around his grandparents, both of whom seem to think that the sun shines out of his backside. As is their right, of course. He's their first grandchild, the apple of their eye and, in their presence, is invariably pleasant, engaging – and basically unrecognisable. After dinner, he stands to clear away the plates and tops up his grandma's drink, as her loving gaze follows him back to the table.

'How about a game of charades?' he suggests. 'What do you reckon, Granddad – are you up for it?'

'Go on then, sunshine,' says Dad, pushing away his chair. 'As long as you don't keep choosing songs I've never heard of. At least do the odd one from my era.'

'Mozart then?' grins Leo.

'Oi!'

What follows is the most enjoyable hour of family fun I've had in as long as I can remember. It would almost have been wholesome if it weren't for my mother's attempt to act out *Baywatch* with the use of two Jaffa oranges as props. As the kids fall about laughing, I can't help wishing Leo would behave like this *all the time*.

Afterwards, Dad insists on going back up the ladder – despite having had two halves of Heineken – while Leo invites his little brother up to his room to play Fortnite, a privilege so rare that it was Christmas Day last time it happened.

'I really don't know why you worry about that boy so much,' Mum says afterwards. 'He's *lovely*. Obviously, he hasn't got that from his father's side . . .'

'I *know* he is,' I concede – because, frankly, the last couple of hours give me genuine hope. 'I'm not lucky enough to see this version of Leo as often as you do.'

She flattens her mouth and raises her eyebrow, an expression that might pass for sympathetic until I realise it's just patronising. 'Are you going through The Change, love? I was moody then too. Your hormones are all over the place. It's easy to lose your temper over the slightest thing. You just need to try and keep a bit of perspective . . .'

'It's not *me*, Mum. It's *him*,' I protest, feeling as if I'm twelve years old again and being – wrongly – blamed for the time my cousin Ali set fire to the curtains on a sleepover.

'All right, love,' she says gently, patting my hand. 'Feel free to talk to me about it. Not that my symptoms were that bad, unless you count biting your father's head off whenever he left the lid off the butter dish.'

'You still do that,' I point out.

'Well, yes. You'd think he'd have learnt by now.'

Part of me wants to tell her about Leo's vaping – and the lying about it – but something always makes me conceal the worst examples of his behaviour. Part of it is because I know it would only upset her (she watched a documentary about them once and is now convinced that fruity vapes are one small step from crack addiction, homelessness and withdrawal from civilised society). But there's some other reason why I don't give her the full picture, which I struggle to define beyond this: I'm ashamed. In front of my own parents.

'All I'm saying about Leo is that I wish he would take his GCSEs seriously,' I continue. 'He needs to knuckle down and start focusing more. He's only going to get one shot at this.'

She opens her mouth, clearly trying to think of a way to blame this on Brendan, but fails. In the end, she settles on: 'Not everyone is academic. Does it really matter in the scheme of things?'

'Of course not. All any of us want for our kids is that they're happy and they reach their potential. But he has *so* much potential – he's been in the top percentile of his cohort throughout his entire school years. He said the other day he wanted to be a rugby player. It's ridiculous.'

'Is it necessarily?'

'Yes, Mum,' I say firmly. 'Leo is great at most sports, better than his classmates, but he's a weekend player, not some future professional. If he thinks this is an alternative to bothering with actual hard work, he's living in a dream world. He's just not good enough.'

At which point, I realise he is standing at the door. Seething.

Chapter 28

To-do list

- Complete first of Philippa Perry's exercises, i.e. unpack the last argument you had and write down all self-critical thoughts
- Find out if Phillipa Perry has an app
- Look up Philippa Perry's agent – has she ever she considered a TV show?
- Speak to Jacob's maths tutor to ensure he is following the national curriculum. Also that he can add up
- Make trampolining child on Bounce-a-thon flyer look less weird
- Sort outfit for forthcoming TV Awards
- Book appointments for nails, tan, highlights
- Whiten teeth
- Charge up all hair removal devices
- Buy shape-enhancing body suit
- Complete daily 'Core Crusher' workouts on Asana Rebel. NO EXCUSES.
- COLLAGEN!
- DIY living room panelling
- Find out where kids are hiding socks
- Fix mortgage rate
- Descale kettle

The Television Critics Association Awards aren't as well known as the Baftas but they have some things in common. First, they take the form of a glittering ceremony, in this case in London's Park Lane, with stars of the small screen flying in from as far afield as LA, Paris and Milton Keynes. Second, everyone in the room desperately wants to win, whatever they say about being honoured just to be nominated. Third, the most eventful parts of the evening tend to happen *after* the main event.

I've been to many an awards do in my time and have *all* the backstage gossip. I've seen famously married showbiz couples suggest threesomes with waiters, newsreaders line up coke on toilet cisterns and – most excitingly – once chased Jupiter from *Gladiators* down a corridor to tell her she had some loo roll stuck on her high heel. She was suitably grateful.

They are, above all, a lot of fun and certainly the glitzier side of my job. It's also reassuring to know that, of the plethora of paparazzi in attendance, most rarely have the urge to photograph me. They want Emilia Clarke and Felicity Jones; they want Helen Mirren and whoever it was that took part in the most recent *I'm A Celebrity*.

Nevertheless, you still want to look good, not least because anonymity is by no means guaranteed. Once, when I was running late for the Baftas, I forgot to shave my underarms, so had to walk round with my hands pinned to my sides like an emperor penguin. Unfortunately, I ended up in the *Daily Mail* like that after inadvertently standing behind the Duchess of York for a red carpet shot. It only made page 34, but still.

I tell myself that *this* is the reason I am putting so much preparation into my appearance for this forthcoming date in the calendar. That it has nothing to do with the – as yet unconfirmed – possibility Zach will also be there.

Since our email exchange the week before last, I have gone to great lengths to make it clear that I have not given him a second thought. When we see each other at work, we exchange a curt hello. We've had a single meeting together in which I refused to meet his eye. I have managed to avoid any one-to-one contact, unless you count once bumping into him in the coffee shop opposite the office. He offered me a sachet of sugar and I mumbled a 'no thanks', before shuffling out as quickly as possible.

If ever my thoughts drift to his muscles and the dimple in his chin while I'm lying in bed at night, I simply whip out the Philippa Perry book and turn my attention to being a better parent instead. My dreams are another matter. I have recently experienced a cornucopia of erotic fantasies involving isolated rockpools on white sandy beaches, the velvet, womblike corners of theatre cloakrooms, the main lift at work and – always, always, always – Zach Russo.

It cannot go on.

But in the meantime, I feel mysteriously compelled to be my best, most polished self at the awards. As nothing in my wardrobe feels quite good enough, I am left with no choice but to go online for a new outfit. It is a frustrating and ultimately fruitless endeavour. I have no idea why Pinterest has taken to suggesting £980 blouses to me in its email round-ups; I feel like sending them a copy of my payslip to prove just how screwed up their algorithm is. But the unedifying result is that I now have what my mother would disapprovingly call 'expensive tastes'. The consequence of this is that I can find nothing I like that's also in my budget.

I'm starting to despair when Daisy, of all people, makes a suggestion.

'Why don't you hire one?' she says. 'It's better for the environment and what everyone our age does when we go somewhere special.'

I'm sceptical at first. I've seen no evidence that Daisy goes anywhere special, unless you count the 'Knit & Natter' meetings she persuaded her local organic juice bar to introduce.

Still, partly in a bid to prove I'm still a trendy young thing at heart, I set up an account for an online rental service and spend every night for a week scrolling through dresses by designers such as Yves Saint Laurent and Elie Saab. They are stunning, every one of them. But they're not exactly . . . *forgiving*. There's a lot of leg on show. And cleavage. And back – not just shoulders, I'm talking all of it, right down to the top of your bum. Frankly, I'm worried about being a bit chilly. Most don't even allow for the wearing of a bra, let alone the Bridget Jones knickers I was hoping to use to suck in my bumpy bits. If you're in any way self-conscious about bingo wings, you've clearly had it.

Problem is, once you've got the idea of Elie Saab in your head, nothing you can pick up in the Monsoon sale is ever going to cut it. I eventually hit on a long, glamourous gown in shimmering teal, with a sweetheart neck.

'A jaw-dropping dress that captures the light and movement of the fabric – ideal for any red carpet!' says the blurb. Neither of these qualities had been among my on-paper priorities, but it is beautiful, there's no denying it. The only issue is that it requires a leap of faith in that you can't try it on before you rent it. But the company provides a 'fit guarantee', so if the item I pick isn't right, it can just be put back into the post and I won't be charged. Which admittedly would leave me squeezing into one of my old outfits. Still, I'm nothing if not an optimist.

When the dress arrives, it's been carefully packaged with a note from its owner. 'Hey babe, thx for hiring! Hope you feel a million dollars in this (word of warning – it's a d*** magnet!!!). Have fun and don't do anything I wouldn't do! LOL!! Love n hugs, Stacey G xx'

I try it on, look in the mirror and . . . honestly, I can't decide *what* I think.

The dress is beautiful, significantly more elegant than Stacey G's message might suggest. But it's also very low cut – both at the front and back – to the extent that, frankly, it's just impractical. How would I cover up my bra?

I turn to look at it from a different angle. Then another. I bite my lip.

No, I couldn't. *Surely* I couldn't . . .

I decide to take a selfie to see if it looks any different on my phone camera than with my actual eyes. I find a position in front of the mirror, as if I'm making a profile on the dating websites I briefly dabbled with after Brendan left, in a futile attempt to make him jealous. I take a photo from a couple of different angles. In the flattering light of my bedroom, the dress looks less revealing than it really is. Instead, I go to my wardrobe and take out a classic, demure black number. It was slightly too big when I first bought it but it fits like a glove now because I've worn it on countless occasions and it never lets me down.

Decision made.

The subject of my outfit comes up that night when Rose and I go for a quick drink at the new bar in the village while Jacob is having his tennis lesson.

'How's your planning for the awards going?' she asks. 'Do you know what you're wearing yet?'

I deliberately hadn't mentioned the event because this is the first year for as long as I can remember when she won't be attending. We've always looked forward to going together; one time, we treated ourselves to a mani-pedi in advance, pretending we were the kind of women who often whiled away half an afternoon on this sort of stuff.

'I hired a dress on Daisy's recommendation but it's going straight back.'

'What's it like?'

'Way too revealing.'

She takes a sip of her drink and narrows her eyes. 'Did you get a pic?'

I click on my phone and hand it over. She looks at it, then up at me.

'Do *not* return that,' Rose says, with a warning tone.

'Really?' I say, stunned.

'Lisa, it's gorgeous!' she gushes. 'You look phenomenal! When did you get abs like that? And your cleavage . . . oh my God. It's to die for.'

'It's just the lighting in my bedroom,' I mumble, a little taken aback. 'Though I *have* been doing this Core Crusher thing . . .'

'*Wear it*,' she says, emphatically. 'Honestly, you must.'

'Hmm . . . no, I've got a long black one I've had for a while. I think that will be better. I always feel comfortable in that.'

There's an ominous silence.

'Can I be honest?' she says. 'That black dress does nothing for you.'

'Are you serious? That dress is sartorial perfection. Carla Bruni has one just like it.'

'Well, I can't speak for her, but it makes you look like you've dedicated your life to religious service and contemplation.'

'Rose!'

'I'm sorry!' she leaps in. 'Look, everything else in your wardrobe is fabulous. Seriously, I'd love a dress sense like yours. But that particular one . . . it's not terrible by any means. But you're 47 not 87. You're still sexy and vibrant. I just *cannot* allow you to send that gorgeous thing back.'

I sigh and look at it again on the phone. 'Is this meant to be some sort of tough love?'

'Exactly!'

'But it's so low my bra would show.'

'You can get bras in all kinds of weird and wonderful shapes these days,' she argues. 'Or even just some of those stick-on nipple covers.'

'Shhhh!' I hiss, laughing, but mainly concerned that the people on the next table can hear.

It's only later, after dinner, homework and a text exchange with Jeff about a play date for the kids at the weekend, that I click on my phone. I'm multitasking as usual – simultaneously loading laundry into the washer, as I idly google:

Where can I buy good quality stick-on nipple covers?

I realise my error the moment I hit 'return' – but by then it's too late. A message arrives from Jeff almost immediately.

I don't know, love – but make sure I'm the first to know when you find out xx

Chapter 29

The following week, after an averagely exasperating morning, I arrive at the station on the day of the awards, buy a coffee and do a good impression of someone who has her shit together. I am booked onto a later train than the rest of the team, unable to join them due to my school drop-offs. Technically, I could have asked Mum to step in – and see for herself exactly how 'lovely' Leo is at eight in the morning – but they're already staying over with my parents tonight so I wasn't going to push my luck.

Ever since he overheard me telling my mother that he didn't have what it takes to be a professional rugby player, he's gone out of his way to be a nightmare. Which he really didn't need to do because I feel guilty enough as it is. So much so that I phoned his rugby coach to dig into this, to make sure I wasn't missing something and hadn't been raising the next star England fly-half, entirely oblivious.

He actually laughed. 'He's a lovely lad and dead keen, but I think it's a question of: don't give up your day job.'

Clearly, I'm not going to break this to him. I've got other priorities after another detention this week. I sometimes feel as if he's ruining his own future just to spite me, though I can't be the only one facing this judging by the fact that, when I googled, 'Why does my teen hate me?' there was NO shortage of articles on this subject.

Anyway, travelling on this train at least means I can get some work done, instead of making small talk with Andrea, Krishna, various execs from post-production and . . . Zach. Yes, he's coming. I thought he might be somehow, though confirmation only came when Andrea's secretary included him on a group email about the hotel she'd booked for the team tonight.

I shuffle along the aisle to find my seat at a coveted reserved table. This is always my favoured position except for one memorable occasion when I was encircled by a stag party on a trip to Newcastle. They were very polite, if a bit noisy, inviting me to join their poker game and even offering me a couple of Jägerbombs. Given it was 9.47am, I declined, adding that I generally stick to gin and tonic for breakfast.

I open my laptop, put on my noise-cancelling headphones and dive straight into my emails, the first of which is from Jacob's school, with the subject, 'A gentle reminder for Year 6 parents.'

I open it up with a sense of impending doom.

Dear Parent, this GENTLE REMINDER is for those of you who have not yet sent in the required resources for tomorrow's art project, when the class will be recreating a scale model of Gaudi's Park Guell for Spain Day. This is a key date in the school calendar – introduced after our twinning with the *Escola Sant Adria de Besos* on the outskirts of Barcelona – and we would be grateful for your cooperation. PLEASE ENSURE YOUR CHILD ARRIVES IN SCHOOL TOMORROW WITH ALL OF THE FOLLOWING ITEMS:
- A toilet roll
- Six rubber bands (any colour)
- A newspaper (offensive or age-inappropriate pages removed please)
- A large cardboard tube, of approx. 7cm in diameter, used to package potato-based, stackable sharing snacks (i.e. Pringles)

- An empty cereal box (not Crunchy Nut Cornflakes or other nut-based brand please)
- An empty washing-up bottle

'Shit,' I mutter, wondering how I'm going to break it to my mother that – as well as collecting, feeding AND giving a bed to both of my children tonight – I need her to gather that lot together too.

I open my to-do list and add: 'Grovel to Mum about Gaudi' before moving onto my next few emails. I deal with them far more deftly than I would in the office, which is just one of the reasons why I love train travel. I get so much done. I think it's the peace, the anonymity, the—

'Hello, Darling.'

I look up as my heart slams into my chest.

Zach reaches up to place a bag on the overhead shelf, revealing the soft underside of his biceps. I realise my mouth has parted and am about to say something – mainly as a reminder to close it – when he beats me to it.

'This is Mila.'

A little girl wearing bright red dungarees and a rainbow cardigan climbs into the window seat opposite me, just as the train begins pulling out of the station. Even accounting for the fact that four-year-olds are cute by definition, she is beautiful. Zach's daughter has inherited those expansive eyes, the wide smile and that little dimple. She has thick, dark hair – with a kink precisely where a bobble once was.

'Hello there,' I smile, gently.

'Hi,' she says shyly, looking up from beneath long eyelashes. 'Are you doing some work?'

I look at my laptop as Zach sits down next to her. 'Well, I *was*, yes.'

'Me too,' she says. Then she takes a pack of crayons and a pad from her rucksack and sets about colouring in.

'We should do some introductions,' Zach says. 'Mila, this is my friend from work. She's called Lisa.'

Her crayon stops and she looks up. 'Like in the Simpsons.'

'That's right,' I laugh.

Her eager little face prompts a wave of nostalgia for the time when my own kids were that adorable, all squidgy cheeks and bubbly giggles. While there's a part of my brain that does remember the odd tantrum, picky eating and – in Leo's case – a frequent desire to try to give me the slip in supermarkets, I refuse to think of those years in anything other than a blissful, rosy haze.

'Mila's with us until we get to Stafford,' Zach says. 'Her aunt lives in the Midlands. She's been desperate to go and stay with her cousins overnight, haven't you?'

'They have a ping pong table,' she explains.

'Well then, I don't blame you for wanting to go.'

'Do you play ping pong?' She sounds like one of those impossibly cute American children they cast in the movies at a young age, promptly ruining their lives.

'Both of my boys love it, especially my eldest, Leo. Every time we go on holiday . . . vacation . . . I have to choose somewhere with a table so he can play all day long.'

'I'd be friends with him then,' she decides and, while my first response is to laugh, I quickly remember that, no matter how vile Leo can be towards me, he's never anything other than sweet to his little cousins.

'I think you probably would,' I decide, as she goes back to her picture.

'So have you been to these awards before?' Zach asks.

'A few times,' I say. 'Don't expect the Oscars, but it's fun enough.'

I'd fully intended to use this journey to finish off a presentation, catch up on emails and work out exactly where I can advise my mother to get hold of six elastic bands (any colour).

In the event, I'm distracted. Because every time I try to focus on my laptop, my eyes are drawn to Zach as he helps Mila colour in a little pony and play repeated games of noughts and crosses. I find myself sneaking glances at his forearms, the direction of hair that feathers upwards into the sleeves of his shirt, and watching the trembles of his face as he laughs and kisses her on the temple.

This is the first time I've properly spoken to him since our kiss, unable this time to dive away and hide behind a potted plant. While in my head this forced proximity should – and indeed could – have been excruciating, in fact, it's something else. As uncomfortable as this is, it's also mildly electrifying, a sensation enhanced when I accidentally brush my calf against his and both of us jolt into eye contact, at which point a smile seems to soften at his mouth before I glance away.

'Will you play "I Spy" with us, Lisa?' Mila suggests, when we're not far from Stafford.

'Oh no, sweetie, Lisa's working,' Zach says.

'No, it's fine, I don't mind,' I say, deciding it's easier not to explain that I've barely managed to get a thing done since they got on.

'I spy with my little eye,' she begins, 'something beginning with E.'

'Hmm. Let me think,' I say before Zach and I suggest envelope, then ears, then *everyone*.

'Noo!' she giggles. 'It's . . . an elephant!'

Zach looks around. 'Where's the elephant? You're meant to be able to see it!'

The smile is wiped off her face. 'Oh.'

'Well, *I* saw an elephant earlier when I went to buy a cup of tea,' I say, defiantly.

Zach smirks. 'Oh you did, huh?'

'Yes,' I say, crossing my arms, 'so Mila wins.'

Her face lights up, before she looks out of the window and starts waving frantically. 'Daddy! It's Ollie and Violet!'

Mila's drop-off – safely into the hands of her aunt and two little cousins – is a rapid-fire affair. Zach helps her off the train, gives her a huge kiss and a squeeze, then jumps back on and takes his seat opposite me, his eyes following her on the platform. He's clearly desperate for her to wave, but she's already holding the other children's hands and hasn't given him a backward glance. The train pulls away.

'Huh. And here was I worrying that this was going to be painful because she'd miss me so much.'

I turn to look behind me out of the window, in time to see her running towards the exit, laughing along with the others.

'She looks like she's coping.'

'Yeah,' he smiles, looking back at me as his eyes soften.

'She's gorgeous, Zach,' I say.

Pride seems to filter into his every pore. 'I think so too,' he confesses.

Chapter 30

By the time I hit the red carpet, I've warmed to the dress. Admittedly, the small glass of champagne I had with Andrea before we left our hotel may have something to do with that. But I'm also partly reassured by the support of a 'plunging backless multiway bra' which I ordered using next-day delivery, having firmly decided against the stick-on nipple covers. It's a bit like a belt with boobs and can be used in a variety of permutations – halter neck, cross back, low back. All options involve contorting into some very complicated positions simply to put it on. Imagine playing Twister with your underwear and you've got the idea.

Tonight's venue is one of those grand Park Lane hotels, all chandeliers and martini glasses, the sort of place that's been here for centuries, welcoming film stars and presidents. We arrive amidst a frenzy of flashbulbs, security guards and autograph hunters, the air filled with a collective waft of expensive perfume. Everywhere you look there is a gleaming, immaculately groomed woman, often with someone equally glamorous on her arm.

As Andrea and I head through security, I feel a tap on my shoulder and turn to see Jamila Abbew, a dynamic young producer from east London who I've been working with for the last two years. She looks stunning in an aqua tulle gown that compliments her dark skin – and so excited she can barely contain herself.

'This is absolutely *bonkers*, Lisa,' she grins.

'Make sure you enjoy every minute of it. I bet you never imagined all this on that first day you stepped into our office with your big idea, did you?'

'Are you joking? I've been imagining *this* ever since I was about five years old.'

Jamila and her colleagues are nominated for Best Entertainment Production Team, an astonishing feat given how hard I had to fight to even commission their programme. But I always loved the concept of *The Greatest Show*: 12 ordinary people, each paired with a professional circus performer, to learn and be judged on a new skill per week. They tackle everything from juggling to trapeze artistry and the result is one of the most awe-inspiring, visually stunning yet simultaneously nostalgic forms of family entertainment there is.

Before the show aired, sceptics – and there were more than a few inside MotionMax+ – were worried that it would fall flat, that the skills (and therefore insurance premiums) would be too much for an Average Joe. I knew all this was a possibility but instantly recognised Jamila as a woman with an eye for detail. She was capable, passionate, energetic – and she'd thought of *everything*.

It was initially a slow burn when it finally streamed, but by the fourth week of broadcast, it had become a water-cooler hit. Audiences liked that contestants were chosen from all walks of life and had all manner of backgrounds – the woman who won had given up gymnastics when she was thirteen and had been working in a chemist's shop for the last twenty years.

We head inside amidst a melee of air-kissing and shrieks of delighted recognition, before we are invited to take our seats. I am walking into the dining room, part of a crowd of black ties and ballgowns, when I feel the warm pressure of a hand on my lower back.

I can smell him before I see him.

When I look up and make eye contact with Zach, my entire body seems to react, with a melting warmth that reaches the dip behind my ears.

He leans in to whisper to me. 'You look the part.'

I raise an eyebrow as we drift forwards. '*The part?*'

He replies with a 'hmm,' more murmur than word, before we are swept apart again.

MotionMax+ has taken two tables and Andrea – fragrant in flowing cerise chiffon – is seated between Zach and Krishna, opposite me. She is in her element at this kind of event and likes to, in her words, 'work the room'. This networking is all for professional reasons, of course, though she does seem mysteriously drawn to handsome, recently retired television doctors and Nigel Farage-lookalikes and once put on an unedifying display at a broadcasting dinner when she was seated next to the Culture Secretary.

She certainly enjoys sitting between Zach and Krishna, judging by the way she keeps playfully slapping the latter's arm and saying, 'Ooh you are terrible,' even though he looks completely bewildered as to what he's supposed to have said.

The awards are handed out after the meal, with a glamorous actor called Joanna Collins as host. A former model and a household name in the 1970s, she disappeared from the spotlight entirely until she was recently cast in the lead role in a gritty – and highly successful – cop show.

There are one or two surprises: Best Cinematography for a drama that many critics snootily said looked as if it was filmed on an iPhone, and Best Make Up & Hair Design for a woman that both Andrea and I had been convinced had retired to Goa to run a yoga retreat.

Before we know it, it's our category. I can feel tension radiating from Jamila next to me and when I glance at her, there are pricks of sweat on her brow. Instinctively, I slide my hand onto hers on the table and give it a fortifying squeeze, which she reciprocates automatically.

'Ladies and gentlemen, now we come to a much-anticipated part of the show,' says Joanna Collins '. . . for Best Entertainment Production Team.'

They're up against some of the big guns – *The Apprentice, The Masked Singer, Cake Ninjas* – so are very much the outsider. But still, I have a good feeling. Everyone loves an underdog, after all.

The nominees are read out one by one, each followed by a five-second trailer. I am vaguely aware of Andrea opposite, crossing both fingers demonstratively as Krishna gives a statesmanlike nod of support. Zach, meanwhile . . . well, I can barely look at Zach, even if I *know* his gaze is fixed on me.

'And the winner is . . .'

The eternal silence is filled by a drum roll tumbling through my head.

'*Cake Ninjas!*'

I feel Jamila deflate before I even get a chance to look at her and see the tremble she's fighting on her lip.

She dips her head to mine. 'I don't think I've mastered the "brave loser" face yet,' she confesses.

'Good,' I say firmly. 'Because this is the last time you'll ever have to use it. Leave a space on your mantelpiece for next year. Just you wait.' A wave of gratitude brightens her sad face.

'Thanks, Lisa,' she says. It's only when she squeezes my hand that I realise I hadn't let go. 'For *everything*.'

Chapter 31

There's a scramble to the ladies' immediately after the ceremony so I wait a little while, making all the right noises about
Jamila's team's loss – namely that awards are meaningless
(which is obviously not what I'd be saying if she'd won).
When I finally make a break for it, I'm crossing the beautiful
art-deco foyer of the hotel, when I lock eyes with a familiar
face.

Martin O'Donoghue, the producer of *Our Girl in Milan*, is
one of those men who looks uncomfortable in a tux, though
maybe it's just the bow tie, which makes his wide neck almost
disappear. There's a strange moment, a bit like seeing someone in a supermarket you don't really want to chat to, when
we both consider pretending we haven't seen the other.

I'm not sure which one of us decides to be grown up
first, but we wave simultaneously and head semi-reluctantly
towards each other.

'Good to see you, Martin.'

'And you, Lisa.'

He's a decent man and a good producer. But my unease
isn't merely because the last time I spoke to him it was to
say we weren't going ahead with his show. It's because the
project that's now dominating my time in its place – *My
Teenage Bombsite* – is not exactly running smoothly. At least
it hasn't been this week. There have been several disagree-
ments between the two production companies, first over the
wording of the 'treatment' – the two-page summary of the

concept – then over whether the title should be adjusted to *My Teenager's Bombsite*, *My Teen Bombsite*, or something else that has no reference to bombsites at all in case it is misconstrued as a programme about terrorism.

'Listen I'm sorry about, you know . . . not being able to proceed,' I say, feeling like it's better to mention the elephant in the room straight away.

'Hey, it's fine,' he reassures me. 'We all know what this business is like. We're over it.'

I nod, gratefully. 'And are YouTime treating you well?'

'Very,' he says. 'I'll admit I was unhappy after that last phone call we had. We were so close to the wire. But now . . . well, we're philosophical. Who knows – maybe one day you and I can make *something* work.'

We chat for a little while, before I excuse myself and finally make it to the bathroom, where I take the opportunity while still in the cubicle to perform a task that's become increasingly imperative as the night has worn on. My multiway bra started out as taut as a parachute harness, but over the course of the evening, the straps have loosened. As a result, the scaffolding that originally kept my breasts in the optimum position has now allowed them to droop by a good three inches, offering absolutely nothing in the way of support.

I tighten them up and look in my clutch bag for some hair pins to fix each side in place, but it seems I haven't brought any. After experimenting with a variety of fruitless solutions, I decide to whip down the top of my dress, wrestle off the bra and secure both sides with a small knot. I'm in a state of slight dishevelment by the time I've redressed, but at least those four years as a Girl Guide didn't go to waste.

I'm about to step outside when a text arrives from Mum who, despite it being 10.30pm, is clearly still awake.

Do you know anything about a washing-up bottle and some loo roll for Jacob?

'Oh . . . fucking Gaudi,' I mutter, though my beef has nothing to with the Catalan Modernists.

I dart out to wash my hands, then quickly exit the bathroom in search of somewhere quiet to call her. I cross a busy landing, saying, 'Hi!' enroute to various industry people – one of whom I realise immediately afterwards was a bloke in *Line of Duty* who I've never met in my life.

I eventually find my way onto a large balcony that overlooks the whole of Hyde Park and the sparkle of London beyond. It seems to be occupied by a handful of smokers and one couple – or maybe *not* a couple – getting amorous in the corner.

I lean on the thick stone wall and press call. She answers after a few rings.

'I was heading to bed.'

'Sorry – I was just responding to your text,' I explain.

'Oh, that,' she says, through a yawn. 'Yes, Jacob seemed to think he'd be in enormous trouble if he doesn't take this long list of things in tomorrow. I told him it definitely *won't* be tomorrow because you'd have organised it otherwise.'

I wince.

'Lisa?' she says, after a moment.

'Well, the thing is . . .'

'Please do NOT tell me I've got to find six rubber bands and an empty box of Pringles before 8am tomorrow? I was about to snuggle up with Richard Osman!'

'No, you don't,' I say firmly. 'Of *course* you don't. This is my fault, so leave it with me. I'll phone the school in the morning to explain.'

'But Jacob seemed very worried—'

'Honestly, Mum. Don't give it a second thought. I'll sort it.'

We have a brief conversation about how Leo spent the evening watching *Fawlty Towers* with Dad, despite the fact that the last television programme he willingly watched with me was *Teletubbies*. Jacob meanwhile has had a fun evening of jigsaws and fairy cake baking, before his homework was done on time without her even having to ask.

I end the call unable to decide whether my overriding feeling is gratitude or an acute sense of my own inadequacy.

'Got a light?'

I look up to see a young guy in his early thirties draped languorously on the balcony. He's strikingly handsome in a foppish, Cambridge Footlights kind of way, tall and tanned with a floppy, dark blond fringe. He's undoubtedly 'talent', an actor I suspect, though I can't recall seeing him in anything.

'I'm afraid I don't,' I reply.

'Ah . . . never mind,' he sighs, leaning back on the wall with both elbows and sliding me an odd sideways smile. 'I should probably vape instead anyway, but it just isn't as . . . *romantic*, is it? You'd never have caught Don Draper with an e-cigarette.'

'From what I hear, vaping is not especially good for you either,' I reply, with matronly disapproval, as my thoughts immediately turn to Leo.

'True,' he says, with a long drawl that suggests he is very, *very* drunk.

I'm about to leave, when he adds: 'Are you an actress?'

I laugh. 'Me? No.'

He pushes away from the wall and starts sauntering towards me in slow motion, his eyes fixed as if he's looking down the lens of a camera for an aftershave advert. It's partly the way he sashays that makes me realise what's odd about the expression on his face. It's . . . God what's the word? *Seductive*.

I blink in frozen astonishment. When he's right in front of me, he rests his elbow on the stone wall and I half expect the next words out of his mouth to be, 'Martini, shaken not stirred.' But, by now, he's not looking at my face. Only my cleavage. In fact, his mouth is slightly parted, tongue near lolling, pupils widening as if in a state of pure hypnosis. I follow his gaze downward and only then register that I might have gone a *little* overboard with my clove hitches.

As a result of my, admittedly excellent, knotting skills, my breasts are positively mountainous. In fact, they bring to mind the *last* papier mâché scale model Jacob's enthusiastic art teacher organised – of Cheddar Gorge.

'D'you know who you remind me of?' he murmurs.

'Um . . . go on.'

'Gillian Anderson.'

I feel a tug of relief that he didn't say someone who works in Hooters.

He leans in, so close now I can smell the whisky on his breath. 'And by the way . . . I've always had a huuuuuge crush on Gillian Anderson.'

At that point, I jerk backwards in a gesture that sets off an unfortunate chain of events, which happens so fast I can barely take it in.

It begins with a ping in the region of my right bra cup, as one end of the strap catapults out of my décolletage. This is followed by a shriek from my young suitor as he crashes away, clasping his eye, like the stuntman in some terrible, tragic scene in a Western movie.

'ARGH! WHAT THE FUCK?'

He staggers across the balcony, emitting a sound of pure agony, as he clutches his face and I scurry after him, muttering apologies and attempting to get a proper look. But he's too busy shrieking and by now a small crowd has begun to gather.

'This is an emergency!' a guest declares heroically as he reaches for his phone.

'Are you calling an ambulance?' someone asks.

'No, his agent.'

Next, a woman pushes through the door announcing that she's a doctor, though it's not entirely clear whether that means she's a cast member from *Casualty*. It takes several minutes before calm is restored and the victim of my wayward lingerie finally removes his hand to allow her to see the damage. She peers in, using the light from her iPhone to give him a thorough examination. Then she stands up and purses her lips.

'Not even a scratch,' she says, with an air of disappointment that very much does suggest the only medical qualifications she has were picked up at the Central School of Speech and Drama.

He pushes out his bottom lip as if he's just lost his teddy bear. 'Well, it's *really sore*,' he says, but by now it seems the drama's over and I take the opportunity to dart back inside.

Chapter 32

I have never been convinced by the idea that it's best to leave a party early, at least . . . I never am at the time. The morning after is a different matter, when on more than one occasion over the years I've cursed not having been tucked up with my Horlicks at 9pm the previous night. But, while life is generally too short not to suck every minute out of an evening like this, those rules don't apply when you've just assaulted a man who, according to Krishna, has been hailed as 'this generation's Hugh Grant' and is currently tipped for the lead role in the latest Sally Rooney adaptation.

Still, judging by how my victim has subsequently swanned about the room, neither his career nor his retina has suffered much harm. In fact, the only thing close to the definition of a catastrophe is my own dilemma following the incident – to have wonky boobs or go braless.

I closed my eyes and thought of Germaine Greer, before binning the multiway monstrosity in the ladies'. I'd now kill for a bit of support, but there isn't so much as a stick-on nipple cover available. After briefly considering whether I should just sit at the bar with my coat on, I remind myself that it's late anyway, I've done my duty and Jamila et al seem to be 'commiserating' well enough without me. It's time to go. I briefly see Krishna on my way to the cloakroom and, while strategically crossing my arms, I tell him I'll see him at breakfast.

'Did . . . Zach already leave?' I ask, idly. 'I just wanted to check in with him about the new compliance guidelines.'

'Ah,' he says with a knowing look that makes my temples redden. 'Those pesky compliance guidelines, eh? I last saw him by the bar in the next room.'

I wave a dismissive hand. 'Oh, doesn't matter. I'll catch him tomorrow.'

'See you in the morning, Lisa.'

I take a circuitous route to the cloakroom, weaving through the tables and past dwindling partygoers into an adjacent function room, where I spot Zach. He's not alone. The woman leaning flirtatiously into him has the look of a young starlet, with long glossy hair and legs that start at the sky-high hem of her sequinned dress and seem to never end. I divert quickly into a side door, but the sight of her seductive whispering makes something bilious rise in my chest.

Am I . . . *jealous?*

I hurry to the cloakroom, give my ticket to the attendant and pull on my coat, snuggling into its collar as I exit the hotel.

It's one of those cool, early-summer evenings when a pleasant chill bites your skin and you could take or leave a coat. I walk along the pavement, past one grand entrance and then the next, all of them gleaming with polished luggage racks and doormen dressed in tails and top hats. It occurs to me after a couple of minutes that perhaps traipsing the streets of London at this time of night – even in these leafy and luxurious parts – might not be a great idea. Yes, it's well lit, my bed is less than ten minutes away and there are still a few people around . . . but even so.

'Hey, Darling! Wait up.'

I turn around to find Zach running towards me, his tux jacket flapping at his hips. He looks so like some charismatic action hero – Cary Grant in *To Catch a Thief* or Daniel Craig as 007 – that I half expect him to pull out a Glock and perform a stunt roll across the pavement. I try to fight the smile that spreads idiotically across my face, but apparently fail.

'What's so funny?' he asks as his feet slow.

'Oh, nothing.' I shake my head as I turn to start walking again and he falls into step. 'How is it that you're hardly out of breath? How much time do you spend in the gym exactly?'

He shrugs. 'I like working out, I'll admit.'

'Do you go every day?'

'Six am before work each morning. And if not, I go afterwards. Never miss it.'

'Oh Lord . . . you're one of *those* people. I suppose you're going to tell me it sets you up for the day?'

He chuckles. 'I never realised I was so much of a cliché. Does it help that I haven't always been like this? I didn't exactly look after myself in my twenties. By then, my sporty teenage years were replaced by too many burgers, too much booze,' he confesses.

'When did the turnaround happen?'

'Hmm. . . I guess when Sara became pregnant. Then, after the divorce, I didn't want to sink back into bad habits, so hit the gym most nights. Part of it was because I had too much time on my hands. Pumping iron kept me occupied on the days I didn't have Mila.'

As we stroll unhurriedly along the pavement, the conversation turns to the highlights of the evening.

'Hope you're not too disappointed about your loss.'

'As a matter of fact, I'm *gutted*.'

'You use that word a lot.'

'Probably because I'm a very sore loser,' I confess.

He slides his eyes towards me and smirks. 'I could imagine that about you, somehow.'

I shrug. 'I can't deny it. I'm very competitive.'

'It's a good quality.'

'You wouldn't say that if you'd seen me playing Trivial Pursuit. It can get messy.'

He laughs. 'Well, maybe this time next year you'll be celebrating with *My Teenage Bombsite*.'

I wince. 'Hmm.'

'What does that mean?'

'Well, I would love to say that it's running like clockwork . . .'

'Oh no. Don't tell me?'

'Ah, hopefully it'll all come good,' I say, though in all honestly I'm currently not 100 per cent convinced. I look up at him.

'Meanwhile, *Our Girl in Milan* is getting PR left, right and centre.'

'You read the piece in *Broadcast* then?'

He nods. The article was on their website today, detailing how filming has already started. 'Well, that's annoying. But I still don't like that show. I don't like that industry.'

'Is this . . . about your sister?' I ask tentatively.

He narrows his eyes curiously.

'I saw your Instagram,' I explain. 'All the charity fundraising you've done . . .'

'Ah. Well, yeah. I mean, maybe things would've turned out the same for Jenna with or without modelling. But I don't think so somehow.'

'What happened to her . . . it must have been hard, Zach.'

'It was. We were real close. She was my best friend, right to the end. I know some twins struggle with jealousy when they're kids, but we were never like that. I just always felt like I was never completely alone, if that makes sense? We were inseparable. Partners in crime.'

A faint smile appears on lips, then is gone as quickly as it came.

'She went from being in high school one year to walking the runways of Paris the next,' he continues. 'As far as everyone else was concerned she was *living the dream*. But she was existing on an extreme diet to try and maintain her figure. Ultimately, she spent thirteen years in and out of eating disorder units across the state. Almost half her life.'

'That's terrible.'

'It's sure hard not to dwell on what things *could* have been like for her. It's corny but she could light up a room with her smile. And she was so damn *smart*. She studied psychology at Columbia and ended up with a 3.9 GPA.' He glances at me, registering that I don't quite know what that means.

'That's really good, isn't it?'

'The top five or six percent. She'd always been a straight A student. Despite that, she was never even well enough to put the degree to any use and get a job before she died.'

'The whole thing must have been devastating.'

Emotion shimmers in his eyes as he swallows hard. 'It was hard for the whole family. My poor mom. I guess the only positive thing we try to take from it is that it had the potential to tear us apart, but it actually made us stronger. Made us love each other even more.' He inhales deeply. '*Anyway. . .*'

The word suggests that the conversation is going to move on to something else. But, for a few silent seconds, it doesn't go anywhere. We just walk. Then, somehow, a levity returns and we end up chatting about some funny guy he used to work with, then Mila, before he shows me a memory that flashed up on his phone about an hour ago: a photo of her aged two, with ice cream smeared all over her face, looking completely delighted with herself.

Every so often, his sleeve brushes against mine and, even through the layers of fabric, it feels like an electric current through my whole body. I find myself thinking that I don't want to go to bed now. What I really want is for this pavement to turn into one big treadmill so I can keep walking alongside him for hours, watching the movement of his Adam's apple and the sparkle of his eyes every time he laughs.

I get a strange kick out of passers-by catching glimpses of us and concluding . . . actually, I don't know what. That we're old lovers? New friends? Or something else, mysterious and unknowable. Two people with an invisible force field that seems to be drawing us closer together.

We reach the hotel far too soon. The concierge greets us and opens the door. We step inside the foyer. Slowly. But, eventually, there's nowhere else to walk.

'Can I tempt you to a nightcap?' he asks.

I look beyond the foyer into a dark, cosy bar area. It's an intimate space, the kind that evokes old leather, whisky tumblers and Cuban cigars. Aside from a lone bartender discreetly polishing glasses under the amber glow of the ambient lights, there is nobody else there.

I look back at Zach and exhale.

'It's kind of late,' I hear myself say.

He nods slowly, then leans into me and says, in a low voice: 'You looked sensational tonight. Just thought you needed to know.'

'The part?' I reply, with a smile, remembering what he whispered to me on the way in.

'Exactly. A leading lady. Pure Hollywood.' He lowers his eyelashes to take in the full length of my dress and my heart performs a somersault. 'Stunning.'

I'm about to say yes to the drink . . . that, fuck it, I've changed my mind. But he beats me to it—

'Come on. Let's head up.'

We walk to the lift and he presses the button. We stand in silence. When it arrives, he gestures to allow me to step in first, before following suit. We stand side by side. He presses the button. The doors close.

I become acutely aware of the rise and fall of my chest. Something that feels like my heartbeat is thumping at the base of my throat. The luscious smell of him is fogging my brain.

An erotic charge is firing through my skin as I turn to look at him.

He jerks his head to me.

And that's all it takes.

Our lips collide in an involuntary blur. He pulls me in around the waist. I slide my hands on the sides of his face. My need for his mouth is as intense as his for mine and heat floods my body in one breathless, fluid rush.

So much so that, at one point my teeth clash gently against his lip, but it only seems to make him hungrier. The shoulders of my coat are halfway down my arms now and he has me pulled in hard, the soft warmth of my breasts pushing against his body. My nipples pinch. There is a building effervescence between my legs.

I am vaguely aware that we're nearly at our floor, that we need to stop, but my senses are so heightened that I don't know how to. I don't need air, I think. I just need his mouth, his lips, his tongue.

Give me more, more, more.

The doors begin to open.

We pull away. Only our eyes are still connected and he's holding my hand. We are both breathless.

'This way,' he says and leads me in the direction of his room.

Chapter 33

Zach has been put in a suite. The difference between where I'm staying is not merely a matter of square footage, though it is definitely bigger. There's also an overall feeling of luxury that unquestionably surpasses mine.

'How did you end up in such a swanky room?' I say with mock chagrin, running my finger along the dressing table.

'Isn't yours the same?'

'No!'

'Huh. Well, now I feel bad.'

'Oh don't, I'm not bitter. *Much*,' I smile, as I wander into the bathroom. It's gorgeous, with stylish dark-green tiles, softly lit by a handful of subtle uplighters, an art-deco vibe and a long marble unit with double sinks, which runs the whole length of the room.

'Even the toiletries are nicer,' I say, pumping body lotion onto my hands and breathing in a heavenly scent reminiscent of some Tuscan citrus grove. I realise I've put a little too much on, as I glance up and see Zach standing at the door, one shoulder against the frame, an amused look on his face.

'Has anyone ever told you that you are an incredibly sexy woman, Lisa Darling?' he murmurs.

'*All* the time, Russo. All the time.'

He smiles. The dimple appears. My heart swoops as he walks towards me, intent in his eyes.

'I'm all sticky,' I say apologetically, holding up the lotion on my palms.

He stands square in front of me and takes one of my hands in both of his. Then he turns it over and slides his fingers in a firm, upward stroke along my palm until they reach the soft underside of my wrist. He begins to massage the cream into my skin, along the heart line of my palm, over my knuckles, all the time maintaining an exact, judicious pressure that robs me of my ability to breathe. There is something impossibly sensual about the movement, the way his fingers slip between my own, meandering to the dip that separates each one of them. When he is done with one hand, he repeats the same process with the other, all the while undoing me with his eyes.

'Better?'

I can only nod. Anything approaching a comprehensible response eludes me.

We find ourselves facing the mirror, him behind me, slightly to the side, a hand on top of mine as it pushes against the cool marble. He brushes my hair away from my neck with the other as I tilt my head and he draws his fingers gently along the stretch of skin that runs from the dip behind my ear all the way along my breastbone. It skims the nub of bone on the top of my shoulder, before caressing the curve down to my arm, my elbow, my wrists.

The whole time, I'm watching him, entranced by the way we look together. His height and strength, how huge he looks next to me. The shape of my body beneath the silk of the dress, the swollen outline of my breasts, the knowledge that the only thing beneath it is a delicate thong and my warm, bare flesh.

He turns me towards him and I think he's going to kiss me, but instead, he scoops me up by the waist and lifts me onto the marble, making me gasp. The fabric of my skirt gathers at my hips as he runs both hands from my knees, all the way up my thighs, sliding underneath to cup me.

He pulls me towards him and I can feel the strain of his crotch. Our mouths draw together in such sensual fluidity;

the polar opposite of what happened in the lift. There is nothing frantic now. It's dreamy and meandering, an indulgence of the senses, that same woozy feeling when you've had too much sun.

He pulls away briefly to undo the top button of his shirt. I have no idea if his intention was to open just the one, to allow some air to his neck. Either way, I take this as my cue to reach up and, with the red gloss of my nails, I pry open the next one . . . and then another. He closes his eyes and breathes slowly. When his shirt is fully open, he wrestles one sleeve off, then the next, before throwing it on the floor.

At the sight of his torso, a pulse quickens between my legs. These are not just abs; they are a work of art. Each muscle is sculpted around his ribs. There is definition in places I never knew existed. A perfect V shape runs from the side of his hips all the way to the hair feathering into the top of his waistband. I have an acute sense of how much I've missed body hair on men. You can keep your waxed, perma-tanned *Love Island* hopefuls as far as I'm concerned. What a gorgeous turn-on just the right amount of body hair is, a smattering across beautiful pectorals. This is what I want. And although the words sound ridiculous in my head, there's no other way to say it: he is *all man*.

He comes in closer. And then—

The knock at his door makes both of us freeze. Our eyes lock.

'Did you order room service?' I say quietly.

He shakes his head.

'I'm sure they'll go away,' he whispers, but as he kisses me again, there is hesitancy in both of us. It's as if the exact same thought is running through our heads. Is this something to do with the kids? Neither of us have checked our phones recently. Why else would someone be knocking on his door at this time of night?

The knocking happens again.

We both pull away.

'Do you think I should—'

'Yes,' I nod quickly. 'I'm sure it's nothing but . . . probably best.'

Chapter 34

I wait in the bathroom while Zach goes to the door. He initially tries to look through a keyhole but gives up on the idea and instead says, 'Can I help?'

'Oh, you're still awake!' It's Andrea. 'Have you got a minute?'

I involuntarily roll my eyes and only then realise I'd been holding my breath.

'Uh . . . well, I was heading to bed. Is everything all right?'

'I've got your wallet,' she says.

He picks up the jacket he'd discarded earlier and pads it down, confirming that it's missing. 'Oh. Damn. Okay gimme a sec.'

He mouths something to me as I grab his shirt and fling it to him. He pulls it on but leaves it unbuttoned. I close the bathroom door and hover next to it to listen.

'Oh!' exclaims Andrea as she presumably catches a glimpse of his torso.

'Well, this was stupid of me,' he says. 'Thank you.'

'It had dropped out under our table,' she explains.

'Good job you're perceptive.'

'I don't know about that!' she laughs, coquettishly. 'So . . . do you like your room?'

'Oh, yeah. It's very nice. Thank you.'

'They offered an upgrade when we checked in and I thought . . . well, I know how you men enjoy all your bells and whistles.'

My eyes roll involuntarily again.

'Thank you,' he says.

There's a short silence.

'You're *sure* you couldn't be persuaded to come and have a little snifter downstairs?'

'A . . . *what?*'

'Snifter, you know. Another beverage,' she clarifies.

'Oh, thanks, but I have an early train.'

'Well, me too but that never stopped me,' she says, with a seductive growl.

Another silence.

'I'll leave you to it then, shall I?' she says.

'Thanks,' he replies pleasantly. 'I'm very grateful for the wallet.'

'Any time!' she sing-songs and I hear the door click.

The bathroom door opens. He's smiling. I'm smiling. We both collapse into a fit of stifled giggles, before I hold my finger over my mouth and attempt to say, 'Shhh!'

He presses his lips together, desperately trying to stop himself laughing.

'Fucking hell, do you think Andrea was trying to seduce you?'

He shrugs. 'I have no idea. Though . . . that lingerie she was wearing just now *was* very revealing . . .'

My jaw drops.

'Kidding,' he says, as I swipe his arm.

Then we stop laughing and I slide my arms around his waist. 'Where were we?' I murmur.

When we kiss, I'm straight back in the moment, a liquid warmth spreading through my core. I can feel the heat rising from his skin, the pounding of his heart, and it's clear that he still wants me as much as I want him. Yet it only takes a few moments before the faintest sense of unease begins to creep under my skin. I can't pinpoint exactly what causes it. A shift in his breathing. A hesitation in the movement of his lips. The way he reaches for my hand and squeezes it hard, as if he's fighting some internal monologue . . .

I tell myself that I'm imagining it and focus on the feel of that mouth on mine, the way my body responds to his touch, like nothing could tear me away except . . .

He is suddenly still. He pulls gently away. I swallow and look at him, as he closes his eyes and exhales. When he opens them again, he draws his gaze over my face. Only this time, it's not just full of longing. It's as if he's hoping I might hold the answer to a half a dozen questions searing through his head.

'What's wrong?' I whisper. 'Did Andrea ruin the mood?'

I'm joking, but it's clear that our colleague's interruption broke some kind of spell. Or perhaps gave him time to start overthinking this . . .

His eyelashes lower. There's a tightness in his features now. He takes a deep breath. 'Come in here,' he says.

He takes me by the hand and leads me into the bedroom, but I already instinctively know we're not here for more pleasures of the flesh. I sit on the bed as he leans on the edge of the dresser, directly in front of me, his shirt still open.

It takes an age before he eventually says, 'This is suddenly feeling a little . . . complicated.'

My heart seems to stop as half a dozen awful scenarios skip through my head. Is he still married? Still involved with Sara? Or someone else?

'That email you wrote me. The one about your reputation and how much that matters.'

I raise my eyebrows in surprise. Surely he knows that my reputation is the last thing on my mind right now. All I care about at this moment in time is the very real compulsion I have to slide my hand into his flies, to bewitch him into grow-ing hard again.

'Zach, I . . . that was then, this is . . . things are . . . I just . . .'

I don't even know what I'm saying. It's nothing more than a series of incoherent protestations. When I finally stop, he closes his eyes briefly and tells me what's on his mind.

'I'm going back to the States,' he says.

The words are like a punch in my gut. 'What . . . when?'

'June 14.'

Three weeks away.

'I only took this position to be with Mila while she was in the UK. She starts school in September, so the plan was that Sara would go back with her at the end of August – and so would I. Only, my departure has been brought forward.'

'Is this about the kickback you mentioned from your senior team?'

'Actually, no. I've been promoted. You're looking at MotionMax+'s soon-to-be-announced Global Head of Partnerships. Susan wants me back, like, yesterday, but we've agreed June 14.'

Our CEO always did have a reputation as being uncompromising.

I swallow. 'So, you're going to be a board member? God, that's amazing Zach. Congratulations.'

'I didn't even apply for the job, but thanks.' He looks at the floor. 'The reason I'm telling you is that I know in my gut that you and me . . . getting entangled is going to make things difficult. For both of us.'

I nod silently. 'Yeah. I mean you're really senior now and—'

'Not because of that,' he scoffs, in disbelief. 'I don't care about *that*. I just didn't want to sleep with you and then tell you in the morning that . . . this *thing* between you and me. It can't go anywhere, Lisa. We're going to be in different continents. We couldn't ever be a couple. Or have a relationship. And . . . I may be wrong but, even before that email, you never struck me as someone who made a habit out of having some mindless fling. Which is all this could ever be.'

'Right.' I cross my legs. Then my arms. If I crossed any more of me I'd be knotted from head to toe.

'I'm sorry,' he says.

'You don't need to be. You've been honest. And . . . I knew about Mila being the reason you'd come here. I suppose I didn't follow that through and put much thought into where she was going to live long-term.'

I finally look up at him. At the tension in his jaw. The regret in his eyes.

'If it means anything, Lisa, I wish things could have been different.'

'Yeah,' I say, forcing a smile. 'Me too.'

Chapter 35

It's not quite afternoon tea at the Ritz, but it's clear that the medical team looking after Rose's IV infusions do everything they can to make the experience, if not enjoyable, then certainly not unpleasant.

'Do you want a splash more milk in that tea, my love?' asks one of the staff as she hands me a cup and saucer.

'No, that's perfect, thank you.'

'And help yourself to biscuits, won't you? They're not just for the patients,' she adds, before disappearing with the plate.

'I feel a bit guilty eating these,' I tell Rose. 'NHS resources and all that.'

'I don't think one chocolate Hobnob is going to make much of a dent into a multi-billion-pound budget, somehow,' she says.

I glance at the IV in her arm. 'How long will that be in for?'

'Forty minutes,' she says. 'You really didn't need to come, you know. I'm getting used to this now.'

'Don't be silly. Besides, you've had to put up with listening to my woes about Leo. You probably won't invite me again.'

'Oh, it's fine. I still don't believe *any* of this about my gorgeous godson,' she smirks. 'It's clearly all *your* fault.'

I snort. 'Thanks.'

'If it means anything, he really is never anything other than lovely when I see him. Nora says the same. A model student.'

'Oh, I know. I hear this all the time. He saves all his vitriol for me.'

She chuckles, then frowns sympathetically. 'Oh, you poor thing. So, come on. Give me all the gossip from the awards. And don't leave anything out.'

She already knows the headlines – about Jamila and the team missing out on their prize – but I fill her in on the stuff she really wants to know about: what everyone was wearing, seeing Martin O'Donoghue, my 'experience' with the young actor, and the fact that while, overall, she was right about the dress, she was very, very wrong about the bra.

'Did the handsome Zach go?' she asks.

I take a sip of tea and study the saucer as I place it back down. 'Yeah, he was there,' I say casually.

'Jeff is adamant that he's got the hots for you, you know.'

I tut. 'Jeff also predicted that Denise Dandy was going to embark on a wild love affair with one of the school governors just because he complimented her handwriting during a safe-guarding meeting once.'

'Well, he seemed pretty determined about it. His exact words were, "He seemed completely besotted".'

I scoff and pull an odd expression, as if I can't decide whether to shake my head or roll my eyes.

She's looking at me now, through narrowed eyes. 'What aren't you telling me?'

I realise immediately that there is absolutely zero point in keeping up any further pretence.

'Oh, where do I start,' I sigh, but as it turns out, the entire story comes out in one jumbled stream of consciousness. I tell her about how I couldn't stand Zach when we first met, partly because I was worried he was trying to win Rose's job for himself.

Then I tell her that I began to realise he wasn't the arsehole I'd initially thought and, besides, he swore blind he was not going to stay in the position. I explain that, as well as being more talented than I'd given him credit for, he is also nice, funny and . . . weirdest of all, he's ignited some long-dead part of me and caused all kinds of confusing and, yes okay, *sexy* feelings that are very nice but frankly can't be normal at my age. And that, as a result, I ended up in his bedroom, ready to spend the night swinging from the chandeliers – which yes, he did have in his room – until we were interrupted by Andrea.

'Did she want to join in?' she asks, raising a mischievous eyebrow.

'Oh God, *don't*,' I snort. 'I was hiding in the bathroom at the time. And either way – just as I was hoping to resume matters – he got cold feet. Told me he was going back to the US. That everything was far more complicated than it had initially seemed. So, the upshot is . . . you really do have nothing to worry about in terms of your job.'

'Wow,' she says. 'So what did you do?'

'I skulked back to my room and read three chapters of my Phillipa Perry book.' I don't add that I was in such a state of frenzied, unchannelled lust by then that even that didn't cool me down.

'Lisa, why haven't you told me any of this?' she says, with a disbelieving tone.

'Because at first you were so worried about the job I felt treacherous for not despising him. After that . . . well, you know my views on getting together with someone else. What I said after Brendan still holds. My judgement with regards to men is abysmal. I didn't even want to go there again.'

'Is it out of the question that you could just sleep with Zach, enjoy the next three weeks and leave it at that? Are you worried about what people will think at work?'

'Of *course* I'm worried about that.'

'But it's nobody's business.'

'We both know that's just not true,' I say. 'Besides, I just can't do no-strings sex. My brain doesn't work like that.

As soon I get physical with someone, my imagination starts leaping forward to something deeper and more significant.'

'I think a lot of women do that,' she sighs. 'Certainly of our generation.'

'Yeah, well look where that got me.'

She's silent for a moment as we both look across the room and watch as a nurse unhooks a woman from her IV and tells her she's free to go.

'Okay, I get it,' she shrugs.

'Do you?'

She nods. 'But for the record, you shouldn't give a toss about what people at work think.'

'Really?'

'Yes. Fuck 'em. People might gossip but you're too good at your job for it to matter. My only concern really *isn't* about your reputation, Lisa.' She glances over and looks at me, flattening her smile. 'It's about your heart.'

Chapter 36

The look on Daisy's face has the same combination of pride, expectation and hope as a child when they're about to show you a picture they've just coloured in. It can only mean one thing. She thinks she's onto a winner.

'This show pushes *so* many buttons in terms of what audiences want these days,' she explains excitedly. 'Number one. Pets. I mean, who doesn't love an animal show?'

'Absolutely,' I agree.

'Number two. The environment. This concept speaks to anyone concerned about climate change, specifically recycling.'

'Sounds promising . . .'

'And three . . . it's original. Completely and utterly original.'

'Go on . . .'

'It's called, *Love . . . and Stuff.*'

'Intriguing title.' I feel a frisson of hope that she could finally be onto something.

'And it's a taxidermy competition!' she declares.

A piece of my sandwich gets lodged at the back of my mouth and I start to splutter. 'Sorry . . . carry on,' I say, tapping my chest. 'Just a piece of cress.'

'The idea is that each week you have three recently bereaved contestants,' she continues, excitedly. 'They've all lost a beloved pet, whether a budgie, a cat or a chinchilla. Each of them has to demonstrate excellence in the art, starting with the removal of skin from carcass, through to the moulding of a perfectly formed mannequin and ending with the final, mounted creation.'

I look down at my egg and cress sandwich, which has become oddly unappetising.

'Contestants are judged not merely on their creative skills but also their ability to create a touching and unique tribute for their wall or mantelpiece.'

'So the "recycling" element of it comes in because they're recycling . . . what, their dog?'

'Exactly! Well, *repurposing*, really. Look, the studio has provided some examples . . .'

She flips around her computer and I'm confronted with an image of what I think was once a cat. While it is unclear what the exact cause of this poor creature's demise was, I could only guess that it involved a few billion volts and an excursion around an electrical pylon. It has moth-eaten fur, demonic button eyes and a tail that has been coiled into what I presume is supposed to be an artistic flourish. Unfortunately, it gives it the look of one of those creepy Victorian effigies – in this case, half feline, half pig – in which two animals were sewn together and passed off by unscrupulous explorers as a newly discovered species.

'Be honest. What do you think?'

'Anyone fancy a green tea?' pipes up Calvin.

'Great idea; must be my turn,' I say, leaping up. 'We'll have a good chat about it later, Daisy.'

I smile at her encouragingly, but her face falls. She already knows this will not be a goer. That no matter how much encouragement I give her when we have one of our private feedback sessions, or how many times I tell her to keep at it, she will still be wide of the mark. Sometimes it's only slightly. More often, it's the width of the Suez Canal.

I head across the office with three empty mugs in my hand. I don't make as many beverages as the others – largely because I have three times the workload – but like to show willing every so often, especially if it buys me a convenient bit of time. I turn the corner to the kitchen area at the exact moment when someone closes the fridge.

That someone turns out to be Zach. He's wearing a pale blue shirt, open at the collar, rolled up to the elbows and tucked into sand-coloured trousers. He looks as if he's wandered in from a photo shoot on the Italian Riviera and I am assaulted by yet another vivid flashback of the muscles that are hiding right underneath that cotton fabric.

'What are you doing here? I'm sure this isn't your fridge,' I say, as lightly as possible.

'We're all out of milk on the fifth floor, so I'm afraid I borrowed some.'

I tut and shake my head. 'You know they chop people's hands off around here for stealing milk? It's a cardinal sin.'

'I can imagine. Don't tell anyone, will you?'

'Consider it between us,' I say, as we simultaneously seem to realise the double implication of the sentence.

He clears his throat and moves closer towards me.

'How you doing, Darling?' he says quietly.

I turn away to flick the kettle on. 'I'm fine. You?'

'I'm okay.' He shrugs. 'A little . . . *weirded out*, if the truth be told.'

I nod, keeping my eyes on the teabags. 'Yep,' I say.

'Part of me wishes I'd kept my mouth shut . . .'

'But then I might have been pissed off with you the following morning . . .'

'Yep . . .'

'Still. Part of me wishes you'd kept your mouth shut too.' I glance up, as he releases a laugh.

Then suddenly, I'm looking into his eyes again and can't turn away. Not merely because of the goosepimples that have swept up my arms. But because I can see almost exactly what is reflected in mine. His hands on my thighs. His lips on my collarbone. The heat of our kisses, like one endless, heart-stopping swoon . . .

'Need a hand with those teas?' asks Calvin, appearing at the edge of the kitchen.

Zach and I look up at him simultaneously.

'That would be great!' I say, before he takes two of the mugs and I quickly follow him back to my desk, without a second glance.

Chapter 37

It was around the middle of a particularly difficult month when I first realised I was in perimenopause and had been for a while. I wasn't just *feeling a bit down*; it was PMS but supercharged, with the kind of migraine that made me never want to get out of bed. Things have improved vastly since I started HRT, but there are still a couple of days of my cycle when I feel as if I'm getting a cold that never materialises, am bone-tired, achy and would rather not have to deal with anything as bothersome as *people*.

These are obviously the ideal conditions in which to find myself at a PTA Bounce-a-thon, having been assigned the dual duties of 'Safeguarding and Socks'.

'How many kids are there again?' Nora asks, as we stand on the edge of the trampolining park, watching children hurl themselves off equipment like wild salmon attempting to swim upstream.

'We started with 71. Whether we'll end up with that many is a different matter,' I say, as two boys collide head-first. Nora and I take a sharp, simultaneous breath, which we hold until it becomes clear that they're not dead, merely dazed. A moment later, they both leap up and sprint to a group of friends. I look at her as we exhale.

'Is it me or do the staff here look far too young to be in a position of responsibility?' she says, gesturing to a guy in a Krazee-Bounce T-shirt, who stifles a yawn before resuming the picking of his acne.

'Most of them are students,' I say. 'They're probably hungover. That's why Denise Dandy insisted we had extra parents in charge of "safeguarding".'

'Well, I don't know why you and I ended up in the job,' she says. 'This has to be the worst task of the night. My nerves are in tatters. I'm a wreck.'

'She found out we'd both been DBS checked,' I tell her.

'Why have you got one?' she asks.

'Oh, I was once involved in a show about kids with an abnormally high IQ.'

'You really should have kept that quiet.'

'I know, but someone had to step in after Santa pulled out of the Christmas fair at the last minute.'

'What happened to him?'

'Twisted testicle.'

'Lucky bastard,' she mutters, as Jeff finally appears balancing three takeaway coffees in a cardboard carrier. 'Here we go! Three delicious cups of grey water that looks like someone's washed their pants in it. Enjoy!'

'As long as it's got caffeine in, I don't care what it tastes like,' says Nora, before she takes a sip and freezes. 'Okay, I've changed my mind. Where *is* Denise anyway?'

'She said a better use of her time was to take the opportunity to try to recruit new parents to the PTA,' Jeff says as he nods over in the direction of a group of unsuspecting mums with whom she's holding court. 'Does anyone else have a sudden urge to shout, "Run for your lives"?'

It's true that, despite her pastel active wear, immaculate blond hair and HD brows, there is something about Denise that reminds me of Arnold Schwarzenegger in that film *Predator*.

Nora gasps as we all turn in time to see a tiny boy performing a somersault with triple pike off the edge of a diving board. Despite it being in clear contravention of at least six rules in the instructional video everyone had to sit through at the start, the closest Krazee-Bounce team member is currently examining her manicure. Jeff, Nora and I meanwhile fail to breathe until the child emerges, apparently unscathed.

'I need a stiff gin,' Jeff says. 'It's bad enough being a helicopter parent to *one* child. How can we be expected to deal with seventy-odd?'

The closing twenty minutes of the event seem to last for approximately five days. They culminate in one particularly trying moment when a Year 4 girl falls off a rolling log and disappears into the gap between inflatables. We give it a few seconds, but when she doesn't emerge, Jeff rises heroically to his feet and instructs us to stand aside. At which point, Nora and I tell him to sit down because he isn't DBS checked.

Instead, she and I spring into action, leaping over the barriers and charging to the scene like Cagney and Lacey in hot pursuit. Unfortunately, even if one of you *is* a tennis coach, there is simply no dignity involved in two middle-aged women boinging from one inflatable to the next, especially when one of them (me) didn't have the foresight to wear a sports bra.

When we finally get there, the closest employee is chatting to his mate about whose turn it is to go and get a Subway, apparently oblivious to the helpless cries and flailing arms and legs rising up from the gulley. By the time Nora and I have created a human chain (well, just the two of us really) and yanked her out, we're both feeling as overheated as we are irritated. Nevertheless, it's me who has a few stern words with the Krazee-Bounce employee, who has a bum-fluff moustache and looks too young to know what a floppy disk is. He looks stunned, a little terrified and mutters something that might be an apology but could also be a comment about what a battleaxe I am.

At the end of the event, Denise waves a triumphant good-bye to dozens of happy, tired, sweaty and, in some cases, bloodstained children, before jumping in her Range Rover Sport, leaving instructions for me to make sure all the damp socks go on a 90-degree boil wash.

Jacob climbs into the passenger seat.

'It stinks in here,' he says.

'I know. I'll open the windows. Did you have a nice time, anyway? Apart from the black eye, I mean?'

'Yes, it was great. I think I'm good at trampolining. I've decided I'm going to join a club.'

Chapter 38

I'm about to start the engine when a new school app notification pings on my phone for Leo. Which is always a source of delight at the moment. The last three have amounted to one detention for failing to submit a piece of coursework, another detention for forgetting about the first one, then a third – for two hours on a Saturday morning – for remembering both but not bothering to go anyway.

Leo's attitude to this is to compare the school to a loan shark. His argument is that, while his initial debt was of little consequence, their now punishing demands are out of all proportion. I take his point but it's not getting him closer to gaining any qualifications and if he doesn't break this cycle and serve his time, at this rate he'll be facing a spell in juvie by the summer break.

I open the notification with weary resignation and discover that it's his school report. An important one by all accounts, because this contains the results of his first mock exams. Gone are the days when a student would have to come home – proud, shamefaced or otherwise – and hand over a paper version of this. Now, there is no opportunity for cunning pupils to doctor their progress with a contraband bottle of Tippex and pass themselves off as a child prodigy. These days, teachers communicate directly, so there's no escape. I click on the link. And the results are . . . *surprising*.

He has top grades in Maths, Geography and Computer Science – subjects he has apparently mastered with his eyes closed. There are a couple of average ones, such as English Literature, which is a feat given I'm not aware that he's actually read a book in the last 12 months. Finally, there are some that I can only describe as, well, abysmal. Contrary to what he thinks, you do actually need to draw the odd picture to be awarded a GCSE in Art. I have a pretty clear overview of what's going on here before I even read the comments by his year tutor.

'Leo is an extremely able and intelligent student, as the grades he achieves in some subjects demonstrate. He is a pleasant and popular boy, but there is an overriding feeling that he will be doing himself a great disservice in the forthcoming exams if he fails to apply even a modicum of effort. Well done on all you've achieved so far, Leo. But I can't underline this enough: it's now time for some serious application.'

I sit back and look at the windscreen, with one question running through my mind.

What would Philippa Perry say?

How do you deal with a boy who clearly might be capable of gaining a PhD one day if only he had the slightest care about any of it? I shake the thought from my head. Give him a break! There's so much to be optimistic about here.

He's got As! That's what these '9' grades are in old money, isn't it? So he must have tried *a bit*. And even if he didn't, how could I be anything other than delighted that he's such a *massive clever clogs?*

I drive home feeling uplifted, which is quite something given my pounding headache and the tangy, ammoniac whiff drifting in from the boot. I rehearse all the words of encouragement I'm going to say when I get home. That I'm so, so proud of him. That I love him. That I'm going to pick him up from school tomorrow and treat the three of us to a trip to Wagamama's. Not to celebrate exactly – we don't want to tempt fate before the real exams – but certainly to underline how proud he should be of himself.

As I turn down our street, I wonder if I should take him shopping at the weekend to buy him some new clothes. I could push the boat out and get one of those ludicrously priced coats he loves, the ones that all the yobs wear while hanging around outside off-licences. I pull into the driveway, let Jacob and myself in, and abandon the sock bag by the front door.

'Leo!' I call up.

There's no immediate response from his room because he's playing an online game with his friends. I know this because I can hear them all yelling the usual terms of encouragement and endearment to each other, such as, '*Why are you doing that, you knobhead?*'

I skip up the stairs.

'Leo!'

I knock on his door and hear him say something, but I'm not sure whether it's 'Coming, Mother, just one moment!' or 'Take cover, you melt!', so I open up.

In the immediate moments before I fully comprehend the scene, I am still beaming like Julie Andrews about to burst into song, full of intentions to be the kind, encouraging parent I always thought I'd be. All I can see is a boy wearing headphones, exchanging a jolly stream of abuse with his mates in an averagely disgusting teenage bedroom, the floor so untidy that finding anything is like one of those *Where's Wally?* games.

The first thing that wipes the smile off my face is the vape pen, hanging out of Leo's mouth and filling the room with a sickly-sweet smell. The next is the bottle beside him, a Sauvignon Blanc that I bought from Waitrose because it was awarded a gold star in the Vintners awards. It's sitting next to his 'Dunder Mifflin' mug, about a third gone.

Finally, I register Leo's eyes. The pure electric panic behind them.

'*GET OUT!*'

He leaps to his feet and squares up to me at the threshold, making me gasp.

'Don't shout at me like that!' I say because, even though the shock nearly knocked the breath out of me, nobody is going to tell me what to do in my own house.

'WHAT IS THE MATTER WITH YOU?' he yells, his face reddening. 'CAN'T I HAVE ANY PRIVACY?'

Disbelief starts knocking in my chest and I feel a rush of blind outrage.

'Do . . . NOT talk to me like that, young man,' I reply, through gritted teeth. 'Who *DO* you think you are? And would you care to explain to me EXACTLY what you think you're doing with a bottle of wine? *Have you lost your mind?*'

This speech does nothing to make him see reason.

'Get. Out,' he snarls, opening the door wide to invite me to go downstairs. 'I'm asking you nicely.'

The slur in his words gives me a sudden surge of clarity. Only one of us has the capacity to de-escalate this situation. And it isn't him.

I need to stay calm.

'Leo. You are fifteen years old,' I say, trying not to sound exasperated. 'It is a Tuesday night. And you are drunk!'

'NO, I'M NOT! DON'T BE RIDICULOUS.'

He's now blocking the view to his gaming desk.

'*You are!*' I splutter, a vein throbbing somewhere in my neck. 'You've got a bottle of wine in there!'

He crosses his arms. 'No I haven't.'

'*I'VE JUST SEEN IT!*'

We continue in this manner for a good five minutes. He lies, he shouts and I call him out, so he shouts some more. He is beyond all reason – and I am beyond getting through to him, so broken and out of ideas that I start shouting too. The result is pyrotechnic.

I feel out of control. I feel irradiated with hormones. I feel *hated*.

And that's before our final, atomic exchange, which goes like this . . .

'Oh, why don't you just . . . FUCK OFF!'

I gasp. Blood rushes to my head.

And I hear myself say: 'No, *YOU* FUCK OFF.'

Even before Leo has slammed the door in my face, I feel a fierce rush of regret. My parenting has hit rock bottom. I've got nowhere else to go.

I turn around, dazed, and trudge down the stairs one by one. When I reach the bottom, I put head in my hands. I want to weep, to let it all out, but my eyes just burn and itch.

'Are you okay, Mum?'

I look up at the sound of Jacob's voice and see the worry on his face. It needles my heart, not least because it doesn't feel so long ago that Leo would have behaved just like that.

How did it come to this?

'I'm fine, sweetie,' I say, forcing a tearful smile. 'I'm really sorry you had to hear that.'

'It's not your fault, Mum.'

This makes me feel so *awful* – on so many levels – I don't even know where to start. As sweet as it is, I don't want my 10-year-old to try and make me feel better. First, because it feels disloyal to Leo, even if he does deserve it. And second, because it's not true. It *is* my fault. Who else's could it be? There's nobody else around here to blame, that's for sure.

Chapter 39

To-do list

- Arrange crisis meeting with Brendan
- Torture self with articles about effects of alcohol abuse on teens
- Ditto vaping
- Install swear box
- Buy bigger notebook for Phillipa Perry exercise: 'write down all self-critical thoughts'
- Reread *We Need To Talk About Kevin* as a reminder it could be worse
- Find PTA member willing to store 71 pairs of socks at home until next year's Bounce-a-thon
- Complete Gaudi-style papier mâché model at home to slot into school project
- Speak to GP about increasing HRT to a point that makes me feel SANE
- Living room panelling
- Fix mortgage rate
- Label Jacob swim cap
- Label black trunks
- Label verruca socks
- Label towel
- Label Johnson's talcum powder
- Buy socks (Leo)
- Descale kettle

Brendan looks troubled as he sits on our sofa. As well he might. In the years since he left, I've kept most of the drama, chaos and mess in this household to myself, preferring to maintain the impression that we're all getting on fine without him. Until recently, I feel as if we have been. But nobody could listen to this tale of woe and believe that we're anything close to fine at the moment.

What makes it worse is how well Brendan looks. Slim and tanned. He's just back from Ibiza with Melanie and, instead of the saggy brown chinos and dusty-looking shirts he wore throughout most of our marriage, he's wearing a T-shirt that says 'Amnesia', has a beaded bracelet at his wrist and leather thongs on his feet. I think he might have had his toes waxed.

'There must be so many hormones floating around this household,' I complain, tearfully. 'Leo's fifteen. Peak teenager. *The pits* of an age, according to most of Mumsnet. And I'm . . . well, I'm perimenopausal, so frankly there are times – and this is one of them – when a person *just can't take any more.*'

His frown deepens. I'm not sure whether this is due to the 'perimenopause' reference – which definitely made him wince – or something else.

'Have you tried to speak to him?' he asks.

'Of course I have. It's like negotiating with a terrorist.'

The look on his face suggests he thinks I'm exaggerating.

'That was a joke,' I add hastily, even though it wasn't. 'I told him to fuck off, Brendan,' I confess, my bottom lip wobbling. 'What sort of mother tells her son to fuck off?'

He exhales deeply, like he's hit on a difficult crossword clue that completely eludes him. 'What happened *exactly* when you tried to speak to him?'

'He just wouldn't engage. He still won't, no matter how hard I try.'

'But *what did you say?*'

'I apologised for swearing at him. I thought that would be a good way in, a sort of olive branch. I'd naively assumed he'd apologise back, that we'd make friends and that would open up a sensible conversation about the drinking so I could suggest we try to tackle the issue together. But when I said, "I'm sorry, Leo," he grunted, "You should be," and went off to play rugby.'

Part of me wants Brendan to say he deserved my F-bomb, that this isn't my fault, just like Jacob did.

Instead, he says, with decisive authority: 'Have you tried sending him to his room?'

I look up, wondering if I've heard him right. 'What?'

'You know . . . to *think* about his actions? That's what my mother always did,' he offers, with the same fist-thumping air of authority he had the year he chaired the Neighbourhood Watch.

'It's not 1962, Brendan,' I point out. 'Unless it's for sport, he never *leaves* his room. No kids do these days.'

'That can't be true.'

'It is. They don't go round to each other's houses to play their new LPs either . . .'

'Then grounding him? Stopping his pocket money? Not allowing him to play rugby? Confiscating his phone?'

'I've tried it all. It's not as easy as you might think.'

This sounds pathetic. I clearly *am* pathetic. 'I outright refused to take him to rugby at the weekend, but then had the coach on the phone complaining that they didn't have a flanker. So I ended up saying he could go, albeit on the bus. The phone's more complicated. *All* his homework is set on that.'

'The homework he doesn't do?'

'Well, quite. But I don't want to hand him any more excuses. I've stopped his pocket money, which he's inordinately pissed off about.'

'Good.'

'But unfortunately, it all amounts to only one thing.'

'What's that?'

'That he's still just as rude, entitled, arrogant and lazy – only now he hates me too.'

'Oh dear,' he says, sympathetically. 'What does this friend of yours think? Philippa, is it?'

'She's not a *friend*,' I sigh, but haven't got the energy to explain.

We sit in silence for a moment, listening as the clock ticks. Then he says the most astonishing thing.

'I blame myself.'

'*Do you?*'

He shrugs and looks down at his hands. 'Maybe if we were still together, things would be different.'

I don't quite know what to make of this statement. On the one hand I should be glad of the recognition that he ought to have put some *work* in to the marriage, like I'd wanted to. On the other, I am oddly irritated by the idea that he thinks if he'd hung around then Leo would've grown into a well-rounded, respectful human being. But then maybe that's true. Who's to say it isn't? Certainly, it's a subject most parents dwell on when they split up – including me.

Back when it happened to us, Jacob was too tiny to really register that it was a big deal. He breezed through it and these days doesn't even remember Brendan living with us. Leo, though older, showed far less distress than I'd been ready for. But maybe, as time has passed, it was all a front and all kinds of long-buried feelings and resentments are only now coming to the fore.

'Oh God, I'm going to have to go,' I say, looking at my watch. 'I've got a vet's appointment.'

'Oh dear. What's wrong with Adrian?' he asks.

'*Alan*. She's got a cold. Apparently hamsters can catch them from humans and a Lemsip just won't cut it.'

'All right,' he says, getting to his feet. 'Well, I'll leave you to it then.'

I nod and we head to the door. He turns to look at me, a peculiar look on his face.

'I'm very sorry you're going through this, Lisa,' he says, softly.

I look up at him and something about the kindness in his expression makes me want to start crying again. I sniff, and nod.

Then something really weird happens. He reaches out and draws me into a hug. I'm taken aback at first, stiff with shock. But after a moment, I feel tension in my spine unfurl. The air trapped in my chest releases. My shoulders slump. My limbs loosen. I close my eyes and allow myself to sink briefly into that once-familiar nostalgic feeling I used to have simply by dint of being in a marriage. Being one half of a couple, having that safety blanket. I haven't thought about this for years, but I am suddenly shrouded by an intense feeling of longing that I still had this. That I was still part of an *us*.

While these thoughts are running through my head, I become conscious of something else too. The tightness with which Brendan is holding me. The way he's breathing in my hair. He feels it too, I know he does. I swallow and slowly pull back, unwrapping myself from his arms before this all gets too strange.

He clears his throat. 'If there's anything I can do again to take some pressure off you, Lisa, just let me know. *Anything* at all. You know where I am.'

I bite my lip and look at my watch.

'Well . . . now you mention it, that vet's appointment is at 4.30,' I say tentatively. 'It would be a *huge* help if you were able to go for me.'

He clears his throat and frowns. 'Oh. Hmm. Tonight's tricky. Spin class.'

He shrugs apologetically and backs out of the door.

'But another time, Lisa. You know you can always count on me.'

Chapter 40

Work is ridiculous over the next few days. Not because of a single particular issue. It's just one of those weeks in which every team meeting, deadline and crisis seem to converge. I see off most of them with the same well-honed juggling skills I employ at home, but it does mean that certain important fringe matters – like mentoring Daisy or supporting Calvin on his first proposal – are a challenge.

I see Zach every so often but resist going out of my way to bump into him. The most I allow myself is to let my mind drift every so often. To that kiss in a rainy alleyway. Our clinch in the bathroom. The sensual warmth of his skin against mine . . .

I tell myself that these short, private moments of inner bliss are a better use of a spare five minutes than anything my meditation app offers. Just a small pleasure all of us surely need, even if these amount to nothing more than scraps of 'free time' while standing in a queue for coffee. But they are, inevitably, just that. Scraps. Mainly, I am pulled in all directions for a full five days and only really decompress on Friday night when Nora and Rose come over for our monthly book club get-together. We spend three minutes discussing *Shadow of the Wind*, then move onto other matters. Namely, Leo.

'Why do you keep banging on about saying the word "fuck" to him, Lisa? He said it first,' argues Rose. I sort of knew she'd say this, which was precisely why I told her. 'You need to get over this.'

'And after pulling the stunt with the wine, he could've been in line for far worse,' Nora adds, supportively.

'I know he said it first, but I'm the parent. I'm supposed to maintain a dignified moral high ground.'

'Look, I'm not a mum, but I do know that this idea that, as his mother, you've got to be this serene, all-knowing, perfect being is bullshit. You're *doing your best*. That is enough.'

'Even if you are a potty mouth,' Nora adds, which makes us all laugh.

As I go to bed that night, a 'memory' pops up on my phone. It's a video of Leo, aged two, all kissable cheeks and sparkly smile. In it, we're in the kitchen in our old house. Brendan is there, working in the background on his computer, not looking up from it. He's got a small but noticeable paunch and is wearing a jumper that makes him look like he's running a post office.

Leo is in his high chair, banging his little hands on the plastic tray as he says, 'MUMMY, MUMMY, MUMMY!'

'What is it, you noisy thing?' I say in that silly, sing-song voice it's impossible not to use with small children.

Then he looks at the camera, his eyes shining, as he declares, 'I lub you, Mummy!'

'That's good because I lub you too,' I laugh.

I click off the phone and close my eyes. The last words I think of before I drift off are: I still feel the same, Leo. No matter what. With every cell in my body, I lub you too.

The following morning, Jacob is at a loose end because he's given up on the basketball and I've refused to even entertain the idea of a trampolining club. So I make a snap decision to go and watch Leo play rugby. I know this is a risk, that he might well shoo us away for cramping his style. But when he spots us, he jogs over during a break in proceedings and ruffles his little brother's hair. 'You come to support me, little mate?' he asks.

'Yeah!' says Jacob.

'Great. I'll score a try just for you,' he says, winking at him.

The rugby union season is over now, so he's been playing league for a few weeks. I can't say I'm entirely au fait with the difference between the two – although I know one has fewer players – but promise myself I'll find out.

In the event, he scores three 'absolute belters' according to the guy next to me, though even if they'd been very average I think Jacob and I would've cheered and clapped just as loudly; my voice is nearly hoarse by the end of the match. It's as I'm watching – and seeing the sheer joy in his eyes as he runs across the pitch – that I start to question everything I've said about the rugby academy. I desperately want him to do well in his exams, to take his future seriously. But his passion for this sport is difficult to argue with.

'You were phenomenal!' I say after the match. Leo shrugs but looks pleased with the comment. I hand over a banana and a drink from my bag. 'Sorry if we embarrassed you.'

'Nah, it's fine,' he shrugs. 'I'm going to get a shower and go out with the rest of them though, okay?'

I nod. 'Of course. Have a great time. Just keep your phone on and make sure you're back for dinner at seven,' I say, even though it's actually at 7.30. I already know he'll roll in at ten past.

As Jacob and I walk back to the car, we pass the swing park I used to take them to when they were small.

'Are you too big for those, these days?' I say.

He looks at me with pursed lips. 'Are you joking, Mum? I'm 10 years old. Of *course* I am.'

'Right. Sorry. I hadn't appreciated you were a man of such sophisticated tastes these days.'

He starts to giggle. 'Course . . . if there was an ice cream on offer, I might be interested . . .'

'I wasn't trying to twist your arm,' I point out, laughing. 'I've got a load of ironing to do at home.'

'I thought you didn't do ironing? You said it was against your human rights.'

This is true. I iron as little as possible, so much so that when Jacob first saw one at my mother's house when he was little, he thought it was some kind of space-age tin-opener.

'A few things have been sitting creased in the utility room for so long that that I am going to have to bite the bullet and just do it.'

'So I'd be doing you a favour by going to get an ice cream at the swings?'

'If you say so. Come on then. As long as I can get one too.'

We enter the park, a pretty urban oasis filled with blossom trees and a large duck pond, and stand in line at the ice cream parlour. It's just as busy as you'd imagine on a sunny Saturday, filled with dog walkers, strolling couples and plenty of small children playing frisbee. Jacob is past all this really, but I think there's still a nostalgic part of both of us that want to have a go.

The queue for ice cream is huge but Jacob's determined, so he stands in line trying to decide which flavour he wants. Bubblegum is a definite, a hideous synthetic taste that he can't get enough of, but he's torn about what else.

'I can recommend the Cookies and Cream.' I recognise the voice as Zach's before I even turn around.

Chapter 41

Zach is here with Mila, who is standing behind him, holding his hand and looking suddenly shy.

'Hello there!' I say, so brightly that my voice sounds strange to my own ears. 'How are you, Mila?'

'I'm good,' she says, in a small voice.

'So . . . this is Jacob,' I say, as he raises a hand.

'Hey buddy,' smiles Zach. 'That's one cool T-shirt you got there. You like *The Amazing World of Gumball*, huh?'

'Yeah, it's my favourite show,' he says.

Zach leans in, and whispers behind his ear. 'Don't tell anyone but it's one of mine too . . .'

We shuffle forward in what seems to be a very slow-moving queue.

'This isn't your neck of the woods, is it?' I ask because, while I've never been to the rented apartments Zach is currently staying in, I am familiar with those long-term lets in and around Media City. They tend to be gleaming, slightly impersonal pads, with great views, but not a great deal of personality. I can't imagine him in them somehow . . .

'No, but Mila's grandparents live around the corner so we come here sometimes before she goes back to her mom. Mila's hoping to tackle that slide at some point before we go back to the US.'

'What, the big one?' I gasp, looking at her shy face. 'Wow . . . you're brave.'

'Well, she's hasn't quite made it down yet. We've been up those steps a few times but . . . you're still working on getting down it, aren't you, honey?'

I am very familiar with the psychological tug of war some kids have when they're desperate to attempt something new and exciting, but simultaneously too terrified to go through with it. Jacob was the same once over a slide in Center Parcs – he spent three days psyching himself up and only finally managed it just as it was time to go home.

'Do you think we'll be much longer in the queue, Mum?' Jacob asks.

'It looks like it. You go and play if you want. I'll wait in the line. Why don't you take Mila with you?' I look up at Zach. 'Assuming that's all right?'

She curls into his body and clutches his hand, clearly not sure.

Jacob smiles encouragingly. 'I'll look after you,' he says.

She considers the prospect for a moment before deciding the lure of the playground is just too much.

As Jacob leads her towards the roundabout, Zach looks astonished. 'Wow. She's usually shy around bigger kids.'

'Well . . . my son is *very* charming,' I tell him, as Jacob helps her onto the ride, before gently starting to push it.

'I can see. What a guy.'

There's a short silence as the queue begins to move again – very slowly. 'This better be some damn good ice cream with a line this long.'

'You know what they say. Everything tastes better when you wait.'

I look up. He locks eyes with me. The tips of my ears redden. 'So I hear.'

Something begins to unfurl inside me. I hastily glance over at the kids. He clears his throat.

'So, what's new at work, Darling?' he says, to my relief. Small talk I can do.

'Oh, you know. Nothing's on time. Everything's over budget. Non-stop arm wrestles with those awkward sods in commissioning . . .'

'We do try . . .'

'Oh, and I've got that huge presentation at the end of the month too. I do it every year and hate it.'

He pulls a face. 'Why? I've seen you present plenty of times. You're *slick*.'

I snort. 'I wouldn't go that far, but thanks. I'm all right in a smallish group, but 200 people? My idea of hell. Don't look so mystified. Just because you can stroll across a stage looking like you were *born* to do a Ted Talk . . .'

'Hardly.'

'Well, you certainly don't look nervous. Is it all a front? Are you a quivering wreck inside?'

'Honestly?' He pulls a pained expression. 'No. Never.'

'Never? I'm sure that's the definition of a psychopath, isn't it?'

'I do hope not,' he laughs. 'Seriously, Darling. There are better things to worry about than whether you're going to stumble over some words or your jokes fall flat. I mean . . . who gives one?'

'Me, apparently. Any tips then?'

He shrugs. 'Just be yourself.'

'Oh Russo,' I sigh. 'That's *so* corny. I expected better of you.'

'No, it's not. It's good advice. *Yourself* is amazing,' he says, holding my gaze in a way that seems deliberately provocative.

I wonder if the smile that's on his lips is specifically designed to make me want to kiss them.

'Have you ever thought of making fridge magnets?' I say instead. 'You'd make a bomb on Etsy.'

He smiles.

We shuffle forward in the queue. 'So did you tell Rose her job is going to be empty again soon?'

I nod. 'I did.'

'She must be looking forward to coming back?'

'Her focus right now is her treatment, but I'm sure she is. She's always lived for that job. Plus, she couldn't get enough of all the gossip from the awards.'

We finally reach the front and order four cones, but as I go to pay, Zach nudges me out of the way.

'Least I can do is buy you an ice cream.'

The server lines up the finished waffle cones in a holder, one by one. Zach picks up mine with a napkin and passes it to me, followed by Jacob's. Our hands brush both times, causing a ripple effect up my arm. I lick a small drip of cold ice cream from one of my fingers and I'm gripped by an unseemly flash of curiosity about what it would be like to do the same to one of his.

We spend almost an hour in the playground, far longer than I'd intended. Zach takes a ton of photos and insists we get a group selfie, which I ask him to send me afterwards. Jacob of course pulls one of his obligatory funny faces – I haven't had a 'nice' photo of him for at least 18 months now – which Mila finds hysterical. From her peels of uncontrollable laughter, it has gradually become apparent that she considers my son to be a comedy genius on a par with some of the all-time greats. Charlie Chaplin, Robin Williams, John Cleese can all step aside as far as she's concerned.

Jacob meanwhile clearly quite likes having Mila follow him around, her eyes wide in admiration. Eventually, he manages to coax her up the steps of the slide as Zach and I stand at the bottom to watch.

'Way to go, Mila!' he calls up, then murmurs to me out of the side of his mouth: 'She's never going to do this. I've been up and down those steps like a yo-yo.'

'How many times has she bottled out at the last minute?'

'I'd say sixty to a hundred.'

And then—

'HURRAYYYY!' Jacob is cheering from the top as Mila whizzes down, looking admittedly more stunned than joyful. When she gets to the bottom, she blinks a couple of times, a dazed look on her face, before leaping to her feet and running to Zach.

'Daddy, did you see?' she cries, as he lifts her up and smothers her with kisses. She's so overjoyed that she promptly wants to do it again. And again, and again – while Jacob heroically accompanies her to the top of the steps every time.

On approximately her twelfth go, at the moment her feet touch the ground, she gasps. 'MOMMY!'

I follow her gaze to the gate, where a woman in a cute denim dress and chunky leather sandals is closing it behind her. She has tousled, chestnut hair that reaches halfway down her back and is sprinkled with natural highlights. She is wearing little to no make-up and has this wide Julia Roberts smile, all warmth and gleaming eyes. She is stunning. I mean, *of course* she's stunning. How could I ever have imagined Zach's ex would be anything else?

'Mommy, come and look!' she says, 'I went down the slide!'

'No way!' she replies.

'Come and watch!'

She looks up at Zach and waves a hello, before seeming to register me a second later. Her expression wavers and, although Mila is now out of earshot, she's clearly trying to persuade her daughter that it's time to go.

'I'll be right back,' Zach says, as he heads towards them.

I suddenly feel like a loose end, so go to join Jacob, now at the swings.

'Do you want a push?' I ask.

He gives me a doubtful look.

'I think I'm all right, Mum,' he says, before flinging up his legs until he's higher than my head.

I sit on the swing next to him and begin to rock, trying to look anywhere other than at Zach, Sara and Mila. They must have been a gorgeous family and, despite the fireworks Zach described, are clearly pretty amicable now.

'BYE JACOB!' calls out Mila, as she runs towards us, stopping at the edge of the swing area.

'Bye Mila!' he replies, returning her wave.

'Can we have a sleepover one day?' she asks.

'Yeah, maybe!' he laughs.

Then she skips away, her day apparently made.

Zach heads back to us after they've driven off.

'What have you guys got planned for the rest of the day?' he asks, as we stroll to the exit.

'Well, I'm going to be panelling the living room and doing some Pilates. But Jacob has a more exciting afternoon than me,' I tell him.

'I'm going to see *War Horse* with my grandma,' he pipes up.

'Oh, the thing with the huge puppets? That looks great,' Zach says.

'But first you've got maths homework, so we need to get back to do it,' I add.

Jacob groans. 'I hate maths . . .'

'What's wrong with math?' Zach asks.

'*Everything*. But fractions mainly . . .'

'They're the work of the devil, according to Jacob,' I tell Zach.

'I can't add them up when the denominator is different. It's too hard.'

'Ah. I see. I used to hate that too when I was your age. But you know what? Someone showed me a trick that I have *never* forgotten that makes them super easy. It's basically cheating . . .'

Jacob's interest is now piqued. 'So . . . what's the trick?'

'Hmm. I'm not sure I could show you here.'

'Come back to ours!'

'*Jacob*. I'm sure Zach's busy . . .'

But he catches my eye. There is a playful glint in it. 'I'll always make time for a little math.'

Chapter 42

I'm not saying my hallway is a disaster area, but there are seismic risk zones in better shape after we've all piled out of the house on a Saturday morning. It certainly doesn't have the serene, tasteful ambience I always imagined when I first decorated. There are several pairs of shoes discarded by the door, half a cup of cold coffee on the sideboard, one filthy sock and the kids' bags, which they both dropped on the floor after school last night and, after a late Friday working and an early start, I didn't get the chance to move.

'It's not always like this,' I mutter, cursing myself that I didn't follow through on that Swedish self-care tip I saw on Instagram – to buy a bouquet of beautiful flowers every Friday to celebrate simply reaching the end of the week. Who am I kidding? If I'd just had the chance to throw the hoover around and clear away the breakfast dishes, it would've been something.

We enter the kitchen and I feel a beat of relief that I cleared away the knickers I'd left drying on the radiator overnight.

'Take a seat, sorry it's such a mess,' I say, shoving a plate into the dishwasher.

'It's not a mess, it's a home,' he says. 'I'd take this any day over the place I'm staying in.'

'Yeah, it must be awful, all those gleaming taps, the 24-hour gym. I bet you've got a nice cleaning lady who comes in and polishes your loo for you . . .'

'Actually, he's a guy called George, but I take your point. It does have some benefits. Charm and homeliness isn't one of them,' he says, looking at my vintage 'Elbow' poster. 'So where's my student gone?'

'Oh, good point. Jacob has a knack of conveniently forgetting about maths homework at the first opportunity.'

'I heard that,' Jacob says, appearing at the door with his fractions book.

Zach laughs. 'Okay, come on over here. But you gotta promise once I've told you this trick, you keep it a secret. Only a very special few get to know it.'

Jacob gives a tentative smile.

'I'm not kidding!' Zach grins and Jacob, unsure, decides: 'Okay, I promise.'

They sit at the kitchen table while I set about bringing some order to the place. Each time I glance over, I have to actively stop myself from smiling and concentrate instead on putting away the mugs.

All in all, it takes about 35 minutes for Jacob to crack it. 35.

And all it's cost me is a cup of coffee, as opposed to the umpteen pounds I've spent on tutoring, which got precisely nowhere.

'This guy was having you on,' Zach says, as Jacob beams proudly next to him. 'He can totally do fractions.'

'I couldn't before! You should do YouTube videos. You'd get *billions* of views.'

'Not interested. You can keep your riches,' Zach says, shaking his head. 'I told you. Only a special few are let into the secret.'

I can tell there's a bit of Jacob that really wants to believe this is true.

'I've *got* to know what this trick is,' I say.

'Sorry,' Zach says regretfully. 'You're not on my list.'

Jacob laughs.

'That's enough of that, you,' I say, glancing at the clock. 'Right, you've now got half an hour before your grandma arrives to take you to the theatre. So go and get yourself changed and smartened up, okay?'

As he disappears to head upstairs, I turn to Zach with an apologetic look on my face.

'So . . . my mum is about to arrive,' I say.

'Cool,' he says.

I scrunch up my face and the penny drops. 'Oh, I see. I should probably go before she gets here.'

'Might be easier,' I squirm, uncomfortably.

'Sure. No. I understand.'

He stands up, looking suddenly slightly awkward.

'Um . . . I'll show you out.'

We are halfway across the hall when the bell rings. Until the moment I open the door, I am convinced it will be Amazon, or something I've ordered from an Instagram link. The fact I can't actually *recall* ordering anything from there lately doesn't mean anything. I'm forever receiving things I have no recollection of buying – as yesterday's delivery of a fermented rice water shampoo bar proves beyond doubt.

I have the door open halfway when I realise my error.

'Mum!' I push it semi-closed again. 'Why are you so early?'

'I told you we were going for a milkshake first. Don't tell me he's not ready. . .'

'No, he is. I'll just get him. Wait there. JACOB!'

'I'm just going to spend a penny before we go,' she says, stepping forward.

'It's blocked,' I say, shoving my foot against the door.

'Oh, not again. What are you *feeding* those boys? There is such a thing as too much fibre you know.'

'JACOB!'

'I'm here,' he says, plodding down the stairs.

'Okay good,' I say, kissing him on the cheek, before ushering him out into the porch. 'Bye, sweetie. Have a great time both of you! Thanks, Mum!'

I go to close the door when it flings open again.

'I forgot my Pokémon cards,' Jacob says, galloping up the stairs. Mum is now standing on the step looking directly at Zach. She blinks.

'Hello, ma'am,' he says, pleasantly. 'I'm Zach, pleased to meet you.'

'Oh . . . hello,' she says, studying him with a look that suggests she wishes she'd brought her reading glasses.

'Got them, Grandma!' Jacob gallops down the stairs and pushes past us all.

'Bye, Zach. And thanks for the trick on fractions!'

'Oh! You're the maths tutor!' she chuckles, with palpable relief. 'Sorry, I thought . . .' she shakes her head. 'I'll just go, shall I? See you later, love.'

'Bye, Mum.'

I close the door.

Chapter 43

I close my eyes and exhale. 'Oh . . . my . . . God.'

Zach starts to laugh and there's something about the awfulness of the situation that makes me join in. 'Oh, I'm sorry,' he says.

'No, *I'm* sorry. I'm cringing. That was ridiculous. I just didn't want my mother to get the wrong impression about you and me.'

The look of amusement that remains on his face makes my temples colour. 'And . . . what's the *right* impression?'

I blow out my cheeks. 'Frankly, who knows?'

I open the door enough to see that Mum's little Mazda has disappeared.

'Is the coast clear?'

'It is.'

I look at the floor and bite my lip self-consciously. When I raise my head again his gaze is fixed on the precise, tender part of my mouth that I've just had between my teeth.

'Thank you, Zach.'

'What for?'

'The fractions.'

'Oh. No problem.' He smiles and I notice for the hundredth time the way the creases around his eyes fan out in the most pleasing way. I have a sudden urge to touch them.

'Well, I'd better go. And leave you to your . . . what was it?'

'Panelling.'

'Right.'

I reach across to the latch on the door again and he turns to leave. But before he steps over the threshold, he leans in to peck me on the cheek. At least, that's what it starts as. Hardly more than the kind of air kiss that happens all the time in our line of work. Only now, when his cheek brushes against mine, neither of us moves.

My eyelids flutter closed as I soak in the warmth of his skin. I tilt my chin just a fraction closer to him and press the corner of my mouth in the dip beneath his cheekbone. I can feel his whole body relax, like a sigh that runs all the way through him. He kisses me again. I return it with another. Eventually, I click the latch shut and move into his arms, allowing my mouth to fully meet his.

There is something about kissing Zach that reminds me of the feeling you get from licking buttercream off a spoon. It invokes all of my senses, sparking every pleasurable neural pathway in my possession. What is it that makes that taste *so* much better than the finished cake, the very thing you are supposed to enjoy more? The intense sweetness on the tongue? Its soft, creamy mouthfeel? Or the knowledge that this is really *not* something you are meant to love as much as you do . . .

A soft moan escapes from somewhere deep inside me, as I run my fingertips along the nape of his neck and his palms meander down to my behind. I wrap my arms around his neck and we continue to kiss as we make our way to the stairs. I recline onto them as he crawls on top of me and I slide my knees either side of him. I get a full sense of how muscular his shoulders are as his lips trace my jaw and I dig my fingernails gently into the ripples of his back.

'Oh Lisa,' he sighs into my neck. There is something wildly sensual about the sound of my name in his mouth. I can feel it tingling and fizzing somewhere in my chest. He pulls back gently and allows his eyes to travel over my face, so luxuriantly that it's as if he is trying to consign every tiny feature to memory.

He reaches up to trace the outline of my eyebrow with his fingertips, then runs it along my cheekbone, all the way to the tip of my chin. When it's there, he tilts up my head and plants another sumptuous kiss on my lips. Involuntarily, I squeeze my thighs against the outside of his muscular legs.

'I cannot get you out of my head,' he says softly.

'Is that true?'

'Completely true.'

I squirm against his body, gently grinding my crotch against his. He is hard. Unbelievably so.

'I wouldn't keep doing that if I were you,' he murmurs, kissing me again.

'Doing what?' I ask, as if I didn't know.

'That thing. With your hips.'

'Oh. This?'

When I do it again, his eyelids flutter reflexively closed and he exhales.

'That it is very. . . *distracting*,' he whispers. I can't wipe the smile off my face. 'I am *endlessly* distracted by you.'

'Endlessly?' I say, in a teasing tone.

There is a dark look in his eyes as he nods.

I reach up and touch his lips with my fingertips, gently tracing the outline of them. 'And during those times when you are distracted . . . what are you thinking about, *exactly?*'

He kisses my finger so quickly it's almost a bite. When I pull it away, it's still warm and wet from his tongue. 'I'm not sure you'd want to know.'

'Oh, I would. I would *really* want to know.'

He shakes his head.

'Come *on*. Did you have a dirty dream about me?' I tease, unable to suppress my smile.

'There was nothing dirty about this. It was beautiful. There were fucking songbirds flying around my head.'

I chuckle. 'Now I *have* to know . . .'

He sighs. 'Well . . . among *many* other things, I have been thinking a great deal lately about what it would be like to . . .'

'Go on.'

The light in his eyes seems to blaze. 'To go down on you.'

My whole body floods with liquid heat.

I look at him for several long seconds. Then, I gently push him away, one hand on his chest, just far enough to give myself space.

I begin to lift up my skirt, inch by tantalising inch. He watches, enraptured, his chest inflated and immobile as he holds his breath. When the hem is skimming the top of my thighs, I scoot up my hips slightly and slide the fingers of both hands under the cool, white cotton of my pants.

He watches every uninhibited movement. Every carefree step. I gently wriggle them past my thighs, over my knees, down to my ankles. Then I kick them away with one foot. I slowly open my legs. He finally releases his breath.

I feel as if I have been reinvented. As a vamp, a vixen, a seductress, a goddess. He slides his hot, dry hands up my thighs.

Then he dips his head.

The kisses start inside my knee, a small corner of my body where I genuinely don't recall ever being touched before. He is unhurried, refusing to be rushed. He moves like someone who is exactly where he wants to be and fully intends to savour every second. By the time he is gently biting the soft flesh on my inner thigh, my need for him is agonising.

His lips find the warm tenderness between my legs. Whatever it is that he next does with his mouth feels like some kind of sorcery. I lean on my elbows and tip back my head, as a mindless hedonistic bliss begins to build inside me.

My to-do lists no longer exist. My schedules are irrelevant. My responsibilities are temporarily suspended.

In the space in my head, there is no room for laundry or work, or *thinking* of any kind. All there is room for is *feeling*.

More and more and more feeling . . .

I feel Zach freeze before I can work out why.

A second later, I realise what he's heard. A key in the door. The rustle of a lock. I draw a sharp intake of breath as my panicked eyes meet his.

The next few moments unfold both in slow motion and way too fast to take it all in. I fling down the hem of my skirt. We scramble away from the stairs. I straighten my hair and rest an elbow on the bannister, like I'm propping up a bar.

The door flies open and in walks Leo.

'What's for dinner?'

He doesn't look up from his phone, just throws his rugby kit on the floor, steps over my knickers and heads towards the kitchen. I squeeze past Zach, grab the pants and scrunch them into my fist.

'Um. . . what are you doing back? I thought you were staying out?'

There must be something in my voice that makes him stop at the threshold and turn around.

'I was. I've run out of dosh.'

I clear my throat. 'This is Zach. Jacob's new maths tutor.'

Leo mumbles something approximating a hello and continues to the fridge.

Zach and I make our way to the door. I open it up and he steps out onto the porch.

'I'm sorry,' I whisper.

'Don't be. I'll see you around.'

I nod. But before he leaves, he leans in one last time to say something, so softly that I can feel his breath against my ear.

'You are . . . *delicious*.'

Chapter 44

It's hard to concentrate on the living room panelling for the rest of the afternoon. Each time I go to measure something, I start reliving what's happened earlier and wondering if I'll be having pornographic flashbacks every time I walk up the stairs from this point onwards. Given that I'd always said this was our 'forever home' and vowed never to move again, this could get a bit strange if I'm still here at an age when I'll need a stairlift.

The problem is, it's not just the sex I'm thinking about. Already, my mind is skipping forward to an impossible place. To a future. A type of togetherness that is simply not available to Zach and me.

I manage to get one wall completed by the time Jacob returns from the theatre with my mum. They both loved the show, though my mother was such an emotional wreck by the end that, to use Jacob's words, 'it was like she had hosepipes coming out of her eyes.'

We have a quiet Saturday night, as Jacob and I snuggle on the sofa for a family movie while Leo spends the evening upstairs on his PlayStation. As I climb into bed later, a text pops up on my phone.

It's no good. I still can't get you out of my head. Yours, The Maths Tutor

I bite my lip and reply straight away.

You do realise I'm changing your name to that in my contacts book?

Seems fair. I am good at fractions, after all.

Among other things . . .

Do not get me all hot again, Darling. I can't take it.

I'll stop. Though . . . that was a very bad thing we did on the stairs today.

Darling . . .

I didn't mean bad. I meant beautiful. With fucking songbirds.

The next text takes forever.

I was hoping to find a songbird emoji so I could send you a whole load of them. My phone is only offering the choice of a penguin, duck or chicken and none of those quite fit my current mood.

I laugh out loud and am considering a response when a series of dots undulate on the screen to show that he's typing. I go to brush my teeth while I'm waiting for his message to appear. When I return, the words on the screen make something burn in my gut.

I'm going to wear my heart on my sleeve here. The idea of not seeing you again after I leave is killing me.

My heart begins to pump queasily at the thought that in ten days he'll be gone. Then, I catch myself.

Don't go there, Lisa. Not again. Do. Not. Go. There.

I type a response. Surely you'll be able to find someone in LA willing to bust your balls as much as me.

Be as flippant as you want. I mean it.

I exhale and try to think of something obtuse to say. I suddenly have neither the words nor the inclination to be anything other than honest.

I know. And I feel the same.

You are amazing, Darling.

Oh shush.

Are you cringing again?

Half cringing, half soaking it up 😂

We text for a long time afterwards, until I'm so tired that by the time we've exchanged goodnights and sweet dreams, I haven't even got the energy to update any of my apps. So I click off the phone and stare at the ceiling.

I *cannot* get this attached to Zach. I can't let what happened on my stairs today make me fall in love with him. I need to act like a grown woman and stop whatever is happening here before it gets out of hand.

I plug the phone in next to my bed. I turn off the light.

Despite everything, somehow I'm still smiling.

The following day, Jeff, Rose and I sit on the terrace of the tennis clubhouse, watching Nora attempt to teach her orange ball kids – who are mainly aged 10 and 11 – how to perform a backhand. The group seems louder than ever today and even Nora, who has a peculiar knack for holding children's attention, is facing an uphill struggle to get them all to listen. So she employs a tried-and-tested method to get them all in a circle for the 'Question of the Week'.

'If you were allowed to have anything for breakfast – anything at all – what would it be?'

The answers range from blueberry pancakes and *pains aux chocolat* to Haribos, a Big Mac and someone's grandma's lasagne. Absolutely nobody mentions Bran Flakes.

'What does this have to do with tennis?' Jeff asks.

'Nothing, it just stops them bouncing around and trying to kill each other for about three minutes,' I say.

Rose turns to him. 'So what would you have for breakfast if you could have anything you wanted, Jeff?'

He thinks for a moment. 'Am I allowed to say Luke Evans?'

Rose chuckles, but it turns into a cough. She got a cold a few weeks ago that went onto her chest and she just can't seem to shake it. She was always one of those people who rarely took a day off work with sickness, but this – presumably when combined with her treatment – seems to have taken it out of her. She looks so pale. I know I'm not the only one worried about her. Jeff texted me last night about exactly this after he'd seen her in the deli in Roebury.

'Okay guys! On your feet and let's get a little backhand competition going!' says Nora.

The kids line up as she starts feeding balls to them one by one. There are some interesting techniques, a few of which actually result in them hitting the ball.

'She must have the patience of a saint,' sighs Jeff. He's in his summer attire today – Italian leather boat shoes, linen shirt, gold-rimmed aviators and a pair of khaki shorts that show just an inch more leg than everyone else.

'She's certainly got more energy than anyone else our age that I know,' I say.

'That wouldn't take much compared with me at the moment,' Rose says, breaking into another cough.

'Maybe you shouldn't have come to meet us this morning,' I say. 'It might have done you more good staying in bed.'

'And miss out on this high-quality sport?' she smiles, as Jacob performs such a forceful serve that his racket flies out of his hand. 'Truth is, I wanted the fresh air and the company. The doctor said if my antibiotics haven't killed it by next week, they'll send me for a scan.'

There's a moment of silence as we all take in this prospect – and what exactly they'll be looking for.

Jeff slaps his hands on his knees and stands up. 'Well, I'm going to grab us some coffees. Is everyone having their usual?'

As he disappears inside, Rose turns to me. 'Come on, spill the beans.'

'What about?'

She employs a 'don't give me that' look. 'Something's happened between you and Zach.'

Jane Costello

'I see your powers of telepathy are as sharp as ever.'

'No telepathy required, Lisa. You're really not that subtle.'

'I haven't even mentioned him!'

'It's not what you've *said*. It's the fact that one minute you're smiling to yourself, then you're looking really wistful and melancholic and looking into the distance. Like you're on the cover of a late-1990s U2 album.'

'My HRT probably needs adjusting.'

'Hmm.'

I look at my hands and start playing with my rings. 'You're going to think I'm an idiot. But I am starting to think I have real feelings for him.'

'Ah,' she says. 'So you had sex with him.'

'No, *actually*.'

She narrows her eyes.

'Not . . . properly, at least.'

'Oh. Is this like a Bill Clinton-type thing?' she says. '*I did not have sexual relations with that man . . .*'

'Something like that,' I concede. 'I'll spare you the detail.'

'You really like him that much then?'

I bite the side of my mouth. 'I think I do. Oh . . . it's probably for the best that he's going back to America.'

Jeff reappears from the clubhouse and puts two coffees on the table, before producing a cupcake for Rose. It's a lovely, irresistible-looking thing, all light sponge and creamy raspberry and vanilla swirls.

'What's this?' she asks.

'It's for you, sweetheart. To keep your strength up. They were all out of cod liver oil.'

'Dad!' We all look up as Bella calls out to Jeff through the court netting. 'My bottle hasn't got any water in it.'

'Oh, damn, I must have forgotten to fill it up. All right, I'm coming!' Jeff says, leaping up to head down the clubhouse steps.

Rose looks down at the cupcake, then up at me. She smiles. 'I feel so lucky to have friends like you lot.'

She picks it up and takes the tiniest bite. Then she swallows, so hard you'd think she was eating sand.

Chapter 45

We have a presenter for *My Teenage Bombsite*. And I'm starting to believe we could have something seriously good on our hands.

She is called Nia Sumarni and, after studying her showreel then meeting her in person, I'm sort of blown away by her. The fact that she's gorgeous helps, but she's also funny, sharp and has that same big sister quality that made audiences love Davina McCall when she first appeared on our screens. I can already tell she will be brilliant with a line-up of hapless teenagers and their filthy living quarters.

By the time it's the middle of the week and I'm back in the office, I'm feeling pretty optimistic about the show, which is good because Andrea is trying to pin down a date for the next monthly scheduling meeting. She sent an email this morning asking for everyone's availability at either 4pm or 5pm on Friday. There is currently a 50/50 split between the two, which prompted Julian Mullins to respond:

'Might I suggest 4.30 as a compromise, Andrea?'

Her response, which I read while sitting in the coffee shop opposite the office, arrives less than ten seconds later.

'ABSOLUTELY INSPIRED IDEA! This is why we need minds like yours in this company, Julian!' You'd think he'd just discovered a cure for cancer.

I'm still tutting at my phone as Daisy walks in.

She's wearing a brown A-line skirt, a humungous matching jacket and Doc Martens. Nobody my age would attempt to get away with something like this, but oddly – with the addition of a frilly cream blouse and a spray of tiny gold cuffs running up one ear – she manages not to look like a giant Christmas pudding. In fact, it strikes me that she could easily pass as the uber-cool curator in a New York art gallery.

'Are you reading through one of my stupid ideas?' she says dolefully, obviously having caught me pulling faces at Andrea's nonsense.

'What? No! And stop putting yourself down. Now what can I get you?'

'No, I'll go,' she insists. 'It me who asked for the meeting.'

'Daisy. Please,' I say, standing up, conscious that she'll be saving for the deposit on that flat until she's eighty at this rate. 'I'll put them on expenses if you feel that strongly.'

She sits down obediently and tells me she'd like a turmeric matcha latte please. Whatever floats your boat, I suppose.

I buy the drinks and when I bring them to the table, she's twiddling with the sleeve on the brown jacket anxiously.

'What's all this about?' I ask.

I have been aware for the last week or so that Daisy has not been her usual effervescent self. I'd partly put this down to Calvin and the fact that things are going so well with his new girlfriend that she's invited him to join her for the weekend at her family home in Devon. But this, it seems, is the least of Daisy's worries.

'I'm here to hand in my notice,' she says.

'What? Oh Daisy . . .' I say, shocked, but not entirely. Working in TV can feel a little like a merry-go-round and I've seen some of the perks Netflix offer their staff if you're prepared to move to London. 'Where are you going?'

'I'm not sure yet. My plan is to sign up for a temping agency. I don't really know. My thought process hasn't got that far.'

'You mean you haven't got somewhere to go? Why on earth are you leaving then?'

She looks down at her hands and gives a long sigh. 'Because I am absolutely awful at this job.'

'No, you're not!' I tut.

She shakes her head. 'That's kind of you, Lisa. I never expected anything less. But it's just not true. I just don't think I'm cut out to work in TV.'

'Well, I disagree. I remember you telling me at your interview that this was your dream job. That it was all you'd ever wanted to do.'

She shrugs. 'That was true.'

'So tell me, what was it that made you want to work in this industry?'

'I just *loved* television. I was like Mike TV from *Charlie and the Chocolate Factory*,' she grins.

I laugh. 'What did you used to watch?

'Oh . . . too many to name. But do you remember *The Secret Life of Four-Year-Olds*? I was only a kid myself but I adored that.'

'It was a brilliant show.'

I admired the format myself, a fly-on-the-wall documentary in which experts in psychology watched children at play in a nursery and gave commentary and analysis on their behaviour.

'I think it was that that made me want to do this for a living. Despite what my parents thought.'

'They didn't think it was a good idea?'

She shakes her head. 'No. Thing is, I did quite well at school.' I already know this is an understatement. I've seen all the A stars she got at A levels. 'Then when I got into Oxford, they assumed I'd follow a similar sort of path to them.'

'What do they do?'

'Dad's a human rights lawyer. Mum's a nuclear physicist. I think they think our line of work is a bit silly.'

I cough into my americano. 'Maybe they've got a point.'

'Well, I disagree,' she says, indignantly. 'Because we make people *happy*. We bring them joy. Personally, I think that's no small feat.'

I lower my coffee cup. 'Well then. If you feel that strongly, why on earth would you be giving it up?'

'Because I've tried to develop more ideas this year than I can count and not one of them has come to fruition. I just haven't got what it takes, Lisa.'

I consider saying all the right things that would make her feel better. But if there's one thing Daisy's qualifications prove, it's that she's not stupid. So I tell her – gently – what I really think.

'You're right, of course. You haven't come up with a concept that would be workable . . . yet. But do you know how hard it is to get a TV programme made, Daisy? I must have seen about 10,000 proposals in the last decade and commissioned only about 500 of them. All the rest ended up in the trash. Some of those ideas were terrible. Some were fantastic but we just didn't have the slots or money. I don't know anyone else who works harder thank you, Daisy. Except possibly me. And the ideas you're coming up with are . . . all right, I'll say it. Some of them are a bit bonkers.'

She winces.

'But that's one of the reasons why eventually I think you're going to come up with a hit. If *everyone* around here all thought in the same way, Daisy, what a seriously boring content we'd be producing. You're a true original.'

'But doesn't that just mean my judgement is way off?'

'It means that, right now, you've got the imagination but not the experience. Stay the course and that will come. I promise.'

She takes a long inhale that suggests she clearly wasn't expecting this.

'Listen, Daisy. Whatever you decide to do – whether you stay or go – I would ask one thing of you.'

She swallows self-consciously and looks up at me. 'What's that?' she asks.

'Don't give up on yourself. Because I haven't.'

Chapter 46

Daisy and I go our separate ways after the meeting. She'd arranged to meet Calvin for a sandwich, or some plant-based alternative. I'm heading back to the office when I hear footsteps quicken behind me – and turn around to see Zach.

My heart triples in speed at the sheer, beautiful sight of him, the way his face lights up when he sees me.

'Hey you,' he says, falling into step.

'Hey yourself. Where are you off to?'

'I came out for some fresh air after lunch. Feel like walking the long way back to the office?'

'Sure,' I reply, as we fall into step with one another. Media City is sparkling this morning. Sunlight bounces off the office blocks and glitters on the gently rippling water. A film crew is setting up in advance of a live broadcast and the faint percussion of clanging bars from the stage being rigged echoes across the piazza.

'So I heard today that they've decided not to make an official replacement for Rose's job. Because there are only six weeks until she returns, the team thinks they can keep things ticking over between them. Whether Rose will agree when she's back and has a mountain of stuff to deal with is another matter . . .'

I force a laugh, unable to truly reconcile the idea of her returning to her desk in six weeks with the way she looked at the weekend. I feel a sliver of anxiety at the thought, even though when I texted her this morning she said she was a little better after a good night's sleep. 'So . . . how are you feeling about leaving?' I ask tentatively.

'Well,' he says, considering the question, 'I'm looking forward to a ton of things I've missed, not least the ranch dressing. But I don't mind admitting that, overall, I am . . .' he takes a big sigh, '*gutted*.'

We walk a few more steps before I confess, 'Me too.'

'Really? I got the impression you were having regrets. Your texts have kind of dried up this week.'

I can hardly look at him. 'I'm trying not to set myself up for heartache, Zach,' I say gently.

He nods thoughtfully.

'Well, I've also been thinking a lot about heartache. And about you and me. And I was wondering . . .' Then his feet slow as he turns to look at me. 'Could we make this work long-distance, Lisa?'

I raise my eyebrows. 'So I'd be *Sleepless in Salford*?'

This at least makes him laugh.

The possibility of keeping something going between Zach and me has obviously occurred to me. More than occurred. I desperately want our story not to end here when it's only just begun. He already feels like one of those rare humans who you meet every so often and just know you want them in your life forever. Him not being here feels so wrong I don't know where to begin.

Equally, let's be sensible here. We are no star-crossed lovers.

'I don't know, Zach,' I say quietly.

The disappointment on his face needles me in the side.

'This wouldn't be like having a relationship with someone in another state. We're talking about another *continent*.'

He looks at the ground and gives an unconvincing nod.

'Also, I would be *terrible* at sexting,' I add.

He gives a sideways smile. 'You managed to get me very hot under the collar the other night . . .'

'Must have been a fluke. Maybe this is a generational thing, but I couldn't bring myself to take a photo that I wouldn't be prepared to show my grandma.'

'What if I said I was prepared to live with the mystique? To just . . . use my imagination?' he says, clearly refusing to continue with this deviation. 'If you were prepared to give this a go then—'

'Zach,' I say, as I stop and turn to him. 'I don't think it's fair of either of us to just hang on in there, our emotions suspended on two sides of the globe. I don't think it would be good for us. Do you?'

As the words come out of my mouth, I still can't muster up any conviction for them. That's not to say I don't believe what I'm saying. I know this isn't just the sensible route. It's the only route.

He blows out his cheeks. 'You know you should be completely unbearable, being *right* this often. Somehow, Darling, you get away with it.'

I release a 'pthwh' sound. 'Well, if ever there was evidence that you really don't know me very well, it's that . . .'

We start to walk again and after a few steps, I feel something brush against my wrist. We can't hold hands in public, so he simply locks his forefinger privately with mine. Even with this one tiny connection, it has fired up nerve endings throughout my whole body. I feel a shot of heat behind my eyes.

'I know enough,' he says under his breath, then he lets go. We are suddenly in front of our building.

'Okay. Well, before you go and break my heart, Darling, would you be willing to let me cook for you this weekend? Could you get a babysitter?'

A big smile filters across my face. 'Russo, I would love that.'

Chapter 47

To-do list

- Ask Brendan to have kids for the weekend
- Undertake emergency shopping for sexy underwear
- Depilate
- Increase pelvic floor strengthening exercises x 3
- Write presentation for school 'careers in TV' talk
- Send Rose flowers
- Sack maths tutor
- Reply to school emails x 6 about the end of term
- Put DIY panelling kit in the loft to avoid looking at it
- Look for socks subscription service
- Descale kettle

Getting ready for a date is nothing like it used to be. Not that I ever really did much 'dating' per se, at least dating that bore any resemblance to the storylines in *Sex and the City*. There was no endless merry-go-round of people trying each other out for size. In all honesty, there never seemed to be that many people available, at least none that were single and vaguely fanciable. But the main thing I'd recall in advance of the handful of dates I went on in the period between Danny and Brendan was that the only preparation I had to worry about was *my own*. I didn't have to think about kids, parents, a hamster called Alan and an ex-husband who is predictably unavailable.

'Can't Leo babysit? He's old enough now,' he says, when I call him to ask. 'Surely it's time you gave him some responsibility.'

The truth is, I did consider asking Leo, even if I haven't left him in charge of so much as a houseplant, let alone his little brother. This has been a long-standing bone of contention between Leo and me for several months now. He thinks that at his age he is more than capable of holding the fort at home. And while in theory I like the idea of giving him some responsibility and sometimes have to remind myself that he'll be sixteen in a month or so, I'm still not 100% convinced. As it happens, he's not available either.

'He's going over to his friend Josh's house for a PlayStation and pizza night. It's his sixteenth birthday. Josh's mum is dropping Leo home afterwards, but it won't be till late.'

'Well, we can't I'm afraid,' Brendan continues, unapologetically. 'We've got people over for dinner this weekend.'

'That's okay!' I reply, brightly. 'If you're staying in, Jacob's never any trouble. In fact, he's *great* when people come over. Whenever I have guests, they love having a chat with him.'

'No. No, that wouldn't work at all,' he says so firmly that it occurs to me that perhaps he and Melanie are planning the type of dinner party that involves guests placing their car keys in a bowl. 'When the children are here, I feel strongly that they deserve my full and complete attention. *Quality time* is the key.' I don't know how he is somehow making me feel bad for having to organise our actual lives instead of just making their every minute as wholesome and fun as a trip to the fairground.

'I think it'd just be easier if your mum had him,' he says vaguely, at which point I have a call coming through from a production company and am forced to end it there.

'I literally don't know how you managed to stay married to that man for so long,' Rose tuts later, when we speak on the phone. 'You must have had the patience of a saint.'

'Hardly.'

'The kids are more than welcome to come over here, you know,' she says, breaking into a cough.

'I appreciate the offer, but I'm not going to inflict my kids on you when you're not well.'

'I love seeing them,' she says weakly. 'Though . . . I'm not exactly on top form, I'd have to admit.'

'It's out of the question. Brendan is right, unfortunately. I'll have to grovel to Mum. Again.'

Thankfully, while she and Dad also have plans this weekend – he's out with his golf club friends, while she's celebrating her friend Shirley's 70th birthday with a spa day – she assures me that both will be back in time for Jacob to have a sleepover at their house.

'You don't have to keep apologising,' she tells me when I take him over there on the way to Zach's place. 'I *like* having him over. We're going to watch *Gladiators* and get a Chinese takeaway. Did Leo not want to come too?'

'He's at a friend's,' I say, as a text flashes up on my phone.

'Who on earth keeps texting you? That hasn't stopped.'

'The PTA,' I say ominously, because my WhatsApp has been red hot this morning on the subject of limo hire for the forthcoming Prom.

Only this isn't Denise Dandy. The contact that flashes up is 'The Maths Tutor'.

Jacob leans in to look.

'Don't be so nosy,' I say, snatching the phone away.

'Is it Zach?' he asks.

'What makes you say that?'

'Because you're smiling,' he says impishly, making my cheeks redden.

'Oh, is he the maths tutor?' Mum asks, narrowing her eyes. 'He was *very* handsome, I must say. From what I could see—'

'Must dash!' I say, grabbing my car keys.

'Are you going anywhere nice? You look lovely with your hair done like that.'

'To the theatre with Nora,' I say, having prepared this alibi in advance.

'Oh. What are you going to see?'

I freeze. Turns out my alibi is a little short on detail and the first thing that pops into my head that's showing locally is *Shrek the Musical*.

'*Hedda Gabler*,' I say.

'What's that?'

'Ibsen.'

'Who?'

'You know. Norwegian. Nineteenth century. It's a tragedy,' I add.

'Sounds it,' she says, scrunching her nose in bafflement.

'It's meant to be really good,' I protest, then wonder why I'm defending an entirely fictitious production of a show I'm not actually going to and isn't even on. I decide to leave it there.

I get into my car and click on the text.

Just checking you're not allergic to seafood? Xxx

I reply, Not as far as I know xxx

I press send as another WhatsApp from the PTA arrives. I read about two dozen messages that start with a request by Denise for someone to host the last PTA meeting of the school year.

'I'd do it myself but we're having our hot tub replaced,' she adds, though with what is unclear. A cauldron possibly?

A stream of excuses follow – including from Nora and Jeff, though at least I know theirs are real: Nora is coaching that night and can only make the second half, while Jeff's dogs get stressed around any more than about three people in his house. The result is a stony silence.

'Come on, everyone!' Denise says. 'We're getting desperate now! Any volunteers? Please?'

Seriously. What's wrong with these people?

'Happy to host, Denise,' I type.

Then I put away my phone in the full knowledge that all I'm likely to get in return is a clapping emoji and a profound sense of self-loathing.

Chapter 48

I turn into the car park at Zach's apartment block and look for the bay he'd directed me to. There is a persistent flutter in my stomach, a long-lost type of feeling, like being fifteen years old and on your way to a party where you know you'll see the boy you like.

I pull into the space and turn off the engine. In the twenty minutes it took to drive here, dozens more WhatsApp messages have landed. I've been invited to log my alcohol units, check the balance of my mortgage, undertake a restorative Vinyasa Flow and look at a video compilation of my photo memories from this day in 2014.

I click on the screen and swipe every one of them away.

Instead, I text Zach to tell him I'm here, as he asked me to. I check my lipstick in the rear-view mirror and release a long breath. Then I get out, open the back door to collect my bag and a bottle of Chablis. When I look up, he's walking towards me, that showstopper of a smile on his face.

He is wearing jeans and a relaxed, white cotton shirt. The top couple of buttons are open, revealing the tanned, muscular notch at the top of his chest. He is cleanly shaven. His hair is still damp from the shower. His skin looks tanned, his lips full and flushed. He is the definition of sexy, oozing masculinity but with just enough softness around the edges.

He touches me on the elbow and bends down to kiss me on the cheek.

'You look gorgeous. You smell gorgeous.' Then he pulls back and looks me in the eyes. 'Damn . . . you *are* gorgeous.'

'That's way too many compliments for one sentence.'

'Have I peaked too early? I'll rein 'em in.'

'Oh, don't do that.' I smile and hand him the wine. He looks at the bottle. 'Nice choice.'

'It's flinty with a long, tingly finish, apparently.'

'Well, what's not to love about that?'

We stroll towards his apartment block and he lets us in. The reception area is nicely decorated in muted shades of peach and cream, offset by a profusion of shiny, oversized plants. We take a lift to the seventh floor and when he opens the door, a delicious umami scent of cooking food ignites my senses.

The flat is bigger than I was expecting and, contrary to what he'd said, less impersonal. It's open-plan and filled with light, decorated tastefully in soft shades, but with splashes of intense colour from the contemporary furniture and pictures on the walls. There's a small corridor leading to a couple of bedrooms, one of which I can already see is filled with an abundance of pink accessories.

'That one's Mila's. Just in case you were in any doubt,' he says, as he takes my jacket and hangs it on a peg near the front door.

'This is *very* swish, Zach. And my compliments to your cleaner George.'

He heads over to the kitchen area to open the wine. He pours two chilled glasses and hands me one, before stirring something in a pan as I wander to a floor-to-ceiling window that leads out to a balcony, where a small table and two chairs overlook the quays.

'Can I go out here?'

'Sure.'

I step outside and look across the network of waterways and skyscrapers of Manchester beyond. Given the weather around here, I don't suppose this always makes for a glorious view. But today it does. Today, it is perfect. Everything is.

A hot summer sun is setting low over the water, creating a myriad of unlikely colours in the sky – deep turquoise through to burnished amber. Looking directly down, I get a full sense of how different the vibe is here at the weekend, the emphasis more on play than work. There are dog walkers and runners, as well as the odd cyclist, while in the canal beneath us, a group of thirty or so swimmers bob about in multicoloured caps.

'They're brave,' I say, as Zach steps out to join me. 'I don't fancy the temperature in that water.'

'No, it's nice in there. Not quite Laguna Beach, but it still gets the endorphins pumping.'

I suppress a smile. 'I might have known you'd have had a go.'

'I'm that predictable, huh?'

He places his wine glass on the table. Then he takes mine out of my hand and puts it down too.

'Come here.' He slides his palms around my waist and draws me in to his body.

I never want to forget what it feels like to be tenderly enveloped by these big, loving arms. As I breathe in the scent on his skin, I want to bottle it and inhale it forever.

I can't decide which type of Zach's kisses I like the best. The soft, sensual ones, like honey running through my whole body. Or the hard, hungry ones when he wants me so much he can barely breathe. Truth is, I'd take either. Anytime, anywhere, as the saying goes. But for now, it's the first kind – slow and sultry and sweet, the type that hints at much more to come.

'I like what you did with your hair tonight,' he says, reaching up as his fingertips play with a soft strand.

'Oh . . . curlers,' I say, entirely ruining any sense of mystique. 'So, what's on the menu? It smells wonderful.'

'Well, you were totally unhelpful when I asked what you wanted to eat . . .'

'I'll eat anything.'

'Precisely. No help at all. After great deliberation, I decided there was only one menu I could possibly serve you.'

'Which is?'

'A taste of home. New York City style.'

'Ah! I love a hot dog!'

He shakes his head. 'Sorry, Darling. You are not getting a hot dog.'

What I get instead is a feast.

As the sun sets, we eat at a candlelit table just inside the apartment, both doors flung wide open to allow a gentle breeze to drift in. It starts with an incredible seafood platter, of fresh-shucked oysters, caviar, clams and shrimp. Next is a chicken dish with polenta and hazelnuts, served with a side of kohlrabi. He tells me this was all inspired by his favourite food from Gramercy Tavern.

'It's one of those perfect places, you know. The kind where everything is just right. A little bit of bustle, great vibe, delicious, fresh food.'

'It's been a long time since anyone cooked for me,' I confess.

'Oh yeah?'

I nod. Brendan did go through a phase once when he developed a sort of love–hate relationship with Gordon Ramsay and vowed to start making a special meal for us on a Saturday night. My main recollection of the experience was the phenomenal number of pots and pans left for me to wash up afterwards, which he seemed to think was a reasonable price to pay given that he'd been toiling over a couple of lamb chops and half a bottle of red for most of the afternoon.

I offer to wash up now, but Zach won't countenance it. He'd done most of it before I arrived and leaves the rest in the sink, telling me he'll deal with it later and that I am not to lift a finger, under any circumstances.

'That might just be the hottest thing anyone's ever said to me, Russo,' I say.

We eat and talk and laugh, all to a playlist he tells me he compiled earlier this afternoon. There's a little bit of Lana del Rey, a touch of The Head and The Heart, a soupçon of the Plain White T's and Tom Odell. I make him promise to send it to me, just so that when he's gone and I'm wondering if I hallucinated these last few months, I can press play and take myself back.

When he finally brings out a lemon tart made with buttermilk, bilberries and thyme, I'm convinced I'm too stuffed, but somehow manage it.

'And now . . . I can't move.'

'My portions are probably bigger than you're used to.'

'Still managed to clean my plate though,' I say, sighing contentedly. 'Zach, this was incredible. You never even mentioned you liked cooking. I'd have been over every other night with a bottle of white if I'd known. . .'

'I've hardly done any since I've been in the UK. When Mila's here, she only wants exactly the same thing – pasta with cheese and veggies – despite my attempts to tempt her with something else. And when there's just me, I tend to just batch-cook and keep things in the refrigerator. It was nice to actually crack open the cookbooks again.'

'Well, I'm honoured. You should keep at it when you go back to the US.'

The reminder that he'll be gone brings a lump to my throat. He forces a smile. 'Yeah. I should.'

I place my napkin down. 'Well, I'm sure I could just do a couple of dishes . . .' I say, standing up.

'Oh, stop it and sit down. If I've only got a limited time left with you I'm *not* going to waste it by doing that.'

'Fine.' I do as instructed. 'What now then?'

He draws his eyes across my face with a slow, sexy smile. 'Scrabble?'

I start to laugh. But then he stands up, walks around the table and offers me his hand. I already know where we're going next.

Chapter 49

There's a soft, thick carpet in Zach's bedroom, the kind your toes sink into, and by now the only thing illuminating the room is a fat summer moon. We fall onto the gentle folds of his duvet, as he massages the hairline at the back of my neck. Everything feels opulent, luxurious and dreamy. When he kisses me, sensitive, hidden parts of me shimmer like the moon. I feel tipsy but not from the wine. It's from his slightest touch, the dry heat of his skin, the hush of the room and the bittersweet melody of some new song drifting in from the door.

I lie on my back as he props himself up next to me and his fingers slide to the sides of my breasts. I watch the shadows of his softly lit face, every perfect dip and curve of his features. In my whole life, I don't think I've ever kissed anyone so beautiful. I feel something hard against my hip as he reaches up to the top button of my blouse. As he pries it open, I become hyper conscious of my breath, the exaggerated rise and fall of my breasts. He draws his eyes over my face and smiles. Then he opens the next button.

I crane my neck to kiss him, to taste those sumptuous lips. He smells of that same delicious scent I caught on the first day I ever met him. Only now, when his skin is close to mine, I can close my eyes and inhale, for no other reason than to breathe him in.

He opens another button.

Now he holds my hand and gently pulls me up so we're both sitting. With a slow, singular movement, he draws my blouse over my head. I'm wearing a new bra, semi-sheer, with just a touch of lace, the kind that made me feel sexy the moment I tried it on. I breathe in automatically, then get a sense that I needn't have bothered. He seems to like the parts of me that squidge. And the look in his eyes suggests that, even if he didn't, he's too far gone to care.

He runs his fingertips slowly downwards from the top of one strap, until they trace the line where lace meets skin and skim the pink outline of my areola. He bends down and places his lips on my neck, before planting a trail of kisses across my décolletage, one after the other, until I'm tingling from his touch.

Our mouths meet and go on another exploration. I cannot get enough of the tender warmth of those lips. The gentle, teasing bite of his teeth. The hot slide of his tongue. I want to taste every inch of him, starting here and ending . . . nowhere. I don't want this to end.

He reaches around and unclasps my bra. The straps fall down first, followed by the rest. My breasts spill out, full and heavy. He looks as if it might just be the most decadent sight he's ever laid eyes on. I reach up to his buttons now, with none of his reserve and patience.

Before we know it, we are both working on them, fumbling and giggling when they don't undo fast enough. Eventually, he tears off his shirt and throws it on the floor. Moonlight reflects on the magnificent contours of his chest. We sink back together, hard muscle on soft breasts, and then—

'Can you hear something?' he whispers.

I freeze. My phone is ringing. It never rings. And I'd silenced it. I'd silenced everything. The only way anyone could get through would be if they were listed on my emergency contacts.

He nods towards the door.

'Go on. You'd better get it.'

I scramble to my feet and dart out of the room, heading back into the open-plan kitchen, where I grab my mobile.

It's Leo's number. I answer.

'Mrs Smedley? This is Josh.'

I'm used to my kids' friends still calling me by my married name. What I'm not used to is hearing any of them sound so shaky and scared. 'I'm sorry but . . . he's in trouble. And I'm not sure what to do.'

Chapter 50

'How long did the taxi say it'd be?' I say, frantically buttoning up my blouse.

'Three minutes, max. He's round the corner. We were lucky.'

I nod. 'I'm sorry to have to leave like this.'

'Don't be ridiculous,' he says, tugging on his trainers and grabbing his keys. 'I'm coming with you.'

As the car hurtles towards the address in south Manchester that Josh gave me, I am delirious with panic, irradiated with fear. I try phoning Brendan, but it keeps going to voicemail. When he doesn't answer on my third attempt, I leave a message.

'Brendan, I need to talk to you about Leo. This is really important. Give me a call when you pick this up.'

A text arrives shortly afterwards.

We've got guests, Lisa! Now is NOT a good time – I'll call tomorrow.

A wave of fury sweeps up inside me that's unmatched by anything I felt when he first announced he was leaving me.

For so long, I have done all the heavy lifting when it comes to our kids. I've been drowning in a sea of homework, sports kits, Seesaw notifications – and absorbing all the worry and stress of our teenager's hideous behaviour. Meanwhile their father indulges himself in the fantasy that the odd trip to McDonald's and a rare overnight stay amounts to anything close to the definition of parenting. I've kept my mouth shut for the sake of staying amicable. I didn't want to be the bitter ex-wife, the angry, unreasonable female.

But you know what? Sometimes, a woman has earned the right to be angry. And I am beyond caring what my ex-husband thinks of me - or anyone else for that matter.

I call him again and, when it goes straight to voicemail, I am unable – no, unwilling – to do anything other than let rip.

'Listen to me, Brendan,' I begin, in the kind of low growl that could get me a job in the Mob. 'I don't give a shit about your guests. I don't care if I'm tearing you and your cycling club chums away from an intense game of Balderdash, a Glastonbury all-nighter or an orgy, for that matter. All that matters is that our son is at a party, having drunk God knows what. He is in trouble and he needs his parents. That's right, Brendan. *Parents* – plural. So phone me back. Now.'

I end the call and glance at Zach, who reaches over and squeezes my hand. I look out of the window, at the bright lights of the city whizzing past, and start to tremble.

'Hey,' he says gently. 'Whatever you find . . . I'm right here with you, okay? You're not alone.'

I clench my jaw and nod, suppressing the tingle behind my eyes.

We finally arrive in one those streets where a process of gentrification has started but never quite finished. It consists of a row of huge Victorian semis, a curious combination of smart homes renovated at great expense and tatty flats with overgrown gardens.

The address I've been given falls into the former category, though I won't be stopping to admire its reproduction pathway tiles. Zach thrusts a ton of notes into the driver's hand and asks him to wait for us while we go inside, adding that there's more if he does. The front garden is strewn with cans of lager, the music pumping out can be heard halfway down

the street and the perspiration streaking down the inside of
the windows suggests there are more people inside than the
house was ever designed for.

Zach and I try ringing the bell, before knocking at the window . . . to absolutely no avail. The music's too loud and the
house is too packed.

'Maybe I could get round the back,' he says, more to himself than me, marching to the side.

'You'd have to climb over the gate.'

He hands me his keys and phone and is about to give it
a go when the front door opens. Two giggling, unfeasibly
young-looking girls stumble out and head into the street.
Before anyone has a chance to close it, Zach darts over and
pushes it open with his foot.

When we step into the dank, crowded hallway, I am
instantly transported back to some of the wilder parties of
my sixth-form years. Two kids are making out on the stairs.
Raucous laughter is coming from the kitchen. The Music so
loud it makes your sternum vibrate and there is an overpowering smell of bodies and spilled booze.

Zach pushes open the first door and I scan what seems
to be a living room, but it's too dark to make much out, let
alone find anyone I recognise. I grab the first random kid
who has the misfortune to stand next to me and shout, 'DO
YOU KNOW WHERE LEO IS?'

He pulls a bewildered expression, so I frantically turn to
someone else. 'LEO SMEDLEY? HAS ANYONE SEEN
LEO?'

The lights flare on amidst a roar of protestation, which
only gets louder when the music comes to an abrupt halt. I
realise that Zach is the one responsible for pulling the plug
– literally, judging by the cable in his hand. A boy tries to
square up to him but quickly realises that this might not be a
good idea when he registers the size of Zach's chest.

'He's upstairs, in the front bedroom.'

I turn around to find Josh – who I last saw at Leo's 12th birthday party at Alton Towers – looking scared and shaken.

Zach and I weave past him and race up the stairs, stumbling over empty bottles and the odd body, as Josh follows us, saying, 'It's first left.'

Zach enters first and there, lying in the foetal position on a double bed, is my son. He is unconscious, or asleep, or something. I rush over and try to rouse him, slapping him gently across the cheek, shaking him by the shoulder.

'What's he taken?' Zach demands.

A lightning bolt strikes at my core.

Josh's eyes widen. 'What do you mean?'

'I mean, has he taken *drugs?* And if so, what?'

Josh begins to stammer. 'I . . . I don't know. He might have just been drinking . . . although he was talking to a couple of kids who had some Molly . . .'

Molly. That's Ecstasy, isn't it?

My heart cracks wide open. My head swims. My hand suddenly feels cold and wet. I turn it over and realise there is blood on my fingers. It's coming from Leo's temple, matted into his hair.

'What the—'

'He fell over,' Josh explains. 'I think he hit his head on the side of the bath. He said he felt weird afterwards. That was when he came in here and I used his phone to call you.'

My bones feel as if they are about to give way. I am initially groping to make sense of all this, when I have a sudden rush of clarity. Of what we need to do to help him.

'LEO! WAKE UP!'

He groans, opening his eyes briefly before closing them again.

'Whose party is this?' I hear Zach asking Josh, who looks as if he's about to cry. 'It's my older brother's, but it was never meant to be like this. He's in the kitchen trying to get rid of people. There are tons of gatecrashers. He'd only planned to have a few mates over but word got out and . . .'

Zach puts his hand on Josh's shoulder. 'You'll be okay. Go tell your brother that if people won't leave he should call the cops. Okay?'

Josh sniffs, nods, then disappears.

'We need to get Leo to a hospital,' I tell Zach.

Despite my son's current state, we manage between us to get him vaguely onto his feet, down the stairs and into the back of the car. I continue trying to keep him awake the whole time, having read somewhere that this is what you're supposed to do in a situation like this. But I'm fighting a losing battle. He does open his eyes and mumble something every so often, but none of it's close to comprehensible. When we arrive at A&E, I wait in the car while Zach runs inside to get a couple of nursing staff to bring out a stretcher.

As they transfer him onto it and take him inside, I follow in a surreal daze, passing images of cartoon characters on the walls. We are in a children's hospital. The same place I brought Leo to when he was five and broke his wrist after falling from a climbing frame. Back then, he went away in a cast, with a sticker and a lollipop. We see a nurse first, who takes his observations, before a doctor comes to take over.

He is young, Asian and has a gentle, unflustered air. In his presence, everything seems to slow down.

He manages to rouse Leo enough to ask the same questions we did on the way here and a few more.

Have you taken drugs, Leo?

You're not in trouble, Leo.

It's important we know.

'His friend seemed to think he'd been drinking and fell over and banged his head on the bath,' I tell him.

'And has he vomited?'

'I think so,' I say. 'I could smell it on him.'

He nods, clicks on a pen and puts it in his pocket.

'He's not showing any signs of an MDMA overdose so my suspicion is that this is all alcohol. It's . . . not unusual for teens to experiment with it. They have a low tolerance and, if they drink large volumes in a short period, it can be very dangerous.'

The plan, he tells me, is for careful monitoring, oxygen therapy and fluids, to be given intravenously. He is also going to order a CT scan because he's concerned about his head injury. So my son is swept away to radiology as I stand, watching, feeling more helpless than I ever have in my life.

Chapter 51

The wait is interminable, but when the doctor returns he gives me a very clear prognosis.

'Your son is going to have a terrible hangover.'

'What about his head?' I ask, anxiously.

'He's had a nasty bump, so that will hurt, but there's nothing on his scan that concerns me. The best course of action is for us to keep an eye on him here for a little while, then when he's sober, you can take him home and let him have a good sleep.'

The nursing staff bring Leo back shortly afterwards. He's conscious if not coherent – though part of me does wonder if he's doing that deliberately to avoid having to talk to me. They set him up on the bed, with an IV and various other pieces of equipment, before he promptly falls asleep again.

Zach puts an arm around me and kisses me on the head.

'Thank you. You know . . . for being here,' I say.

'Any time,' he smiles. 'Did you phone your mom?'

'Yes, she's on her way. You should go, Zach. It's nearly 4am. There's only meant to be two people at a bedside,' I add, for good measure.

He nods. Stands up. 'Well . . . that was *almost* a perfect evening.'

I give a little laugh. 'Almost.'

'Take it easy, Darling,' he says, planting the softest kiss on my lips.

'And you, Russo.'

It's only a matter of minutes after Zach has left that the curtain swishes and my mother appears, like a magician's assistant.

She looks at Leo, her eyes as wide as dinner plates. I'm not sure if it's the sliver of drool out of the side of his mouth, but I am suddenly all out of ideas about how to put a positive spin on things.

'You'd better sit down, Mum,' I say.

She lowers herself onto the chair next to me.

I take a deep breath. And I tell her everything. Not just about what happened tonight. But about the run-up to this. The lying, the vaping, the non-stop clashes and his almost wilful resistance to his schoolwork.

She listens silently as I go on and on. When I've finally finished, she sits back in her chair as if she's been winded.

'I didn't realise things were that bad. Why didn't you tell me, Lisa?'

'Because I was ashamed.'

'Of what?' she says, shocked.

'Oh, I don't know. Because you and dad were such great parents and I seem to be making an almighty cock-up of the job. If I'd pulled a stunt like this when I was a teenager, you'd have killed me. Quite honestly, Mum,' I say, feeling my lip begin to tremble, 'it's hard not to feel like a bit of a failure sometimes.'

The expression on her face darkens. 'Do *not* do that, Lisa.'

'Do what?'

'Blame yourself. We mums get enough flack as it is without heaping more on ourselves. Now, you listen to me. You are a fantastic mother. And I am horrified that you think I'd have ever considered you anything else. As for Leo . . . well, he might be the light of my life, but he's been an idiot. However . . .'

She leans in.

'I hate to break this to you: you weren't an easy teenager either.'

'I never did anything like this,' I protest.

'You did *plenty*. And I'm sure you don't need me to remind you that you ran off at the age of 22 and got married to a boy we'd hardly even met. Do you think I felt like a "great parent" then? I didn't do much patting myself on the back after that, I assure you.'

'I'm sorry.'

'You don't need to be! The only point I'm making is that you were young. We all do silly things when we're young – it's part of life. Leo's growing up. He's becoming an adult. But like a lot of teenagers, he's tripping over his own feet and trying to get there faster than he's ready. His brain hasn't quite caught up yet. But it can be horrible for you, I know.'

'I just feel like he's out of control sometimes.'

She shakes her head. 'You just don't feel like *you* have any control over him any more. And the truth is: you don't. The days when he was little and you could just put his shoes on for him if he was playing up are long gone.'

I swallow, look down at my hands.

She looks at him and shakes her head. 'I'll be having words with him when he's sobered up, believe me. But in the meantime, just know that he *will* get there, Lisa. One day, you'll look back on this and it will feel like a distant memory. Look, Leo's no angel. But there are enough glimmers of light in him for us all to know that he'll turn out to be a wonderful young man. You've just got to hang in there.'

'I really hope you're right . . .'

'I am. Because he's got you – his *rock*. You're his and I'm yours. Okay? Now come here.'

I stand up as she envelops me in a hug so tight I can hardly breathe for a moment.

She pulls away and looks at me before a smile appears on one corner of her mouth.

'So what was the maths tutor doing here exactly – teaching you Pythagoras's theorem?'

'I—' I begin to blurt an explanation, then spot the wry smile on her face.

'He is very handsome,' she says, for what I can't help noticing is the second time. 'How long have you been dating?'

'We're not *dating*. We're not anything. He's lovely but he's going back to the States soon so it can't go anywhere.'

'That's a shame.'

She frowns at my expression. 'Why do you look so surprised?'

'Well . . . I assumed you'd disapprove.'

'Don't be ridiculous.' Then she stops herself. 'Maybe I would have . . . a bit. But not about you *finding someone*. Not about you *being happy*. That's all I've ever wanted for you. I just don't think you should rush into getting married again. I don't mind admitting that I think you've got appalling taste in men. Generally, at least.'

'Mum, I can promise you now: I am never, ever, ever getting married again.'

'Good girl,' she smiles, patting me on the hand as if I've just passed a Grade 3 piano exam. A nurse arrives and announces that she's here to take Leo's observations.

'The doctor has also asked me to give a leaflet to take home about potentially getting help for alcohol addiction,' she says.

'That's all she needs,' Mum says, rolling her eyes. 'She already thinks she's a bad mother as it is.'

'Course you do, love,' the nurse deadpans, gesturing to Leo. 'They make all the mistakes and we get to do all the suffering. Though, to be fair, I think he'll be doing plenty of that by the time he wakes up. If I were you, I'd just sit him down in the next day or two and have a proper conversation with him about the risks of drinking. If you feel you want to be referred to any support services afterwards, speak to your GP.'

Leo begins to stir.

'Oh, here is. George Best is awake,' sighs Mum, as his eyes flutter open to leave an almost comical where-am-I look on his face.

I lean in and kiss him on the head.

'You're in hospital, sweetheart,' I whisper. 'You're going to be all right. But just so you know, you're grounded – until you're 35.'

Chapter 52

Mum drops Leo and me back home in the morning. The sun is bright and clear after yesterday's rain. Church bells are ringing in the distance and there's the usual weekend roar from the sports ground a few streets away. It is a new day. We pull up in the drive to find the unexpected sight of Brendan sitting on the step, his head in his hands. When he looks up, despite the Superdry T-shirt and On Cloud trainers, his face is creased, his eyes craggy. He looks old.

On spotting him, my mother releases a grunt of derision. Then she remembers that Leo is in the back seat and focuses instead on parking. She pulls on the handbrake and I kiss her on the cheek.

'Thank you, Mum. For everything.'

She pats me on the hand. 'Are you sure you don't want me to come in?'

'We'll take it from here.'

She nods. 'I'll ask your father to drop Jacob off after his golf lesson.'

I nod and step outside. Leo follows, muttering a 'Thanks Grandma,' that's too muffled from remorse to come out fully formed. She still gets out to give him a hug, which only seems to exacerbate his shame.

Brendan stands up and, as Mum drives off, he immediately starts on Leo, having presumably decided that he needs to make up for his absence last night, and indeed the last eight years.

'What happened? What have you got to say for yourself? Do you have *any* idea what you've put your mother through?'

'Not now, Brendan,' I say quietly, as I put my key in the door. 'We'll talk to Leo later.'

Our son shuffles inside, his head hanging so low that if he could make it disappear beneath his shoulder blades I suspect he would.

'Go on up and get a shower, love. Then I think you should get yourself into bed.'

He plods up the stairs as I turn to Brendan.

'Come in. I'll put the kettle on. Sorry you had to wait a while. We weren't sure exactly what time they were going to let us out.'

'What happened, Lisa?'

I make some tea while I fill him in on as much of the detail as I can muster the energy for. He listens silently, his expression becoming more and more pained. When I finish, there is a short, numb silence as we both gaze at our mugs.

Then he says: 'No wonder you sounded so irate in your message.'

'I was stressed. And I was angry you weren't there to deal with it, like I was. Quite honestly, I still would be if I wasn't so shattered.'

He begins to chew his lip.

'Listen, Brendan—'

'Don't say *anything*, Lisa,' he says emphatically. 'Not a single thing. I agree with everything. Wholeheartedly.'

'I was just going to let you know your flies are open,' I tell him.

'Oh.' He looks down. Fiddles with his trousers. Turns away when they're not immediately fixed, then back again.

'Last night gave me a lot to think about. This is hard to admit, but I know I haven't been very . . . *present*, I think is the word. As a father, I mean.'

'No. You haven't,' I agree. I take a sip of my tea and take a moment to work out what I want to say about this. 'And sometimes I think that's *fine*. When you first left, I constantly told myself that I'm perfectly capable of raising these kids by myself, so why would I need you?'

He lowers his eyes.

'But all I could think of last night was not, *oh, how will I cope without Brendan*. But that our child had done something stupid. He'd got himself in trouble. And that, despite all that, he deserved to have his father there to help get him out of this mess. Not just me and my *new friend*.'

He freezes and registers these two words.

'Look, Brendan, I don't doubt that you love those kids. I know you do. But fatherhood doesn't start and finish with five hours every other weekend. Being a parent is about more than McDonald's Happy Meals and the odd pet hamster.'

'I know.' He looks up. 'But can I outline my defence?'

'Go on.'

'I am acutely aware of how surplus to requirements I am around here, Lisa. Believe me, I am. But that's partly it. When the boys come to stay with me, all they want is to be back home with you. They *tolerate* me. They *want* to be with you.'

'It's nothing personal,' I insist. 'They just want their Play-Stations. And their friends.'

'You're wrong,' he says, more firmly than I'd been expecting. 'I'm sorry, but you are. I know you get all the hassle from Leo, but you also get the love. He adores you, Lisa.'

'I don't think so,' I scoff.

'No, it's true,' he says emphatically. 'You should hear how he describes you to Melanie. He goes on about how his mum has this amazing TV career, lots of friends and goes running and does DIY in her spare time. She gets a little . . . paranoid about it.'

'Right.'

'Look, I'm digressing. This is not about Melanie, it's about me. And the point I'm making is that it's hard to have to *force* two kids to spend time with you when they'd rather be with their mum. You've made this their home. My place is not somewhere they want to be.'

'Maybe you need to do something to make it feel more like home or just spend more time over here supporting them – and yes, I'll say it, supporting *me*. It's not fair that my mother has to pick up all the slack. She doesn't mind, but it's not her job, Brendan. It's yours and mine.'

I don't spell it out that she might hate him a bit less if he did pick up the reins a little more. That's *might*.

He nods, takes a deep breath, then says: 'All right. This is what's going to happen. Things are going to change around here. You have my word.'

Brendan's word has not always been worth much, but for once he looks as if he really means it. And what option do I have but to give him the benefit of the doubt?

'Those kids do mean the world to me, you know.' I register a slight quiver in his bottom lip. 'I'd do anything for them.'

'Good.'

He takes on a thoughtful, determined expression. 'Do you think . . . Lisa, this is a big question I know. But . . . do you think we should try again? As a couple, I mean.'

I nearly spit out my tea. 'Good God, no.'

He pulls back, clearly affronted.

'Don't be ridiculous, Brendan,' I add.

'All right, *steady on*,' he huffs.

But after a moment, his piqued expression makes way for a smile.

'I didn't mean any offence, but I think we're past all that, don't you?' I add.

He shrugs. 'Yes, I suppose we are.'

'And don't pretend you're not relieved.'

He chortles and sips his tea. 'I *could* potentially look at moving back to this end of Manchester though,' he suggests. 'Not necessarily Roebury itself, but somewhere closer.'

God, that would make life so much easier.

'How would Melanie feel about that?' I feel obliged to say.

'I'll talk to her,' he says. 'And in the meantime, whatever happens, I promise things are going to change. I'm going to arrange something special for them next weekend.'

'Excellent.'

'Peppa Pig World is meant to be good.'

I freeze and look up.

'Gotcha!'

'That's very funny, Brendan.'

'Thanks. I'll get my coat, shall I?'

Chapter 53

I decide to make dinner for the kids before I have a conversation with Leo. That's THE conversation. This doesn't feel like a discussion any of us want to have on an empty stomach. So, as Jacob does his homework at the kitchen table, I throw together a spaghetti bolognese, not having the energy for anything fancier today.

'Mum, shall we make Tanghulu tonight?'

'What's that, Jacob?'

'Chinese candied fruit. All you need is some bamboo skewers, some pieces of kiwi, strawberries and grapes, and some sugar water, which you need to keep at 300 degrees Fahrenheit for ten minutes.'

'Let me guess. Did you see this on YouTube?'

'Yes! Do you want the recipe?'

'Not really, sweetheart,' I confess. 'But we'll do it another time, all right? Now crack on with that homework,' I say, placing a lid on the bolognese as Leo appears at the door and says, to my surprise: 'Can I talk to you, Mum?'

This is a new one – I'd put the chances of him actively seeking out a heart-to-heart with me as somewhere around the nil to one per cent mark.

'Of course you can. Just give me a minute.' I tip out the cooked pasta, turn the sauce off and decide to strike while the iron's hot.

We go into the front room, away from Jacob, both preferring to keep the youngest member of the family blissfully unaware of recent events. As Leo sinks into the sofa opposite, the grave look on his face makes a feeling of deep unease run through me. A series of possibilities swipes through my head from left field. Like, he wants to leave home to join the Army. Or live in Bangkok to train in Muy Thai like he told me he planned to do at thirteen. Or, God forbid, go and live with Brendan.

'Are you ready to talk about Saturday night?' I ask.

But he doesn't reply.

'Leo?'

When he finally raises his eyes, they are already pink.

'Oh, Leo.'

I go and sit on the sofa next to him and before he can argue, I wrap my arms around him. He doesn't resist and from the movement of his shoulders, I think he begins to sob.

'I'm sorry,' he mumbles. An actual apology.

'I know.'

Eventually, he pulls away and clears his throat. But it seems that he still can't talk, or doesn't know what to say.

'I imagine waking up in that hospital scared the life out of you, didn't it?'

His mouth turns downwards and he puts his knuckles in his eye sockets to give them a hard rub.

'I *never* want to feel that sick again in my life.'

'I bet you don't.'

'Why do people even drink?' he asks, incredulously. 'It's . . . horrible.'

'It certainly can be. Especially if you have that much. The problem is that it can be hard to judge.'

He shudders. 'I can't believe Grandma saw me like that. I am *never* doing that again. I mean it.'

The look on my face must suggest I find this hard to believe.

'It's true,' he leaps in. 'I don't want to be some arsehole who messes up his life.'

'Okay . . .'

'So I'm staying at sixth form,' he declares. 'I've decided. I've looked at the rugby academy's academic results and I know they're awful. So I'm not going to go.'

I let his words settle in my head. I've been pushing him to study and work hard for his GCSES for good reasons – namely that I want him to have options and truly believe that education is the route to a life well lived.

So I should be delighted that, as unpleasant as this whole experience has been, it's clearly been the wake-up call he needs to knuckle down.

Equally, I am suddenly aware that this is not my future we're talking about. It's his.

'Is that what you really want, Leo? Because . . . I know what I said. Yes, it's not the place to go if you want to get great A level results and go on to university. But I also know how much you love sport. I suppose what I'm really saying is . . . this is up to *you.*'

He takes a moment to take this in. 'Really?'

'One hundred per cent. This is your future, your decision. Wherever you end up – whether it's sixth form, rugby college, or joining the circus . . . I'll support you.'

His mouth seems to harden as he fights back emotion. 'Okay. Thanks.'

'You don't need to rush into any decisions.'

He nods, looks at his hands.

'Come here,' I say and pull him in for another brief hug.

'Just so you know, on balance, I'd rather you *didn't* join the circus,' I say.

He snorts and pulls back. It's so nice to see a smile on his face. 'What's for dinner?'

'Spaghetti bolognese. It's nearly ready if you want to go and set the table.'

'Sure.'

The three of us sit down to dinner together and I dish up. As the boys begin to tuck in, Jacob tells us a joke he heard on YouTube.

'What do you do if you see a fire man?'

Leo looks at me sideways and smiles.

'I don't know matey, what do you do?' he says.

'Put it out, *man!*'

He's so delighted with himself that it doesn't matter how unfunny this is, all Leo and I can do is join in.

'I've got a better one,' Leo says. 'What's the best part about living in Switzerland?'

'I don't know,' Jacob replies.

'Neither do I but the flag's a big plus.'

His little brother roars with laughter, even if the private frown on his face afterwards suggests he doesn't get it at all.

So begins our terrible joke competition. The worst one wins.

I wrote a song about a tortilla . . . but actually it's more of a wrap.

What do you call a crocodile that's also a detective? An investigator.

They go on and on. They get worse and worse.

And all the while, as I watch these boys, it strikes me that I really have no idea whether Leo's good intentions will last, or indeed whether he'll decide to devote his life to sport or academia.

I also know Mum was right.

Before I had kids, I assumed that raising a child would be like taking a piece of Play-Doh and moulding it into your desired shape.

But by fifteen, Leo is already his own person. In all honesty, he always was. All we parents can do is our best, in the hope that our best is good enough. I never expected it to be easy. I also didn't expect it to be this hard. But in the meantime, there are moments like this.

When my boys and I are laughing, and my heart is so full it could burst.

Chapter 54

'Are you heading upstairs, Lisa?' Andrea asks, as I hit send on my umpteenth email of the day. 'We haven't had a catch-up before the scheduling meeting. Maybe we could talk as we walk.'

'Good idea,' I say, grabbing my bag, pens and folder as she and I walk along the corridor together.

'I read your script notes for *My Teenage Bombsite* and I must say this project sounds excellent,' she says.

'Well, it hasn't been without its teething troubles.'

'Nothing good ever is.' I open the door for her. 'Oh, by the way – this is going to be a marathon meeting, so when you do the notes, would it be possible to try and send them round before tomorrow? It would be very helpful.'

I keep walking. I consider not saying anything. And then—

'Actually Andrea,' I say casually, 'I think it's probably someone else's turn to take the notes.'

She looks at me, confused. 'Um . . . all right,' she says, shiftily. 'I'll ask Angikka to take them.'

'Angikka is in the south of France.'

'Suzy then.'

My feet come to an abrupt halt.

'Andrea, can I level with you?'

She clutches her necklace. 'What is it?'

'Look, I'm sure this is completely unconscious but . . . do you realise you only ever ask the women to take notes? In all the years we've worked together, I don't think I've ever heard you ask one of the men.'

Her mouth pinches. 'That can't possibly be true. Can it?'

I nod. 'I think so.'

We start walking again, slowly. 'Good Lord.'

'Thing is, none of us mind doing our bit, Andrea. I'm the last person to try and—'

'Has anyone else noticed this?'

'Well . . . some of the women certainly have,' I confess.

'Oh my God,' she says, horrified. 'I hope people don't think I'm some sort of . . . dinosaur.'

'Nooo,' I say dismissively. 'Not at all. You're far too young for the thought to have crossed anyone's mind.'

A flash of satisfaction appears across her face before we speed up again. 'Hmm. Well, duly noted, thank you.'

We reach the lift, where Julian Mullins from Reality is already waiting.

'Are you heading to the scheduling meeting, Julian?' she asks.

'I am, Andrea,' he says.

'Do be a love and go and grab your notepad then,' she smiles, as the doors open and she steps inside.

The meeting goes on for more than two hours, not helped by the fact that Julian keeps telling people to slow down so he can make sure he's captured everything on his notepad.

But that's fine, because I am sitting opposite Zach Russo for the final time and frankly I can't help thinking this is a moment to savour. He's wearing a blue shirt today and looks so ridiculously gorgeous that it's hard to tear my eyes away from him and concentrate on the latest budget figures instead. Especially as, each time I look up at him, his eyes meet mine and hold me captive for a few moments all over again.

When the meeting is finally over, I have to dart to the ladies' straight afterwards, wondering how anyone can be expected not to empty their bladder for that length of time and trying to think back to a time when I didn't have to.

Then I head downstairs and find Zach at my desk.

'You left your bedtime reading behind,' he says, handing over a folder that contains a handout from the digital department.

'Oh, thank you.'

'How's Leo?'

'Alive but shamefaced I think sums it up,' I say, as Calvin clears his throat.

'Er . . . Lisa, Daisy wanted to mention something to you,' he says.

She frowns at him furiously, but he ignores her. 'She's got an idea for a show. It's good. I mean, I think so anyway.'

'I think we need to hear this,' Zach says.

She looks suddenly uneasy.

'All right. Well, remember that show we almost got involved in – *Our Girl in Milan*? Well, I just wondered if the producers might be interested in something similar . . . but different.'

'Go on.'

'You know how on most catwalks there is still this crazy obsession with being thin? Well, there's a movement away from that. I was listening to a podcast which interviewed the owner of an agency for models who are an average size and a healthy weight. You wouldn't believe the brick walls she's hit because the industry wants most girls to be either super skinny or pigeon-holed as "plus size".'

I glance over at Zach, who is listening intently.

'But the tide is changing,' Daisy continues. 'This agency has just won several big contracts. So, my idea was a sort of fly-on-the-wall format for one or more of their models? I think it'd be so much more interesting than any old agency. People would be interested to see which companies were willing to use them – and which weren't. It would shine a light on this aspect of the fashion industry and I guess be a talking point about our own weird prejudices based on people's body shapes.'

Zach looks at me.

Daisy swallows.

'I like it,' he decides, approvingly.

'Hands off, Russo,' I warn him, with a smile. 'Don't go trying to poach my department's talent and offer her a job in LA . . .'

Daisy inhales and her eyes begin to sparkle. 'Does that mean you like it, Lisa?'

'I do. I think you could be onto something. In fact, I'll be dropping Martin O'Donoghue a line this afternoon.'

Chapter 55

I make a point of leaving work on time so as not to leave my mum at the helm for any longer than is necessary. I have already sent her a huge bouquet today and, although she told me off for wasting money, she clearly loved them. I phone Rose as I'm walking to the tram.

'Hi there,' I say, when she answers. 'I texted you earlier to see what the GP said. Thought I'd give you a ring when I didn't hear back. Call me your stalker . . .'

She releases a sound that starts as a sigh and ends in a cough. I wince. 'I need to go for a scan. There's a two-week wait but I'm going to go private and they can fit me in tomorrow.'

'I'm sure they're just taking precautions,' I say quietly, because the possibility that the cancer on her breast had spread to a lung before it was removed does not need to be said out loud. 'Should I come over?'

'No, Angel's making me some food and then we're going to watch a bit of TV and get an early night.'

'Okay. Well, if you need me at any time – day or night, I'm serious. Just phone.'

'I will. Thank you.'

'And try not to worry. Stupid thing to say I know, but until you know what's going on . . .'

'Actually, I feel oddly calm and a bit defiant. Part of me thinks, if this *has* spread, I'm not going to take it lying down.

'Good,' I say, through a clenched jaw.

She sniffs. 'Tell me about something nice to take my mind off this. Has Leo's hangover gone yet?'

'Yes and he's turned over a new leaf, apparently.'

'Well, that sounds positive.'

'I mean, I'll believe it when I see it . . .'

'How about you and your grand passion with the office stud muffin?'

The phrase makes me laugh, which she joins in with. 'I'm serious! Fill me in. Let me live vicariously!'

'There's not much to say. I hate to disappoint you on the passion front but I haven't even made it into bed with him. Please don't mention Bill Clinton again . . .'

'What's stopping you?'

'Kids, parents, work. And the small matter of him flying out of the country on Friday morning.'

There's a short pause. 'You know, I've been thinking a lot lately. About making the most of time.'

'Oh Rose, don't,' I protest. 'That's premature. That's—'

'It's not premature. I've *had* to think about this. If Zach makes you feel like I *think* he makes you feel . . . then I think you should do everything in your power to make it work between the two of you. There *are* such things as flights. You could make long-distance work. We don't live in the 19th century. If you really think you've got something with this guy then, Lisa, what is the alternative?'

'I've always been happy being single,' I say.

'That's because you were comparing it to life with Brendan.'

I can't help but laugh.

'Look, I'm not saying you wouldn't be fine on your own. God, we *all* know that – we've seen you juggling everything. But life is about more than spinning plates, Lisa. At least it should be. Take it from me, we all need to have as much fun and joy as we can – *while* we can. Look, it's your life. But if I were in your shoes, I'd be doing everything in my power to keep hold of someone like Zach, for as long as he makes you feel as great as I know he does.'

I feel the faint spit of rain on my face, so I open my bag to try and find my umbrella.

'Are you still there?'

'Yes.'

'Listen, I'm going to have to go. But one last thing.'

'Go on.'

'For God's sake, just go and . . .'

'What?'

'Tell Zach how you feel.'

I splutter. 'Sorry. I thought for a moment you were going to suggest something more *physical*.'

She starts to laugh. 'Well, now you mention it – that too.'

Chapter 56

As I start walking away from the tram stop, rain getting heavier, I make two phone calls. The first is to my mother, to check she's on board with what I'm about to suggest. The second is to Leo.

'Hiya, what's up?'

'Do you think if I ask Grandma to drop Jacob off, you could hold the fort for an hour or so? I'm going to be a bit late tonight, that's all.'

'Yeah,' he says, surprised. 'That's fine. I'll look after him. I mean . . . should I make our dinner? I can if you want.'

'If you like, or I could order you both a pizza.'

'Ooh yeah. Good idea. I'll do his homework with him too.'

I raise an eyebrow.

'Thanks, Mum. See you later. And don't rush home. I'll really look after him, I promise.'

Zach mentioned earlier that he'd got into work at 5am so was planning to leave early. Which means he must be at home.

I turn away from the tram stop and look in the direction of Zach's flat. Am I really going to do this?

Oh, fuck it.

It takes less than five minutes until I'm in the car park of his apartment block. I'm still trying to work out whether this is a bad idea and I should just head back to the tram. I check my phone, but he hasn't responded.

I head around to the side of the building. The gym is on the ground floor, with a waterside view. The moment I turn the corner, I see him through the glass on a treadmill, his arms and legs pumping at an unfeasible speed, his expression one of total concentration.

He sees me immediately and I have a pang of concern that he might think I'm stalking him.

But the look that spreads across his face is one of pure delight. He slams on a button, slows to a walk, then a stop. He gestures to the entrance, then steps off the machine to go and let me in.

'Come for a workout?' he grins, holding open the door.

'I'm not dressed for it, sadly.'

The room isn't huge but it's bright and airy, with a handful of state-of-the-art machines, as well as some of those ceiling-mounted suspension trainers that I'm not sure what you're supposed to do with. Zach is wearing pale grey shorts and a slate-coloured T-shirt. His muscular limbs glisten with fresh, clean sweat.

'I was actually passing and thought you might be around for a drink, but if you're busy . . .'

'What about the boys?'

'Brendan's in town. Last-minute thing. He's taking them to Wagamama's, so I've got a couple of spare hours. But, honestly, if you're still working out . . .'

He narrows his eyes. 'I think you know already that I'd take you over a treadmill any day, Lisa.'

'Well, I didn't like to be presumptuous.'

'Get outta here.' Then his smile fades and his eyes lower to my lips. 'Damn, I want to kiss you, but I'm super sweaty,' he murmurs, stepping back as he pulls his T-shirt away from his body.

I reach out and pull him back. 'I don't really care.'

He sinks the briefest of kisses into my lips. He tastes of salt and spearmint.

'*I* care,' he says. 'Come on. I'll take a quick shower then I'm all yours.'

We head out of the internal door and he calls the lift. We step inside and he presses the button to the seventh floor, before swiping his pass.

We stand side by side.

'Well, this is bringing back *very* pleasant memories,' he says, smiling to himself.

'Still, if you don't want me to touch you until you've showered . . .'

He turns to me. 'I'm regretting that decision.'

The door pings open.

We step out and walk to his apartment, where he lets us in.

'Help yourself to anything. I'll be three minutes tops,' he says, heading into the bathroom.

It's not quite as spotless as the last time I was here, but it's clear that Zach leads a relatively well-ordered life. Or maybe that's just compared with me, because it's a damn sight more presentable than my house was when he caught me unawares. I slip off my shoes, not daring to walk on that cream carpet, and head to the dining table. A printed-out packing list sits next to a highlighter pen. The reminder that soon he won't be here makes an unexpected shock of heat prick behind my eyes.

Just don't think about it.

Next to that is one of Mila's pictures – a depiction of what I presume to be her and Zach. They have stick limbs and she's wearing a triangular dress, while he has a scrawl of curly black hair on his head.

'I really hope that in real life my hair doesn't look quite so *pubic.*'

I chuckle and look up, but the laughter dissolves in my mouth the moment I see him. He has a white towel around his waist. His tanned skin is still damp. I'm not sure if he's still pumped after his workout, but every sculpted contour of his torso seems to glisten in the soft evening light.

'I . . . wouldn't worry too much.'

'Gimme two minutes to get dressed.'

But as he goes to turn around, I touch his hand. He stops. Turns around again. Moves into my arms.

'Or . . . maybe not.'

Chapter 57

The backdrop of the window is a melodramatic, grey watercolour. The percussion of rain against the glass is the only thing I can hear over the catch of my quickening breath. He draws me into the warmth of his chest and, the moment my mouth finds his, I am hungry for him. The thought of his touch has been in the back of my mind all day and, each time I've indulged it, a snare drum has begun to faintly roll somewhere inside my core.

His tongue teases open my lips, as I smooth my hand along the flesh of his lower back, the line where it meets his towel. Tiny goosepimples rise beneath my fingertips. He gently tugs the fabric of my top out of the waistband of my skirt. He lifts it over my head and drops it over the back of a chair. Then he pulls me in closer, the lace of my bra grazing his skin.

His hand sweeps slowly up the side of my ribcage until it reaches my breast. He caresses my nipple with his thumb, making it tighten. He slides one strap down off my shoulder, bends to kiss the freckled curve of it. Then he moves to the next as my chin tilts upwards and he presses his lips against my throat.

I reach around and unclasp my bra. It falls to the floor. He brushes his lips in a pathway all the way to my breast. Then my nipple is in his mouth and he's playing with it with his tongue. I have to hold the back of the chair to steady myself.

I whisper his name, in a breath, a heartbeat, and the sound of it seems to make some feverish new pressure begin to build inside him. Our lips collide and he reaches down and unzips my skirt. I wiggle my hips so it falls to the floor, pooling at my feet. I step out and kick it away, before we stumble towards the bedroom in a frenzy of heat and kisses. We pause at the open door, my back pressed against the threshold as I reach down to smooth my palm over his towel, gaining a sense of how hard he is. His head tilts back and he groans.

We make our way to the bed and he sits on the edge. I climb on, straddling him, my thighs gripping the outer edge of his hips. His pelvis bucks, pressing into me, and I can feel his precise, rigid shape against the nub between my legs.

My body has never felt more fluid. The way we move together is like two instruments being played in complete harmony. I glide my fingers through his still-damp hair as his hands grip my waist, his palms just above my hip bones. The curves and dips of my body feel exaggeratedly feminine against the athletic bulk of him.

'I think about this with you . . . *all* the damn time,' he murmurs. 'I swear my head has been taken hostage by your body.'

He traces the lace on my pants with his fingertips. Heat starts to gather in my core.

I begin to unknot his towel, making a point of doing it with purpose, as if I'm unwrapping a gift. The sight of his erection sends waves of melting pleasure through me. It twitches at my first touch, as I stroke my hand along it firmly and he releases a soft exhalation.

He slides a hand around my face and kisses me once more. The feel of his skin against mine is my new obsession. He runs a finger along my bikini line and skims the fabric between my legs, before he slides them off, all the way down my legs. Then I'm naked too and something inside me seems to fold in on itself. For a long time, we are a tangle of meandering limbs and hot skin.

'Gimme a moment, okay?' he whispers.

He stands to walk into the living room as I lie on his bed, wrapped in his sheets and utterly entranced. He is an exquisite vision of masculinity. The muscular form of his buttocks. The ripple of his back and triceps. The supreme curve of his shoulders. Right now, in the grip of desire, I feel as if a Renaissance sculptor couldn't do him justice.

He picks up his wallet from the table, unfolds it, and takes out a condom.

When he returns to the room, he plants a brief, tender kiss on my lips before he sits and puts it on. Then he turns back to me and crawls on top of me.

We luxuriate in the undulating feel of one another to the point at which my need for him is agonising. But then the tip of his erection is right there, nuzzling at the soft folds between my legs. I have never wanted another human being like this in my life.

When he looks into my eyes, I can see some deep, elemental part of him. Then he slides inside me and something opens, like the time-lapse of a blossoming flower. A moment of surrender, a feeling of pure obliteration. When he withdraws, my insides grip around him. Then he pushes into me again, as far as he can go, and I groan because I just can't keep it in any more. Every thought in my head is eclipsed by the mystery of his body, the poetry of his flesh. I begin to work my hips, intoxicated by him, by *this*, mindlessly grasping for more and more.

I am close to the edge of some primitive oblivion for so long after this that, in my head at least, I start to beg for mercy, scream out his name. The hair around my forehead is stuck to my skin. Sweat has gathered in the creases behind my knees. I am alive in places that never existed before this.

And then . . . and then . . . *I'm there.*

It is transcendental, otherworldly, a blissful skyscraper of a feeling.

Please, I think. *Make this never end.*

Chapter 58

Of all the things I'd rather not have to do the following day, hosting a PTA meeting is right up there at the top. As I potter around the kitchen diner, serving white wine and Kettle chips to twelve other parents, I can hardly bring myself to engage in any of it.

Not the endless debate about how to maximise profits from a sponsored Crazy Hair Day. Not the passive-aggressive chat about the correct price point for a speakeasy-themed Gin Night. And certainly not the arm-wrestle I was convinced would break out earlier – over whether we'd ever be able to make a 'Fun Healthy Tuck Shop' work at the school production of *A Midsummer Night's Dream*, or should we just go for broke and stock up on Starburst and Skittles?

There are only two things I can think about right now. Number one is Rose, who should have had her scan by now and whom I'd hoped to have heard from about her results.

But for me, this is a classic case of the head versus the heart. I can't speak for Zach, but my heart has made enough mistakes for one lifetime.

Every fibre of my being wants to think a transatlantic relationship could work. The alternative makes something erupt in my chest every time I contemplate it. But I am completely convinced that a long-distance love affair is unworkable for anyone.

Zach only gets 10 days paid vacation, which he will obviously devote to Mila. And what about the physical side of things? While meeting him has opened my eyes to certain ideas – not least falling in love - I can't ever see myself performing a striptease in front of Zoom, no matter how good the lighting.

More than all of that, there's the simple, over-riding fact that I'd miss him more than I could bear. Three thousand miles is too many. I couldn't stand it. So while the subject has been open to a debate between us that still hasn't officially concluded, I already know what's going to happen. Tomorrow will be the end of us. It has to be. The day we pull off the sticking plaster and get on with our lives.

Know what the worst thing is?

I think deep down he knows it too.

'So that's two non-uniform days, a talent show, a balloon raffle, a half-term disco, Bonkers Bingo, a drive-in movie and, to kick it all off in September, a Gin Night.'

Denise Dandy peers at the Year 2 mum next to her – who she chose as her 'volunteer' to take minutes – to check she's got it all down.

Denise looks immaculate tonight. Glowy skin. Silky, blow-dried hair. Lips plumped with pink gloss. She's even ditched her trademark athleisurewear and is wearing a silky, safari-style jumpsuit.

'There are still several outstanding jobs for the upcoming Gin Night and it would make far more sense if they were all done by one person. Lisa, I think you're the only one who knows how to use that special shareable spreadsheet thingy, so I'll put you down.'

I look up, snapping out of my daze.

'Isn't Lisa already doing the communication?' Jeff leaps in. Nora is next to him, giving me a look. A glare. One that says, *Don't you agree to do this, Lisa. Do. Not. Dare.*

'We *all* have to pull our weight, Jeff,' Denise says sweetly, though I can't help but notice that since she created the new role of 'PTA CEO' – and promoted herself into it – the only thing she actually does is come up with more jobs for the rest of us to run around fulfilling. 'I was going to ask Lisa to phone the council about the alcohol licence, but maybe you could do that?' she adds.

Jeff starts sucking an invisible lemon. 'Sounds right up my street, Denise.'

'Excellent. So, Lisa, that just leaves the posters, the e-flyer, touching base with the school secretary, sourcing raffle prizes, speaking to the class representatives, updating the PTA Facebook page and Twitter. Are you around on the night itself too? We need someone to clean the toilets beforehand.'

I realise I have been my own worst enemy.

The first to raise my hand. To offer my help. I am one of life's doers, someone who prides themselves on being capable, indispensable and absolutely not afraid of hard work. I've always told myself that the school needs people like me.

But this is not indispensability.

This is being a mug.

Well, enough is enough.

'The thing is, Denise. I've been trying to find a moment to tell you but . . . I'm *out*.'

I didn't intend to sound like Deborah Meaden but, once the words are out of my mouth, I realise I quite like it.

Her beautiful eyebrows twitch in consternation.

'What do you mean? The Gin Night is the first big event of the PTA season. Who else is going to be able to design the posters?'

'I did them on a free app and it's really easy to pick up. I can show you how if you like, Denise?'

From the look on her face, she does not like.

'To be honest, it's not just the Gin Night,' I continue. 'I didn't appreciate when I got involved in this PTA just how demanding it would be. I've got a lot going on at the moment and I'm afraid, once this term is over, I'm not going to be joining you next year. I'll help you with the tickets for this event, but I'm afraid it will be my last.'

I'm not saying that the last few months have made me realise that I'd much rather spend the rare pockets of free time I have enjoying pleasures of the flesh with a super-hot man (though, come to think of it, *I would)*. But it has made me realise just how easy it is for women like me to put themselves last. And while it's one thing making sacrifices for my kids, this is quite another.

I've done my bit. Now it's someone else's turn.

Denise clearly does not see it this way.

'Well, this is *far* from ideal, I must say.' From her clipped tone, you'd think I'd just cleared out the PTA bank account and run off to Mexico. 'Let's hope everyone doesn't take the same attitude. After all, it *is* our children who are going to benefit. Still, if you feel happier sitting around and leaving the rest of us to do everything . . . that's *fine.'*

I'll admit it. Her speech nearly breaks me. Nearly.

'Look, I'm sorry—'

'You don't need to be, Lisa,' Jeff interjects.

'Can I make an observation?' Nora says. 'Look, I haven't been a member of this group for a long time. But it strikes me that what the PTA really needs is *more* people doing *less*. There's too much of a burden on too few people.'

There is an explosion of agreement, though nobody says out loud that the way Denise has managed things – by running a small group of put-upon individuals into the ground – has done absolutely nothing to help recruitment.

'Well, I don't see how leaving helps!' she protests, her voice rising a pitch. It's a fair point, but I know I'll regret it if I let her sway me.

So I stick to my guns until the end of the meeting, when I see everyone out. I even offer to carry my crate of Bounce-a-thon socks out to the boot of Denise's Range Rover Sport, though she declines, snatches it from me and staggers along the path instead.

Afterwards, Nora and Jeff stay for a glass of wine so we can deconstruct the evening's events.

'I hope you can live with yourself after leaving us to the mercy of Denise and her raffle tickets,' Jeff teases.

'I'm sorry. I do feel guilty about leaving others to deal with all this.'

'You *mustn't*,' says Nora. 'You've got to do what's right for your family.'

'I know but—'

The doorbell rings. 'God, I hope Denise hasn't changed her mind about the socks,' I mutter.

But when I stand up and open the door, it is Rose and Angel standing on the step.

'I . . . I expected you to phone. Come on in,' I urge them.

'Has your PTA meeting finished?' she asks, stepping inside. There's something about the way she says it that makes my blood vessels contract.

'Yes, only Jeff and Nora are still here. Do you want a drink?'

'I think we could both do with one,' Angel says.

They wander in to join the others as I close the door. By the time I've gone through myself, I can already see the concern in Jeff's eyes.

'So what happened?' I ask, bringing over two glasses.

I pour one and hand it to Rose, who takes a sip.

'Maybe I should've bought fizz . . .' she says, smiling at Angel.

Nora and I exchange a glance. 'Does that mean—'

'It's just a post-viral cough, apparently.' She shrugs but her voice is trembling with relief. 'A bit of inflammation, that's all. The scan was clear. The cancer hasn't spread. I'm going to be absolutely fine.'

Chapter 59

To-do list

- Book afternoon off for school sports day
- Dig out summer workwear wardrobe to avoid repeat of cashmere jumper and boots hell on hottest day of the year
- Buy sandals for Jacob
- Get Leo to measure inside leg to avoid him looking like Victorian chimney sweep in stupidly short school trousers
- Contact Philippa Perry on Twitter to say thanks and offer self up as case study
- Book Chinese in the village to treat parents to Sunday dinner
- Text Mum to reassure her chopsticks are not compulsory (though either way, Jacob will show her how to use them)
- Buy litter for Alan
- Fix mortgage rate
- Descale kettle
- Call Rose about career bombshell before she does anything hasty

I sit at my desk ploughing through emails, but I still can't really get over what transpired during the course of last night.

As well as the good news about her lung scan, Rose made another announcement: that she isn't coming back to work in August. In fact, she isn't coming back altogether.

The money they had set aside for a new extension will instead be used to fund her way through college. At 48 years old, my best friend is having a career change and plans to retrain as a teacher. She repeated something I've heard her say a few times since I've known her. That she felt so unbelievably lucky all those years ago when she got that trainee position at the BBC that she never actually stopped to question whether it was what she really wanted to do. She's loved broadcasting and has had a tremendous career at Motionmax+. But teaching – at a secondary school or an FE college ideally – remains an itch that she has never scratched. So that's exactly what she plans to do.

I take a sip of my tea and lower it to my desk. I click on my to-do list and cross out the last item. Then I return to my emails.

> Hi Lisa,
>   As promised, I'm delighted to attach the completed sizzle reel for *My Teenage Bombsite*. Enjoy!
>   Jake

The short promotional video helps people understand our concept and gives them a taste of the main concepts, characters and locations audiences will expect to see, all set to the punchy music that's been created specifically for the show. I click on the link, sit back and watch. It is less than a minute long, but that's more than enough to make a smile spread across my face. I know you can never guarantee a hit, that in the past I've loved the odd show that's bombed and hated others that have gone on to unfathomable success.

But I'm calling this now.

It's going to be huge. I close the file, create a link and compose an email.

Subject: Some in-flight viewing

Russo,

Thought I'd share a little bit of pure gold with you before we send you on your way. Hope you like it as much as I do. Just realised I don't think I ever said thanks for your steer on this, did I? Well: <u>thank you</u>. For this and a whole lot more that I will attempt to articulate tonight at your leaving drinks. In the meantime, I hope you're enjoying your last day. Has Andrea been over with her X-rated novelty cupcakes yet?

Darling xxx

I hit send as another email comes through, from Martin O'Donoghue.

Hi Lisa,

Great to catch up on the phone yesterday. I ran the idea of the mid-size model show by a few people here and everyone loves it. Can we say Tuesday 15th at 11am for our meeting? We'll host. Will it just be you coming at this stage?

M

Dear Martin,

That date is perfect – it's in the diary. I'll be bringing Daisy Fellowes, who came up with the concept. I think you'll like her a lot. See you then.

Lisa

I hit send as a WhatsApp message lights up my phone, followed by another one, then another. Soon, the handset is almost jumping from the number of pings. I click on the PTA group chat. Denise Dandy, it seems, has spoken.

Dear all, I am writing to let you know that I have just informed the Principal, the school governors and other relevant staff that, when my current tenure as CEO of the PTA comes to an end this term, I will be stepping back from duties.

'Oh, shit,' I mutter.

It goes on to give a heartfelt and almost Trumpian address about how it has been a great honour to lead the PTA to 'triumph after triumph' during her time in charge. She lists her personal highlights, including introducing a Crochet-a-thon, a Pedicur-a-thon, a Car Wash afternoon AND 'Roebury's Got Talent' (I'd be the first to admit that this was an unforgettable evening, thanks to Jeff's duet with the Head of Chemistry). It goes on and on and on, before adding a final PS: that anybody interested in taking over the helm of the PTA should send an email to the governors by close of play next week.

The words 'not if my life depended on it' spring to mind.

I'm midway through joining the throngs of well-wishers with a nice message thanking Denise for her commitment and hard work when a different WhatsApp group lights up. The Roebury Besties. This message is from Jeff.

What do you reckon? Should I go for it and take the helm at the PTA?

Nora replies first. I'd vote for you. Though . . . is this all because you enjoyed being on that mike so much at the Wine Quiz?

Jeff doesn't miss a beat. As a matter of fact, I thought it would be nice to do my civic duty. Still, any opportunities to take the stage are always welcome

For the rest of the day, I am hit by a variety of, let's say, challenges. Locations that have fallen through, presenters that have dropped out at the last minute, health and safety certificates having expired several months before filming was due to start. It's only as I'm approaching 5pm that I realise Zach still hasn't responded to my email. I start to get an ominous feeling about this. In truth, I start to develop a theory as to why.

I haven't explicitly said anything about our future, my concerns that this is never going to work long-term. But he knows. Of course he knows. Having flip-flopped back and forth between decisions, unable to imagine the word 'goodbye' actually coming out of my mouth, I have a horrible feeling he's going to solve this problem for me.

I push open the door and spot Andrea by the bar, chatting up a guy I recognise as the presenter of a property show. Most of the people here are from Scheduling . . . including Rose, who has popped by briefly, after a meeting with Krishna about her future. I spot her chatting to a couple of her colleagues, most of whom she hasn't seen since she went off for her treatment. She's wearing a floaty dress, soft make-up and looks brighter than she did even 24 hours ago.

'You look lovely.'

'That's what a good night's sleep does for you,' she says. 'I haven't had a decent one for ages, but after the relief last night, I even had a lie-in.'

'Good for you. So, what did Krishna say?'

'He was predictably lovely. Said all the right things and tried to persuade me to stay. But then said he understood and gave me his blessing to go.'

'He's far more understanding than me then,' I smile.

She laughs. 'Do you think this is bonkers?'

I shrug. 'I can't deny I was surprised, but actually . . . no, I don't,' I decide. 'I think this is your stunning second act, Rose.'

'Ooh, I *like* that,' she grins. Then she nods to the other side of the bar, which is being propped up by Daisy and Calvin.

Their heads are virtually pressed together, as Daisy twirls her straw coquettishly.

'They look very cosy. Are they an item yet?'

I shake my head. 'No. I think they really are just friends. They spend a lot of time gazing into each other's eyes and talking about *Antiques Roadshow*, but that's about it.'

'Unfathomable. Come on,' she says, nudging me. 'We need to make this happen.'

We head over to find them deep in conversation.

'It's *really* plump and firm to the touch,' Calvin is saying, as Daisy listens enraptured.

'Has it got a strong upward curve?'

'Very much so.'

They spring apart as we approach.

'We were just talking about Calvin's succulent. It's magnificent,' Daisy breathes, wide-eyed. 'Look.'

He holds the phone to me and shows me a photo of a potted aloe vera.

'Calvin and Daisy know *a lot* about plant care,' I tell Rose.

'You two have so much in common,' she tells them, very unsubtly. 'Tell me, have either of you ever watched the movie *When Harry Met Sally*? It's a sort of friends-to-lovers story. I'd really recommend it . . .'

I glance up as the doors open and see Krishna walk in, followed by Zach. The moment he sees me, his eyes light up.

I excuse myself and head over, as Zach breaks away to greet me.

'Hey,' he says, a smile dancing at his lips.

'Hey yourself,' I reply. 'You are seriously honoured. I don't think I've ever seen Krishna in the pub before.'

We're amongst a crowd of colleagues but all I want to do is kiss him. Still, as he glances around the room, I register there's a peculiar look on his face.

'Everything all right?' I ask.

'Um . . . kinda,' he says. 'Have you got a minute in private?'

I feel a sliver of unease. 'Sure.'

He nods towards the door. 'Wanna step outside?'

We stroll along the canal as an orange sun is beginning to dip behind the office blocks. A band that was setting up in the piazza earlier is rehearsing a live performance. I don't know what it is they're playing but the music is mellow and earthy and the singer has a sort of soulful voice, reminiscent of Nat King Cole or Gregory Porter.

Zach turns to face me. There's some hesitant emotion in his face that I can't interpret. I'm already worried that he's about to say the words I'm unprepared to hear. Even if it is the precise thing I've been thinking for days, if not weeks.

'This is awkward,' he begins. Tears prick in my eyes. 'So, here's the thing. I met up with Sara today. And she asked me a pretty big question. One that has a huge effect on her life, my life . . . and, most of all, Mila's life.'

I feel as if the ligaments in my limbs are going to give way.

Is he telling me what I think he's telling me?

Are they getting back together?

'Her dad is not going to get better, so the priority now is simply making him comfortable, looking after him and giving him the best quality of life he can have for as long as possible. It's going to be a lot for her mom to deal with on her own. Her brother is here, but that's a lot of heavy lifting for one young guy.'

'Of course.'

'And, while we're all trying not to think too far ahead, this whole experience has made her feel like she doesn't want to be too far away from her mom as she gets older. So, she's made a decision and that's that she want to stay here with her parents. She doesn't want to go back to the US. She wants to raise Mila here.'

I blink, taking this all in. 'So where does that leave you?'

His jaw tenses before he answers. 'It's like I said, Lisa. I *cannot* be a continent away. I just can't.'

The breath seems to be sucked out of me.

'Are you telling me what I think you're telling me?'

He can't keep it in any more. 'I'm staying.'

I actually gasp. 'You're not!'

He laughs. 'I am!'

'But what about your big promotion?'

'The one I never asked for? Who cares?'

He grabs me round the waist and pulls me in towards him. Then he kisses me. It's such a sweeping kiss that it makes me feel like I'm in a VE Day photo, heart soaring, limbs softening, the strength of his arms near holding me up. If anyone sees us, I can't say I care. All that matters is the feel of him against me and the dreamy thought that this doesn't have to end after all. When he finally releases me, we're both smiling.

He takes me by the hand and we start to walk back to the bar.

'So what about employment?' I ask. 'Rose isn't coming back but that job doesn't quite match the heady heights of "Global Head of Partnerships".'

'Krishna and I have been discussing it.'

I slide a glance at him. 'Really? Does this mean I've got to carry on working with you?'

'Maybe. I didn't mention it, but I was also approached by Streamflix recently. They have an opening . . .'

'Our biggest competitors? Are you *serious?* I'm going head-to-head with you – in direct competition?'

'I haven't decided yet,' he grins. 'But thought it could be fun.' We are now almost back at the bar, which, judging by the view through the window, is even busier than when we left.

'That's your leaving party going on in there, Zach. Except now, you're not actually leaving.'

'Like I said. *Awkward.*'

I chuckle. 'Come on. You need to face the music,' I say, but he stops dead and pulls me back by the hand.

'There's something else I need to tell you. It's been on the tip of my tongue for as long as I can remember.'

'What is it?'

His eyes are shining with some inexpressible feeling. From the way they sweep over my face, I almost know what's coming before he says it. 'I love you, Lisa.'

I can suddenly hear my heart.

Never again. That was what I said, wasn't it?

This wasn't in the plan. It wasn't part of the programme.

But then, none of it was. And if I've learned something recently, it's that all any of us are doing is winging it.

I stand on my tiptoes to press my lips gently against his. Then I say a sentence that is so true and real that I just can't argue with it any more, whether I like it or not.

'I love you too.'

His face breaks into a luminous smile.

'Come on, let's go face the music.'

Just before we reach the bar, a notification appears on my phone and I pause. It's my to-do list. A reminder to tick off all those I've managed to complete today.

'One moment,' I tell him, as I begin clicking. I check one item and the next, until even 'descale kettle' is highlighted.

Then I hit a single button.

Delete.

BONUS EPILOGUE AVAILABLE
Find out what happens when Lisa and
Zach go on their first mini-break together, to
romantic Seville.

Visit www.janecostello.com and sign up to Jane's
newsletter to see what happens next!

Acknowledgements

This is the tricky bit. Not because I don't like saying thank you – I generally try and do it as much as possible – but there are so many people involved in the publishing of a book that I will inevitably miss someone off. Allow me to extend the usual apologies in advance.

There is however, a handful of people who have collectively represented a shining light during my career over the last couple of years.

First and foremost, thanks to Jo Dickinson at Hodder & Stoughton. It's not the first time we've worked together, but I was lucky enough to win her support for *It's Getting Hot in Here* when it was only a one-page concept. It's a joy to be back in her capable hands, alongside her brilliant team.

Thanks to my agent Sheila Crowley at Curtis Brown for her unstinting support and expertise. A special mention too for the powerhouse that is Tanja Goossens, who has shown so much passion for my writing from the moment we met.

Thank you to Helen Wallace, partly for helping me get all the medical facts right in this book; mainly for being a magnificent human being all round.

Thanks to my unofficial focus group and tennis friends: Jane Haase, Dawn Collinson, Karen Swanson, Kate McCormick, Alison O'Leary. And to my fellow authors for just *getting it*, in particular Debbie Johnson, Milly Johnson, Paige Toon and Clare Williams.

Finally, thank you to my family: my parents Jean and Phil Wolstenholme, husband Mark O'Hanlon and three boys Otis, Lucas and Isaac. You really are a lovely lot.

Read on for the first chapter in Jane Costello's next laugh-out-loud rom-com ...

FORTY LOVE

Chapter 1

One tennis session. That's it. If this is what it takes to get everyone off my back, then I'll do it. But I'm certainly not going to buy anything special for the occasion, except possibly a racquet. Even I'd concede it might be a challenge trying to play without one of those.

I head to Sports Direct after work one evening buy the cheapest model I can lay my hands on. It costs £12.99 and I suspect has all the aerodynamic properties of a frying pan. As I'm heading to the till, I wander past the clothing, where I find further affirmation of my decision to give up this sport when I was a teenager.

The tennis skirts only come in two lengths – short and very short.

I may not be a self-conscious thirteen-year-old these days, but there is still no love lost between me and my thunder thighs. Hate might be too strong a word for what I feel about them, but I've never considered my limbs to be long enough, slim enough, Cindy Crawford's enough. And I'm always happy when wide leg trousers come back in fashion. I know this makes me a bad feminist *and* a hypocrite, having banged on for years to my daughter about body positivity. But I'm also a realist whose knees haven't seen sunlight since the early Eighties and I can think of a hundred other issues I'd rather bother blazing a trail over than this.

Instead, when I arrive at the gates of Roebury Tennis Club on Sunday afternoon, I'm dressed in one of the trusted combos I wear to the gym: a vest top and 'power leggings', with fabric that has the suction of a Dyson and a magical ability to smooth lumps and bumps.

There are ten of us booked onto the class, seven women and three men, covering a broad spectrum of ages, from mid-twenties to early seventies. The group is reduced to nine after one guy cancels at the last minute, citing a veterinary emergency involving his German Shepard and a pack of Crayola crayons. Concern for the dog proves a rich topic of small talk while we wait for the final player, my brother Jeff.

As the class is about to get started, he arrives in a pair of small, retro ivory shorts, a matching zip-up track top, white sports socks pulled to mid-calf and, never one to do things by halves, an elastic headband.

'I'm not late, am I?' he says cheerfully, swinging an enormous racquet case off his shoulder and onto a court-side chair.

'Just starting, Jeff. Come on over,' says Nora.

He slides into line between Lisa Darling and me.

'You've certainly dressed for the occasion,' I say, suppressing a smile.

'It's all new,' he confides.

'I'd hope so given that you haven't played tennis since you were ten.' I look him up and down. 'You look like you're on your way to a fancy-dress party dressed as Bjorn Borg, circa 1984.'

'Do I really?' he says, delighted. Lisa snorts.

'It's *very* you,' she adds, approvingly.

'Oh, don't encourage him,' I say.

'What makes you think I need encouragement?' he grins.

'Welcome to Rusty Racquets,' Nora says to the group. 'For those who don't know me, I'm head coach here at Roebury Tennis Club and today we're going to be focusing on your forehands. I know we've got a couple of complete beginners for this session, as well as some players, like Jules, who are returning after a bit of a break.'

I smile self-consciously as the class looks at me. I feel like reminding her: thirty years is not *a bit of a break*. It's eons.

'At this stage, please don't worry about your level. We're all friends here and the emphasis is on fun,' she continues.

'Think you can manage that?' Jeff asks, nudging me.

'I'll try my best.'

We begin with a warm-up drill, which Nora demonstrates with the help of a heavy set guy in his late 50s, dressed in an enormous, turquoise polo shirt and baggy shorts. He is hesitant at first, but immediately gets the hang of the exercise, which involves standing relatively close to the net opposite another player and tapping the ball back and forth in – to use Nora's words – 'a nice, controlled fashion'.

It's an optimistic instruction.

As Lisa and I pair up, we don't exactly get off to a flying start. At first, I keep hitting too gently and the ball repeatedly ends up in the net. So I add more force, which only makes it fly off in one direction, then another. On the plus side, I do at least manage to make contact, unlike Lisa who, spends most of the time on the court next to us chasing after balls she's missed completely.

'They made this look easy in the demo,' she says.

'Things can *only* get better, Lisa . . .'

'Are you *sure* about that?' she chuckles.

'So how are the kids? Leo must be, what – fifteen now?'

She hits the ball into the net and bends to pick it up. 'Sixteen, thank God. I never want to repeat the year he was fifteen again.'

I smile. 'Was he a handful?'

'I'm his mother, I love him, but yes, I'll say it: an absolute nightmare.'

'Oh dear.'

'Then he had his birthday and it was like the clouds parted. Overnight, he became a nice, considerate human being again. He's got a girlfriend these days, so that helps. It's easy to be in a good mood when you're in love . . .'

'So I hear.' I glance up in time to see her stifle a smile as the tips of her cheeks redden.

'Did you have a lucky escape from any teen trouble with Olivia?'

'Oh . . . I've been through *plenty* with Liv,' I assure her, resisting the temptation to expand. If people knew half of what we've had to contend with over the years, it would blow their minds. As ever, I find it's easier to keep it to myself.

'She's on a gap year, isn't she?' Lisa adds.

'She is. In Italy as we speak.'

'Oh, good for her,' she says, enthusiastically, which I want to concur with. I really do. But the mere mention of this subject is enough to set off a freeze frame in my head - of horrifying possibilities about what Liv might be doing right this minute. Bungee jumping? Having something pierced? Or – as per last night's dream - being kidnapped by a roguish Captain Jack Sparrow lookalike, who threatens to hold her hostage until I sell the semi and transfer ownership both of that *and* the Honda Civic.

'Time's up, folks,' Nora announces, as we finish the rally. 'I saw some great shots on display there. How many points did you and Jules get, Lisa?'

Lisa and I lock eyes, both realising that we've singularly failed to keep score while we've been chatting.

'About . . . eighteen, wasn't it?' she asks me, with a hopeful, possibly deluded, note in her voice. It was more like three, but Nora jumps in before I can correct her.

'Oh, well done. Very impressive!'

We both look away, sheepishly.

In the forehand drill afterwards, it becomes apparent that things have moved on a fair bit since I last played tennis. Now, it's all about the 'topspin', Nora tells us, which is absolutely nothing to do with a tumble dryer. Instead, the trick is to brush upwards on the ball with your strings, to send it spinning through the air and pull it down on the other side of the court.

The players line up to give it a go and I hit one ball, then the next. By the time I've hit my fifth and sixth, an odd and unexpected sensation begins to creep in under my skin. There's something about the pop of the ball as it hits my strings, the whoosh of the racquet as it moves through the air, the small beat of jubilation when it ends up vaguely where it was intended, which forces me to ask: Am I *actually* enjoying this?

I push the thought away, telling myself that what's nice about this situation is simply getting to spend time with Jeff. Having a laugh with friends. Breathing in some fresh air. It's not the tennis per se.

And while there's something undeniably satisfying about the act of hitting of a ball, it's no better than, say, getting to the bottom of your laundry basket or popping bubble wrap. Still, as Nora praises a shot of mine - even though I strongly suspect she says the same thing to the seven year olds she teaches - I feel a stupid, girlish swell of pride.

The final half hour is devoted to what Nora generously terms 'match play' although this is about as far from anything you'd see at Centre Court in Wimbledon as you could imagine.

We play doubles and Lisa is paired with Annabel, an attractive Scottish doctor in her mid-sixties. I am with Jeff. It's the first competitive *thing* we've entered together since a school talent show in which he sang 'I Don't Know Much' by Linda Ronstadt, while I accompanied him on the bugle, after a mere two practice sessions with the brass band.

'Would you like to serve?' Annabel asks Jeff.

'Honestly? I can't think of anything I'd like less.'

Our game begins with a minor sibling debate between us about where exactly the net player is supposed to stand at the start of a point, before Nora comes along ushers my brother into place. Annabel heads to the back of her court and fires off her first serve, with Jeff receiving.

It becomes immediately clear from the speed and precision of her shot that there is little about Annabel's game that qualifies as 'Rusty'. Jeff is so taken aback when the ball skims past that he lets out a gasp then stops to look at his racquet as if the only possible explanation is that there is a hole in it.

The next points are over equally quickly and Annabel and Lisa are winning one game to love without breaking a sweat. We switch ends.

'I don't know why you're looking so smug, Lisa Darling,' Jeff calls over, teasing. 'You haven't even touched the ball yet.'

'I'm clearly just a very intimidating presence over here,' she fires back. 'Because something has got you two flummoxed . . .'

Jeff turns to me. 'I'm not having that,' he says, deliberately within earshot. 'We need to win at least one point. Come on, Jules. *Get your head in the game.*'

I roll my eyes and, while this is all very amusing, I don't mind admitting that I don't really want to lose *every* point either.

Sadly, the first three of the next game disappear in the blink of an eye. But at 40-Love, there is a bona fide rally between Annabel and I, which lasts for nine shots and only breaks down when she mishits a backhand and Jeff cries, '*YESSSS!*'

'Don't get too excited,' I mutter, but even my heart is thrumming now and not only from the exertion.

To my astonishment, we win the next four points. Jeff even hits the ball a couple of times. Somehow, we find ourselves at Advantage.

I serve and it goes in.

What follows next on our side of the court is less of a performance and more of a pantomime. Annabel returns the ball and, when it's unclear who's closer, Jeff and I both dive for it, clash racquets, but by a small miracle manage to get it back. Lisa, in what she'd be the first to admit is a fluke, performs a lob over our heads.

I'm closest so scramble for it, headless chicken-like, before the ball plops directly at my feet. I somehow get it back over the net in a technique I last used on Shrove Tuesday when flipping pancakes. Annabel dives for a volley, Jeff manages to return it and for the next four shots the three of us play a game of ping pong – the ball going back and forth, as I am vaguely aware of gasps coming from the five other students in the session, alongside Nora.

The rally finally ends with an overhead smash from Annabel that is impressive in every way but one . . . it goes out.

Jeff flies towards me, flings his arms around my shoulders and spins me round.

'You are amazing!' he laughs, before pulling away with a grimace. 'And also *very* sweaty. . .'

A burst of applause makes me look up and realise that our fellow students aren't the only ones who have been watching. There's also a handful of people on the clubhouse terrace including, at the very front, the handsome guy who I've been trying to place for days. I register his wide smile and playful eyes, as something unhinges in the back of my knees and I finally realise who he is. Sam Delaney. My first ever crush.

Pre-order *Forty Love* now

An invitation from the publisher

Join us at www.hodder.co.uk, or follow us
on Twitter @hodderbooks to be a part of
our community of people who love the very
best in books and reading.

Whether you want to discover more about a book
or an author, watch trailers and interviews, have the
chance to win early limited editions, or simply browse
our expert readers' selection of the very best books,
we think you'll find what you're looking for.

And if you don't, that's the place to tell us what's missing.

We love what we do, and we'd love you to be a part of it.

www.hodder.co.uk

@hodderbooks

HodderBooks

HodderBooks